DARKNESS AT THE STROKE OF NOON

DARKNESS AT THE STROKE OF NOON

DENNIS RICHARD MURPHY

HARPERCOLLINS PUBLISHERS LTD

Published by HarperCollins Publishers Ltd

First edition

Darkness at the Stroke of Noon is a work of fiction inspired by the Franklin Expedition of 1845; however, the characters and events portrayed in the book are products of the author's imagination.

HarperCollins Publishers Ltd
2 Bloor Street East, 20th Floor
Toronto, Ontario, Canada
M4W 1A8

www.harpercollins.ca

Library and Archives Canada Cataloguing in Publication information is available

ISBN: 978-1-55468-321-5

Printed and bound in the United States

9 8 7 6 5 4 3 2 1

For my father, Robert Joseph "Pat" Murphy, who would have been proud, and my mother, Helen Mary Murphy, who is.

To work by twilight were to work too late,
And Age is twilight to the night of fate.

John Donne
"Satire 3" (versified by Thomas Parnell, 1714)

SUNDAY, NOVEMBER 8

Victory Point, King William Island, Nunavut

The paper is frail, pages more by custom than constitution. It's a record of sorts. A diary, it seems. The writing is decorative, leaning towards calligraphy, the words and script of a literate man with tools and time on his hands.

> *Sunday, May 18, 1845*
> *Greenhithe, Dartford, Kent*
>
> *I write in some haste as we prepare to weigh anchor tomorrow and sail to Arctic shores . . .*

"Jesus," he says aloud. He inhales deeply the frigid air, open-mouthed, slowly, as if he is about to be ill, that high stomach nausea habitually resolved with a heave in the pub pisser. But this is different. Deeper, somehow. Below the stomach. Closer to the groin, as if his balls were fat with bile.

He tugs off one thick mitten and turns the pages slowly, using the padded tips of his fingers—delicately, singly, sometimes as groups when some seem stuck to others. He hears his shallow breathing over the keening bitter wind and gusts of granular snow pebbling the canvas. He flinches unconsciously each time the tent walls snap like rifle shots.

Turning pages without pausing to decode words or meanings, he sees the long and ornamental entries reduced to shorter accounts towards the end—lunges rather than sentences, single words, odd abbreviations, with poorly formed characters. He arrives finally at a blank page, brittle brown at the extreme edges, fading inwardly through a pale yolk halo to cream in the centre near the hand-sewn binding. Carefully pulling the reluctant leaf away from the one before it, he stares at the final entry. Pokes of pencil lead pierce the page. There is a madness about the few words, the frustration of an incomplete life.

He feels hot. Gulping air like a tank fish, exhaling slowly through whistle-pursed lips, he watches the thin stream of his breath splay in the freezing air. The beads of sweat on his brow cool quickly and his thick eyebrows grow hard with frost.

"Jesus," he says again, his freezing fingers resting gently on the final page as if feeling for its pulse. "It's the holy fuckin' grail."

Yellowknife, Northwest Territories

The exhaust fan groaned, infusing the steamy bathroom with the carbon smell of electrical faults hidden somewhere in the ceiling. Its loud, arrhythmic whine drowned out the surround-sound audio from a flat-screen television perched on the dining room table, raised four inches by sitting on its own box.

Booker Kennison towelled off in the narrow hall between the bathroom and the dining room. The oak parquet floor was water-stained; others had stood dripping here before him. He rubbed his too-long-for-regulation dark hair and peeked through the towel to watch a Senators defenceman skate towards the penalty box, shaking his fist and spitting blood on the ice to a chorus of jeers from Flames fans.

Even to his uncritical eye, the one-bedroom apartment was a mess, the transient nest of an unsettled man. Single pieces of used furniture had been salvaged, on the advice of others, from the landfill site where those who abandon the city dumped their goods rather than paying more than they were worth to ship them south. His odd finds had been placed where they'd landed on scarred floors in bare rooms with noisy radiators covered in thick coats of eggshell paint.

The thin TV set, its box, and the disfigured teak table that supported them filled a dining alcove six feet from a living room dominated by a brown vinyl reclining chair with a rip in its right armrest and its footrest permanently raised. Beside the chair, dependent as a drunk on the neck of a new best friend, was a two-level wood-grained Formica side table. Wobbly on its splayed brass-capped legs, it was overpopulated with empty long-neck beer bottles and hardcover books with stains resembling disorderly Olympic rings on their dustcovers. A pile of discarded newspapers, some folded to crosswords completed in ink, lay on the other side of the chair, and a large foil bag of salt-and-vinegar potato chips gaped slack-jawed where it had fallen on a once-white long-haired rug.

The only thing worse than being exiled to Yellowknife by your superiors, thought Kennison, was being suspended in your first week of duty for a stupid bar fight with a loud-mouthed local and forced to sit in this apartment in this nothing frozen town, drinking beers and watching hockey games until you fell asleep in a time zone three hours earlier than home. Except *this* was home now. The Northwest Territories, for Christ's sake. Like it or not, Kennison, this was home.

The place wasn't really named Brenda's. It was a block and a half from his apartment, past a prison-like tenement called Sir John Franklin School, across 48th Street and up 50th, or Franklin Avenue. Kennison thought they needed a few more heroes to name things after up here and wondered idly what this guy did to deserve all the hero worship. Probably discovered one of the diamond mines up north, he guessed. In the States he might be a military man, but not here. Canadian heroes are scientists or successful businessmen, not soldiers or politicians. Or cops.

The restaurant was overheated, smelled like toast and employed Brenda, according to the plastic sign pinned low on her left breast. She was bottle-blonde and about Kennison's age—mid-forties, maybe two or three years older—although she looked more at ease with it, more settled. Either life suited her or she was resigned to acceptable sacrifice. Below her smile she was buxom, broad in both the hips and in humour.

"Cold enough for you?" She staked his territory with a thin paper placemat, utensils pre-wrapped tightly in a paper napkin twisted on itself, and a cardboard six-pack beer carton of condiments. Her breath smelled of tea and mints that didn't mask an honest whisper of working sweat. Her heavy rings clacked on the tabletop, a small diamond and a broad gold wedding band dulled with wearing. Her nails were cut very short. Practical, or maybe she bit them when things were slow.

Kennison looked at the specials scrawled in red marker on a whiteboard next to the kitchen pass-through. Through it he could hear the hockey game and see the television set's magic lantern shadows on the kitchen wall. He removed his regulation heavy coat and fur hat and hung them on the stainless steel pole at the end of the booth, feeling in the coat pocket for his book. Seamus Heaney. Poetry in lieu of conversation. Made the food go down easier, and the time as well.

"No more meatloaf." Brenda spoke quickly as if there wasn't much food or time remaining. "Fish is frozen factory-battered square pieces don't even look like fish you won't like it." Kennison opened the plastic-coated menu. "Give you a second take your time." She rattled off to the coffee stand for a Pyrex pot. She wore extruded-foam shoes, vibrant purple, with thick soles and breathing holes in the tops—shoes for people who spend a lot of time on their feet. Her calves looked smooth, muscled, and Kennison realized she was wearing shorts under her server apron. Shorts in Yellowknife in November. Her legs were pretty good, he thought, as he watched her walk between the booths to refill the cup of the only other diner, a man with a backwards-facing baseball cap huddled behind a newspaper at the far end of the joint. Without asking she banged down a thick cup and saucer and poured a coffee for Kennison.

"How's the burger?" he said.

"Frozen, but Dooby's on tonight, so it'll be fine. Want the combo? Fries and coleslaw?" Kennison nodded. Without moving she yelled at the kitchen hole over the sound of the hockey game: "Dooby? Listen up. Burger. Works . . ." She looked to Kennison. "Works?" Kennison nodded again."Works. Combo." She scribbled down the order as she yelled it. "That it?" she said.

"Bottle of Blue," said Kennison. She paused a beat, and Kennison had the naked feeling she knew exactly what he'd been doing all day, all week.

"You drink that coffee down first, Sergeant. Then we'll see about a beer." Kennison looked at the placemat, covered with gaudy, colour-saturated pictures of the freshwater game fish available in the cold lakes of the Northwest Territories. He'd been in town two weeks and she knew who he was. It was a very small world up here.

He traced the sharp, V-tailed outline of a lake trout with the tine of his fork. He'd never caught a lake trout. Have to fish deep for them. Use metal leaders, too. Maybe in the spring, if spring ever came up here. He'd have to find something to do—some hobby. Keep his mind off things like Kolchak, and Ginny. He heard the metal-on-metal screech of the aluminum street door opening. A blast of cold air made him shiver, as if in anticipation of the large shadow that crossed his table.

Victory Point, King William Island, Nunavut

The mud ruts connecting Heaven and Hell were frozen in place by early November. The barely visible path wove westward for two kilometres from the base camp to the dig site through random rocks and ice-skinned pools of meltwater. Marie-Claire Fortier walked the road in a twilight that would last for less than five hours today. The sun would not be seen for a hundred more days in this land as dark and as fated as death.

Every day was noticeably shorter now, each day colder. The temperature hadn't risen above zero Celsius for two months, even when the sun was still visible low in the sky. Everyone in the camp knew these details. Apart from comments on routine tasks and Lillian's attempts at cooking, the only topics of shared conversation were the erratic weather, the phobia of encroaching darkness and the number of days, hours and minutes they had left in this desolate place.

Poncey reminded them hourly that they were cutting it too close this year. Winter had already claimed much of the landing strip of open water between the dig on shore and the ice cap in the strait. The channel grew narrower each day, and without open water no plane could land until after freeze-up, and then only if the ice set smoothly, without the natural heaves and hummocks that can flip a bush plane on its back in seconds.

Everywhere Marie-Claire looked was a lifeless limestone desert dotted with large boulders covered by an ash of granular snow. Only the black wound of open water and the orange rust of lichen on the wind-worn rocks broke the infinite greyness, two brushstrokes barely visible on the vast canvas of snow and ice, rock and sand.

She smiled in spite of what she saw. Marie-Claire had come to find this place inexplicably beautiful. Today, rather than riding the team's ATV trailer to the dig with Anne or Trevor, she was walking the summer road to bid Victory Point farewell, to pledge to some Arctic essence, newly and parasitically entrenched in her heart, that she would return to this place, that she and Kenny would come back. Together.

Ice crystals hung like tinsel in the air, then tossed her way, pricking her cheeks. Penilik's random rifle shots, from directions and distances impossible to gauge, shattered the silence into shards of frosted glass. The twilight was flat and dully grey as slate, its daily diminution a tangible pressure on the mind and in the heart.

She neared the small storage shack that marked the halfway point between Heaven and Hell. In the distance a small squall swirled, crystal confetti played tag in a whirlwind. Marie-Claire shivered and picked up her pace.

The temperature faded as quickly as the light. Ice formed like scabs on the puddles and the crystallizing mud squealed under the pressure of her thick-soled boots. The tiny storm was closer now, not dissipating—coming on faster, if anything. An unanticipated advance of ice crystals rattled the plastic lens of her goggles. Daddy had bought these goggles, smiling at her and stroking her hair as he muttered about what things cost these days. The storm was upon her now, surrounding her, stinging her face, sticking to her hat, whiting out the halfway shack even though it was just metres away when she last saw it.

Gusts tore at her clothes, stole inside her loose hood and shoved it off her head. Her blonde ponytail thrashed in the wind, slapping at her face as she slipped while climbing the icy windrow and banged her knee—on ice, or a rock? Visibility was zero, her view so completely obscured that she walked suddenly into the side of the rough hut and bruised her cheek. Even with her hand against it, she couldn't make out the weathered wooden wall. The narrow border of skin between her goggles and the scarf covering her mouth stung as if shot with pins.

She fumbled at the hasp, covered with a protective piece of leather made stiff by the cold. By pushing the lever up and pulling it towards her she managed to open the wooden door, but it took the wind like a racing jib and flung her back into the road. Her elbow hurt. Crawling slowly, painfully, close to the ground in a futile attempt to stay under the gale, she found the edge of the road again by striking the ice bank, then located the hut by the banging of its door as it slapped madly on its leather hinges against its own wall.

It took almost everything she had to crawl inside the shed, and she exhausted her last vestiges of strength to pull the door closed and secure it with a wooden latch against the ripping wind. For a moment she lay back on the floor, catching her breath, sweating with exertion, shivering from the drafts rising between wide gaps in the floorboards.

It was as dark as tar and reeked of vermin, mildew, damp straw. There was a sour smell as well, a curdled stink like a blown fuse, though there was no electricity here. Even as her eyes became inured to the murk, she saw only degrees of darkness. At least she was safe, for now.

2100 North Service Road, Mount Winans, Maryland

The fastest way from midtown Baltimore to the western industrial suburbs on a late Sunday night is to drive through Washington Village to Carroll Park and pick up the I-95 at the south end. There's little traffic on the interstate at that time of day, just the odd minivan stuffed with tired parents and sleepy kids on the way home from a visit to Grandma's cramped apartment in the city.

Ruby Cruz set the cruise control on Harry's old Camaro to 60 and covered the fifteen miles to the off-ramp in as many minutes. "Mile a minute," her father used to say. She missed the old man. In some ways. She hadn't known he or Harry were so much a part of her life until she'd lost them. Back to back.

Keith Dickerson's call came when she was dozing on the couch. It wasn't until the ring tone woke her that she realized she'd fallen asleep. Her neck was stiff, her back cramped. A hardcover whodunit lay closed on the floor where it had fallen, and an untasted glass of California red wine sat on the glass-topped chrome table beside her. The remnants of a Dante's medium pizza curled in the open box on the coffee table.

She'd been thinking of—dreaming of—the new house. She should have crept up and pushed the For Sale sign down between the dead perennials in the front garden when she visited it earlier in the evening. There was one other offer, but the agent said it was conditional on something that could not be completed until next week. It was hers if Ruby was ready. And she *was* ready. Ready for change. For a new start. She would sign Monday, four days from now. Move in by Christmas. Launch her new life with her new job and her new home. Watch your back, Mary Richards—Ruby T. Cruz is going to make it after all.

She recognized she was desperate to share this with someone—like Harry—but shook the feeling off. This was about her, about her life. Nobody's but hers. She'd spent long enough mourning and moping and feeling sorry for herself.

In her job search, she'd tried to put as much physical distance between her and the Bureau as possible. Her new employer, AEI, was off the interstate just west of Baltimore. No need to go anywhere near D.C. or the J. Edgar Hoover Building, where, after Harry died, her fellow agents smiled at her as though she'd lost a favourite pet in a car accident and speculated among themselves in hushed tones as to whether she was lonely enough to sleep with them. She was glad to be out of the Bureau, tired of the relentless games of one-upmanship, even though she usually won them. She was even farther away from Quantico, where people who'd known Harry longer than she had gave her hugs she didn't need, squeezed her hands like they understood something, kissed her cheek without asking.

What was there to understand? Harry was a soldier. Harry went to war. Harry was killed in an ambush by the same Iraqi cell he'd ambushed the day before. Tit for tat. Harry was raised and trained to answer the call, to serve his country without question. It took her long enough to become angry, she thought. She couldn't blame the president—she'd voted for him. But even unplaced anger helps more than companionship, more than friends she didn't have anyway.

Daddy was old when he died. Nobody mourned him but Ruby. Whatever he'd done, or hadn't done, he deserved remembrance. She'd given it to both of the men in her life. Now it was time for Ruby.

Victory Point, King William Island, Nunavut

Marie-Claire stood and reached out in the dark. Something soft lay against the wall opposite the door. She poked at it suspiciously with her mitten. Mattresses maybe, thin ones, five or six of them stacked on their edges. That was where the old straw smell came from. She pulled two away from the wall and laid them on the floor. They seemed to impede the draft blowing up through the floorboards.

She could build a nest here, with walls and a roof, a child's mattress fort to keep her warm until they came for her, until Kenny noticed she was missing and came for her. Even with the shelter, she wouldn't last too long in this cold. She shuffled clockwise in the dark, striking her hip on a corner of a piece of furniture. She moved her mittened hands over its top. It was a hard surface, metal maybe, with large holes in it. She felt cautiously, and her cold fingers touched something at the back. She leaned forward, hitting her forehead on some superstructure she couldn't see. Her hands felt a camping lantern like the one Daddy kept in the green metal case, the one only he was allowed to light at the picnic table while she and Karen watched the flames burn off the excess gas. When Mummy was alive and they all went camping.

The rattle of the wire handle on the glass confirmed it. She shook the lantern. It weighed little and made no sloshing sound.

She put it down carefully, avoiding the holes in what she now guessed was a woodstove with missing burner plates, and pushed it to the back, where it bumped something. The wind increased, shaking the cabin as if it knew she was inside and frightened. She felt a tin, a tall, rectangular can with a screw cap and a metal handle, like a maple syrup can. She lifted it and felt its weight. She took off her mittens and unscrewed the cap, resistant with rust at first, and lifted the container to her nose. The acrid smell made her smile. It was camping gas.

The wind shook the door, demanding entry. Marie-Claire's fingers were numb. She undid the zipper of her jacket, crossed her arms and shoved the tips of her bare fingers under her armpits to warm them up. When she put her mitts back on they felt colder than her hands. The cold up here sucked the heat out of everything in seconds. Poncey had told them that. Lillian had agreed.

She felt a tinge of real panic, a hollow feeling somewhere between her heart and stomach. Someone would miss her, right? Kenny would wonder where she was if he wasn't too wrapped up shutting down Hell or waiting out the storm in one of the shacks there. Even Trevor might worry when he saw the ice blow, if it was blowing up at Dr. Kneisser's dig. Although probably not—Trevor only thought of himself. Anne might notice if she wasn't lost in a book, or in a thought or talking to herself. Or Poncey, or Wayne . . . even Lillian, maybe.

2100 North Service Road, Mount Winans, Maryland

There were three vehicles in the parking lot: an industrial white van, its doors decorated with AEI's polar bear logo and the word security; beside it, a dark BMW 5 Series that Ruby imagined was Dickerson's; and parked away from the other two, barely visible in the shadow of the building, was a mud-spattered black Toyota Camry. Ruby had to press the key fob several times until the car lock chirped. It didn't always work, but she couldn't see a way to open the black fob and replace the battery—if it had a battery.

The building was a tinted-grey glass cube five stories high. It sat unimaginatively centred in its large groomed lot, surrounded by a moat of November-brown lawn that looked yellow under the powerful roof-mounted security lights. Over the double glass entry doors was the white polar bear logo matching the sign at the driveway entrance. Affixed to the building in three-dimensional brushed-stainless-steel letters were the words Arctic Exploration Institute and the address number, 2100.

Ruby heard the door latch click open as she approached. Through the glass she could see the silhouette of a slope-shouldered security guard slumped behind the reception desk in the dimly lit lobby, a finger in his nose, unaware he could be seen. When she entered, he stood and smiled as if obeying a memo and limply held out his hand. Ruby backed away. He smelled unwashed under cheap cologne. He'd shaved badly and had recently returned from a smoke break.

It took her a moment to realize he wanted to check her ID card, which she pulled forward on its retractable cord. He nodded and gestured with the flourish of a maître d' towards a chrome and leather bench while he called upstairs. Ruby checked her hair in the copper-tinted mirror behind the lobby bench. In the top light she could see the grey strands. She hadn't started to dye them yet. She hadn't been that concerned. Maybe that sent a message to others. Maybe once she was settled in this job and her new house she'd turn her attention to herself. Dye her hair, bleach her upper lip, wear more makeup, get her colours done. Maybe lose some boob. Did they still do people's colours? She wondered briefly what hers were. Summer, she hoped. She could handle summer all year round. It was already too cold for Ruby Cruz.

Telephone to his ear, the guard watched her covertly in the mirror. He nodded into the telephone, then stood and pointed out the elevator, but she shook her head and took the stairs, part of her new fitness plan. The guard shrugged and returned to his long night of sitting as Ruby climbed the stairs in the fluorescent glare of exit signs reflecting off unfinished concrete walls and metal plaques advising of fire escape routes and smoking bans. She sniffed. This was where the security guard went for his smoke break.

When she reached the fifth floor, she pushed open the heavy metal door to a carpeted hallway. Dark offices were ranged around the perimeter. The sunken central support area was lit only by security lights. Small dots glowed on some computer screens. One displayed a screensaver of the user's name careering madly around the monitor. The few car lights passing outside on the service road appeared starred and distant through the grey-tinted glass.

Ruby heard male voices coming from down the corridor,

where light spilled from a glass-walled office onto grey industrial carpet. She thought she recognized Dickerson's voice, even though it seemed more strained, with more tenor than when she'd heard it before, when he'd introduced her, welcomed her, nudging and winking and touching her too much and too often.

The other voice was a bass rumble, unintelligible from this distance. Whatever it was saying was in disagreement with Dickerson because the latter kept interrupting in his high-pitched tone. She realized she'd crept closer to hear, that she was consciously making no noise. Like on a stakeout. The way Harry had trained her.

". . . and she should know what the hell the situation is, Norm. We can't send her to hell and gone with a shopping list she doesn't understand, for Christ's sake. She's smarter than that. Let her hear the tape. She needs to know the lay of the land, the tilt of the jib, know what I mean? Sure you do. If the old bugger really finally struck gold, goddammit, we have to act on it. Now."

The bass voice responded—prodding, it seemed, rising and falling with a statement rather than a question.

"She's no pussy, for Christ's sake. She's an employee—like Kneisser—not a summer rental like the whiney Patel kid. We'd better watch that little bastard, by the way. She's signed on, Norm. Oaths taken. Sealed and delivered. She'll be loyal. We'll keep her in line. Ex–FBI goddammit, checked out, vetted from birth, for Christ's sake. By you, am I right? Huh? By you yourself, dammit."

The bass voice rumbled a sentence or two.

"Jesus. We don't have anyone else. Bennington's in fucking Denmark, Norm. Karel's in Moscow on the Lomonosov thing. And I can't ask Starovic to leave the Alaska conference in the middle of the goddamned—"

More rumbling response. Ruby was perspiring. Dickerson's

voice was rising in pitch. Her thighs ached from standing still, leaning forward.

"Well, I think you're wrong, dammit. Hate to pull rank, but there it is, Norm. She'll be here any second. So what d'we do? D'we just tell her to escort Kneisser and nothing else? Just let her fly blind? Let her babysit him all the way home without knowing what the fuck he's holding and hope he just keeps his goddamned mouth shut and doesn't pack it in his fucking carry-on or cargo shorts for the pleasure of Homeland Security? Jesus, Norm."

Rumble, rumble.

"If anyone else gets it, there'll be hell to pay. You know that. The partners'll scatter like fucking deer to a shotgun blast. If it proves what I think it proves, we got to keep it quiet or it could take AEI down—and us with it, Norm. And I mean you 'n' me, fella. Don't think the shit won't stain you too."

It struck Ruby that she should back up and leave, just walk away and pretend to ignore what she'd heard—though that was impossible, like a judge asking a jury to ignore testimony ruled out of order. Besides, she'd already been announced by the guard downstairs. By using the stairs, her arrival hadn't been tipped by the chiming of the elevator. As the bass voice rumbled again, Ruby walked towards the light, coughing to proclaim her presence, calling out in the dark corridor: "Hello? Hello? Is anybody here?"

Victory Point, King William Island, Nunavut

The storm shook the shed again. Standing in front of the woodstove, Marie-Claire felt above her head and found a handle. She opened a door that swung down and felt inside. Something seemed to scuttle and she screamed like a young girl, unheard in the storm. There were some papers—newspapers, maybe. She could smell them, old and dry and mousy as dust. In her mind they were brown, steeped in the tea of time. She moved her mitts to the right, where they struck a rectangular box that rattled when she shook it. She removed one mitt to feel the rough granular strip on the side of the box, and her heart leapt as she realized it contained wooden matches.

She scraped one on the side of box, feeling only the soft, silent disintegration of the match head. Punky. She removed her other mitt and took out another, rubbing the match head quickly between her bare hands like a Boy Scout starting a stick fire. It warmed her hands as well as the match. Scraping it on the box offered a hopeful spark. It took three more matches before she managed to get one to fizzle and burst into flame, cupped from the wind between her palms. The heat was painful and foreign, worse for the cold, and the light blinded her so she held her eyes closed tightly to maintain her night vision. Her chest below her breasts still ached oddly as if it contained an expanding tumour of fear she must ignore lest it grow to choke her. The match went out.

Blowing into her hands and giving them another heat treatment from her armpits, she unscrewed the lantern base gas cap and that of the can, mostly by feel. The gas poured out too quickly and spilled, running into the holes on the stovetop. It smelled bitterly alcoholic and chemical and made her gag. The pressure mechanism was stiff from lack of use, but she managed to unscrew it and pressurize the lantern. The tips of her fingers ached with cold. After one more pump and a prayer, she warmed and lit another match. When the brittle, broken mantle sputtered and caught, filling the hut with the hiss of hard, white light, she cheered aloud, unheard under the wail of the wind.

Yellowknife, Northwest Territories

Kennison looked up from the lake trout to see Dutch Duchesne standing over him, the bulk of the man made larger by his Royal Canadian Mounted Police parka and the regulation fur hat he clenched in his large hand like roadkill.

Inspector Duchesne had a walleyed face, his large slabs of cheeks permanently blotched with red veins too close to the surface, making him look like he was blushing or fresh from a cricket game on a common, bridged by a thick brown military mustache under a large nose with a prominent arch. His eyes were large and brown and he seemed not to blink. His hair, although regulation length, seemed softer, blonder, as if the mustache had been store-bought or his hair dyed.

Other than welcoming Kennison to Yellowknife, assigning him one domestic murder and suspending him for the bar fight at the Sly, Duchesne hadn't established much of a relationship with him. There hadn't been time. Kennison had wondered why there wasn't more to do in this place. He knew why he'd been posted here—a not-so-subtle message from the brass that he'd better keep his mouth shut—and that Duchesne was part of the plan, but it seemed odd there wasn't more going on.

The ball-capped newspaper-reading man at the far end of the diner disappeared as if he had his own distant early-warning system for cops and a private exit from the building. His fresh coffee still steamed on the table.

"Java, Inspector?" said Brenda, holding up a half-full Pyrex pot. She waited until he nodded. "Make fresh if you want." Duchesne pointed for the coffee, shook his head against fresh, unzipped his parka and sat down uninvited. Kennison smelled a sweet mix of deodorant and aftershave that rose from the man like steam from a two-loon lake at dawn. This man had come from home, not the office. Before he came here he had been sitting comfortably in his favourite chair, probably watching the hockey game with his wife. Duchesne waited until Brenda poured the stewed coffee into a chunky, chipped mug and left before he spoke. The wind howled at the metal door.

"Been trying to reach you, Sergeant. At home and on your cell."

"I'm not at home, and I left the cell there, Inspector." Kennison looked him in the eye and felt like an adolescent jerk, despite which he continued: "Besides, what's the panic? I'm in a strange city, banned from bars and on suspension. The only fun I'm having is watching Calgary lose to Ottawa and not answering the phone."

Duchesne nodded, as if he understood, as if he expected to hear exactly that, as if he'd heard it from recalcitrant children and reluctant sergeants many times before. His mouth was open and he breathed through it despite the size of his nose. His teeth were large and stained, as if he smoked, but Kennison hadn't seen him smoking and he didn't smell like it. He seemed uncomfortable, inexperienced in small talk, incapable of repartee, defeated by wit. Kennison regretted his smart-ass banter. Duchesne leaned forward, a conspirator.

"I need you to be off suspension, Sergeant."

"But it was you who suspended me, Inspector." Brenda arrived with the burger and fries. The platter was huge, and she smiled as though she was proud of that, proud of making hungry men happy. If only Ginny had a dram of that desire, thought Kennison, just a taste of wanting to make someone happy beside herself, snorting herself into delirium. Brenda returned to the pass-through and brought back a small ceramic bowl of greenish coleslaw before disappearing into the kitchen. A cheer went up from the kitchen television, a hometown cheer too loud to be a response to an Ottawa goal. The coleslaw was cold and crunchy, thick with real mayonnaise. He pushed it across to Duchesne.

"Try some. It's good." Duchesne shook his head again. "How'd you find me, Inspector?"

"I'm a cop, Sergeant. Just like you." Their eyes met and held. Dutch Duchesne came up through the ranks, Kennison knew. Slowly, in rural postings. He wasn't an urban MBA cop—Kolchak said that stood for Mystified Boring Assholes. Poor Kolchak. Still, the inspector was part of that bastard Cosentino's network.

"Fair enough." Give the guy some room.

"One of the clerks at HQ said you liked this place."

"That's impressive. I don't know any clerks yet. Must be my personal magnetism."

"It's a small town, Sergeant. People tend to know what other people are doing. Some people make it their hobby." Duchesne said "'obby" with a hint of a French-Canadian heritage. "Works both ways. Everyone knows your business, but they'll support you, feed you, save your life and defend you to the death. Like family, you'll find. Hardest part of the job is sooner or later you'll arrest family. Bad guys live with good guys. Sometimes the good guys are the bad guys."

"So who knows you're here talking to the man you suspended last week?"

"No one. Margit, my wife. No one else. Yet. Although you can bet Sue has already broadcast it around town."

"Who's Sue?"

"The waitress."

"You mean Brenda."

"Sue. Susan. Susan O'Sullivan. Lives with Eddie Bretanno—LD trucker—out on the Frame Lake Road."

"LD?"

"Long distance. Calgary to San Francisco or San Jose, mostly."

"Why she wear that tag says Brenda?"

Duchesne shrugged. "Keep the hustlers away, maybe. You know, those lonely guys with nothing better to do than come on to every diner waitress they see? Like those rings of hers, those rings she's got on . . ." He said "dose guys, dose rings"—definitely out of Québec, or maybe St. Boniface. "Camouflage, I'd guess. She's not married. Anyway, anyone who'd mess with Sue would have to deal with Eddie, and Eddie's a mean son of a bitch even when he's not drunk."

Duchesne's cheeks went red at his own swearing, as if he'd been caught in some systemic trap he promised to escape when he became an officer. Kennison liked him better for that.

Victory Point, King William Island, Nunavut

Marie-Claire heard larger ice crystals battering the shed now, as if someone was hosing it with gravel. She imagined that the shed outside was covered in snow, that the ice was meant to bury her. Inside its glass cover the lantern light wavered but held in the storm assault. She'd done it. Succeeded. The sailors on those ships long ago must have tasted these small victories. The ones who survived. Except that none survived.

She felt frightened, suddenly breathless as if the lantern light was stealing her oxygen, as if her lungs weren't large enough to absorb the air she needed to live. She opened her mouth and tried to inhale deeply, but something in her chest prevented it. She wished Kenny were here with her. Daddy would understand about Kenny. After a while. He'd understand why his "Little MC" needed to carve her own path, why she couldn't spend her life as a political wife no matter how much everyone thought it was preordained.

Holding the lantern by its wire handle, she waved a mitten above her head, feeling for a suspended hook, something on which to hang it before it became too hot to hold. Her reach raised the hem of her parka, and cold wind rushed inside her sweater. She could feel it cool her sweat, stiffen a nipple, raise the pores on her belly.

Shivering, lantern held high, she turned away from the stove. She cried out. A guttural moan as the pale circle of light revealed the ragged rictus of Dr. Karl Conrad Kneisser, chin pressed tight to his chest, unseeing eyes staring into hers, his bearded jaw wrenched off bias in a mute mask of unquestionable death. A congealed black stain covered the collar and bib of his down vest like unbidden vomit. Ice pellets crusted his beard and mustache. Frozen tears evidenced his last breath.

Marie-Claire's heart stopped dead. She screamed and reeled. The lantern crashed to the floor and a volatile conspiracy of wind and flame and fear and fate levelled the shack in seconds.

2100 North Service Road, Mount Winans, Maryland

When she called out "Hello" and entered Keith Dickerson's office, he was standing next to an oversized faux-leather chair, behind a large desk with nothing on its surface except a modern lamp and a framed photograph angled so that Ruby couldn't see it.

Dickerson was a large, mustached man with longer-than-usual sideburns that, despite his expensive suits, gave him the aura of an unsuccessful country and western singer. His speech pattern of four-dollar words mixed with ten-cent redundancies further emphasized a confusion of higher education and homespun habits. He did not ask questions, but made statements with eyebrows raised while he waited for agreement as answers. His lips were weak, his eyes moist; he might have been most comfortable hitting on women in a singles bar. By the smug look on his face, Ruby guessed he'd won the argument with the deep voice.

Across the desk from him, leveraging his bulk out of one of two deep tub visitors' chairs, was a man with a combed black brush mustache and skin the colour of caramel pudding, who held a folded document in his right hand and tapped it against the knuckles of his left.

"Miz Cruz. Good evening. This is Norman Fernandez. Norm, this is Ms. Ruby Cruz, our new paralegal eagle for the NorthAm sector." Dickerson pointed to the ground, indicating the office on the floor below where Ruby worked. Fernandez transfered the document to his left hand and they shook. His eyes were oddly cold for being brown, but his hand was soft and warm, and he held hers for just a beat after the shake. Polite. Gentlemanly. Not like the smarmy little tugs and finger tickles from the adolescents at the Bureau. "Mr. Fernandez is one of our top international security people, Ruby. Speaks six languages. That right, Norm?"

"Five." His voice was as warm as his hand. Like Lou Rawls, thought Ruby. She liked Lou Rawls's voice and she had three of his CDs. She knew all the words to "After the Lights Go Down Low" and sang along to it in the car.

"Five, then. Lotta languages. Highly intelligent smart man, is Norman. Clever fellow." Dickerson seemed to be fishing for a response, so Ruby nodded. They sat down, Fernandez still toying with his paper. Her chair, like his, was small with high sides, pushing her shoulders towards each other, forcing her forward; the sides were too high for her to rest her arms, so she interlaced her fingers and rested them on her knees like an obedient child, knees together, legs angled to the side like a soldier's pinup. Dickerson stared at her knees and coughed into his manicured hand several times before speaking.

"Ms. Cruz . . . Ruby. As you are probably just beginning to comprehend and understand, AEI has operations in several parts of the polar universe, and our people—academic, technical and administrative, teachers, engineers, managers—are integrally involved at many of those locations." She nodded. She could smell herself and wished she hadn't answered his call like an obedience-school puppy but had shown some spine and taken time for a shower.

"Partnerships are complicated animals, Ruby—like marriage, huh?" He paused and posed like a standup comic, waiting for a laugh, but when she didn't deliver, he proceeded. "People say that a moose is an animal designed by a committee. You'll have heard that one." Ruby nodded, even though she hadn't.

"We here at AEI must offer our partners reasonable representation, as defined by the total population divided by the dollars each one of them contributes, huh? These are not simple negotiations in the first place, Ruby, and as time goes on and more factors enter the picture, there tend to be even more difficult . . . er . . . mathematical or, say, management problems. Management problems." He hesitated, raised his eyes to look at Fernandez, and must have received some signal of support as he continued, fluent now, hitting his stride.

"What you will not have yet personally experienced yourself is our attempted endeavour to establish a credible presence on many operations that may not be ours or directly involve the members on our partner list. These are sometimes delicate . . . uh . . . delicate and, shall we say, clandestine, confidential situations." He leaned heavily on the word "clandestine," using his fingers to suggest quotation marks. Ruby frowned. What the hell was he talking about? Dickerson sensed her confusion and appeared bothered by it. He looked over to Fernandez, who spoke in a soothing tone—softly, so she had to lean even farther forward to hear him.

"Ms. Cruz, it's critical to our mandate and to our clients that we are sensitive to the actions and explorations of others in those areas we consider to be within our corporate geographic jurisdiction." Fernandez's eyes sought Dickerson's, but the large man was staring at his long fingernails. Guitar player's fingernails, she thought. "Even if they are in what one might consider the sovereign territories of other politically defined entities."

"You mean other countries?" asked Ruby. Fernandez stared back at her, brown eyes unwavering, unapologetic. He nodded to corroborate, or at least she thought he did. Dickerson adjusted the height of his desk lamp and the angle of the photograph on his desk. Was it a photograph of his wife? His family? Of his horse? His car? Of himself, maybe? He took back the conversation.

"When required, we necessarily consolidate our knowledge base by having credible, uh, representatives attached to the projects or investigations of others so that—"

"Agents," said Ruby. "Spies." Fernandez looked her in the eyes and she stared back, unwavering. "Corporate spies on other people's projects? In other countries, correct?" After the years in the Hoover hot tub of American paranoia, Ruby was weary of double-entendres and double agents behind every tree. After 9/11, life in the Bureau had gone manic, with half the agents looking the other way while the rest redefined the bad guys and rewrote the history to credit themselves. She'd heard it was worse at Langley, and even worse inside the NSI. The delusional madness ended for Ruby with Harry's death. That was reality. Bang. No more Harry. Say it like it is. Dead in the water. Over. Period. Move on. That's when she started fantasizing about wearing sarongs and slinging beer in a beach bar where the only issue was local rainfall.

In the midst of the madness, she'd quit the Bureau, bailed out of the conspiracy blimp for good, she'd thought. And now, damn it, it seemed she was back in it, but at the corporate end. Was America simply divided into those who conspired and those who believed in conspiracy? Fernandez frowned at her as if re-evaluating her loyalty to the corporation and the country.

"Ms. Cruz, Ms. Cruz, Ms. Cruz," soothed Dickerson from behind his desk. He said it as if he was writing a lyric, fingertips joined and knuckles flexed slightly to emphasize his sensitivity. His fingers had thick tufts of black hair between the knuckles. "We are in a global business. One in which certain worthy and valuable items that lie beneath the Arctic and Antarctic ice caps have become . . . uh . . . attainable, shall we say, whether through advances in technology or global temperature realignments.

"Guaranteed access to these parts of the world is critical to their—and our—survival. We have clients from many countries. Promises have been made to them, and we have contractual requirements to live up to those promises. It's business. Their business is our business. Let me cut to the chase." He glanced at Fernandez and waited until he nodded agreement. Ruby's mind was racing. She was beginning to feel excitement. Maybe this job wasn't as tame as she'd thought.

"Please," said Ruby. "Let's cut to the chase." Dickerson turned to see if she was mocking him, but Ruby wasn't smiling. She focused her gaze to look directly up into his eyes, the angle making her appear serious, pious, perhaps attractive. His eyes were grey in this light, or perhaps light blue. There was a yellow tinge. Lying eyes, untrustworthy, like those of a misbred Husky.

"Ruby, listen," Dickerson said at last as he sat down in his large chair and leaned forward, elbows on his desk. "An esteemed colleague of AEI—an employee, one might say—an internationally respected anthropologist named Dr. Karl Kneisser is working at an Arctic archaeological site to which we provide . . . assistance . . . provide support." Fernandez stared at his hands in his lap and cleaned a fingernail with the corner of his folded paper.

"And we're not talking Alaska here, are we?" said Ruby. "We're not talking the American Arctic."

"We need a person legally capable and competent, someone representative of our corporate credibility, someone onside with a skilled, judicious mind to accompany Dr. Kneisser back here, back to where we can accord him the proper respect and give his accomplishments the credit and exposure they deserve. You have an active passport?" Ruby nodded. After the twin towers she had made sure she had one so she could escape to that beach bar.

"Why does Dr. Kneisser need help? Is he crippled?" she said.

"And you have the passport at home?" Ruby nodded again.

"Why does Dr. Kneisser need help getting home?" The two men stared at each other, and Ruby realized they hadn't completely settled their difference of opinion. She pushed herself forward in the chair, ready to rise. The move drew Dickerson's attention, and without looking at Fernandez, he spoke.

"For eight years, Ruby, we have funded—our clients have funded—Dr. Kneisser's explorations in northern Canada." Ruby stared back at Dickerson, thinking she could hear Fernandez's deflated sigh in the corner and sense his shoulders sagging in defeat. "We have not only provided Dr. Kneisser with the tools and support to continue his celebrated explorations into the mysteries of the Franklin Expedition—you know about it?" Ruby shook her head. Dickerson looked at Fernandez as if to apologize, but Fernandez misread him.

"I'll get the books from my office," he said, and left the room. Dickerson moved forward on his elbows, more intimate with Fernandez gone. Ruby moved back in her tub chair.

"This year, with the unexpected collapse of funding for the annual British archaeological exploration Dr. Kneisser attaches himself to, we stepped in with funding, or rather, our clients did."

"What's he looking for? Wouldn't whatever he found be Canada's anyway? Surely, they're not going to let anyone take what's under the ice, no matter who pays to find it. Or do you think they'll be too stupid to notice?"

"Those are good questions, Ruby. It's not just what's in the ground that's important. It's the land itself and what it borders." Dickerson hesitated as Fernandez rejoined them and placed two softcover books on the desk. He picked one of them up and showed the cover to Ruby.

"The Franklin Expedition set off from England in the mid-1800s, twenty years or so before the country of Canada existed. Although there's no proof they traversed the Northwest Passage—they disappeared off the face of the planet—there's no proof that they did not."

"What does this have to do with Dr. Kneisser? "

"Please bear with me. Canada claims the Northwest Passage is an inland Canadian waterway because they claim the land on each side of the waterway. With the melting of the ice cap, that passage is becoming more navigable, perhaps soon clear of ice. I can't emphasize enough what that means. Shipping between this continent and Europe is reduced by four thousand miles, an annual saving of billions. For America, the northern sea link between the Pacific and Atlantic becomes a viable shipping corridor, let alone what it means for defence, for Homeland Security, for—"

"Unless Canada denies access."

"Unless Canada denies access. Or unless we can establish that that country's claim of sovereignty over the passage is spurious."

"How would you prove that?"

"By establishing that the Northwest Passage was traversed as an international waterway before Canada became a country."

The light dawned. "Your Franklin Expedition." Dickerson nodded. Fernandez stared at the floor.

"If Franklin or any of his men of the British Admiralty traversed the Northwest Passage before Canada was a country, that passage is arguably unclaimed. An international waterway . . ."

"So we don't really care about the land."

"Only to the extent that it will support supply services to, and shelter for, American ships. Otherwise, Canada can have it. For the present."

"Is there precedent for such an argument?" Whenever Ruby became excited, she reverted to legal process. She checked her emotions with the tedium of law.

"Several. The Panama Canal remains international despite Panama having claims to the land on both sides of the waterway—and Americans fought hard to make it so. The Gulf of Sidra, off the coast of Tripoli, lies between sovereign Libyan lands. Despite that, America has negotiated a guaranteed right of passage. There are examples in Indonesia and—"

"So this Dr. . . . What's his name?"

"Kneisser. With a K. Silent K."

"This Dr. Kneisser has discovered something that will prove our case, something from that expedition that disputes Canada's claim that this passage is an inland waterway?" Dickerson hesitated and looked to Fernandez.

"Perhaps. Yes. We believe so. That's why we need Kneisser and his findings, his evidence, here."

"So we can use it to dispute Canada's sovereignty over the Northwest Passage, or at least take it to an international court." Dickerson nodded and opened his mouth, but before he could speak, Fernandez interrupted in his warm tones.

"Or, if it helps establish a Canadian sovereign claim beyond doubt, so we can destroy it."

"Play her the Kneisser tape, Norm." Ruby thought he sounded victorious.

Yellowknife, Northwest Territories

"How can I help you, Inspector?"

"Thank you, Sergeant Kennison. Thank you . . . Booker."

Kennison could tell he was uncomfortable with the name. He'd have been more uncomfortable with the real one if he knew it. Or even his nickname—he'd grown up being known as Balls. Sister Cordelia's boy's class roared when the new nun read his initials—B.O.L.—as his name at role call. Kennison, the punk teenager and Difficult Placement, kept it because it sounded like what he wanted to be—tough and American. Balls Kennison. A man's name. The nickname had carried over onto the street and into the army and, to a few close colleagues, into the Mounties. None of them knew its origin, and none of them ever would. It existed only on his birth certificate, and that was locked up in a safety deposit box in Hamilton.

"I'm in a bind, Sergeant. I have seven men on a course down south, and the rest are assigned to the annual Dog Derby running in town this weekend. I can't bring in officers or men from the North or South divisions because of staff directives."

"It's about time, Inspector, if you don't mind me saying. I feel like I'm being kept in the closet like some secret Christmas present." Duchesne hesitated a moment, raised his large head and nodded. There was something he didn't want to say.

"Sergeant. I . . . look, this is a low-profile job, eh? A straight in and out. We've had a satellite telephone call from Jensen, the constable stationed at Ross Haven." Duchesne reached into his left chest pocket and pulled out a small spiral-bound notepad he read from. He seemed more comfortable when he wasn't looking into Kennison's eyes.

"There's been a fire at a camp about a hundred miles northwest of Ross. Two people dead. Non-natives . . . visiting scientists, Jensen thinks. Accident. She can't get away to investigate. DVs coming to Ross on their annual sovereignty rah-rah parade, and there's a substantiated rumour about a Turqavik protest, or worse. I can't let her leave Ross, so I need you to go there, Kennison. In and out. Write it up and copy me. That simple." Duchesne stared at the upside-down placemat and played with the spoon in his coffee cup.

"Turqavik?"

"Native group. Inuit, mostly. Land rights and all that, but Jensen thinks they're about to get radical." Duchesne tapped his spoon on the rim of the cup. "Sort of thought process that happens when you're on your own in an isolated community sometimes." Kennison bit his burger and mopped the juices off his chin with the thin paper napkin. It was very good. The mess on his face gave him time to think. DVs—Distinguished Visitors—were a pain in the ass for any police or military force. Kolchak called them DTs because he said they all drank too much on the road. The Mountie's job at such events is more "suit up and smile" than real policing, but it's unavoidably part of the federal hype, especially up here with the new emphasis on Arctic sovereignty. And if there are rumours of a protest . . . Kennison rolled his eyes at the thought.

They'd all read emailed copies of interdivisional memos about politicians planting flags on more and more remote Inuit villages, and even uninhabited sterile islands that Denmark thought belonged to them. With the Big Melt, everyone was in on the grab. The Russians were claiming the North Pole because their Lomonosov Ridge ran through it. Ottawa kept making speeches, and the Canadian Rangers, a paramilitary group made up mostly of elderly Inuit snowmobilers, converged on some remote Arctic location every so often in the name of sovereignty. As the ice cap melted, the world saw money. Duchesne was still talking.

"I need someone senior—someone experienced—to sift through the ashes, so to speak, talk to the colleagues of these two dead people . . . you know the drill. Go there. Do the job. Wrap it up quickly. Low-profile. Do it so neither the case nor your name rings any bells here or in Ottawa or anywhere else . . ."

Kennison measured his next bite and turned the burger to ensure it included pickle and bacon.

"Ricky Monteith's Otter is booked to pick them up tomorrow or the day after if the weather holds," said Duchesne. "You can use it to get a ride there in the morning, weather willing." He dropped his spoon in his coffee mug. "They're closing camp very late in the season. I'm surprised the water's still open. Must be that global warming." Duchesne rose and began putting on his heavy coat.

Kennison ate a french fry slowly. They'd been good, but they were cold now. Gone soggy. Mealy. Like him. Kennison couldn't tell anymore who was protecting him and who was setting him up. Duchesne wanted him out of town. Why? "Suspension wiped off the books?"

Duchesne put on the fur hat that added six inches to his already impressive height. He raised his eyebrows as Kennison pushed the plate of fries towards him like a twenty-dollar bill palmed to a headwaiter. Duchesne leaned down and forward and took a long piece of potato.

"Off the books. Just stay out of fights and bars, especially the Sly. There's people like nothing better than—"

"Full pay restored?"

Duchesne stood tall, hesitating, looking at the french fry. He was uncomfortable and wanted to go home.

"Retroactive. Next pay period. Reflected in direct deposit." He held the french fry up like a fish, turning it with sausage-like fingers, measuring the risk.

"Personal apology in writing from the Division Chief Superintendent?"

Duchesne froze and looked down at Kennison.

"Not a fucking chance, boyo."

Duchesne put the french fry in his mouth and looked sideways furtively as if Brenda-Susan might tell his wife he'd been eating forbidden food or taking a bribe or using inappropriate language in a public place.

237 West Fayette Street, Baltimore, Maryland

It had been a foreign voice. Ruby, in her sensible underwear, spread the coats in the hall closet and reached to the back, leaning forward on her toes, feeling with her extended hand for the slippery nylon skin of the ski jacket. Not like a Middle Eastern or Arabic language or anything like that. A European accent of some kind—German or Dutch, probably, given his name. Kneisser.

She grasped a sleeve and pulled it towards her. The coat was stuck on something, so she yanked it towards her and the wire hanger hook bent straight to release the jacket. With it came a pair of ski pants with a lift pass attached by a wire. It was bent. That was what had been caught on the hanger. It said "Stowe, Vermont." The first time she skied. Harry took her, spent half an hour with her on the bunny hill before he became impatient and handed her over to an instructor who looked twelve years old.

She'd been so angry at being dumped that she'd refused the lesson and stomped into the clubhouse, where she'd spent the day sulking in front of the fire, drinking too much wine. The next morning, they'd driven back to Washington in silence, and she hadn't worn the outfit since. Would it fit? The half-glass of red wine and curled slices of pizza lay on the coffee table where she'd left them when Dickerson called. She glanced out the apartment window. Fernandez was idling in his car three stories below, exhaust fumes disappearing into the cold night air. She could sense his impatience from this distance. He could wait. She had a lot to think over.

"There. There. I'm recording now. Put him through, Donny."

"Signal's lousy, Mr. Dickerson."

"Just put him through, Donny. Now." The quality of the recording wasn't good. The signal varied, made randomly weaker and stronger by weather or location. The voice pronounced "have" as "haff," "will" as "vill," "think" as "sink."

"Hello? Hello?"

"Dickerson here. Is that you, Dr. Kneisser? Karl?"

"Hello? This is Karl Conrad Kneisser. Hello?"

"It's me. Keith Dickerson. Is that you, Karl? Dr. Kneisser? Can you hear me?"

"Yes. Yes. If I move . . . one moment bitte . . ."

The signal had faded, replaced by a howl that made Ruby cover her ears and Dickerson lunge for the small machine's volume control. Before he could find it, the caller's voice had sounded clearly: "Can you hear me better?"

"Yes. Yes, I can. Much better. Where are you, Karl? Are you still at the site?"

"*Ja. Ja.* I'm using the satellite telephone from the site. I am told that the batteries are low and I have not much time."

It was a gruff voice, not angry in tone, more rusty from lack of use, the voice of a man used to thinking before speaking, yet talking quickly and excitedly like a child in a theme park. The wash of static that had come and gone had sounded like massed crowds applauding at a college football game. In the pool of light from Dickerson's desk lamp, the three of them stared at an MP3 player the size of a keychain.

Ruby sat on her bed and pulled the ski pants on. A year of Dante's pizza and glasses of red wine hadn't helped, despite the jogging. They were tight across her butt but they'd have to do.

"Are you okay?" Dickerson was talking. "Anything wrong? Shouldn't you be on your way back by now?"

"*Ja. Ja.* We are packing up today the site. I have news. That's why I call. Big news."

"What kind of news, Karl?"

"I have found a journal here. *Ein Buch.* How do you say . . . a diary."

"Just a moment, Karl. Let me write this down . . ." Ruby had heard the click of a hold button and a buzz.

"Fernandez here."

"Get in here, Norm. It's Kneisser. From the dig. He's found something." There was another click and Dickerson resumed his conversation. "Okay, shoot, Karl. What have you found? Is it one of the ship's records? Is it Franklin's journal?"

"*Nein, nein.* It's better than that. It's a crew-member diary, full of things no officer would record. There is murder. Cannibal . . . cannibal . . . ?"

"Cannibalism?"

"*Ja.*"

"Proof?"

"*Ja.* It is priceless, my friend. It will ensure the name of Karl Conrad Kneisser is forever remembered, that the history of anthropology will forever include—" Ruby heard the noise of someone entering the room and pulling up a chair.

"Sure, Karl. Happy for you. Norm Fernandez is here. I'm putting you on speakerphone. How does this diary help us?"

"This is without question the most important archaeological and anthropological discovery of modern times . . ." Static washed in and covered the words " . . . whether it helps you with your quest is not the point, Mr. Dickerson. This is history. This is the solution for one of the greatest mysteries of the last three centuries, *mein Freund . . .*"

"Karl, we're happy for you. Really. But listen to me. We haven't been paying you and your expenses for seven, eight years now so you can become more famous. You know damned well what we're after, what we need for the partners here . . . just a second . . ." Ruby heard whispering between Dickerson and Fernandez. "Here's Norm, Karl. Answer his questions."

"Dr. Kneisser." Fernandez's voice sounded like a late-night FM radio announcer compared to Dickerson's increasingly strident tones. "Norm Fernandez here. Do you have this book, this journal, on your person?"

"*Ja.* I do."

"Who else knows you found this?"

"Patel. The assistant. He sees me cut it from the pocket of the man in the grave. Trevor Patel—how do you say, 'crybaby boy,' always talking about cold and hard work . . ."

"Anyone else?"

"*Nein.* This Masterson suspects, I think, just as I suspect him. The others? *Nein.* The archaeologist only thinks of herself and her assistant is a child. The rest are natives and kitchen help. They know nothing . . ." The static washed in again, and out to reveal: " . . . we are leaving today, tomorrow, next day. This little Patel already looks at me like I am carrying millions of dollars. He is hungry, this boy. He envies me, wants my success after so little work and so much complaining. And he owes money to this Masterson. I do not trust him."

"Dickerson here, Karl. Does this journal incontrovertibly prove that Franklin completed the Northwest Passage? Does it establish beyond doubt that—" The static wash rolled in like hurricane surf, receding only so that they could hear a comment including the words "storm" and "batteries." "Damn. Karl, are you there? Are you there, Karl? Damn it, Norm. Do something . . . Karl. Come in, dammit. Karl? Kneisser?" A sustained whoosh increased in volume and tonic range until it stopped abruptly. "Shit. Shit, shit, shit." They listened to the recorded sound of Dickerson pounding his desktop as he tried to find the off switch for the MP3 player. While he fumbled, Ruby continued to listen.

"The signal seems to have ended, sir."

"Who's that? Donny? Is that you? Have you been listening? For Christ's—"

"Well sir, I didn't know I shouldn't be. You didn't say . . ." The security guard's voice became muffled, as if the receiver had a hand over it.

"Jesus, Norm." Dickerson's voice. "He's heard fucking everything. See to him. Now. Lemme . . ." Ruby heard a final click and the recording ended. Dickerson held the small player in his palm, his face red with embarrassment.

It reminded her to take her iPod.

Ruby ripped back the Velcro strap that held her iPod to her

jogging jacket and fed the earbud cords through the vent. She might as well pack her music. Earlier tonight, before the pizza, before Dickerson's summons, she'd been running beside Camden Yards, turning from South Paca onto Fremont to steal a look at the new house. She was listening to "Slow Down Baby." Ruby privately believed that Christina Aguilera was her animate opposite—blonde where Ruby was dark, raucous where she was reticent, focused where she wandered. She was proud that the two of them shared a birthplace in Staten Island and a childhood in urban Pennsylvania, even if Christina was unaware of the coincidence. If the crossing of their paths had ever been possible, it had become highly unlikely when pretty Christina joined the New Mickey Mouse Club and plain Ruby, with her bad hair and skin problems, had hidden behind the locked door of her small room and transferred her adolescent sense of injustice into dreams of being a federal agent.

She'd never seen the house from the Camden Yards angle. She watched her feet, cautious of the uneven cobbles and what they could do to an unwary ankle. There was already ice in the ditches, early this year for Baltimore, for Ridgley's Delight. She was going to live in Ridgley's Delight. Take that, Christina. Come by for tea someday. Lah-de-dah, Ms. Ruby Cruz.

The late-afternoon air was dry, wintry, without humidity, fresher for its temperature than the Indian summer day only a week ago when she'd found the house on one of the meandering drives in Harry's car that she used to fill the weekends. Cooler was better. She liked the sour, damp smell of fallen leaves that still lay on the street, matted by rain, pestled by traffic. The leafless beeches and maples were old, sedate even in their nakedness, genteel, like Ridgley's Delight. Like Ruby Cruz someday soon.

She'd sat on a wooden bench, eyes trained purposefully on the ground, pinching the damp apple-green T-shirt and pulling it away from her body to let the chilly air rush between it and her skin. Her sports bra pinched, too small for her breasts, a wishful purchase rather than a practical one. Men stared at her body no matter what she did to compress or obscure it. Especially this last week in the new job. It would pass. It had better, although the jerks at the Bureau never stopped, did they? Her black Lycra cycling shorts fit well, smooth over her small hips, stretched over long, thin thighs of which she was proud. She'd only ever told Harry.

Ruby Cruz. Thirty-five years old, ex-federal agent, newly widowed, newly employed as a paralegal in the private sector, virtually a new homeowner and finally her own woman. Lah-de-dah. Independence at last.

She stuffed a pink angora sweater, another undersized gift from Harry, into the suitcase and sat on it to close the clasps. Fernandez tooted the horn impatiently in the street. The suitcase was heavier than she'd thought it would be.

Victory Point, King William Island, Nunavut

It was after supper before he could get back to his tent unobserved. Somewhere out there continued the sporadic single pops, as much a part of the ambience as the cold and dark, that said Wayne Penilik was shooting at things. The bloody Eskimo was never around to help with the shit work. Better off without him, to tell the truth—always looking at you like you were crapping on his front lawn, as if this shit hole had some real estate value and you didn't belong here.

Lillian seemed to have no power over the boy, grandson or not. With him always bloody well out shooting, there was only himself and Monk to set breakfast and pack the pots they wouldn't need for meals the next day.

With the grace of good luck—and Ricky Monteith—they'd be out of there in two days, although tomorrow they'd probably have bloody guests for lunch since the cops had been called. Lillian would have to make pasta again, or maybe more bloody frozen fish if the Inuit kid came back to camp without game. Stores were running low, though with Kneisser and the girl dead there were fewer mouths to feed.

He removed the small book from his backpack and unwrapped the pale blue towel in which he'd rolled it. He turned again to the first pages, where the bold, confident loops and strokes implied the anticipation of adventure, and read from the beginning.

Sunday, May 18, 1845
Greenhithe, Dartford, Kent

I write in some haste as we prepare to weigh anchor tomorrow and sail to Arctic shores. I wrongly presumed I'd have more time to watch these proceedings, to record my observations for future publication perhaps, but with church services on the wharf this morning and senior officers bounding about, yelling endless commands to the Warrants, Petty Officers and Able Seamen, I have spent today and much of the past week staying out of the way, overseeing my small part of this expedition of hearty men to discover the elusive Northwest Passage to the Orient. Better them than me, I think.

The wharves and buildings of this harbour town are dusty with the shipping residue of chalk and lime from the inland mines. Despite the overriding pallor and stench of industry, the village is middling charming and the fanciful new pier upstream vouchsafes a burgeoning nautical enterprise as carefree Londoners can now travel their beloved Thames on steamers as far as Gravesend. Good for them, I say. Not my cup of tea.

Today on these piers there's no holiday atmosphere. There's anxiety in the air, as if departing an hour or a day late will alter the course of history. Perhaps it will, or perhaps it's just the seamen's sullen response to the gruff demeanour of Commander Sir John Franklin. The Captain and his wife appear daily with a retinue of uniformed Admiralty types, one of whom I'm informed is Sir John Barrow. Formerly a teacher like myself (albeit Mathematics, I believe, rather than Language), he is now the famous explorer (Cape Barrow, Barrow Strait, Barrow Sound), published author, and chief organizer of this Franklin Expedition. It was he who chose Franklin to lead, though not a few question his selection, and the leverage that Lady Jane Franklin may have brought to bear. They stand in small groups in the rain, arms folded, epaulettes dripping, whispering to each other in low voices, pointing at the ships and frowning often.

Lady Jane points and frowns more than most. She has a rather detached smile that she turns on and off like a gas lamp for passing sailors, yet, to my eye, is maintained with unflickering radiance in the presence of Sir John Barrow. He seems quite taken with her as well, even as she hangs on her husband's arm. An ambitious woman, it's said, probably more than capable of the commission she's captured for her husband, although rumours persist of her insensitive failures in Van Diemen's Land.

Franklin looks older to me than his 59 years, but that may be due to a portly mien that transforms a naval strut into his ungainly waddle. I overheard a group of rough men say that the Commander may die of old age long ere they return to these shores. The apparent leader of this gang, a man with a deep, raw scar from his left ear to the deep cleft in his chin, said the departure date is immutable so that Franklin doesn't expire before the expedition departs.

As I am only employed to set up the libraries and teaching schedules for four months, I have not the long-term concerns of the others who have inured themselves to three years away from their loved ones. Alice Maud Lort may pine for me for a few months from St. Dunstan's in Maidstone, but I shall return to her ample bosom mid-October, whereupon I have vowed, at her insistence, to apply myself more strenuously to our future together.

As for the pressures of timely departure, I have heard from a Quartermaster, an older man called MacDonald, that upwards of 8,000 tins of meat, vegetables and soup were ordered from Goldner's in London as recently as the first of this month and are consequently late in arriving. Perhaps that alone explains the concerned countenances of the senior staff. I certainly hope it's not disquiet regarding the safety of the ships themselves.

I am being summoned. My books are being loaded on the ships, and my desks as well. As the latter are made of fine mahogany, I must ensure they are treated with some delicacy by hands more used to lading coal.

MONDAY, NOVEMBER 9

Cambridge Bay, Northwest Territories

Kennison walked the wooden pier in the morning dark, smoking a cigarette he had to hold up his sleeve to save his fingers from frostbite. The frozen wooden boards creaked under his black snow boots. In his other hand he clutched a Styrofoam cup with an insulating value of zero, containing rancid coffee laced with clotted powdered creamer. He watched as a ground crew of one elderly Inuit man unhurriedly unloaded a box that seemed to be made more of duct tape than cardboard.

Through the brightly lit window of the site trailer that served as a terminal, Ricky Monteith chatted up a plain-faced and impossibly young local airline rep wearing a tight tank top and push-up bra that would have demanded attention in St. Tropez. Every building up here was overheated and overlit. It's compensatory, thought Kennison, like guys with short dicks driving long red cars, or small towns with a surfeit of one-way streets and stoplights.

Beside the terminal, lit by a harsh yard light, sat a dark-coloured snowmobile with a vibrant sport graphic and a small rusted Chevrolet truck with a cracked windshield. An orange extension cord ran from under the truck's hood to an outlet on the wall. How did a truck get here, Kennison wondered? Where would you drive it? Up and down the main street of Cambridge Bay? Did Cambridge Bay *have* a main street? Or any street at all?

With stoplights? He shivered and nodded as the Inuit passed him with the box, nodding and smiling, revealing missing teeth, saying something Kennison didn't understand.

"Sorry?" said Kennison, more polite than interested. Let's get this thing gassed up and go. The man ducked his chin towards the box in his arms and grinned.

"Shrimp," he said, batting his lips together, licking them with a pink tongue to mime delicious. Frozen shrimp to a frozen land, thought Kennison. Coals to Newcastle. Owls to Athens. Refrigerators to Eskimos. And Sergeant Booker Kennison to bloody Yellowknife, N.W.T.

Two days after the bullets stopped flying in the Roadkill Riders raid, he'd been called on the carpet by Superintendent Gino Cosentino. One of the bullets had been Kennison's, and it had entered the mouth of Patrice "Patsy" Prévost and blown out the back of his head in a parking lot in Gatineau, on the Québec side of the Ottawa River.

Plenty of witnesses had seen Prévost draw a gun and fire at Kennison's back as the Mountie dove sideways onto the gravel and rolled to his knees, drawing his gun and popping a single shot down the perp's throat like a breath mint. The cops from Ontario's Provincial Police, Québec's Sûreté and the local Ottawa and Gatineau forces were thrilled. A few civilian tourists applauded as if the shooting was an unexpected theme park presentation enacted for their benefit.

"I'm not saying you weren't doing your job, Kennison," said Cosentino. "Not saying that at all, you understand." The superintendent had a reputation for explaining what he was not saying.

He was a shorter-than-average man with clean-shaven and fleshy cheeks, a desk cop carrying out orders from those who held jobs he coveted. Kolchak had called him "Ginotino," though not to his face.

His desk was clean, except for a multi-line telephone at which he kept glancing as if willing an incoming call. There were no framed pictures on the desk or matching credenza. Either the man had none or was caught up in his work. The office had been carved out of a retrofit, so the windows were mullioned and narrow and the ceilings disproportionately high. Cosentino offered Kennison a chair so that their height difference wouldn't be obvious.

"And I can't truly complain about how you performed, Kennison, except to say . . ." He paused as if trying to recall rehearsed words. " . . . that we have an image out there, and that image—like it or not—is not rolling around parking lots in civvies like the hero on an American cop show, yelling and shooting at citizens in public places where stray bullets can harm the innocent."

There was so much unspoken between them, so much history and baggage and the death of a good man, that Kennison couldn't hold onto his temper. "You would prefer I'd been wearing dress scarlets and a Stetson, maybe carrying a lance and riding a black horse, sir?"

"Sarcasm is not welcome here Kennison, nor is it—"

"Neither is criticism, sir." Kennison watched the words escape from his mouth like a cartoon balloon and wished he could suck them back before they reached the Superintendent's little ears. Too late. Cosentino's face went beet red so quickly that Kennison thought he was having an aneurysm. The man's eyes bulged until they seemed to touch the inside of his thick lenses. In for a dollar . . .

"I do my job and I do it well, sir. You know that. Every officer and member of senior management here knows that. You may not like me and I may not like you, but Patsy Prévost is—was—a very, very bad man. He's now a very, very dead biker, and no one except the Admin staff seems to have a problem with that. Sir." Kennison couldn't stop now. He was angry—angry about a lot of things beyond this piddling affair.

"Maybe it would have been better if he'd killed me, sir. Then you could have killed two birds with one stone—got rid of me and had a parade. A musical ride, sir. You could make a moving speech at the memorial right outside there. Prévost would get bail, the high school kids would get their happy pills, the press would have a story, and no citizens or small animals would be harmed in the making of this movie. Everyone would be happy." Kennison stood quickly and Cosentino exhaled hard, rigid in his chair.

"Well bullshit, Superintendent. You want to transfer me to chasing odometer cheaters or vinyl siding salesmen, that's up to you, but I'm not going to stop doing my job. I'm a cop, a Mountie, not a damned tourist attraction."

"That's enough, Kennison. More than enough," Cosentino said tightly, his upper lip quivering uncontrollably as if he had palsy. "Why in God's name do you always make things worse for yourself?" He was having trouble opening the drawer of his desk, rattling it loudly until it sprung loose. The sound echoed in the room. He reached inside for a translucent orange bottle and put a small white pill on his sharp pink tongue. He stood, fingertips spread on the shiny top like a pianist, wrists high. His face wouldn't pale and his shaved red neck swelled over his doubly starched collar so that Kennison thought he might cut his own throat and bleed to death in front of him.

When Cosentino spoke again, he hissed. "I'm certain we'll secure a position suitable to your . . . skills, Kennison. And to your extremely high opinion of them. Somewhere less visible, somewhere you'll have time to think about the consequences of your actions. That'll do, Sergeant. Dismissed."

Dismissed was right. Out of A Division down to G Division, an alphabetic descent that probably had the HQ keyboard cops still laughing up their dress uniform sleeves. A slippery slide from the tulip-lined canals of the National Capital Region to the ice-bound inequities of Yellowknife's Ragged Ass Road. In less than a heartbeat.

But it wasn't really about the death of Patsy Prévost, thought Kennison, no matter what the Superintendent was saying. That was just the excuse they needed to get him out of town. There was something big happening, and Kennison was being put on ice because he had made some very important people very uncomfortable. And some very bad people, too. He knew a whole lot of secrets, and it went a whole lot higher than Cosentino. He just hadn't blabbed it like Kolchak. Not yet.

Ricky Monteith walked down the dock with a smile on his face. Kennison smiled back grimly and climbed into the co-pilot's seat as Monteith warmed up the port engine and coaxed some of its heat into the cabin, whistling to himself as if he'd just got lucky—or would after the Dog Derby dance.

Lucky wasn't one of the cards in Kennison's deck.

Victory Point, King William Island, Nunavut

The wind ripped at the tent flaps. There was little else to hear other than the constant whining about rocks and dark and food and weather as they prepared another load for the Otter. They were trying to pack up the dig at Hell, as well as up at Kneisser's site, and be ready to leave. In this bloody wind. Fat chance. Be frozen here for a month if they couldn't get out. At least they were at it now—and none too bloody soon. He paused to ensure he was truly alone, then unwrapped the towel and opened the book to the next entry, directing the weak beam of his flashlight onto the brown-edged pages.

> *Monday, May 19, 1845*
> *At sea*
>
> *It is late in the day and I put pen to paper, sitting at a writing desk in the Library, now situated amidships in the* Terror. *The room they have given me is smallish, but I've found all rooms—cabins, they call them—are small on board ship. My mood, however, one of some sadness, perhaps tinged, to be honest, with regret, has neither to do with the allotted quarters nor the leaving of England. Rather, my ennui concerns a letter I received moments before embarking. Miss Lort informs me that she is with*

child—mine, she suggests, and it is to be presumed. She prays her letter will reach me before we sail, and it did. I was unable to respond, or perhaps incapable of doing so in the short term before sailing. I do not, in truth, know what to say. As the letter was delivered through the Purser, I can perhaps feign lack of receipt and justify no immediate response.

I am of the opinion that absences refresh relations rather than weaken them and that the unexpected shock of impending fatherhood demands time to weigh the personal consequences and immediate future. Besides, I shall be back long before the child is whelped.

I realize in this first moment of respite since boarding that I have not recorded my name and place among the crew of this ship. My name is William George Bearman, a singular name in Kent, perhaps descended from the Dutch, we surmise (Behrman perhaps?), who came to England under the protection and parliamentary reforms of William III and Queen Mary 150 years since. I am by birth a Kentish Man as opposed to a Man of Kent, coming from west of the River Medway, Sevenoaks in particular. I am 25 years of age and fit. I've been told I am of better than average appearance, that I have good legs and bearing (by several, including Miss Lort), despite some facial scars from acne and the sulphur treatments taken to cure it. Like me, much of the 134 crewmen of the Terror *and* Erebus *are in their 20s. Unlike me, most cannot read nor write.*

It was Lady Franklin who convinced the Admiralty (or perhaps only Sir John Barrow, as I think on it) to provide monies for books and lessons for the sailors on her husband's expedition.

I was found teaching British naval history and literature to ill-behaved children of the newly wealthy in Sevenoaks, and welcomed the opportunity to establish a library on each ship and the classroom materials for the education and edification of the crew, should they desire it. The offer was perhaps less avocation than escape. I have done well, I believe. The library in which I write on Her Majesty's Ship Terror *comprises 1,200 volumes in glass-fronted cases fixed to the walls—they call them bulkheads. Each shelf has decorative wooden stops to prevent the volumes slipping onto the floor when we're heeling hard to port or starboard. HMS* Erebus *holds 1,700 in a slightly larger space. With the bookshelves taking up all of the bulkheads save the entry door, the desks are somewhat cramped in the centre of the room. I could have made do with fewer, I suppose, but it is difficult to deduce how many sailors might take advantage of the available schooling, either out of desire for self-improvement or as an antidote to utter boredom. As an amateur naval historian, many of the books I chose for each Library are narratives of earlier Arctic or Antarctic explorations, as I thought it wise to provide context to these gallant men and allow them the opportunity of whiling away the dark winter nights with the successful tales of others in similar climes. For lighter entertainment, and with a mind to homesickness, I have included a smattering of popular novels, including the Irishman Goldsmith's* Vicar of Wakefield *and Mr. Dickens'* Nicholas Nickleby, *the latter so recently having its serial parts bound into a rather handsome and worthwhile book despite the many sordid aspects of its story. I have always found it easier to impassion the illiterate by using popular texts, preferably the short ones.* Lectio brevior lectio potior*—the shorter book is that more likely read.*

Although the wind is presently picking up and the afternoon sky darkening, it was a fresh spring day when we departed this morning, somewhat cloud-covered but with gaps for the spring sun to find us standing on the pier at dawn. Goldner's victuals finally arrived late yesterday. The group led by the scar-faced man swore that some of the tins were still warm from the ovens. It's a simple matter for one to speak of three years' worth of sustenance, but to see it piled on the wharf—8,000 sealed tins of various shapes and weights—is a sight to behold, and one I shall not soon forget. I have heard that we have a "camera" aboard for scientific use and thus jealously guarded. If such a thing could capture the image of tins on the pier I see in my mind, sales of the new Illustrated London News *would increase measurably. Today's departure ceremonies were somewhat curtailed by the men's exhaustion. They loaded provisions all night long, making sleep difficult for all, yet there was still a pallet or two remaining on the wharf at first light. During the speeches, many of the men were falling asleep standing on the pier. I sensed Lady Franklin's displeasure from where I watched at the edge of the crowd. Her husband, resplendently clad in his dress uniform and surrounded on each side by his officers, seemed tired, his face drawn. A rumour circulates that, a night or two since, Lady Franklin proudly draped a Union Jack over her husband's sleeping body to give him warmth. When he woke to find himself covered in the Jack, he felt it a premonition of death and tore it from his body. A superstitious man, it seems. During the ceremonies, Lady Franklin placed something around her husband's neck and kissed his sallow cheeks. Those close or on the dais applauded, and the rest of us politely followed suit without knowing or understanding the purpose. I could not hear the words nor see what she gave him, but he spent the rest of the hour rubbing it with his fingers (like a Turk with his "komboloi") as he listened to speeches and looked downriver towards the sea. It took a dove landing on the main mast of his flagship* Erebus *to break his mood, an agreed omen of peace and harmony that is utterly lacking in the names of his ships,* Terror *and* Erebus, *the latter classically being the "gates of Hell."*

We sail north now, England to our port side. We're to touch land at a port on the Orkney Islands for reasons I do not know—at Stromness, I think. Perhaps I can send Miss Lort a note from there. The weather seems increasingly rough, and this ship yaws constantly to starboard. I am reminded that I am a teacher, not a sailor, and, to be truthful, I am feeling ill and somewhat faint. There are no portholes in the Library, no fresh air that I can sense . . .

International Airport, Edmonton, Alberta

Ruby Cruz slept curled up on three cloth seats in the Arctic Air pod waiting room. The overnight Gulfstream flight from Washington to Edmonton had been comfortable enough, but she couldn't sleep on planes. The pilot and the flight attendant had been civil, but only just, deeming her not high enough up the corporate ladder to deserve red carpet treatment. When she boarded at Dulles, as Fernandez watched dully from the tarmac, the attendant had given her a fruit plate covered tightly in clear plastic wrap and pointed to the snack cabinet and small refrigerator. After the standard speech and a seat belt check, she closeted herself in the cockpit with the pilot and stayed there for the duration of the flight.

Ruby needed a shower. Her dark hair was naturally coarse and became oily and frizzy soon after it was washed. In her teens, she'd been the poster girl for everything that could go wrong with hair and skin, and not much had changed despite all the conditioners and potions she'd tried. Maybe she'd have time for a hot bath in Yellow Knife if damned Yellow Knife had any hot water or a tub to put it in.

She shifted her hips on the chair. Fernandez's two paperbacks protruded from a pocket of her backpack. She'd leafed through them on the plane but quickly grown disinterested. The Franklin story was all so terribly English and depressing and so very long ago. History wasn't her cup of coffee unless it was American history. The speculations about what agonies might have met the freezing British sailors eventually bored her to sleep.

She'd felt pumped when Dickerson finally explained her mission—excited the way she'd been when she first joined the Bureau and felt she was part of some force that could save America from itself under Reagan's benevolent leadership. The real drudgery and stupidity of the job, and of her colleagues, dulled that edge quickly, but this mission sounded like it was about something important, something that could make a difference to America, something she could fight on the front lines. At forty-one she didn't feel too old for a fight, although fighting Canadians seemed like the punch line of a bad joke. They were just French-speaking wannabe Americans who spent their winters in Florida getting melanoma until they ran home for free operations.

The paper in Fernandez's soft hands had been a map that he spread out over the mahogany acreage of the desk. The three of them stood around it, and Dickerson swung the lamp to illuminate a high school–like map of North America, densely detailed throughout the forty-eight contiguous states with insets of Hawaii and Alaska. Canada and Mexico were comparatively vacant, pale netherworlds letterboxing the multicoloured U. S. of A. Dickerson sidled uncomfortably close to her. She could smell his musk cologne and stale breath.

"The AEI jet is at Dulles," said Fernandez, jabbing at Washington, D.C., with the butt end of a white Cross pen tugged from an inside jacket pocket. "It will fly you up to Edmonton in Canada." The white Cross arced high in the air and landed half a continent away on a city in the middle of a large rectangular state north of Montana. "There's a seat booked on a connecting flight tomorr . . ." Fernandez checked his watch. " . . . yes, tomorrow morning, that will take you from Edmonton to . . ." His white Cross stayed on the paper and traced a path north over an area almost devoid of names and roads to settle on the northern shore of a blue lake. Dickerson was watching her reactions, so she kept still, revealing nothing, moving away from him, turning her head to see the map.

"Yellow Knife." Dickerson said it as two distinct words and repeated it the way a child repeats a phonic. "Yellow. Knife." Fernandez tapped his pen on the small dot and looked at Ruby.

"From there, we've booked a local airline to take you—"

"How long will all this take?" said Ruby. Dickerson looked up, eyebrows raised. She flushed. "I have an important personal meeting on Thursday afternoon . . ." They continued to look at her blankly, as if her personal life was of no interest or relevance. She felt suddenly small, as if she'd misspoke, as if she'd been caught putting herself ahead of America.

"If things go as planned, depending on flights and weather, you will be meeting Dr. Kneisser at his camp on Victoria Point sometime tomorrow afternoon," said Fernandez, looking Ruby in the eye. "My guess is that you'd be twelve hours in transit, a day on the ground, and an another day to return, given time zones . . . That would have you back here Wednesday evening for your . . . for your, uh, personal business." Ruby clenched her teeth, wishing she hadn't mentioned the real estate appointment. Dickerson broke the silence with a fake cough.

"This has already taken longer than expected, Ms. Cruz. You can leave your car here—give the keys to Dwight at reception. Norm will drive you to Dulles—right, Norm? You'll be able to pick up proper clothing in Edmonton or Yellow Knife. Whatever you buy will be reimbursed. Keep your receipts, please. Any questions?"

Ruby leaned forward over the map. "Where exactly is this place . . . where I'm going? The end place?" Fernandez ran his pen from the Yellow Knife dot across a solid white expanse without a single name or designation, without a village, a road, or a river. Dickerson moved closer. She could feel his thigh against her hip. The point of the pen stopped on the northwest tip of a small white island. Dickerson watched Ruby Cruz carefully. Holy Mother of Jesus, she thought.

"Oh my gosh," she said aloud, stepping back from the desk and from her boss. "That's really up there, isn't it?" Her high-pitched cackle embarrassed her.

The flight call for Yellowknife caromed off the hard walls of the temporary waiting room, bringing her back to the uncomfortable present. Her nose and throat were dry, and the chemical odour of the newly cut carpet was nauseating. She swung her legs to the ground and sat up, stretching her lower back. One foot was asleep. She felt a trickle of sweat run between her breasts to her belly. It was hot in here. On the walls were pinned posters of planes with owls and cougars and winter animals painted on their tails. Outside on the tarmac, there was a dusting of snow that seemed to blow in all directions. Her mouth tasted like acid, and she wanted a toothbrush and a long, hot soak in a long, hot tub.

She sensed someone staring at her and looked to her right. A worn backpack rested on the seat beside her. Beyond it, still close enough to smell her sweat, slouched a pale man with perhaps a day or two's growth of sketchy blond beard. What she could see of his face was round, jowly, most of it obscured by a Blue Jays baseball cap with the brim severely hand-rounded and tugged down over his eyes and nose. He seemed to be asleep, but Ruby was certain he'd been staring at her. From what she could see, he was her age, perhaps, maybe a little older. She wondered why she judged every man she saw in terms of their eligibility. She wasn't on the prowl, wasn't even interested in men. It worried her a little, this withdrawal from life.

Under a puffy, black, thigh-length, down coat better suited to an L Street federal accountant, he wore a tartan flannel shirt, unbuttoned to show a white T-shirt with a beer company logo on the chest. She guessed it was a Canadian beer—it was no brand she'd ever seen. The open shirt also revealed a large silver belt buckle with a relief casting of a semi-trailer designed to make it look as though it was zooming out of its frame. He wore clean, faded jeans and new, toffee-coloured work boots with one scuffed toe. Ruby felt self-conscious in her ski suit. It was tighter than she'd thought—uncomfortably so. In the Duty Free shop she'd purchased a hot pink scarf. She'd stuffed the matching wool hat deep into one of the pockets.

People were standing and stretching, collecting their bags to board the plane. Most of them, she saw, looked like the man she'd been studying—working types, forties or younger, with a sense of adventure tinged with a dust of desperation. She decided, after overhearing two of them talking, that they had flown in from eastern Canada to work in some diamond mines somewhere farther north and make some good money in a short time. This was the new Wild West, she supposed, the Wild North. It thrilled her slightly to see there was still something to discover in the world, some place where people could still be pioneers. Even if it wasn't

America, although maybe Alaska was the same. More advanced, probably.

A large woman with the flat features of an Eskimo and dressed in an ill-fitting blue uniform was announcing the boarding call for Yellowknife, pronouncing the city's name as if it was one word, emphasizing the "yell." Ruby said it quietly: *YELL'owknife*. She found herself staring at the woman until she looked back, her coal-chip eyes diffident, her smile shy, her voice not designed for announcements. Ruby scraped the roof of her mouth with her tongue and wished she had a breath mint. She stretched her back again and sluggishly joined the line to board. The man in the Blue Jays cap struggled into his backpack, picked up two long plastic cases and followed. Fishing rods, maybe. Something to test diamonds with? Who cares? Just get me home. Get me out of this cloying heat.

Wednesday, May 21, 1845
Off the Faeroes, bound for northern seas

Sometime late yesterday we docked at Stromness on the west rim of the Orkney Islands, off the north coast of Scotland. A raw and desolate place, I have heard, although I saw none of it and failed to respond to Alice Lort. The noise of the men shouting and belaying lines woke me where I lay face down on the desk in the library. I had been sick on myself.

The scar-faced man and one of his colleagues carried me, dragging my feet, to my berth where, with a weariness beyond anything in my experience, I fell into a deep, deep sleep. By the time I woke we were under way again. One of the cabin boys, a Tom Evans who says he looks forward to classes, found my sick in the Library and came to report that he had cleaned it up, but that my gastric acid had removed a streak of varnish from the mahogany desktop. One forgets the toxic power of our natural juices. He brought water and lemon juice. The water was a cooling balm on my parched throat, and the lemon extremely tart but good, I'm told, for preventing scurvy.

On deck, the cold wind felt fresh in my face, a better antidote for my mal de mer *than anything a ship's doctor might prescribe, although I could not stay out long for shivering. There are no actual doctors aboard, in fact, only a surgeon and an assistant on each ship. On the* Erebus *it is Stephen Stanley, assisted by young Harry Goodsir—I know his brother Robert. Here on the* Terror *we have John Peddie, assisted by Alexander McDonald, whose brogue is so thick he seems to speak a guttural foreign tongue. All competent men, I am certain. These ships are peopled with tested men, many of them experienced with sickness at sea and the treatment of injury.*

The muster rolls on both ships are similar. HMS Erebus *has 13 Officers with Sir John Franklin leading and James Fitzjames as ship Commander.* Terror *has 11 with Francis Crozier as Captain. Each ship has three Warrant Officers—an engineer, a boatswain and a carpenter.* Erebus *has 22 Petty Officers and* Terror *21 (including me and my two colleagues). Both ships have 19 Able Seamen and two boys. Troops of well-trained and armed Royal Marines—seven on* Erebus, *six on* Terror*—provide policing duties and will prove their worth should the ships become threatened in any way. These combined crews total 134 men, a sum that will be reduced by one (me) when I have organized the classes and set my curriculum for the two I have chosen to teach for the duration of the expedition. I shall return to England on the* Barretto Junior, *the supply ship that trails us through dark seas like a loyal dog his master. She carries, among other supplies, 10 live bullocks which are to be slaughtered and delivered as fresh meat to* Terror *and* Erebus *at the last possible moment. The men will not go hungry. I know of the* Barretto *from my naval studies, and her role as the supply vessel to the Franklin*

Expedition is the venerable old vessel's end to a dutiful career. She has conveyed troops to and from Gibraltar, Malta and Corfu in northern climes. She has delivered a load of female prisoners to Van Dieman's Land, stopped at Sydney, Australia, and thence to China. She should carry me home safely as well, and I look forward to her final voyage, one that will return me, one supposes, to the mysteries of fatherhood and the eminently beddable charms of Miss Lort. But whatever the reason, better a return to England than three years on the northern ice, I think. Others disagree and are in high spirits.

Postscript: I'm not the only ill passenger. I hear others rest in sickbay, one with a cut hand, some with dry cough and one with blood in his sputum.

In Flight, Cambridge Bay to Victory Point

Monteith pointed east, where a herd of musk oxen splayed at the approach of the airplane, the circles of white hair on their backs targets unknown to them. Kennison stared obediently at the tundra far below. The bush pilot was from suburban north Toronto and resented it. He loved the North like a convert loves Jesus, treasured his job and adored the De Havilland Twin Otter he flew. He babied it, coaxed it and waggled its wings for the sheer joy of proving its strength and sensitivity. He loved it with tires, with skis or with the present floats, and expressed several times an hour that "this baby can lift off straight up in a forty-klick headwind."

Kennison watched the musk oxen flee, stumbling over hummocks on the tundra, breaking through newly formed ice, splashing through puddles and over tussocks that made him wonder if the land was littered with lakes or the water crammed with islands. The herd regrouped after the plane passed. If there was a single remarkable thing about this land, it was that there was so much of it. And most of it where no one had lived or canoed or fished or walked or claimed ownership. It was a good place to hide, if hiding Kennison was what Duchesne had in mind. Did they think Prévost's gang would track him down? Maybe it was a setup. It wasn't the first time the thought had crossed his mind in the past week or two. He wondered for the hundredth time who they suspected was after him. Was it the third-party sharpies who laundered the insiders' pension-fund money? Or was it the insiders on the pension fund scam—people from his own force, afraid he knew their names and crimes who wanted him shut up for good? It could be a lot of people. Knowing who was gunning for you didn't make it any more comfortable.

Kennison had expected a pathologist or some basic forensic help to meet him at the floatplane dock, but no one showed up. He wondered if Ricky was prepared to help him wrap the bodies and bring them home. The medical community of Yellowknife provided forensic and pathologic services to the RCMP on a rotating basis, and Kennison's only experience hadn't been impressive.

The day after he arrived, Kennison had been sent by Duchesne to check out a domestic dispute on the road to Detah, about twenty-five klicks by winter road out of Yellowknife and less inhabited in the winter than the summer, when it became a fishing camp only minutes across the inlet by boat. He was accompanied, on Duchesne's orders, by Dr. Dugald MacIntosh.

Mac the Knife was an old-school doctor who had delivered more babies to the North, and later declared more of them dead from stupidity and violent acts, than anyone else ever would. He'd seen so much senseless drunken violence that he no longer wondered or cared what motivated crime, and he'd done it all before four-wheel drives, snowmobiles or all-terrain vehicles made it easy. Ten years before, at seventy, he'd retired and departed Yellowknife with his wife after a big party in the Anglican Church Hall. After only three months in Victoria, B.C., they returned, complaining that the place had too many tourists and too many old people driving too many cars badly. Mack had inserted himself back in the pathology rotation, and no one had the nerve to suggest he shouldn't.

In Detah, the old doc had nodded to the wife and muttered "Hi Debby" before declaring the crime unpremeditated. The wife—Debby, guessed Kennison—had all but decapitated her common-law partner in a booze-fuelled argument over a hockey game in the overheated trailer. Interesting call, thought Kennison, seeing as the woman must have sawn away for an unpremeditated half an hour to slice that far through her mate's neck with the serrated bread knife. When Kennison helped her stand up, she'd vomited litres of hot beer onto her late husband's bloody head—and onto Kennison's boots.

Monteith pointed to another musk ox herd. Kennison nodded for the tenth or eleventh time. Seen one herd, seen them all.

"So tell me, Rick. Who's stuck here on Gilligan's icebound Island?"

"Well, let me think back. I flew all of them in, except an old Inuit woman who makes her own way up from Ross Haven every summer to cook. The rest arrived about the same time about two months ago," said Monteith. "Early to middle September." He flicked some switches on and off, checking dials. "They arrived in groups, some from the States, some from England. A couple from here—Canada, I mean. Usually come here in July, soon as the water opens up. Came really late this year."

"You know them all?"

"Not 'know' them, no. Don't know any of them really, 'cept to see. The camp chief—Masterson is his name, but they all call him Poncey, I'd guess because of his English accent. Foul-mouthed guy, sometimes. Been around the block twice or more, to look at him. Mid-forties at a guess, but looks older. Runs the place for some Brit group going on five or six or maybe more years now." Kennison scribbled on the inside back cover of the Heaney book.

"Know the dead ones?" Monteith shrugged and trimmed something that made the engines quieter.

"The old man—this Kneisser—is a German. Comes up every year, too. I think he's actually the one who first discovered the site, but don't quote me on that. He's an anthropologist, I think, and is—or was—well respected, the way some of the others bow down to him . . ."

"And the other vic?" Kennison checked the notes he'd scribbled when Duchesne had briefed him. "This, um, Fortier? Marie-Claire Fortier."

"Well, I remember her, that's about it. Hard not to. Pretty girl. Blonde, pony-tailed sporty type, turned-up nose, nice, hard little body, know what I mean? Early twenties at a guess. Great teeth, I remember. Expensive clothes—big-name designer stuff that costs a fortune, y'know? She was just a junior helper of some sort, a student, maybe. Canadian, I'm pretty sure—Quebecois, maybe, but you can't tell where they come from once they're dumped off in Yellowknife." The pilot lightly tapped the altimeter with the nail of his right index finger. Kennison's throat was dry, and he licked his lips and scratched them with his teeth.

"Run the rest of them down for me. The living ones."

"Well, like I said, there's Poncey Masterson—Paul, I think his real name is. He arrived first to set things up. Knows better than most that they were dangerously late in coming this year for some reason. Course, they are really pushing it staying this long. Should be coming out today, tomorrow at the absolute latest. Lose even the twilight in less than a week."

Monteith was a talker. People up here either were or weren't. Kennison fought to stay on topic.

"Who else?"

"Masterson has staff to cook and clean up and so on. One's the

Inuit woman I mentioned. Lillian something—an Inuit name—who comes up from Ross Haven on her own. This year she brought her grandson with her—don't know his name. Kid in his late teens, maybe early twenties, always on the land shooting at something. Great Inuit hunter type. There's another kid, about the same age maybe, from Alberta—Calgary, I think—a real extreme specimen with dyed hair and tattoos and piercings all over his face, cheeks and everything. I think he was sent up by some social agency or whatever. Y'know, one of them troubled kids . . ."

"So this Masterson is like the quartermaster. He and the Inuit woman and the pierced kid cook and clean for the scientists? Is that it?" Monteith nodded and leaned forward to trim adjustments on the console.

"And the grandson too, I guess. He works in the kitchen." The plane further lowered its tone and ran smoother for it. It made it easier on the throat to talk. Kennison realized they were losing altitude and that his head was throbbing less. He'd never realized that flying in small planes meant listening to them drone on and on. It was boring, not the seat of the pants ride he expected. Fucking uncomfortable. Monteith was still talking.

" . . . an English woman named Anne something-something—one of those hyphenated names. She's the Brit scientist—archaeologist, I think, the expedition leader or whatever. Horsey-looking, you know? Lots of teeth. Dull little woman to look at. Knows how to fly, though. Told me things about this Otter even I didn't know. Flown everything, she says. Small planes, anyway. She's pretty accomplished, I hear, pretty fit despite being kind of old and tired-looking. Been doing hard work on sites all her life, I guess.

"Then there's an Indian guy—India Indian, not a local Dogrib or a Dene. Named Patel—who came up this year with the old Kraut and acts like a serious scientist, although he seems a bit young for it. Got an opinion on anything and everything. At a guess, he's a graduate student or something. Treated me like a city bus driver. Didn't exactly call me 'my good man' or slip me a keep-the-change fiver, but came damned close—"

"So there's eight of them?" Kennison used a headset to keep the book pages from closing in his lap and counted on his fingers. "There's the dead Kneisser, his helper Patel, Anne double-whats-hername and her late helper, um . . . Fortier. That's the science end of things. Then there's this Paul Masterson and his cook, Lillian, and his gofers Pierced Boy and the Eskimo—I mean Inuit—kid. Right? That it?" Monteith nodded and fiddled with the pitch of his engines.

"Minus the Professor and Mary Ann—sorry, Marie-Claire—leaves six." Monteith nodded and sat forward, pointing at something below. Kennison searched briefly for another musk ox herd but could only see an endless white desert scarred by black open water.

"We're here," said Monteith. "Be down in a minute." Kennison looked down and finally picked out an antlike grouping of brightly coloured tents.

"In and out as fast as we can, right, Rick?"

"You betcha, Sarge," said Monteith, pushing the plane lower, yawing to the left. "Hot date for the Dog Derby dance, doncha know?" If he meant the child from Cambridge Bay, Kennison might have to jail him. "Best bands up from Edmonton. Beer tent 'n' everything. Kinda kicks off winter every year." Monteith pointed again and tilted the nose farther down. "Here we go."

As they flew closer, Kennison saw that the collection of dome tents was arranged in an orderly manner and neighboured a nearly invisible cross-shaped structure. On closer inspection it was a collection of like-sized structures, four of them equal bars of a cross and the fifth at their intersection. Their canvas roofs were the same stained eggshell colour as the snow, which made them difficult to see from the air. The entire tent compound was enclosed by a fence made of snow blocks and was a kilometre or more inland from the shore, where four tiny dots stood waiting. Two waved into the air. Monteith made an extra circuit to duck the westerly crosswinds and came in low over a narrow strip of black water.

"Less open water every day," said Monteith. "Freeze-up could be days away. Hours even, if the wind shifts. You'll hear Masterson whining about it every chance he gets. Usually thinks he knows more than the rest of us put together, except this time he's right on the money. If you wanna go back today . . . let's see, it's 11 a.m. now, so I'm leaving by three, three-thirty absolute latest, to make it to Yellowknife with some light left for landing. 'Kay?" The pontoons hit the water with a jolt as if the liquid was thick with cold. Kennison tasted blood where he'd bit his tongue.

Fifty metres away, three people waited on shore in the dim twilight, facing away from each other, huddled against the wind. They looked posed for an oil painting, thought Kennison. The fourth moved closer, rowing a fat grey rubber raft.

Kennison slid back the window. He took a deep breath through his nose to shake the cobwebs and the engine drone out of his head. The cold air felt good, instantly freezing the moisture in his nostrils, reminding him where he was, as if the snow and impending dark weren't enough of a reminder. Moments later, standing on a pontoon, watching the black water slosh over his boots, he looked out at the most desolate landscape he had ever seen. He wanted to leave as soon as he could. Maybe it's just barren in context, he thought. It's all relative. Yeah, right. Relative to this place, posing in a red uniform holding sour-smelling infants at the Yellowknife Dog Derby sounded like a viable career option.

In Flight: Yellowknife to Victory Point

Ivan Krevaluk was a big-boned man. Even securely belted into the worn seat of his Cessna, he looked like he'd been built for a larger universe. His legs were spread wide, the large knobs of his knees touching the console on either side of the steering wheel. His huge hands sat lightly on the wheel, and from where she sat in the co-pilot seat, Ruby noticed the delicacy with which his sausage-like fingers touched the various switches on the dash. She turned in her seat to glance back at the sleeping man slumped in a webbed seat, legs stretched across the narrow cabin. His fishing rods were propped between his legs, his Blue Jays baseball cap tugged forward over his face.

By the time Ruby had found her way to the Yellowknife terminal exit, weaving past the luggage carousel, dodging hugging couples and children shouting "Daddy, Daddy, lookit what I got," there were no taxis left at the cab stand. A sign above the old-fashioned black telephone on the wall between the double glass doors read "Taxi. Pick up." She'd put her overnight bag on the floor and lifted the telephone. A male voice at the other end answered.

"Taxi."

"I need a taxi?"

"You got one, eh? Where are yah?"

"I'm at the airport."

"How'll I know yah?"

"Huh?"

"Whaddya look like?" Ruby hesitated. "So's I can find yah, eh?"

"Um. . . ." She felt the woollen hat in her pocket. "I have a pink hat. On. A pink hat. On my head. And a scarf."

"Nice. Gotcha. Five minutes." In the time it took the cab to arrive, the terminal had emptied. The car was a late-model Ford Focus, although judging by the dents and chips in the grey paint it could have been twenty years old and rolled several times. A large, starred crack in the windshield made it impossible for Ruby to see out, so she watched this strange world go by through the rear passenger glass. It didn't look pretty.

"You know Ivan?" said the driver. He was a small man of indeterminate age, dressed in layers as if he was smuggling smelly clothes from a rummage sale, smoking constantly without using his hands to take the cigarette from his lips. "Krevaluk. Your pilot? You know him?"

"No," said Ruby. "No, I don't. I was told to—"

"Good guy, Ivan. You-kranian, eh? Wife isn't. Pregnant, eh? Been here ten, maybe twelve years. Ivan. Not her. Long time. Longer'n many. Most last a year, maybe three. Miss the south, eh? Not me, though." He waited for Ruby to ask how long he'd been a Yellowknife resident, but she didn't. "Been here twenty years next May twelfth. Came up from Tronna May twelfth nineteen years ago and never went back. Ivan's been here twelve years. You know Ivan?" Ruby shook her head as the car pulled up alongside a string of docks stretching out into a lake. "At yer service, lady.

Ivan's shack is third one down." Ruby realized she didn't have any Canadian money, but the driver took the U.S. cash without comment.

When she stepped out of the cab, the day was surprisingly beautiful. The sun shone on the ice and sparkled in the patches of clear water of the lake. The silhouette of a low strip of land across the inlet marked the horizon, and closer, a surprising number of sailboats and powerboats sat for the winter in cradles on the shore. The dock was long and high above the water, constructed of substantial lumber. The third wooden building on the dock wore a newly painted sign in a red italic script that read "Fly Krevaluk Air." The sign was oversized, bigger than the building it identified, wrapping it like a city bus poster. A small airplane on pontoons, tied to the dock like a tethered pony, wore the same logo. She heard a deep, accented voice behind the door.

"It's up to the lady, eh, Mims? She's the one who booked me, sir. Paid up front without a bother. Company did, anyway. If she doesn't mind taking you along, I sure don't mind. You seen her? Supposed to be here by now. I can take you to Taloyoak after I drop her. No problem, sir. Eh, Mims? No problem . . ."

The voice stopped when Ruby pushed open the door. Inside, it was very warm. A very pregnant woman, pretty but no youngster, sat splay-legged on a castered chair. Her hands were red and puffy, as if she'd been washing laundry in lye soap or had circulation problems. Her face was thin and the worried lines stretched across her brow. At her side stood a large man, well over six feet tall, with big features, a Jack Palance nose over Mick Jagger lips smiling to reveal a mouthful of Chiclets. Beside him, dwarfed by the man, was the fisherman with the Blue Jays cap.

"You must be Miss Cruz, I bet," the large man said, stepping forward to offer a warm hand that could have encompassed her head. "I'm Ivan. Ivan Krevaluk. This is Mims. She's gonna have a baby. Our baby." Mims Krevaluk smiled feebly as if she was weary of hearing that she was pregnant. Krevaluk looked at his watch. "Right on time, Miss Cruz. That all you got?" he said, nodding at Ruby's suitcase and the plastic bag from the Duty Free shop. "Let's get a move on, then. Gotta leave now if I'm gonna be back in time for the baby, eh, Mims?" Mims nodded slowly. Blue Jays Cap coughed, standing with a fishing rod case in each hand like walking sticks.

"Oh, yeah. This fella wants to hitch a ride with us, Miss Cruz. I told him it was up to you. He wants to fly to Taloyoak—Spence Bay, used to be. Hour or so past your drop-off at Victory Point. Said it was up to you. You're the one who booked me, or your company did. Course, it'll keep me overnight, won't it, Mims? But fella here says he'll pay extra for the room. Am I right?" Blue Jays Cap nodded.

"I guess it's okay with me," said Ruby. "As long as I can get back here tomorrow."

"That's a fast trip, ain't it, Mims? Be dark most of the time you're there. Maybe all the time. Tomorrow, eh? Well . . . if I stay over in Taloyoak I can pick you up on the way back here." Ivan raised his eyebrows. "Saves me gas and you money, Miss. And I'm at your service. Let's go."

Once they were airborne, Mims waved a slow-motion goodbye from the dock, one red hand high in the air, the other resting on the top of her belly.

Victory Point, King William Island, Nunavut

When the inflatable reached the pontoon, Kennison stepped into it, standing on the hard wooden floor, holding onto one of the Otter's float struts while Monteith tossed an anchor into the frigid water to secure the plane. The pilot shoved a black backpack emblazoned with yellow diagonal reflective stripes into his arms.

"Your crime kit, Sergeant," he said. "Guess Dutch figured you didn't have one." Kennison unclipped the plastic catch and looked inside. Of course he didn't have one. He didn't know they existed. He'd been out of uniform too long. "And the body bags, Sergeant." Monteith held out two plastic bags that looked like domestic garbage bags but were darker and of a thicker stock with coarse zippers heat-sealed to the plastic. Kennison stuffed them under his arm as a mittened hand came into view.

"Masterson," said the man at the oars. "Paul Masterson. Factor here. You are?" The man's long, sun-bleached hair stuck out from under a thick wool toque at the back and ears. He wore a puffy dark green parka with a thin, windproof hood hanging behind him and a pair of quilted, lined navy blue ski pants over thick-soled hiking boots. His face was superficially handsome, with a strong chin and jaw and a straight nose, weakened by insecure lips and a pox of acne scars that had cauterized the pores on each side of his mouth. His beard was red and spotty, and a skimpy mustache barely covered his upper lip. "A man of estimable weakness," Ginny would have said, before she snorted away her wit.

He had an English accent, a much more upper-class tone than his looks or language suggested. *Mawsterson,* he'd said. Poncey was a good name for him. The lines on his face made him look older than he probably was. It was a spoiled face, flawed by failure and reflecting a weariness of experience. When he spoke, he showed large upper teeth, English teeth. Kolchak always said that British teeth, like British golf courses, were natural, blemished things. In America, both were cosmetically perfect and utterly artificial.

"Kennison. Sergeant Booker Kennison. RCMP Yellowknife." Masterson nodded and said something unintelligible to Rick Monteith. Both looked at the dark sky, and Masterson mumbled something that ended with "time is short." With Kennison and Monteith sitting on the inflatable's side tubes, Masterson turned the craft to shore, rowing efficiently and quickly across the strip of black water towards three people who huddled in the wind. It must be ten degrees colder here than in Yellowknife, thought Kennison. And hours darker this far north. He glanced at his watch. It was not yet noon and this was as good as it got. There was barely enough natural light to read. The sun was permanently below the horizon here and would not reappear until spring. What struck him most was that, for the first time in months, he felt like he didn't have to keep checking over his shoulder. There was a peace to that.

An icy crust formed where the water lapped the shore. It was only a matter of a degree or two until the gelid brine became ice. Masterson gave the oars a final pull, impelling the rubber raft onto a pebbled shore. A boy with several rings in both ears and a large grey metal stud in the side of his nose steadied the boat. His eyes were wet and red—maybe from the cold, thought Kennison. Metal studs must hurt like hell in this temperature.

Kennison stepped out of the boat onto a beach of coarse sand and stones. Surprisingly, there was little snow on the ground—an inch or two at most, granular stuff, dry enough to blow around like Styrofoam packing beads in an unrelenting wind. He stood, knees bent for balance, and surveyed the land. Beside him was an olive-drab four-wheeled ATV with a long, black metal sled attached. Further up the beach, white patches of snow appeared in isolated random clumps on coarse sand where three wooden buildings, one the size of an outhouse, the other two slightly larger, stood sentinel. He scanned the rocks, the ice, the black water and the permanent white ice cap a kilometre or two offshore. The utter desolation here made Yellowknife seem civilized, southern.

For a moment, he thought he saw movement on the horizon to the north.

"What's that?" he asked. Masterson looked up.

"What's what?" Though Kennison hadn't moved his eyes away, the image was gone. Masterson followed his gaze. "Ice pellets, maybe, snow on the wind. Happens all the time."

Fifty metres away, the small welcoming party stood silently, ignoring him and one another. Maybe they were grieving, or maybe they had nothing left to say to each other, thought Kennison. Perhaps they were just giving him a moment to share the unqualified isolation and come to some superficial understanding of the hell they had been suffering for the past two months. Kennison's throat was sore after three hours of dry air and yelling over the twin engines. To his ears, this world was deathly silent, but for the wind.

He lit a cigarette, hunkering down until it was burning. His disposable plastic lighter was low on fuel. He inhaled deeply and exhaled slowly before approaching the group, where Masterson was already lecturing Monteith on the probabilities of weather and the capabilities of his Otter. The cigarette grated on his throat. A monochrome grey-haired woman who looked like a frozen house sparrow in a fat beige parka with thin, black-clad legs eyed Kennison's cigarette with undisguised disgust and turned away, muttering to herself. By the slope and shake of her shoulders, Kennison thought she might be weeping.

"Hi there. Trevor Patel." A strong tobacco-coloured hand with long fingers and broken, discoloured nails took his and shook it firmly. Kennison looked up at a fine-featured young man with a strikingly handsome face. It must have been the Indian assistant to the late professor that Monteith had mentioned—not Indian anymore . . . what was it? Asian? South Asian. His smile of perfectly even white teeth and a slight upward twist to the left corner of his mouth made him appear a friendly, if somewhat superior, confident. His voice was deep and warm. His eyes, with irises the colour of stout, hovered on the edge of a wink, thought Kennison, eyebrows slightly raised as if the world was mad and he had tales to tell they'd both enjoy.

"And you'd be Kenneth Monk," said Kennison, turning to the boy with piercings. The boy had loosened his parka collar and Kennison could see the rough tips of amateurish blue tattoos on his neck, peeking above his collar like weeds above a curb. The boy—a man of maybe twenty-three or twenty-four if you looked closer—shook hands weakly, reluctantly, as if Kennison's palm was wet or touching him symbolized some previously avoidable truth. The sparrow woman—she'd be the Anne Double-Something—continued to look away, up the shore. Monteith was right. She didn't look like she could fly a plane or pick up a shovel.

"Mr. Masterson," said Kennison, ready to get the show underway. The man stopped nattering at Monteith and stepped away from the group as Kennison indicated. Kennison wished he had a real notebook, and he did—on his dresser in Yellowknife. He opened the inside back cover of the Heaney book.

"You called in this accident, Mr. Masterson?

"Paul."

"Beg your pardon?"

"Paul. Call me Paul."

"You reported this accident?"

"Yes, I did. My responsibility. The fire occurred at midday yesterday, give or take a half-hour." Kennison had to listen closely to make out the vowels. "Hawf" was half, and hour sounded like "awe." He nodded and scribbled translations in his book.

"Ice storms aren't uncommon this late in the season, Sergeant—it's sergeant?" Kennison nodded. "But this one rattled the bloody place, I'll tell you and Jesus. Bit more lasting than most here. Couldn't see a bloody thing, I swear. Didn't even see the fire through it all—least not from Heaven. Not that we were looking. When the weather cleared, the shed was burned to the ground. It held the flammables, sir . . ."

"Sergeant," said Kennison. Masterson shrugged.

"Sergeant, then. Propane, kerosene, even some wood shipped up a year or two ago. Far above the treeline here, as you may have noticed, and some of them like the rustic old Canadian campfire in the summer. Keeps the spirits up and the bloody bugs down." A shot sounded in the distance. Only Kennison and Monteith looked up, both in different directions, Kennison straining his eyes to see the shooter.

"Who discovered the bodies?"

"I rushed down there—soon as the ice storm cleared of course—and saw the ruin. Smelled it first, truth be told."

"How did you know who the dead were?"

"Simple head count, Sergeant. Process of elimination.

Elementary, dear boy, eh? All present and accounted for except for the old man and the girl. And Penilik the Eskimo boy, but he's always missing in action. Bloody shooting. Hear him?" As if to corroborate Masterson's statement, another shot sounded far away. "Put a pall on us. No matter that relationships aren't always the friendliest here. Close quarters. Lot of pressure on all of us, Sergeant, especially lately. We must depart this bloody place before the freeze, Sergeant. Tomorrow latest. Can't tell you enough how important that is."

Kennison understood why they called him Poncey. "So you contacted the police?" he asked evenly.

"On the satphone. Battery-operated. I called Ross Haven first. Spoke with your colleague Miss Jensen there—a constable, I think. Seemed a bit preoccupied, uninterested in my little problems even. I guess she called you blokes. I don't really know."

"Did you call anyone else?"

Masterson nodded. He seemed uncomfortable.

"Yeah. Yeah, I did. Part of my job. They make them list their next of kin. On the forms. For insurance purposes. Names, numbers, closest relatives in case of emergency—that sort of thing."

"And?"

"Well, the batteries were low. That damned—don't speak ill of the dead, eh—Kneisser had drained them the day before, jabbering away to his people in the States. Still on the poor side, I can tell you. I called the number on the girl's record first, but there was just one of those answering machines. Office somewhere. I left a message, said what had happened."

"You left a message that there had been an accident?"

Masterson nodded, looking away.

"And that the accident had been fatal?"

Masterson said nothing.

"You left that message on the answering machine." It wasn't a question. Masterson looked everywhere but at Kennison. He shuffled his feet in the shallow snow and looked to where the others stood in silence, stamping their feet and beating their arms for warmth. Finally, his eyes stopped darting around and the man looked at his boots.

"Guess I did. But the phone's battery-operated. Solar-charged. Delicate device. It's our only reliable source of communication with the world, Sergeant. Without any sun, there's little charge on it, so we have to use it as little as we can. No time for proper manners, have we?"

It occurred to Kennison that Masterson was one of the people who spent their lives blaming their lives on others. Nothing was ever his fault. But somewhere, sometime soon, the shit would hit the fan on this one, Kennison knew. He had a good nose for shit after years spent too close to the fan.

In Flight: Yellowknife to Victory Point

Ivan was talking. He hadn't stopped since the takeoff. Now that they were at altitude, he steered with his knees, nudging the Cessna left to right, up and down while leafing through one of Fernandez's paperbacks. It looked small in his big hands. "This Franklin fellow was fifty-nine years old when he led the expedition," he said. "Old man, eh? 'Specially back then in . . . what was it? Eighteen forty-something?"

Ruby Cruz ignored him, staring from the meaningless dials that surrounded her to the endless tundra below, playing with a loose thread on the label of her knitted pink hat. She was thinking about Ridgley's Delight, about having a warm home far away from this godforsaken place. With a full bookcase. And a real Christmas tree, with decorations that meant something to her.

"Wife seems to have been behind him getting the job," said Ivan. "Lady Jane. Griffin, her name was. Strong woman. He left England with 139 men in two ships." He ran down the page with his large finger. "Last seen somewhere up in the Davis Strait by a couple of whalers. Let's see . . ." He thumbed through the book for a map to identify the Davis Strait, but there was none.

"Map's in this one," Ruby grunted, passing him the other book. In the centre was a map that ranged west to east from Alaska to Greenland, from the North Pole south to the Arctic Circle. It showed a jigsaw collection of islands that, depending on the permanence of ice between them, might border a passage through which a ship could travel west from the North Atlantic to the Beaufort Sea off Alaska, then south to the Bering Sea and Pacific Ocean. Ivan found the Davis Strait, the eastern channel between Denmark's Greenland and Canada's Baffin Island. He passed her the book and pointed at the map.

"After that sighting, they were never seen again." Grudgingly, childishly, she raised her eyebrows. "Not one of them. Not alive, anyway."

"When was that?" she said. There was nothing else to do but stare into the semi-darkness at the boring land below.

"Mid-nineteenth century, eh? Let's see . . . 1845 to be exact. They spent the winter near Beechey Island. Find that?"

"Yeah. Here." She turned the book towards him and pointed with her finger. Her deep red nail polish, almost maroon, had chipped since the last application. The colour looked good against her dark skin.

"Did you turn the heat up?" said Ruby.

"Nope. Engine heat. Want it down?"

"Please," said Ruby and pointed behind her, wrinkling her nose at Ivan, then pinching it to signify the body odour coming from the man in the back of the plane. Ivan smiled, tripped a switch, turned a dial and kept reading. The plane was flying itself, for all the attention he paid it.

"Later found three bodies buried at Beechey Island," he said. "One lad looked like the day he died. Found he died of lung disease, eh? Maybe tuberculosis even. 'All three bodies had high levels of lead poisoning,' it says."

Ruby grunted. She was reading the other book. Loud snores rumbled from the back of the plane.

"Never seen again," said Ruby. "Look here." She held the book forward, pointing at something. A lurch of the plane threw her forward then shoved her back in her seat.

"Sorry. Really. Air pocket."

Ruby grimaced.

"Where were we?"

"I was pointing out our destination," said Ruby. "Victory Point. Why are they digging there, do you think? What was the victory?"

Ivan shrugged. "Maybe some bodies from back then. Maybe minerals. They say there's a lot of them up here, and now the ice is receding you can bet people are lining up to cash in, like with the diamonds north of Yellowknife. Like a gold rush up here. More diamonds there than have been discovered on earth, someone said. Can't see that anything good will come of it . . ." Ruby was reading. Both were silent until she spoke.

"It says they found an abandoned lifeboat once. Oh. Look here. Wow. Dr. Karl Conrad Kneisser led the group that found it. That's who I'm going to see. That's why I came here. To get him. Kneisser. It's him." Ivan looked at her with a half-smile. "There were . . . oh, yuck . . . skeletons in it—in the lifeboat—and, get this, chunks of chocolate, books and, Holy Cow, curtain rods. What's that about, huh?" This stuff wasn't as boring as she thought. Kneisser might be an interesting companion on the ride home. The plane dipped its nose and the engines slowed as Ivan took the wheel. His hands danced over the console.

"There it is," said Ivan, nodding. Ruby stretched to look down, but couldn't see anything but white.

"There what is?"

"Victory Point."

"Where?" The Cessna moved closer to the ground, but still she couldn't see anything but snow and rocks. There was a black strip. Coal? Or water, maybe. She smelled, rather than heard or saw, the presence of the man in the Blue Jays cap as he leaned between their seats, staring out the cabin window at the land below.

Victory Point, King William Island, Nunavut

Masterson pulled nervously at his thin mustache with his red fingers.

"And the professor?" said Kennison. "Did you call his wife and children and leave a message he was dead?"

"Hold steady, Sergeant. I was only doing my best, wasn't I? You have to be parsimonious with these devices. Besides, I told you, it was Kneisser who drained the bloody thing jabbering on with the States for hours the day before yesterday. Not my bloody fault. Not me that held up the bloody money that didn't get us here until September. Simple facts. No sun, so power. No power, no satphone."

"Not your fault at all, Mr. Masterson," said Kennison, staring at a man who would not look at him. "What about the call to Dr. Kneisser's next of kin?"

"Didn't call anyone," said Masterson. "The batteries were done. No more calls out or in."

"Don't you have a generator? Couldn't you charge the telephone some other way?"

"Generator? Yes, of course we have a bloody generator. Small one. Japanese. Low on juice to run it, though. Need the petrol for this ATV here. Have to budget use of things up here, Sergeant, and I don't need some southern copper coming to tell me how to do my job, thank you." Masterson raised his eyes towards Kennison. "Deaths or no deaths, telephones or no bloody phones, Sergeant, it's best if we could deal with these matters quickly and leave this place today. I'm serious about getting trapped here. We can't support ourselves, feed ourselves or keep ourselves warm now the fuel shack burned up."

"Yes, Mr. Masterson. I understand. I'll need to see the accident site and speak formally with each of you before we go anywhere."

Masterson relented. "Of course. Heaven'd be the best place to talk. Lunch will be served shortly so everyone will be gathering there." He removed his mitt to raise his sleeve and see his watch. "We can head over now and stop at the site on the way." He looked up, as if remembering something, and gestured at the group. "You met everyone? Dr. Anne?" The sparrow turned and came towards them. Her eyes watered, perhaps from the wind. "Sergeant Kennison, this is the lead archaeologist for this year's dig, Anne Ferguson-Crewe."

"Miss Ferguson-Crewe," said Kennison.

"Doctor," she said, almost inaudibly. At close range, she was younger than Kennison had thought. It was the grey hair sticking out of her parka hood that made him think she was in her fifties, but the grey was premature, perhaps, or maybe all other women of her age dyed their hair. What he knew about women her age—*his* age—wouldn't fill a beer bottle. Whatever the norm, the archaeologist had let her hair go grey. Her eyes were grey. Her face was grey. Her teeth were grey. She wore black tights. Wool, thought Kennison.

"You are the head of this operation, Doctor . . . ?" Kennison had already forgotten her name, and she had guessed it.

"Ferguson-Crewe. Anne," she said. "Doctor Ferguson-Crewe?" It was a British accent, but not the manorial speech of

Masterson, or proper like the announcers on the BBC news. This one had angles on it, a hard edge on some words that could split rock. Still, she had the superior attitude that Kennison thought all those with Brit accents seemed to have. Or perhaps that was the Canadian inferiority complex speaking, forever sandwiched between the class-consciousness of the Brits and the aggressive middle-crassness of the colonial Americans. His toes were beginning to freeze in his boots, and they hurt when he stamped his feet to get the blood moving. Masterson, for all his questionable judgments, was right about seeking comfort.

"The lead archaeologist, it's called? I am in charge of this dig?" The woman Kennison identified in his own mind as Grey Anne was answering questions he couldn't remember asking. Her habit of making every sentence a question at the end confused him. It was as if she were interviewing herself.

"The dig," he said. She nodded and pointed vaguely up the shore to the construction site. The pile of rocks and snow he now saw was divided into equal sections by stakes and taut strings with small yellow labels flapping in the wind over a portion of the shore half the size of a football field. "What are you digging for? Gold? Dinosaur eggs?" The woman snorted loudly, then blushed for it. Her nose dripped, but she didn't seem to notice.

"We call it a 'dig,' Sergeant? An archaeological dig? We're marking where the skeletons lie and photographing—"

"Skeletons?" Kennison looked again. What he'd thought were clumps of snow and ice on the rocky shore he now realized were the domes of human skulls and lengths of long white bones half buried in the sand. "What the hell . . ."

"The bones are those of some men who died on the Franklin Expedition, Sergeant. You're not familiar with it?" Kennison shook his head. Franklin again. Like the school and the street on the way to Brenda's. Susan's. "There are knife marks on many of the bones, and we are removing each with great care after photographing it *in situ,* recording where we found it. We then photograph each against a scale and catalogue each photograph. Then we replace them exactly where they were found? It's a delicate and time-consuming task."

"Cuts on the bones? Knife cuts?" Anne Ferguson-Crewe nodded patiently, as if Kennison was a backward student and she'd already explained things in detail to the rest of the class. Her nose dripped again.

"Yes. It's believed that some of the men survived for a time by eating the flesh of their peers."

"You're joking. Cannibals? Really? Here? In Canada? Up here?"

The archaeologist nodded. She looked up at him and seemed to blush, but she could not hold his eye and turned away. "There are some who argue, but I think the evidence is incontestable. That's why I'm here. Why we're here. To prove that members of the Franklin crews ate others to survive. To find out what happened to cause such behaviour."

"Jesus." Starvation, for one thing, he thought. Kennison stared at the field of bones, shaking his head. He felt strangely offended, oddly trespassed against. Cannibals came from other countries, people with bones through their noses in tropical places with boiling iron pots in jungle clearings, or survivors of plane crashes in the Andes. He was embarrassed by his ignorance. Apparently this Brit, this Franklin guy, led an expedition to the Canadian North and some of his men ate some of the others, and they still named streets and buildings after him? What was that about? Some kind of Northern survival joke?

"Was this recently?" he asked. Ferguson-Crewe snorted again

and put her hand to her face to wipe her nose. She reached into her parka pocket for a mealy white tissue and dabbed at the raw red rims of her nostrils.

"Oh no, Sergeant. Over a hundred and fifty years ago? Surely you learned this in school. I'm sure it's been on your History Channel. It's quite a well known—"

"Mr. Masterson mentioned Heaven . . ."

Anne Ferguson-Crewe didn't smile. "That's the base camp, Sergeant. Where we live, been living. When those with the late Dr. Kneisser first discovered this beach of death and bones, they called it Hell. We still do. Some wag called the base camp Heaven, and it stuck."

"Thank you. Doctor." She dipped her head slightly, like the Queen acknowledging a courtier, and without looking at him walked over to join the group by the ATV. She'd succeeded in making him feel stupid, and Kennison had the feeling that was important to her. How the hell should he know about some old sailors freezing themselves to death way the hell up here a century and a half ago and eating their mates for lunch?

"Mr. Masterson? The deaths. Our deaths. The new ones. Where were they?" As the rest bowed their heads in what Kennison assumed was shared sorrow, Masterson pointed up a barely visible rough road that wound through rocks and ice.

"About a kilometre up the road. Halfway back to Heaven. We'll pass it. You see that black thing sticking up on the horizon? It's a stove. A woodstove. It's all that didn't burn other than some exploded propane tanks tossed around the site. Sergeant, I'm deadly serious about the weather. Aren't I, Monteith? We have to be off the island today, absolute latest tomorrow. I'm depending on it."

"I guess I would be, too. It's a godforsaken place."

"It's not that. Not really. One gets to quite like it after a while."

"Yeah, right," said Kennison. "There are four of you here. There should be six, by my count. Who's missing?"

"Lillian, of course. Lillian Ooqlooq, our cook. She's preparing lunch. And Penilik—Wayne Penilik, her grandson. Both Inuit from Ross Haven. A hunter by birth and destiny, I suppose, isn't he? Shooting at anything that moves all bloody day long. Keep hoping for a hare in the pot. Been waiting a bloody long time." A shot sounded to the north as if on cue. "Drives us all quite mad, and he's not much of a help—"

"So the fire happened at this wooden shack halfway between Heaven and Hell?" said Kennison.

"We call it Purgatory, Sergeant," said Trevor Patel, speaking up for the first time, long lashes winking, teeth shining in the twilight.

"Of course we do," said Kennison.

June 10, 1845
Off Cape Farewell, Greenland

I am staggering proof that an interest and expertise in naval issues and Admiralty accomplishments does not guarantee satisfactory sea legs. Although the delicate state of my belly improves daily, I am still greatly affected by the movement of the Terror *as it traverses the majestic waves of the North Atlantic. We presently wallow at the conflux of the Denmark and Davis Straits at the southern tip of Greenland on a western heading. I have seen the profile of this misnamed place through clouds and fog. Perhaps it was titled for the facial hue of those who tried to sail around Cape Farewell in crossing currents. For some days now we have been climbing massive moving mountains of slate grey water and sliding down the nether sides like frightened children on a steep winter hill, crashing into each trough with a shudder of oak and a shake of stomach instantly dismissed in the ascent of another briny mountain and the sequential freefall to another unyielding trough.*

I pity those in the sick bay, tossed like rag dolls in their bunks, secured by straps across their chests. The boy Tom Evans—who is surely not the eighteen years in age he purports—tells me some are losing weight and spitting up inordinate amounts of phlegm. One is the colleague I have chosen to teach lessons here. He sweats so much his sheets must be changed in the night. I hope this fever is a sign that his sickness has peaked and he will begin to heal quickly.

Due to my mal de mer *I have been seeking the curative smell of fresh air and the sense of stability offered by a visible horizon on deck. I hover, hunched out of the worst of the weather at the flapping door of a rear gangway, holding grimly onto the brass doorknobs with both hands as I watch the helmsman wrestle with the big wheel. The scar-faced man sneers and mouths unheard curses at the sky as he keeps the* Terror *square to the wave as it climbs and hangs on for dear life as we fall, trying to see through the waves and the spray of icy water that washes over the decks as we hit what feels like the rocky bed of the sea itself. He is tied to the helm should the water try to claim him, his beard (which does not grow where he is scarred) and eyebrows are rimed and his clothes soaked solid with the spray. When he bends his arms or legs, sharp shards of thin ice fall to the deck to be washed overboard with the next wave. Crouched by the gangway, I feel he sees me, is laughing at my weakness as he proves his strength. Like a yoked ox he works for an exhausting hour before another man, mocking the storm and cursing the crosswinds, takes his place. But for the grip on these cold brass knobs, I would be like the knives of ice, washed clean from the deck, returned forever to salted seas from whence all life comes (if Darwin is to be believed. In truth, the scientist's divisive views seem less credible in these cruel climes than in his fecund southern seas.) Though protected from insidious spray, I soon grow too cold to stand erect and must work my way carefully down the gangway with stiffened legs, one hand always on the rail lest a rogue gust rip me from the safety of the* Terror *and toss me in waters so frigid they seem clotted with cold, a grey congealment of inestimable depth. I feel the disparaging eyes of the helmsman on my back as I seek the warmth and safety of the berths below.*

Despite the incessant pounding of their hulls, the Terror *(launched in 1813 at 340 tons) and* Erebus *(launched in 1826 at 370 tons) are well fit for this Arctic voyage. Both were tested by Sir James Clark Ross in the Antarctic with our own Captain Crozier commanding the* Terror *as he does today. The ship has northern experience as well, as part of George Back's explorations since nine years past. Both are barque-rigged Hecla class bomb ships, reconstructed to withstand anything man or nature can deliver. If strength is not overlooked, nor, I must say, has comfort been ignored. Both ships boast steam heat systems whereby hot water is piped through cabins to keep them warm and cork insulation to contain that warmth. Beside the large boilers, in a mysterious arrangement reminiscent of both Druid circles and poteen stills, Machines remove the salt from seawater and make it potable, though I have not yet tested it personally. Whatever one's personal discomfort, one need have no fear that ice or the cold will threaten these proud Royal Navy ships, nor their hardy crews under officers adept in extreme conditions.*

Victory Point, King William Island, Nunavut

Kennison took the last drag on his cigarette in the lee of the Salon Tent. He dropped it and watched the sparks burn hot in the wind before he ground it out with the heel of his snow boot. A mile south, he could make out the silhouette of the wood stove at the accident site.

He'd asked Masterson to stop the ATV briefly when they'd driven from the shore on the sled trailer it towed. While Masterson and Patel had stared after him, Grey Anne and the pierced boy averted their eyes from the scene. With Ricky's help, Kennison had quickly surrounded the site with the roll of yellow tape from the crime bag. There were few places to attach it other than the gaping maw of the woodstove and spikes of charred studs. At the west end, they'd had to lay the tape on the ground and secure it with rocks and two of the dented propane tanks that lay scattered about like dud mortars on a battlefield. The tape whip-cracked in the wind, and the bright yellow looked more out of place in the empty landscape than graffiti on an ivied cottage wall.

Through the compound's canvas roof, he could hear the murmur of people inside gathering for lunch, the cook clacking plates over a general grumble suggesting time was being measured by the ever-declining quality of food. The afternoon smelled like fried fish. He heard a crunch on the snow somewhere behind him.

"Plane coming," said a voice, deeply pitched, rumbling below the hiss of the wind. Kennison hadn't heard anyone approaching. He couldn't hear a plane, either. Maybe they were sending the forensic help he needed. He hoped it wasn't old Mack. The shape that moved past him was silent on the snow, walking from side to side as if alternating his weight to each foot. He was hunched over with hands in large pockets, invisible inside a large fur-lined parka hood. It wasn't until the shape reached the kitchen door and pulled it open to spill light outside that Kennison saw the Winchester rifle strapped across his back and the silhouette of a man who must be the Inuit boy. Wayne something. He carried no game. With a final scan of the empty slate sky, Kennison followed him inside.

Kennison removed his jacket and hung it on a hook inside the entry door of a tent with couches stacked on top of one another behind three empty bookshelves. The coat rack was fat with the down coats of others. Beneath it, a clutter of oversized insulated boots spilled over rubber trays onto the rough plywood floor where they sat in small puddles. Kennison kept his boots on.

It was already becoming darker outside, the twilight dimmer by invisible increments, as if there was a delicate hand turning a rheostat, causing the sky to lose light so slowly you couldn't see change unless you closed your eyes and opened them quickly, measuring difference rather than progress. Monteith kept looking at his watch. It was barely past noon, but the pilot was serious about his departure.

He hoped there was enough light to give a cursory site inspection, take some pictures, bag the bodies and leave on time. He could do his rough notes on the ride home and type the final copies tomorrow. It struck him odd that not one inhabitant had yet commented directly on the deaths of the girl or the professor. It was only a day ago. Maybe it wasn't real to them yet. Maybe they hadn't processed the loss. Maybe some were glad they died.

Boxes already packed for departure lined the canvas walls, making a narrow corridor to the central tent where food was served—what Masterson called the Mess Tent. In his heavy boots, Kennison walked around the place, clumping loudly on the plywood floors, poking his nose in doors. It was a simple layout. The Mess Tent was central to four equal arms of a cross. He'd entered through the western arm, the Salon Tent, a room that looked as if it had been used for relaxing before being turned into storage space. To the north was the Kitchen Tent, where, peeking his nose in, Kennison could see a woman who must have been Lillian Ooqlooq presiding over a large cast-iron stove amid the smells of soup and steam and fish. By the door, Masterson berated an unresponsive and silent Penilik.

"Where the hell've you been, boy? This isn't a fuckin' Butlin's, is it? No, it isn't. Monk here and me have been packing and washing up, cleaning out the fuckin' showers and shitters, and where the hell've you been? Playing great bloody Northern Inuit fuckin' hunter in the rocks. So get to bloody work, and you'll be doin' the cleanup by yourself after lunch, you can bet your bloody bullets, boyo." Penilik said nothing, or if he did he said it in a voice too quiet for Kennison—and perhaps Masterson—to hear.

To the south was the Dormitory Tent, divided inside by a thick hanging canvas wall. Boys' and Girls' sides, thought Kennison, like the entrance doors at elementary schools of a certain age. He guessed that most of the dig crew would be sleeping here in the colder weather rather than in the individual tents outside, which were probably meant for warmer weather. Kennison poked his head around the canvas wall to see Trevor Patel and Grey Anne whispering quietly. Patel spotted him and nodded, raised an eyebrow as if with the promise of a good joke shared one day soon. Anne did not look up. Kennison nodded in return and backed out, thoughtful at what he'd seen.

The eastern section contained portable toilets and sinks and jury-rigged showers. A sign on one toilet informed users it was the only one in operation, and a similar sign was taped to the plastic curtain on one of the showers. The rest of the room was piled with plastic storage boxes bearing stick-on labels reading "Kitchenware," " Drygoods" and "Books/Boardgames," all absorbing the smell of a powerful industrial deodorant that, to Kennison, smelled worse than the odours it was applied to mask.

Masterson or someone had set a separate table in the Mess Tent for Kennison and Monteith. There were small, unlit votive candles on each of three tables. Faded orange crepe-paper streamers crisscrossed the ceiling from corner to corner, probably part of a planned departure celebration before the fire killed two of the group. Last night should have been the final main meal at Victory Point, the end of the dig. Following on the Heaven, Hell and Purgatory theme, Kennison would bet cash money they'd called it "The Last Supper."

He wished he had a beer and could smoke inside. He idly clicked his lighter until the flame caught and lit the small candle as Monteith joined him. The others arrived from all directions, silent, uncommunicative, as if subject to unshared priestly vows, their soft slippers making no sound on the wooden floor. There was probably a rule about keeping your boots on. There were probably a lot of rules. Kennison guessed they sat in the same seats they always used. The places so recently vacated by Kneisser and Marie-Claire Fortier were defined by gaps as if their deaths hadn't registered or their absences misunderstood.

From the open door to the Kitchen Tent, Masterson frowned

on the gathering. Behind him, Lillian Ooqlooq sweated over steaming pots and Kenneth Monk and Wayne Penilik slaved steadily, Penilik scrubbing large iron vessels, eyes on his job. He was short in stature, yet wide across the shoulders. His complexion was dark, like Patel's, but with a greener tint, and shinier, oilier, which was probably diet. His face was round, his features blunted, brows thick and joined over the bridge of a dough-ball nose pressed flat on his face. He had little facial hair, and his eyes moved quickly without landing on anyone's face. He was frightened of something or someone, thought Kennison. Maybe Poncey. Maybe cops like Kennison. Maybe his own shadow.

With the breaded fried whitefish, mashed potatoes and some anemic, seedy broccoli came comfort and the return of light laughter to the room, as if the task of the living was simply to dig in and get on with life, even if the food was substandard. Kennison sipped at a thick, cracked mug of stale water and stared at his plate, lost in thought. He wished Monteith would stop looking at his watch and trading knowing glances and nods with Masterson. The subject of time and dark and freezing were getting on his nerves; the two of them were quickly becoming boring. He knew the pressure of time well enough, but you'd get nowhere questioning nervous people.

At the other table, Patel jiggled his right foot like a drummer playing sixteenths on a hi-hat, talking aimlessly and glancing at Kennison regularly. Grey Anne sat two seats over, looking worried. Monk ate as if hypnotized, staring into the middle distance, sitting beside the gap that was once Marie-Claire Fortier, unresponsive to Patel's prodding, uninterested in camaraderie. Masterson shovelled food into his mouth as if his job was to start last and finish first. Penilik wasn't eating. He washed pots as penance, and Lillian stayed with him in the kitchen.

Kennison chewed slowly, planning his investigation. He'd look at the site first, take advantage of the remaining light, then do the interviews. Masterson had two industrial work lights and a limited amount of fuel to run the small generator. The food made him relax, and his shoulders sagged. He felt extremely tired. The room was hot, and he'd been up since five this morning. He wanted that beer and a nap, to lie down and pass out for an hour or more.

His lethargy was snuffed with his candle flame as a gust of freezing air blew into the room through the open Salon Tent door. All turned to stare at a person in an ill-fitting white ski jacket with quilted blue pants and hot pink wool hat and scarf, stamping feet on the plywood floor, making an inordinately loud noise. Kennison noticed Penilik duck quickly behind the kitchen counters, out of sight, taking cover from something. His frightened brown eyes peeked around the stainless-steel counter at the newcomer.

The person tore off a hood and the pink accessories, revealing an unsmiling woman with frizzy black hair and dark Latin features. She hadn't yet closed the Salon Tent door behind her. In the distance, the airplane that brought her, a small single-engine by the sound of its whine, revved in the strait, swinging into the wind for takeoff. The draft tore at the streamers and rattled the plastic tablecloths

"Close the jeezly door, you fucking eejit," yelled Masterson. The woman glanced severely at the few gathered in the room as if counting them, as if taking attendance and finding it wanting.

"I'm from the Arctic Exploration Institute in Washington . . . in Maryland," she said. "I've come to escort Dr. Conrad Kneisser home."

"That will be difficult." It was Kennison speaking, standing as he addressed the woman.

"And why is that?' She looked impatient, as if she wanted to leave immediately.

"Because Dr. Kneisser is dead," he said.

"Oh shit," said the woman. "Oh, goddammit all to hell." She aimed a kick at a bookcase and yelped when the action hurt her foot. "I knew it. Damn. Wouldn't you just know it? Shit."

Wisps of smoke still rose from the charred rubble that was once a small shed—or maybe they were eddies of ice crystals playing in the wind. Steam haloes crowned the heads of two telescoping work lights, bright yellow in their own beams. Kennison had extended each to its maximum height, where they waved slowly like masts at rest, top heavy in the wind. Under each, separated by fifty feet of dark and listening in the wind for instructions from Kennison, stood Wayne Penilik and Ruby Cruz, neither of them pleased.

The relentless sound of the wind was lost in the hum of a small red generator. Masterson didn't think there was enough gasoline to run it for long, so Kennison had been impatient to begin and use as much twilight as possible. He'd wanted to call Inspector Duchesne on the satphone, but Masterson said it was charging in what little light the sky provided. Those last calls had drained it and Kennison would have to wait.

Was it like Kneisser to talk so much to his employers? Kennison realized he didn't know anything about the man. Or the Fortier girl, for that matter. It was important to know your cast of characters as well as yourself in an investigation. Even the dead ones. Especially the dead ones.

The fire didn't reek like a full-fledged burning of a wooden structure, perhaps because no water had been poured on the charred lumber. There hadn't been the time. Or the water. The shack and its contents had burned quickly and completely, extinguished only because there was nothing left to feed the flames, not even the two bodies, side by side humps that, from outside the yellow tape, resembled discarded cocoons.

Twenty-four hours after the deaths, the weather was restrained in grief. The twilit sky resembled the gauze of a funeral shroud. The bright electric lights made the sky seem darker than it was. Kennison had assigned the American woman and the Inuit boy positions beside the work lights in case he needed them moved. At lunch, the woman had been annoying, asking questions about Kneisser that Kennison couldn't yet answer. She didn't seem interested at all in Fortier's death, only in her own agenda. Kennison didn't trust her. She seemed in a hurry about something. Maybe to get out of here. With that, Kennison could sympathize.

Subdued now, either by the scene of death or the cold, she stood beside her light, shivering in the wind. Her bright skiwear looked out of place, underlined by the fact that Wayne Penilik was all but invisible in his Inuit clothing. Both performed without vocal complaint, and Kennison ignored them.

First, he studied the scene from the rough road, imagining how the victims had entered the shack. Were they walking together, running for shelter when the storm came up? The ragged black ruin of a surviving wall stud, angled against this slate sky, reminded him of a cast-metal sculpture, rough-edged, newly free of its mould. He could hear the ATV over-revving at the Hell dig, where Monteith and Monk were hauling another load of packed boxes to the Otter. From the corner of his eye he saw Penilik and Ms. Cruz standing glumly beside their lights, looking in different directions.

The stark superstructure of the woodstove rose above the rubble, arrogant in solitary victory. The chromed script "McClary

Queen" shone undiminished on the oven door, blued and polished by the intense flames that had destroyed everything else. The door of the upper food warmer gaped like a mouth struck dumb. He stepped closer and inhaled a smell that was pervasively sweet, a blend of burned straw and smoked crackling.

Holding the crime kit by its shoulder straps, Kennison stared. He thought he sensed something behind him, something moving in the plain rock field to the east, but there was no movement when he looked and, from his perspective, nowhere for anyone to hide. The humps of the two bodies were near the southern edge of the site, camouflaged by the charcoal ashes that had settled on top of them. He shouted to Penilik to turn his light clockwise towards the bodies. There was no answer, no adjustment. Damn the kid. A simple job like manning a light. No wonder Masterson had ripped a strip off the guy. Kennison yelled again and stared into the increasing dark. He called to Ruby Cruz and watched her hot pink hat move to the other lamp and turn its beam as he directed. Damned Penilik. Disappeared like an aboriginal walkabout. Just up and gone.

Kennison placed the crime kit on the snow at his feet and searched its contents. He found a digital camera and walked the outside perimeter of the scene, muttering in a monotone to himself, taking flash pictures, asking Ruby to run between lights and adjust their angles, a man lost in investigation. The generator absorbed all sound. Ruby Cruz watched him.

Kennison made some notes in his Heaney book, unconsciously turning his back on her to hide it. From outside the perimeter he couldn't tell which body was which. The two bulges looked equal in size where they huddled beside each other. Kennison didn't understand his sudden sense of foreboding, a sharp sensation of complication, of being somewhere he didn't want to be, of discovering things he didn't want to find. He shook off the thought and asked that Ms. Cruz aim her light towards the corpses. He thought he saw another movement on the western horizon, far away—ghosts, perhaps, dead sailors in the dusk stumbling across the ice ridges. He looked again and they were gone, dissolved back into history perhaps. Cannibals. Unbelievable.

Surely this was just a professor and his student getting it off in a hut before they never saw each other again, sharing a mutually embarrassed post-coital smoke and burning their borrowed bedroom down. Hot sex indeed. He took pictures of the bodies *in situ* with and without the flash. The flash made everything look trapped and removed the detail and textures that shadows provided. Kenneth Monk drove past on the ATV without a glance, going for another load of boxes. Kennison shuffled his feet through the ashes, feeling for unburned evidence.

What was the Cruz woman thinking? She'd been shocked that Kneisser was dead. No, that wasn't it. More angry than shocked. It was obvious she hadn't known the man, and she certainly wasn't here because the professor was dead. She hadn't known. No, whatever Kneisser had said on the long satphone call to his company had directly resulted in her coming here or, more likely, being sent. She wouldn't care if the old man and the girl had a relationship or not. Kennison wanted a cigarette, but he wouldn't smoke inside the tape. He no longer had cigarettes after sex. He had cigarettes instead of sex.

He replaced the camera in the bag, kneeling on his haunches, ignoring Ruby Cruz stamping her feet under her light. The light white wood ash he'd stirred up had blown away, carried across the land to the east by the ceaseless wind and tucked like dustballs in ruts and ridges of snow and ice, augmenting the landscape with yet more melancholy. He asked Ms. Cruz to turn her light to her right as he used his hand to clear the ashes and other ground residue covering the two black bulks. He touched each corpse tentatively in case it retained heat. A recently burned body could yield second-degree burns long after death. Both of these bodies were very cold. Up here, the wind neutralized all heat, quickly sucking the warmth out of anything more temperate than itself.

From the crime pack, Kennison pulled out a yellow flashlight that he stuffed in his side pocket and a fuzzy implement with a long plastic handle like the windsock on a film soundman's microphone. He wasn't sure what it was for, but he used it like a duster to brush the ashes gently away from the side of the face of the corpse farthest from what had been the south wall. At closer range, it was identifiable as the smaller of the two. Although the hair was completely burned away and the flesh cooked and cracked, Kennison could see the elusive, delicate features of a female, even in death. By the curve of what was left of a cheek, he imagined her young and attractive, like Monteith said. It was a failing of his, he knew. He always tried to give the dead life, especially the young ones, yet in giving them life he received only grief in return.

The male corpse was much older, the roasting of his facial features muddled with the charred grizzle of his former hair and beard. It lay on its side in an unnatural fetal position, head tucked too tightly to the chest, knees pulled up to almost meet the chin as if the heat of the fire had shrunken the tendons and tightened the cast of the man. The size of the skull and a fuzzy tuft of hair in one ear, miraculously uncharred, told him this was Kneisser. He worked delicately, slowly, dusting thin layers away, asking for light adjustments as he went. Ruby Cruz ran obediently from light to light. Probably keeping her warm, thought Kennison. Damned Penilik. Where had he gone?

The bodies were more badly burned than he had imagined. He'd assumed their deaths, like most fire deaths, would be from inhaling smoke, from asphyxiation, the flame damage secondary, occurring after death. But it seemed these two had been literally boiled to death in their own juices, then baked once those juices were spent, cooked before they could inhale the poisons that could kill them. A postmortem would let the lungs tell the story. Kennison could hear Cruz stamping her feet again, patting her chest with opposite hands to keep her blood flowing in the cold. The lights shook with the motion, which didn't help.

Kennison crouched close to Kneisser's corpse, wiping more ashes away from his nose and eyes. His knees hurt—he wasn't as young as the last time he'd leaned over a corpse. He was able to roll the body onto its back, but the extreme fetal position held. The man was curled into a ball with limbs. Kennison had seen a dead sheep on a trip to Wales with Ginny, a black-faced sheep, dead on its back in a ditch, four stiff limbs raised to the sky. Kneisser looked the same. Was it rigor mortis, or was the dead man frozen in this position? He lifted an arm up and let it flop down beside the body. Not rigor, then. The joint was loose, the rest of him frozen like a human Popsicle in a natural icebox.

He yelled to Cruz for more light on the larger corpse. He needed both lights. Where the hell was Penilik? He bent down, his weight on his elbows, his head almost touching the ground beside Kneisser's corpse, eye to eye with irises that had boiled out of their sockets and dried like raisins in the heat. Without moving his head, he reached into his pocket for the small yellow flashlight and shone it on the face of Karl Conrad Kneisser.

"Ohhhhh shit." He heard himself as if the sound came from another. He exhaled and straightened as air-light ashes danced on Kneisser's skull. Kennison's shoulders sagged and his head dropped again to the ashy ground as he stared sadly, resentfully, at the bullet hole in Kneisser's temple.

Ruby Cruz screamed. Why? She couldn't see Kneisser's skull. Suddenly, her work light toppled and smashed on the ground as the sound of a shot split the gloom. Kennison dove to flatten himself, cramming his body between the two corpses, dropping the flashlight in the rubble, trying to roll to his side as he had done when Patsy Prévost died. He felt a bullet hit the body of the dead girl and he waited for its pain, scrambling frantically to find the flashlight that betrayed his location and turn it off. He doused the light as two more shots sounded from a different direction. A different rifle. A team? A siege? Then silence.

Kennison raised himself slowly, opening eyes he didn't know he'd closed, peeking over the body of Marie-Claire Fortier. In the beam of the remaining work light he could see Ruby Cruz sprawled on the ground. Had she been shot? There was something else—someone else—in the shadow at the base of the operating light. Kennison couldn't make it out. It wasn't Wayne Penilik, because the Inuit boy was walking slowly towards the shape, arms outstretched with his rifle at the ready, stopping to stand tall over what seemed to be the prone body of a man.

June 28, 1845
Davis Strait

After some time battling currents and crosswinds around Greenland's tip, we have turned north, sailing close-hauled against a fresh but bitter breeze coming, one imagines, directly from the North Pole. The Erebus *leads, just visible on the horizon ahead, and the* Barretto Junior *tracks* Terror*'s wake in dutiful manner, seeming none the worse for the rough weather we have endured. I swear today I could hear the bullocks on board lowing astern, but it may have been the luff of our sails as the helmsmen try pinching the course for maximum headway. The weather has cleared somewhat and the seas, although we sail against both wind and current here, are calm enough to abide a quick turn on deck for all of us mobile and dressed warmly enough. I fear for those in the sick bay. Today I visited my colleague G., who is still feverish, yet pale-faced and lethargic and complaining of pains in his chest. He continues to cough up extraordinary amounts of phlegm and his night sweats continue unabated. He has lost a great deal of weight, noticeable on a man for whom the description "portly" was a polite understatement. He is an extremely good teacher, however, my first choice, even* *over L. on the* Erebus. *He has a fine mind that has not damaged his affinity with the labouring class. He enjoys his students, revels in the expansion of their abilities and vocabulary and regularly crows that they teach him more than he instructs them. I fear for his condition and cannot think what is to be done. Dr. Peddie, the ship's surgeon, trained to remove gangrenous limbs rather than treat internal diseases, seems at a loss. He and I avoid mentioning "consumption," as if by not labelling our real fear the dreadful inevitability of diseased tubercules will somehow right itself. I must think on the resolution, if there is one—not in the sick bay, but elsewhere contagion is less likely.*

The library is my haven and now properly set up. I have grouped the volumes under subject headings, and within those categories arranged books alphabetically by author when possible. This task could not have been accomplished before now, as arrival of books ordered was not guaranteed, nor was the degree of duplication across two ships known. I have grouped the books into two general sections of Fact and Fiction, the latter of which has been lately produced in inordinate numbers. The novels are arranged alphabetically by author so, for example, we have John Agg's MacDermot *abutting Charles Brockden Brown's* Wieland, *James Fenimore Cooper's* The Pilot, *Charles Dickens'* The Life and Adventures of Nicholas Nickleby, *and so on down to William Frederick Williams'* Sketches of Modern Life.
Early in the process of accumulating fictional volumes, I decided to limit the number of fanciful books written by women. It is not an easy task, as the bulk of novels written recently seem to be by those unencumbered by the practical necessities of making a career or supporting a household. Women with cats or small dogs, I suspect. One named Catherine George Ward has written

17 novels, including such prosaic tomes as A Bachelor's Heiress *and* The Widow's Choice, *neither of which have I read (nor any other). I shall be the first to suggest that there may be some talent there, but I have avoided female authorship because the subject matter is of minimal interest or value to sailors. Further, men at sea for an extended period need not muse on women or distaff perspectives of English society more often than they already do.* Caveat lector.

The factual books, mostly explorations and the history of great ships, are arranged alphabetically by the surnames of the primary explorers (Back, Barrow, Franklin, Ross and so on) or the class of vessel should ordinance be the issue. The system works, as I've spent many hours setting myself logistical problems and solving them until I am pleased with the consistency of the search path. When we stop to resupply the ships, I shall share the system with L. on Erebus *who, if I know his ways and passion for order, has already invented a cataloguing system of his own.*

The separation of the ships is somewhat bothersome for regular communication, and I do not feel I can prevail upon the Terror *signalmen to include notes to L. on book categorization amongst their important messages concerning weather and navigation. We drew close to* Erebus *today, close enough to make out the faces of men waving on deck, although there are not many I know by name. I believe I saw Franklin himself pacing at the bow, recognizable by his way of walking and his hand to his throat, fingers rubbing the gift from his Lady, which I am now told is a valuable stone of some kind on a gold chain, a bauble awarded them when Governors of Van Dieman's Land. Now it serves as a love charm, a talisman, though it will not last if the Commander continues to rub it with the frequency he seems to favour. Soon L. and I will be able to speak in person, and a recovered G. too. Other than an inexplicable and irrational attractionto the emptiness of the bleak landscape here (magnificent iceberg sculptures pass us like ships ten times our size, as if* Terror *is a lad's toy boat in a village pond), I am looking forward to returning in time for the fall semester and, with trepidation as I muse on it, the role of husband to Alice Lort and father to her spawn, however forced by circumstance.*

The Fortier girl's corpse had taken the single bullet meant for him. The pros—like Kennison—never planned for a second chance. Unconsciously, instinctively, he'd placed his fingers on the dead girl's throat, checking for a pulse as if the bullet had struck a living woman. Her arms were crossed near her neck as if she'd died protecting her face from the heat. The joints were stiff, making the taking of her pulse a difficult and, with the slow return of logic, pointless procedure. He realized he was operating in shock, using rote to make sense of the ridiculous.

He stood warily, unsure of what had happened. Penilik stood frozen in place, rifle raised like a character in a crashed video game. Ruby Cruz was sitting on the ground by the fallen light, holding her knee now and chanting a mantra to Kennison's confusion: "What's happening? What's happening? What is it? Who is it? What's happening?" With his eyes fixed on the body at Penilik's feet, Kennison stepped back outside the tape and moved towards Cruz, feeling his way through the rocks with his feet rather than looking away.

"You okay, Ms. Cruz?" He didn't look to see if she nodded. "You okay?" he repeated.

"Yes. Yes, I'm okay." It was a whimper, qualified by some insight that her situation wasn't the primary issue at the moment.

Kennison moved slowly towards the Inuit boy, worried that he'd spook the young man holding the rifle, approached him as if he were a ledge jumper in the financial district. He carefully drew his Smith and Wesson.

"Okay, Wayne. Go easy now. Lower the rifle. It's all right. It's over now . . ." Penilik looked up, expressionless, at Kennison. He turned quickly and walked away into the dark. He disappeared immediately as if he'd become dusk. Kennison heard Cruz grunting to her feet and breathing heavily as she approached from behind. He stared down and rolled the dead man over on his back with his foot, revealing the AK-47 pressed into the snow by his body. The man's face was fat, his blond beard thin and scraggly, his hair thin and stuck to his head in a circular nest. A Blue Jays baseball cap lay on its side in the snow.

"The fisherman," whispered Ruby Cruz. "It's him."

"What fisherman?" Kennison whispered as well, as if they were in a confined, secret place instead of this vast and empty land. To the north, Kennison could hear the ATV starting up at Heaven. Someone must have heard the shots, or Penilik had already reported the kill. Kennison realized he was using his investigative skills not to solve the crime but to avoid the reality. This man had tried to kill him, and Kennison knew from experience that this would take its toll emotionally sooner or later. Later, he hoped. When he was at home with a carton of smokes, a hockey game and a case of beer.

"The man who flew with us here," said Ruby. "With Ivan. I saw him before, in—how did he get here? He was going somewhere else." Kennison crouched and checked the body on the snow for vital signs the way he had the Fortier girl. Two inactive pulses in as many minutes. He looked up to Ruby, frowning, still confused.

"He was trying to . . ." Ruby stepped forward and put her hand on Kennison's arm. " . . . kill you?"

"Yes, he was."

"Do you know why?"

Kennison felt the sweats begin. The ATV was approaching. He needed to be alone to deal with this.

"Wait for the ATV, Ms. Cruz." His voice croaked. "Please ask them to help you take the body back to the camp. Gently now, so we can look him over later." Ruby Cruz looked like she wanted to go with Kennison, but she stayed with the body and watched its recent target walk the path that led to Hell.

Who was he? Kennison had more questions than he could form—and a major discovery he had yet to be able to share: Kneisser had been shot in the head.

Kennison looked back as an ATV driven by Masterson revved and negotiated a turn on the narrow path, arriving to take the sniper's body back to Heaven, leaving the two other corpses inside the tape awaiting his attention. The attempt on his life wasn't about Kneisser or the girl. This guy had just arrived, had come for what seemed to be the express purpose of making Kennison dead. Was Prévost's gang tracking him down, all the way to the end of the earth? It didn't seem their style. They liked to hit a man where he lived, not tucked away where no one would see the message they were sending. More likely the sniper was sent by people he knew, people he was supposed to trust.

It was clear to Kennison exactly why he'd been posted to Yellowknife, even if Ormerod and Cosentino thought he didn't know. Kennison was evidence. Kennison's single testimony could indict senior members of the force, including his former father-in-law, for corruption, for fiddling the pension plan, for installing their friends and relatives in high-paying jobs in which they shored up the rotten foundations of their bosses and hid the deal that had made them all rich. Ormerod was Ginny's father. Cosentino was his mewling sycophant, dependent on Ormerod for the small favours thrown to him like meat scraps from the table. The man had used the Patsy Prévost affair as an excuse to move Kennison out of Ottawa to somewhere they could keep him quiet or shut him up.

They couldn't have pulled it off without Duchesne's agreement, thought Kennison. With the help of Duchesne, they'd stashed him in Yellowknife, out of the glare of investigators and the media. Hoping he wouldn't testify. Like Kolchak had. Or making certain he couldn't testify. It had to be about that. This guy had to have been sent by them, by his own leadership. To kill him. To save their sorry asses. Duchesne had sent him here with that bullshit story about Turqavik terrorists, set him up to be killed. He shuddered involuntarily. Here it comes, he thought. Soon he'd shake, maybe vomit. It was a process as inevitable as death and mourning, and there was no way to cheat it.

If you pretended it didn't happen, if you thought that this time you'd escaped it, you'd find out tomorrow or the day after—or, more likely, in the middle of the night—that it was only waiting for you to drop your guard. Then it would come, step by step, the order of events never changing, never faster, never easier for your knowledge of what they were.

Kennison breathed deeply and walked again. The faint passed. He thought of Edgar Kolchak. He and Eddie had accepted desk jobs when they'd returned from the former Yugoslavia. Cosentino—an inspector then—had smiled and shaken their hands and said desk jobs would aid the decompression of their return to Canada, act as an antidote to the body counting and graphic and sickening war crimes evidence they'd waded through for six months.

Ironically, the desk job had become an investigation. They were plucked from HQ to serve on the Cavan Commission. Named for the former auditor general who headed it, the commission was an unannounced—government talk for secret—investigation into the financial and hiring practices and pension fund corruption within the RCMP.

The commission had coloured Kennison's view of politics ever since. He'd done a good job. Kolchak had helped a lot, although he wasn't operating at the level that Kennison was as lead investigator. They'd dug deep, uncovered a dirty world the average Mountie and most citizens knew nothing about. After seven months, he'd filed his report with Cavan and then . . . nothing. The press weren't clamouring for accountability because they didn't know about the investigation. Politicians knew little, and those who knew the most had the most to lose by leaking the story, so they weren't going to talk.

The good guys, Kennison and Kolchak, naively thought that their report would cause heads to roll. The bad guys knew better. In the end, nothing was done either to eradicate the parasite or contain its growth. Two middle-rank officers were chastised and retired early to their expensive homes in Alta Vista with full pensions; Kennison was made a plainclothes sergeant and the rot continued to fester, aided and abetted by top insiders who turned the other way or, worse, joined the corrupt. Even a resurgence of guilt three years after the investigation didn't touch the real criminals. The Commissioner himself resigned, but those responsible for the embarrassment and the crimes remained untouched. Until now. Until a young politician from Québec had started asking questions out loud and received no answers.

"I know too much," Kennison said into the night air, as if putting words to a funeral dirge helped lighten its despondency. "If

I testify, they'll lose." Everything. Big time. Ormerod, Cosentino. Maybe Duchesne—even Dutch Duchesne? It was worth so much to them they were willing to ship him to some goddamn place and then send some guy to kill him. And if they'll send one guy, they'll send another . . . and another.

His chest heaved, and in the bitter cold of Victory Point, sweat rolled from somewhere in his hair, down his brow and into his eyes. A halo of self-generated steam surrounded his head. When he began to shake and cry, he couldn't tell if the tears were from the sting of his sweat in his eyes or the pain of process. Whatever their origin, they dropped to the ground and froze into small pellets that blew away in the wind.

It was the fisherman, all right. Even in death, Ruby could smell the body odour that had made her gag on the plane. His fat face was the unshaven one she'd seen in the Edmonton airport, his beard swarthier in this light, heavy and oddly dark in comparison to his wispy blond hair. His backpack was still on his shoulders. Old habits made her want to search it, but she held back. Kennison wasn't the kind of man you wanted to piss off. It was his sniper. It would be his investigation. Why was this man trying to kill him? she wondered. And who was he?

At the crime scene, Masterson had moved to pick up the rifle, but she'd stopped him and picked it up herself—carefully, mindful of evidence, using bits of paper she found in the pocket of her ski clothes to keep her fingerprints off the gun. She held the rifle where the barrel met the stock as she rode on the high seat behind Masterson, her other arm around his waist for lack of anywhere else to put it and to steady herself as the ATV rolled through the ruts on this excuse for a road.

She couldn't help but think about Wayne Penilik. He scared her, even though he was little more than a shy native boy. When she'd seen him leave his post by the light and dissolve into the dark shadows, she'd taken for granted he was simply uninterested in helping. But he'd obviously seen a movement or sensed something neither she nor Kennison had noticed. The ATV rocked in the ruts, almost tossing her off. She held the rifle high over the bumps, like a commando.

She realized now that what she thought was Penilik returning was the shooter's shadow. She'd looked up and screamed. The noise must have caused a slight hesitation, a momentary disruption that caused the sniper to miss Kennison and give Penilik time to fire his gun. What the hell was going on? Who was this guy, and why did he want to kill Kennison? And why should she care anyway?

Masterson was asking her some of the same questions, but the wind and the roar of the ATV made them inaudible or at the least gave her an excuse to ignore him. Whatever the events involving Penilik or Kennison or this dead man, it was not her business. In fact, with everyone's attention on shack fires and snipers, her search for Kniesser's journal could prove easier than if she was under their microscope.

She was able to turn just far enough to see that the body of the sniper was still secured with yellow polyester rope. How hard could finding the journal be? She knew it existed, and perhaps no one else did. Kennison hadn't referred to it, and surely he would have mentioned it in passing. Kneisser wouldn't have hidden it under one of the ten million damned rocks she could see in every direction. Why would he have hid it at all? He was an anthropologist, for God's sake, a scientist. Didn't scientists usually want to brag about their finds to their colleagues, like anglers about their catches? Recognition of the find, especially from peers, was what scientists worked for, wasn't it? Not fame or money. Ruby doubted, no matter what the promises or contracts, that Kneisser and Dickerson's motives were the same.

Maybe Kneisser had told everyone else. Maybe they knew

about the journal, maybe they'd all read it. Maybe it was sitting there in plain sight on the bookshelf in the damned tent compound. At least that was a place to start. How hard could it be? She remembered that Dickerson and Fernandez didn't even know their star employee was dead in a fire. Had the journal burned to powder with him? Was she searching for dust?

Masterson aimed the ATV over the last few bumps to its usual resting spot near the exterior door to the Kitchen Tent. Inside, she could hear someone preparing the evening meal, chopping something punky, like limp vegetables. Between the two of them they managed to lift the dead weight and lay it on a blue plastic tarpaulin Masterson pulled from beneath the steps. Ruby placed the backpack and rifle on the dead man's chest, barrel pointed up at his chin like a contemplated suicide as Masterson drew the tarp over the body and secured it with the yellow rope. The corpse would freeze before rigor mortis set in. This climate was good for something. She waited, watching Masterson head for his yellow tent before she walked into the compound.

Trevor Patel would be her best bet for a first chat. He was Kneisser's assistant, or junior partner or gopher or whatever they called it, although she didn't know what their day-to-day relationship was. He'd tell her that, as well as the location of their work and how much Kneisser had shared about his discovery. From the tape of Kneisser's call, Patel knew something, she just wasn't sure what. She thought she remembered Dickerson or Fernandez questioning Patel's ethics, or maybe they just didn't trust him. Perhaps all that meant was that he was capable of conspiring, of seeing some advantage to working with her to find the journal if he didn't already have it in his pocket.

In the kitchen, Monk stood over a bag of reedy carrots, chopping them under the Inuit woman's direction. A shot in the distance confirmed that Penilik was back on the barrens. Would he have any emotional reaction to having killed a man? Do hunters ever feel for their prey? Did Penilik distinguish between man and animal? She wondered how Kennison was making out. Poor bastard. Monk didn't look up or speak. He looked like he'd been crying, or maybe he'd been slicing onions or had allergies. Allergies in the Arctic? Somehow she didn't think so.

Trevor Patel was not in the compound. Ruby checked the Salon Tent and peeked without hope at the empty bookshelves. He was probably at Kneisser's dig, wherever that was, packing up. She needed to go there as well. She checked the Dormitory Tent and finally the Wet Tent, where she found Anne Ferguson-Crewe weeping behind the closed door of a toilet cubicle.

"Anne? It's Ruby. Ruby Cruz. Can I help?" There was no answer. The weeping was replaced by sniffles and Ruby heard the rattle of a toilet paper roll, then a nose being blown. After that, silence. "Anne, I'm sorry but I need to ask you some questions—not just you, but everyone. I thought I'd start with you because you're the lead scientist here." Sugar catches more flies than vinegar, her father always said. "It won't take long, I promise." No answer. "I'll be in the bedroom . . . the Dorm Tent, Anne. Just you and me. Won't take long. Private chat. I promise."

It was more difficult with the one remaining work light, but by adjusting it himself just outside the tape, Kennison was able to do a cursory examination to corroborate what he thought he'd seen before the attempt on his life. The steam from the heat of the work light made it look like a leggy alien creature.

Kennison was feeling Masterson's pressure of time now. It was getting darker, and Monteith had mentioned more than once that he was sticking to his departure schedule. There was no way, with what looked like a murder on his hands, that Kennison was leaving with him. Monk drove by on the ATV with another trailer full of labelled boxes, and Kennison moved quickly to the Fortier girl's corpse, the butt of the small flashlight in his mouth, checking her head for a hole that matched the one in the forehead of Karl Conrad Kneisser. It struck him as obvious that he was prepared to use her as a shield again should another sniper be on the ground.

He tried to turn her skull upwards with his hands, to examine the temple and neck and nape for bullet-entry wounds, but he couldn't move her. The cold had stalled the process of rigor mortis and she was still stiff as a board. He stood to stretch, then crouched on his heels to think for a moment, his concentration subject to his vigilance. He sensed rather than saw another movement in the far distance. A bird maybe? A fox? A bear? He doubted there was much left out there with Penilik shooting everything. Still, it made him uneasy. The sniper had crawled out of the dark.

He looked back to the bodies. What the hell was this really about? Did these two have sex and then she shot him and torched the place to hide the evidence, to murder her guilt? Did he rape her, so she killed him and burned herself in some misdirected shame? Did someone else shoot him, and maybe her, too? Or kill her by some other method? And then burn both of them? There was no way he could answer these questions in the encroaching dark, no way he could begin to examine these bodies here. He leaned forward and knelt close to the ground, shining the flashlight on Kneisser's charred forehead. The skin had cracked and dried, and he had to peel skin off with his fingers to properly see the bullet hole.

Somebody shot him. No question. From a distance, though. He shuffled over to the light and turned it towards Kneisser's forehead. There were no visible powder burns or residue or pitting on the man's temple, although perhaps that would have been burned away with the flesh. The wound seemed clean, the hole perfect, not ragged from physical force like it would be if he'd been shot close up and the skull casing had absorbed the impact of the explosion as well as the penetration of the bullet.

Whatever this might be, it was no longer a quick fuck in the furnace room. He needed to get these bodies somewhere they could be examined more carefully, get them off to the morgue in Yellowknife, and right away. He heard an engine of the Otter turn over. He pulled up his sleeve to see his watch. It was already three o'clock. He had half an hour left at the most.

Maybe the red herring here was the fire. Fire wasn't rare up here. Fuelled stoves and heaters and generators were everywhere and used often, all year round. Gas, electrical, oil-fired . . . it's a wonder the whole North didn't burn to the ground on one windy day. Charred ruins in villages were as ubiquitous as gravel-cracked windshields and sled dogs. But murder was rare—at least premeditated murder, murder like this. A bullet hole in the temple isn't an accident. He shook his head and backed outside the tape.

Kennison lit another Rothman's and stared back at the scene. Something was bothering him, hovering on the edge of his thoughts, masked by his constant attention to the 360-degree horizon, to his fear that someone else was lurking out there, waiting for the right moment.

It's a southern crime, he thought. Not a crime from here. Here, there's nowhere to hide, no back alleys between tall buildings, no chain link fences to vault, no Dumpsters to hide in while the cops run by. People kill up here, but they kill relatives and friends and sworn enemies over misunderstandings, embarrassments or betrayals. They stab, punch, strangle or kick people unconscious or split their heads with a fire axe across the kitchen table, and they usually do it while one or both are extremely drunk. They don't snipe like professionals, don't shoot their enemies in the head from a safe distance. Karl Kneisser's death was a deliberate killing.

Was it the girl who killed him? Kennison thought not. There was no weapon detritus in the rubble, no pistol or metal rifle remains he'd been able to find by shuffling his feet through the ashes. The stock might burn, but the barrel and the trigger mechanism wouldn't. Kennison put out his cigarette, shaking his head for clarity. Something sensible was scratching at the door of his logic. Something he'd missed, something he should see or had seen and hadn't processed. Something that would answer a question if he knew what the question was. His mouth tasted like smoke and vomit. His eyes ached from focusing on distant movement, real or imagined. As he stared mutely at the crime scene, willing understanding, the generator coughed twice and the work light dimmed briefly, then died with the last of the gasoline.

July 10, 1845
Whalefish Islands, Disko Bay, Greenland

We have docked off the Whalefish Islands, south of the Svartenhuk Peninsula (say my maps) on the east coast of Davis Strait. I have appealed to officers with sextants to allow me access to their latitudinal and longitudinal calculations so I can regularly record them in these pages, but they are loath to take the time and have dismissed me, to my thinking unnecessarily and without good manners. Out in the Strait, large chunks of ice float south with the aplomb of a regal march past, colossal crafts of clotted cream, each worthy of fastidious study as the blue ice and white snows change colour with the waxing and waning of the light. A truly moving and magnificent sight.

The sky is clouded and the winds constant, but the temperature is tolerable today, even in the open tender they use to row us to shore. Ah, shore. This barren rock of island is oddly attractive to all of us. Is it that no man was born to live at sea? I worked to disguise my childish glee of being back on land, wobbly as a foal on my new sea legs, far in body and mind from the verdant blush of Kent's soft summer. Others, less constrained by class or mien, whooped and leaped and made acrobatics on the gravelly sand beaches while others laughed and sported. I watched with fascination as the Able Seamen—for that is what they certainly are—hauled on heavy lines to bring the Barretto Junior *into a stern-facing position from whence she whelped the ten bullocks like a litter of pups into the frigid sea.*

The cattle were driven through the roiling shallows, herded to shore with shouts and whips and sticks to a land where no grass grows, wet with sweat and salt water, yet shivering with the cold, bolts of steam shot in splayed spikes from their broad nostrils as if their core heat was expelled by an apocalyptic pressure of fear.

First Pestilence lunges onto shore, mad with cold and confusion. War is flanked and tripped to the sand with a shudder. Famine trumpets with terror as its legs are tied, and Death twitches witlessly with humiliation when hauled by its rear legs high on a tripod of poles transported for the purpose—there are no trees to fell up here. Knowing their fate, I still cannot take my eyes away, even when L. approaches, excited to see me at last, overflowing with pride of the sorting system I knew he would design. Beyond him the stark silhouettes of Terror *and* Erebus, *starboards to shore, bows high and shoulders turned away like townswomen affronted by rude events beyond their ken. I rebuffed L. unfairly, rudely I suspect, as the beach on which I stood transfixed by gore echoed with the baritone screech of frightened cattle, each voice rising in pitch as death comes closer. Still-spastic carcasses, slick with steaming, freezing blood, are hauled by tethers to hang head down. Writhing throats are nicked with knives and unimaginable volumes of blood soak the sand and creep to where I stand, petrified with nausea, trapped between murder and the sea.*

The scar-faced man—Bealls is his name, I'm told—and his friends seem to enjoy the bloody holocaust and snigger together pointing at me and my too obvious distress. I shall not forget this day of death. May there never be another like it.

Ruby Cruz balled her fist and used the fleshy end to melt ice from the glass on the Salon Tent door. It was unnaturally dark outside, and she looked again at her watch to see if the second hand was moving. It was, and the time was just past three-thirty. Minutes took hours to pass in this damned desolate place.

Maybe she should leave with the Otter pilot, she thought, except there wasn't room in the plane with all the boxes and three bodies. In any case, Dickerson and Fernandez would be furious if she showed up without Kneisser's body or possessions—especially the journal—and besides, Kennison had not offered her the opportunity to leave. In fact, no one here paid any attention to her. She would use that to her advantage.

Ruby looked south, her head pressed close to the glass pane in the door. Even in the encroaching dark, the crime scene at Purgatory was marked by the silhouettes of unnatural totems, the expired work-light pole and the wood stove. Farther to the west, she could barely see movement on the shore where Kennison and the pilot loaded the bagged bodies into the Twin Otter in the last of the light.

She backed away from the window and shivered. The shape of her cheek remained, sculpted in ice on the glass window. The cold had crept into her feet and lower calves and wouldn't leave, even with the heavy socks. Anne Ferguson-Crewe hadn't said much about the Kneisser journal, other than that, judging by his recent personality about-face, she and others suspected the esteemed scholar had found something. A day or two ago, the normally dour and brusque Kneisser had turned into a grinning and garrulous grandfather. But that's all she knew. He certainly hadn't told people about any find, or at least hadn't told the lead archaeologist. She agreed with Ruby that Patel might know more.

When Ruby shivered, Anne had plunged into her packed suitcase and given her a pair of thick woollen socks with a white ankle band and a red rim. They looked like socks that Maine woodsmen wore under thick boots. Ruby asked her where Dr. Kneisser spent his leisure time or where he slept, but she'd clammed up, shaken her head quickly and left the room as fast as she could, her hand cupped over her mouth as if she was going to be ill. Ruby sensed there was no love lost between Anne and Kneisser—perhaps between Anne and anyone, even herself.

It suddenly struck Ruby that she didn't know what Kneisser looked like. Dickerson and Fernandez hadn't supplied a photograph. There had been no need. She'd imagined a large, stooped man with large glasses and a stylish but unpressed wardrobe, a romantic Indiana Jones in a worn fedora, but of the Far North. A treasure hunter, although judging by what Dickerson had said, and Fernandez's recent order to obtain the journal at any cost, the treasure was more valuable to AEI than the man.

There was a small flashlight perched on the bookcase closest to the door. She put it in her coat pocket and sat on one of the futons to pull on her snow boots. The thick socks made them fit tighter than she liked, and that would probably make her feet even colder. She hated this place. Get me back to Baltimore, she thought. If she didn't leave tomorrow, there would be no Ridgley's Delight for her. Damned Dickerson. Damned Fernandez. Damned Kneisser.

On the shore, the Otter idled, warming for takeoff. She didn't have much time. Kennison would be back soon after the plane left. To her right, the individual tents shuddered in the wind, protected only by a four-foot-high wall that looked like it was made of snow blocks, like an igloo she'd seen constructed on a PBS program. The unremitting winds had eroded the loose-packed snow used as mortar between the blocks, and the entire structure looked porous, as if it might collapse at any moment. This whole place might have been more welcoming, even more appealing, if it weren't so damned dark and in the midst of being abandoned. She tried to imagine it in sunshine, but the picture wouldn't come. The neglected wind wall, the piles of boxes everywhere and the constant talk of abandonment didn't make it any more attractive.

There were seven small dome tents arranged north of the Kitchen Tent door, each of them designed, at first glance, for one or two people. It seemed strange to Ruby that here, where the land was endless and space at no premium, the tents were pitched in a pattern designed to reflect the unimaginative order of suburbia. The four tents to the north, farthest from the main compound, were lined up and equidistant, as if on a subdivision street. Between them and the northern entrance of the Kitchen Tent, three more tents were pegged, square to the others as if laid out on a grid. Maybe this forced and narrow order was an antidote to the vastness of the land, she thought. If she lived here—perish the thought—she'd have her tent far from the others and without reference to any of them.

On closer examination, the tents weren't pegged. The ground was either too frozen or too rocky. They were larger than they seemed at first, four- or five-person tents reduced in size by a ring of rocks piled on top of the wall material at the outer edge, ensuring the wind wouldn't send them sailing across the wasteland. These individual tents were for privacy, she imagined, for escaping one's colleagues, for reading or thinking or sleeping in better weather without the lip smacks and snores and farts of strangers that made good rest improbable. Even now that the cold forced them to sleep inside, it would be important to know you had access to a shelter of your own when you needed to get away from it all—from *them* all.

The three tents closest to the Kitchen Tent were similar, possibly identical, as if issued by a single supplier. Each was the same bright yellow. The zippered doors of each faced south to the main compound. She'd watched Masterson head for the one nearest the snow wall, farthest from the kitchen door.

The four tents to the north were not part of the same standard issue. Each was a different colour and style. From west to east, they were pale green, beige, orange and a dark blue, the last three squared with their yellow neighbours. Only the green tent farthest west, the odd man out, extended beyond the suburban design. For no reason she could support, Ruby imagined that it was Kneisser's. It was the one she would have chosen, the one calf that refused to be corralled.

The Twin Otter gunned its engines. She couldn't see Hell over the main compound, but she imagined the plane turning, taxiing down the narrow channel and turning again to face the wind. If she couldn't see them, they couldn't see her, so she moved quickly to the yellow tent nearest the kitchen and rattled the door with her mitten. As she expected, no one responded. She removed her thick mitt, undid the zipper with cold fingers and poked her head inside, pulling it back immediately.

It smelled like something had died in there—a strange perfume of fish oil, rotting meat and human sweat. She took a deep breath, held it and poked her head and arm through the opening to shine the flashlight inside. A plaid-lined sleeping bag was roughly folded in quarters and tossed in a far corner. A piece of the ubiquitous blue plastic tarpaulin covered the floor area and was itself covered with a large, dark, unidentifiable animal skin. In the corner opposite the sleeping bag, the corpse of a large white rabbit or hare lay on its back, feet stretched to the extremes and the stomach wire-lashed like a corset where it had been eviscerated. There was nothing else visible—no backpack, no books, no personal items. The smell was overpowering, and she pulled her head back outside. Whoever lived here, she didn't think it was Dr. Kneisser.

Ruby zipped the tent closed and moved to its yellow neighbour.

Kennison watched with mixed emotions as the Otter took off. He'd been in many firefights, in the army and on the force, but not since his later peacekeeping days in Bosnia had he been a target for snipers, played the grinning, utterly unaware, pocked metal duck in a Serbian shooting gallery. In the end, he decided, he was safer here than in Yellowknife. It was harder for anyone to fly here, let alone stalk and kill him in this place. Maybe Dutch Duchesne was on the side of the good guys. Maybe he'd sent Kennison here to prevent him from being unwittingly blown away in the middle of the Dog Derby. At least out here, he now knew it was someone's agenda to kill him.

But whose? The Ormerod and Cosentino HQ link seemed obvious. No love lost there, especially because Ormerod blamed Kennison for Ginny's descent into hell. It was a hell of her own junkie making, and Kennison was past blaming himself. But Ormerod wasn't. And where did Dutch Duchesne fit into all this? Kennison liked the guy, felt good talking to him, joking with him. What was his agenda? Was he amenable to trading a Mountie's life for a few bucks from the pension fund?

Kennison's mind had raced as he and Monteith used the two body bags for the corpses from the fire and the blue tarp for the sniper Penilik had killed. Carrying them up the steps and negotiating the tight turn into the packed cargo area was like moving a sectional couch into a third-floor walkup. Kennison had left the sniper rifle and the man's backpack back at Heaven. He'd examine them later when he had the time.

Kennison clapped his mittened hands together as if to brush the death from them. He had never been comfortable with corpses. He couldn't bring himself to believe they were just dead things, especially if they were young—dead before what Sister Sinestra used to call "their time." He'd been told a woman named Giles was the best of the pathologists in Yellowknife. He'd advised Rick Monteith to avoid Mack the Knife if possible. Monteith knew Mack and had confirmed Giles's expertise. Kennison kept forgetting that everyone knew everyone else up here, that the city of Yellowknife was home to only twenty thousand people on a very good day.

"Jennifer Giles is—was—the wife of a cop," Monteith had said. "Husband died last year investigating a domestic up towards Wha Ti. A Dene couple was murdering each other in a trailer and making too much noise to hear his warnings from outside. When Tim Giles finally busted through the door to stop them, they both turned guns on him and shot him in the head. Twice. Too bad. He was a very nice guy. Came from down in Manitoba somewhere, I think. Left Jen—Dr. Giles—with three little kids." Monteith hadn't told Kennison that he was the replacement for the late Constable Giles. Everyone else knew, and not a few wondered if the new guy would take over where Tim Giles had left off, especially with Jennifer and the kids.

Kennison waved as Monteith dipped a wing after takeoff. Behind him he heard the ATV, but ignored it. He wanted to walk back to Heaven, take some time to think. Kennison watched the plane grow smaller in the southwest as if it was the last one on earth. He thought he could still see it as one of the stars after its sound was eaten by the wind. For that single moment he felt lonelier than he'd ever been, suddenly more anxious then the first night in a foster home, more depressed than lying in his brown iron bed, staring at the shadows cast by the wall crucifix, after being returned, once again, to the sisters. They would flutter and whisper after they'd put him back in his room. "D.P.," they said, sad for him, and shook their heads knowingly. "Difficult Placement."

Kennison turned to walk back to Heaven, forcing himself to clear his mind of all thoughts except the investigation into what now looked like the murder of at least one of the two in the shack fire. No other plane had landed, and they wouldn't have sent two snipers, so he had some time. Or was there someone out there on the horizon? Had they sent one in by plane and a backup somehow by land? Kennison shook off the thought and tried to concentrate on Kneisser's murder.

Suspect number one had to be the Inuit boy. Penilik. He was the only one with the skills to run and hide on this land, and he was the only one with a rifle, as far as Kennison knew. There must be others here with guns—this was polar bear country, and for all their sleek beauty at the zoo, they were mean bastards. Attack you as quick as look at you, they said.

Kennison walked towards Purgatory and Heaven, picking his way through the rocks on a road barely visible had it not been for the ATV tracks in the shallow snow. He was warm as long as he was moving—hot, even. He unzipped the neck of his parka and the zipper of the fleece beneath it. The suspicious something on the edge of his mind still hovered like a July deerfly, circling somewhere above his head, unseen and always out of reach.

If the Fortier girl hadn't been screwing the professor as a

goodbye gesture, what were they doing together in that shack? Exchanging email addresses? Plotting next year's explorations? Unless someone else torched the place to get rid of either or both of them, to cover something up. Or maybe whoever torched the shed didn't know it was occupied. But why would anyone just burn the shack? To burn all the fuel? Why? To expedite the leaving of this place? No, they were leaving anyway.

Maybe the two vics were already dead in there and the shack was burned to hide some evidence of wrongdoing. Like Kneisser's murder. Maybe the Fortier girl was a red herring. He stooped to light a cigarette out of the wind and stopped while he smoked it. He was running low and he wanted to enjoy it rather than heat it up with the exercise of the hike.

Maybe the Giles woman could prove Fortier killed Kneisser. But how? The wind gusted and tossed ice pellets at his face. They stung his cheeks and he stamped out the cigarette and tucked the butt in his pocket before zipping up again, pulling his collar around his chin and his brow flap down to just above his eyes. Christ, it was cold. Kennison walked on.

Whatever the reason, someone had killed Kneisser. It wasn't a suicide, not with that neat hole in his head. He hadn't been shot in the shack. He had been shot elsewhere and brought there. Why? To burn him as evidence? To prove something to someone? All Kennison knew was that Kneisser had been killed, killed after he'd made an extensive call about something to his office or employers in the States. A rare call, he assumed, as Masterson would have whined even louder about the issue if calling the States on the sat-phone was Kneisser's daily habit.

Whatever he'd said to his people down south, it had motivated them to send Ruby Cruz north immediately. In fact, they'd reacted so quickly that she'd departed before they knew Kneisser was dead. So she wasn't here because of the death. She was here because of the satphone call.

There had to be some connection, some motive to kill him that had something to do with the content of the call he'd made. Cruz would know. Was it something Kneisser had found? Something he knew? Is that what he'd reported? Is that what he had been killed for? Or maybe for the money it was worth? For the envy of discovery and the fame it would bring? Or was it just a murder rising out of that frustrated insanity that comes from living with people for too long in a confined environment, like the young priest sworn to silence?

Sister Beata had told the story one evening when young Booker couldn't sleep. The room, with its yellowed walls and dark corners, frightened him, even into his teens. The hard hall light on the graphic crucifix on the wall cast disturbing, angular shadows on the walls and kept him awake. He made it happen more often when Sister Beata was on duty.

Sister Beata's plain storytelling was seldom comforting, but she was the youngest sister in the convent, and to have her sit on the edge of his bed and say anything at all fed the fires of eroticism when he was eleven years old. He couldn't tell her that her presence left him more awake than the imagined fears that went before. He couldn't tell her how much he wanted her. He watched her perfect cheek as she told him a story, her eyes unwaveringly on the crucifix as if she too had something to confess.

Her story was about a young priest sworn with other priests to silence. Every day, the priests ate together, walked together, prayed together and worked together without exchanging a word. The young priest began to notice the customs of another, older priest—how he sloppily spaced the three knots for the Holy Trinity in the rope tied around his cassock, how he ate with his fork in his right hand, moving it to his left only when he had to cut meat, how he ignored the long, untended hairs growing out of his nose and ears, how he slurped soup loudly and sniffled constantly, how he shuffled his sandals on the flagstones in the cloister like, in Sister Beata's words, "a Chinee man." Each day, the young priest looked for these faults. Each day he found them and was angered by their repetition.

After some weeks, the silent young priest fell into an obsession of intolerance, so that even when he saw the old priest from a distance he would flush red with anger, his nostrils would exhale hot air and gummy spittle would form in white pellets where his pressed lips came together.

One evening at the dining table, in the subdued yellow glow of ensconced candles, the old priest slurped his soup and sniffed loudly as he sliced a small piece of meat. He placed his knife on the table and moved his fork back to his right hand, stabbing the meat and raising it to his lips.

Beside him, ever mindful of piety and his devout vow of silence, the young priest stood quietly, picked up the discarded knife, drove it through the old man's heart and sat down to finish his meal.

Was that why Kneisser had died? Because someone could no longer abide him or some of his habits? With no tangible clues as to motive, perhaps it was better to look at opportunity.

Excluding suicide, there were only seven people who could have killed the professor. The late Marie-Claire Fortier, who perhaps died with him; the rifle-toting Inuit boy, Wayne Penilik; his grandmother, Lillian, who could probably handle a rifle as well as her grandson. That's three. Then Paul "Poncey" Masterson; Kneisser's assistant, Trevor Patel; the boy, Kenneth Monk; and Grey Anne. Kennison looked up to realize he was already at the remains of Purgatory. By some ambient, sourceless light he could see the exhausted red generator and the yellow work lamps, one still waving in the wind, one lying prone on the rocks like a carcass with its spine shattered, the only colours in a slate world fading quickly to black.

He shivered, less from the cold than from the knowledge that Kneisser's killer was on the loose and that he'd met that killer today. Somewhere to the north and east, a single shot had been fired. Kennison looked and thought he saw the hunter. Or the animal being hunted. Or perhaps nothing at all.

August 1845

A reader of my previous entries will expect this to be written in the comfort of The Horns in Otford as I command my corner table near the fire and sip at Mr. Keefe's notable bitter. They would rightly expect this entry to be a coda to my brief symphony of life at sea as the Franklin Expedition plunges westward through the frozen seas of the high Arctic and I return safely to Sevenoaks and the maternal brooding of Alice Lort. I myself imagine scribbling this in haste, paper stained by the overflow of ale, as I await her imminent arrival, flushed and heavy with her child, to sip from the schooner of dry Spanish sherry that warms beside me, and to witness my devotion to her health and plans for our future. Alas, I write this in my library on the Terror, *a full-fledged member, despite many misgivings and very little welcome, of the Franklin Expedition. I shan't be home for birthing.*

I write under oil lamps this afternoon, now that the rays of the sun are lost earlier and pass more time below the horizon than above. Instead of dozing after one of Mrs. Keefe's proud roasts, I'm sleepy from the effects of another of Goldner's tinned pot pies and no little cabin heat. The ship's steam system provides a comfort that my flat in Bligh's Court could not imagine. (I am somewhat relieved I need not now give up those bachelor rooms nor seek, nor suffer the expense of family quarters.) The warmth does not dispel an increasing gloom. As we sail north in Davis Strait towards Baffin Bay, I find the increasing darkness oppressive, as if light was somehow the source of the air I breathe. I know that to be untrue, but a heaviness weighs on my heart, as I'm certain it does in the hearts of others, although few speak of it, and none to me.

The unexpected turn of events that sees me a full-fledged, if yet unaccepted, member of this expedition is worthy of the telling, if only so that, by recounting it, I can myself understand the chain of events that has me here. After the events at Disko Bay (I still wake wallowing in fancied pools of bullock blood to the laughter of rough-mannered men) the Barretto *was preparing to depart, and me with it. But for a perhaps misunderstood visit to the hospital quarters, I would be home. G. was still ailing, although recovering, by his most recent account. I thought it apt to visit him before his departure, as his parents live nearby in Tunbridge Wells and he owed me not a little money from some evening games of whist. Despite prognostications to the contrary, he looked ghastly, barely able to raise himself other than to hack and spit. Dr. Peddie, at times a man of wry wit, simply shook his small head. Ever-dour Dr. MacDonald rumbled with brogue and medical jargon I could not ken, especially with the chorus of groans and coughs from the hammocks. Into this maelstrom walked Captain C., Master of the* Terror *and a man I had previously only seen from afar.*

A decisive and forthright man, it seems, because, without quite knowing how and why it happened, now G. is on his way home to England in a sickbed and I have been installed by my Captain's orders in my hireling's place as teacher and librarian on the Terror *for the duration of the Expedition. Four others returned home as well, three sick, one from the* Erebus *in chains for crimes unexplained, depleting our numbers from 134 to 129.*

In private, I am not, I think, of clear mind on this life-altering decision of the Captain's, nor do I feel I was afforded opportunity to ponder it. However, I have reasons to celebrate, although I feel that is perhaps too strong a word. With no commitment made to Miss Lort prior to sailing—she cannot know for certain her letter reached my hands—and a proffered salary paid into a solid British bank for the term of the travel, I will be wealthy and single when this voyage is over a year or two hence. The promise of a refit and refresh at journey's end, (as directed, whispers Bealls, in the Admiralty's Instructions to Sir John) amidst the tropical splendour and tan native women of the Sandwich Islands will not seem unattractive to a single man of means.

Further, I am afforded new purpose for this journal. There are two formal expedition records commissioned—one on the Erebus, *one on the* Terror. *Those records will be, of course, Admiralty documents, written for our naval masters, our newly crowned Queen, and for history under the career-sensitive eyes of the senior officers accountable for the success of the expedition. As ever, historical record is the purview of those charged with making it. I, however, have it in mind to keep notes from a less lofty yard, a lower spar of observation, one might say, from a simple sailor's position "before the mast," as the American writer Dana has coined.*

On reading the entries to date, I feel they are, perhaps, too florid in style for public consumption, so I shall attempt a more reportorial stance henceforth. Perhaps someone in London may one day publish it, as a family saga, like Mr. Goldsmith's. Or perhaps as a serialized social commentary tucked behind a fictional mask such as Mr. Dickens' weekly tales in All the Year Round *and, I'm told,* Household Words *although I have not read the latter. I am proud to have both men's works in my libraries.*

(One's journal, to be of value, is of one's private and honest thoughts, and I feel it incumbent upon me to share those, especially in light of my literate intentions. To wit: I had thought Goldsmith a Jew, but it seems he's Irish, of all things, Son of a curate, graduate of Trinity College and pure Church of England. Curious. Dickens, on the other hand, is the son of a former Navy pay clerk and his mother born a Barrow, which may explain his voluble and uncritical support for the Admiralty, Lady Franklin and this Expedition.)

More anon.

While she was searching though what she guessed was the Monk boy's middle yellow tent, Ruby Cruz heard the ATV enter the compound yard. She peeked out the unzipped door, afraid that the boy would discover her rifling through his meagre possessions, but it was Trevor Patel, newly arrived in the dim light with a trailer load of picks and shovels, probably from the dig where he and Kneisser had been working.

In the next tent over, Masterson unzipped his door and she quickly pulled her head inside just as he peeked out, as curious as she. She heard him zip his door again and cough loudly, returning to whatever he was doing in there. Napping, perhaps.

Monk's tent provided her with no information. A few comic books—the new ones with Japanese illustrations and lots of graphic violence—a small black iPod wrapped in a white headset wire ending in only one earbud, some clothes, folded and stacked, surprisingly neat. But nothing else. No journal.

Carefully, quietly, she unzipped the door so Masterson wouldn't hear and walked quickly to the Kitchen Tent door, holding her breath until she was inside, pulling the door behind her until it clicked quietly into place.

Patel was in the Mess Tent, drawing himself a coffee from an urn that, from the stains of the floor beneath the spigot, Ruby guessed was available all day. The cook Lillian sat at the end of the stainless-steel prep table, engrossed in a well-thumbed and outdated *Maclean's* magazine. She was short and overweight and her rear end seemed to envelop the stool on which she perched. Ruby waited until Patel was through and poured herself a cup.

"You a serious coffee drinker?" he asked, his eyes flashing, his smile in place as it always seemed to be. "'Cause this isn't very serious coffee." Lillian did not look up, inured to insults like all camp cooks.

"Not really," said Ruby. "Nothing else for me to do here. I see you're busy. Closing down your work?" Patel nodded and stirred some powdered creamer into his coffee, pressing out the lumps on the sides of the Styrofoam cup with the brown plastic stir stick.

"Gotta get out of here fast. Today would have been best, but tomorrow at the latest."

"Must be tiring—do it all yourself, I mean, without Dr. Kneisser to help." They walked together into the Mess Tent.

"No difference to me. Kneisser wouldn't have helped anyway. That wasn't, shall we say, his way." Ruby sat at one of the tables and nodded for Patel to join her, using a combination of pretended authority and eyelash batting. Something worked, because Patel sat down across from her, exuding charm, smiling like he knew what a prize he must seem to women who weren't beautiful.

"What was he like? Kneisser, I mean," said Ruby. "It's strange that we three work for the same company and don't know each other. I'm new. Last week."

"AEI, you mean? I wouldn't work for those bastards if they were the last money on earth," said Patel.

"Oh. I didn't realize. I thought—"

"Another bullshit American lobby group," he said. "As bad as the rest of them—worse, in fact. These buggers meddle in countries and territories that aren't theirs, messing with cultures they don't begin to understand, and it's only about money. Nothing else, no matter what they say—"

"But it's their money that—"

"Oh, you'll be a perfect employee, Ms. Cruz. That's the American way, right? Loyalty to the funding source negates any serious thought about intentions or consequence. America right or wrong . . ."

"I thought you were an American . . ."

"I am. Third generation, despite my visible-minority complexion." He framed his face with his hands, raising his eyebrows in a magazine cover pose. "More American than you, maybe. But that doesn't mean I'm a fan of the current regime or the big-business power complex. Only half of us voted for the president, Ms. Cruz. Maybe less than half." He laughed at his own joke. "I'm with the half that didn't. You're probably not. It's organizations like yours, you know, that make our science such a joke. Old Kneisser didn't know how to say no, so they bought him, simple as that. Well, not me, baby. Not me."

"What was he like?"

"Kneisser? Old. Doddering. Self-centred. A naive fool in some ways . . ." Patel stopped, re-evaluating the question and his answer. "A good scientist, though; a bright and thoughtful anthropologist. Successful man, but all science, and no little ego."

"I never met him. What did he look like?" Harry's training on the good interview: agree with or ignore anything they say that bothers you and play to their superior knowledge. Never argue. Express only interest in anything they say.

"Big man. Six-three, six-four maybe. Stooped a bit lately. Age, I guess. Remarkably strong when he needed to be. Big arms. Huge hands, but soft—not soft, really, but sensitive, you know? If he found a shard of something or a shaped piece of horn, he held it like a dragonfly in those massive mitts of his, as if he was afraid he'd crush it with his pulse."

Ruby nodded, smiling.

"Big head, in more ways than one. The original absent-minded professor, I guess. Never cut his hair or beard or cleaned his nails, at least not up here." Patel looked at his own hands. "Though I should talk. Never took the time to wash at all, as far as I know. Devoted to his work, his science . . ."

"Good at his job?"

"The best. That's why I fought to work with him. Best man for your resume if you can stand him. He hired me, not AEI. Besides, I knew everything about the Franklin Expedition—as much as you can know." He looked away from Ruby as if embarrassed about something. She would swear he blushed, although with his skin colour it was difficult to be certain. Whatever tripped him, he recovered quickly.

"I'm a grad student in anthropology with a minor in nineteenth-century British history. Perfect for the job, but I think he had to push them to allow me in. In fact, Kneisser's the reason everyone is here. He's the one who rediscovered the cairn McClintock found here more than a century ago. Before that, he followed a trail of skeletons from Todd Island and Starvation Cove up to Terror Bay and Erebus Bay—those two were the names of Franklin's disappeared ships, you know?"

Ruby nodded. She hadn't learned much, but she'd learned that.

"It was Karl Kneisser who tied together the sites at Starvation and Todd with McClintock's Boat Place and the NgLi-2 site down south at Little Point. It was Kneisser who plowed north through Point Le Vesconte and Gore Point to the cairn. If it wasn't for

Kneisser, there'd be no dig here, no news of the expedition since the Beechey Island discoveries—"

"I've heard of Beechey Island."

"Oh really?" He sounded disappointed, as if she wasn't the ignorant soul he'd hoped for. "It's north of Lancaster Sound, north of Baffin. It's where the expedition wintered the first year, where three men died and were buried. The following spring, they sailed through Peel Sound and what's now known as Franklin Strait to Victoria Strait." She thought he blushed again, as if he'd said something he regretted, but he stood and went into the Salon Tent, beckoning her to follow him to the door, where he pointed to the water. "That's Victoria Strait. See the ice cap out there? The white?" Ruby nodded. "That was the end of the expedition and the beginning of something quite sinister. We believe it was cannibalism."

"Cannibalism? Here?"

Patel looked sideways at her, the white of his eyes bright against his dark iris and skin, suspicious of her now.

"That's what the Hell dig is all about. All those bones and skulls that Anne Ferguson-Crewe is cataloguing?" She nodded, noncommittal. No one had told her this. "Many of the long bones—femurs and ulnae—have marks on them, marks of what Anne assures all of us are the knives and other implements of the sailors who killed and ate their peers . . ."

"You don't agree?" Patel stared at her.

She shrugged. "You sound like you have another theory, that's all."

"I do, as a matter of fact. Not one that our Queen Anne credits, but one I will be able to prove. Even Dr. Kneisser came to see I was right, and from him that's tantamount to my career being made."

"What is it? What do you think?"

"I think there was cannibalism, all right. I think men were eating men. I just think it was someone else doing the dining."

"Who? Who else was there?"

"It's well known that Inuit tribes—they called them Eskimos then—hovered around the horizon for the entire time the Franklin Expedition foundered and expired. The Netsilik, specifically. Not a new thing—the transient tribes always found it advantageous to stop near Arctic explorations, trade stuff, get food maybe . . . I think it's possible they did the killing and the eating."

"The natives?"

"Why not?" Patel looked through to the Mess Tent to see if Lillian was listening. He lowered his voice conspiratorially. "Fact: The winters of 1846 through '48 were terribly severe. There's historical and meteorological proof of that. Fact: There was no food anywhere on the land for anyone. Fact: The natives had nothing to eat. They were starving. Fact: The sailors had food, whatever anyone thinks about its toxicity now. Don't try to tell me that the Inuit would sit back quietly, happily resigned to dying by starvation while they watched the British sailors eat pot pies from tins and sip sherry. Noble bullshit. They kill bear cubs and infant seals to eat, to survive in this godforsaken place. That's all this place is about—survival. Not proper manners."

"But the native peoples, I mean—"

"It's not an anti-native thing, like Queen Anne insists. Show me a starving person of any background who won't kill to survive. Kill anything. Eat anything. For Christ's sake. Men have been known to drink their own piss to live."

"And Dr. Kneisser thought you could be right?"

"He knows I'm right. Knew I'm right. We can prove it. I can prove it."

"How? How can you prove anything from so long ago?"

"Well, that would be telling, wouldn't it, Ms. Cruz? Let's just say the British Admiralty once protested that the only accounts of their sailors being cannibals came from Eskimo sources. I'll be the first to grant that there's a strain of romantic human that can't bring themselves to believe the poor naive savages have a dark side. But I'm in the business of science, not politics, and certainly not political correctness." Ruby was excited. He must be talking about evidence discovered in the journal. He must have it, or have read it, and know where it is.

"So you and the Penilik boy probably wouldn't see eye to eye?"

Patel laughed. It wasn't a pleasant laugh.

"You could say that. He goes on about Inuit honour and ancestral land rights and Canadian sovereignty and all that political bullshit. I don't buy it, any of it." Ruby's coffee was cold. Patel's must have been as well but he sipped at it anyway. Maybe cold coffee was normal here. Like cold everything else.

"So why did Dr. Kneisser think you were right? What did you find?" He looked at her sharply. "There must have been something that convinced him."

"At the site—it's just under a kilometre north of here. Up the shore—Dr. Kneisser found pieces of wood—oak, we think it is—that could be the remainder of a lifeboat. The wood seems to match that of identified lifeboats found down at Crozier Point."

"It still exists? After a hundred and fifty years?"

"Oh yes, the skeleton of it. For all the terrible weather and climate here, it does preserve things. That's what the big deal is about finding Franklin's grave, if there is one. That's the real prize, the thing that people like us dream about in the night. It's imagined that he'll be mummified by cold, perfectly preserved. One crew member buried at Beechey, a young stoker, was in remarkably good shape when Owen Beattie exhumed him in the early '80s. I suppose some think Franklin will be sitting up in his grave, saluting and posing like his statue."

"There's a statue?" said Ruby. Patel laughed out loud. In the Kitchen Tent, Lillian looked up from her magazine and smiled. She had few teeth, and there were bristles of coarse black hair on her upper lip and chin.

"There most certainly is," said Patel. "In London. Waterloo Place, end of Regent Street, erected in the mid-1860s with all the names of the crew and Franklin standing up like the important man the Admiralty wishes he was instead of an incompetent who cost 129 men their lives. The damned thing even says that he discovered the Northwest Passage—"

"Did—?"

"He most certainly did not. But on the statue it's even vouched for by the British Parliament, for Christ's sake. Talk about nineteenth-century spin-doctoring. Talk about unscientific bullshit. History is written by the rich and well-positioned, Ms. Cruz."

"Tell me about what you and Dr. Kneisser found."

Patel looked at her, frowning, trying to discern whether she was interested in the science or had some other motive. Self-interest made the decision for him.

"It doesn't look like much. Just a pile of rocks now, marked up so we can replace them when we're finished—when *I'm* finished. It's a grave with a perfectly preserved skeleton in it, still bits of clothing around it, and even some tough tissue on the bones that was once flesh." Patel shifted his legs under the table and began jiggling his right leg at double speed.

"But it's nothing. It's not Franklin—that's what we hoped, of course." He was lying, she knew. Not about it being Franklin maybe, but about it being meaningless. They had discovered something. She already knew that, and Patel didn't know she did.

They'd discovered a journal, and Kneisser had called Dickerson to tell him. Either the scientist hadn't shared the discovery with his junior, or Patel knew exactly where the journal was. Maybe he'd read it. Maybe that was where his theories came from. His evidence. She flushed to think that she was this close to it. Maybe it was in his pocket.

Ruby waved her arm to take in the area. "So this was the end of the Franklin Expedition," she said, backing away from the hunt, giving the fish line the way Harry had taught her.

"Not at all. This was the beginning of the end, when after two winters and summers the men abandoned the ships icebound in the strait and landed here. Historians make their cases based on wishful thinking or good storytelling, but we scientists provide the evidence when we can. There is evidence of bodies to the south, as I said, all the way to Starvation Cove on the mainland."

"Tell me," said Ruby.

"There is a story that a number of white men—*qabloonas,* they were called by the Eskimos, means bushy eyebrows but is usually translated now as "white men"—were seen by a Netsilik tribe heading south across the Simpson Strait that separates this island from the mainland a hundred miles south of here. They could have been some of the group who were trying to find Back's Fish River and food. The Netsilik said the men they saw were dead, but the man they told the tale to didn't stop to check the evidence. Instead, he sent word to the British Admiralty that the Franklin Expedition had no survivors."

"Who was he?"

"An Orkney Scot who worked for the Hudson's Bay Company. No friend of an Admiralty that was sending men out with sherry and literature to a land where you had to live like a native to survive. This man had gone native—wore Inuit clothes and ate Inuit food and survived. He embarrassed the Admiralty, laughed at them, and they hated him for it. In fact, he was the only Brit explorer in the Arctic in the nineteenth century who wasn't knighted—that's how much they disliked him. John Rae was his name."

"What happened to him?"

"Oh, he claimed the ten-thousand-pound reward offered to the man who found out what happened to the expedition—a pile of money then. In fact, he was the man who actually mapped out the route of the Northwest Passage, although he never sailed it. No one did until Amundsen in 1906. And that's all she wrote." Patel stood up, smile back in place, eyes flashing again.

"But that's not evidence that the natives killed and ate the survivors."

"No, it's not. But the only evidence of the sailors eating each other came from natives. Period. No other witnesses. Besides, when this guy was told the story of the *qabloonas* dying and eating each other, he didn't go to check it out. He just told the Admiralty what he'd been told. He didn't see the evidence, and he didn't share the prize money with the Netsilik, you can bet on that."

Booker Kennison stood smoking near the door of the Kitchen Tent, watching the sleeping tents expand to a ghostly sailboat race, coloured spinnakers fat with wind, barely visible in the night. It was almost completely dark now, the twilight quickly dissolving to no light at all. He inhaled slowly in case the extremely cold air made him cough and ruin the pleasurable feeling of the smoke in his throat. He was coughing more lately.

Despite the temperature, he wanted a cold beer, but there seemed to be no liquor allowed here. Probably a good idea, he thought. If he were stuck here for any length of time, he'd drink it all very quickly and send out for more. It was a long way to the nearest liquor store.

Kennison took another deep drag and stared at the tents. He had never been camping in a tent. He'd built forts with overturned chairs and blankets in the yard of one foster home. Under a willow tree, he remembered, with sticky narrow leaves dotted with some infestation on the back. He'd tried to peel the bugs off the leaf with his thumbnail, and someone had slapped his hand and told him to stop.

When he was older and back with the nuns for a spell, he'd been sent to church camp for a week, but there weren't tents there. They slept in groups of six in wooden huts with deep wooden bunks and scratchy tick mattresses. He had blankets, he remembered, and was embarrassed because the rest of the kids had zippered Woods sleeping bags with dark green shells and plaid flannel linings. His feet stuck out and he was cold at night. Kennison had been in the Touareg cabin, but hadn't known what a Touareg was at the time. Later, he found out that each group was named for an African tribe.

He remembered the din of the summer rain on the corrugated-metal cabin roof and watching it gush to the ground outside the open windows, too much and too fast to be absorbed at first by the hard-packed earth. He remembered being awake when no one else was, sitting in the open doorway with its worn wooden threshold, listening to the snuffling, sighing and smacking of boys sleeping, smelling the rich mud when the dirt finally became soaked with water. One boy with gold chains on his neck and a speech impediment had shown them a package of condoms and been sent home by ever-smiling priests the same day.

Kennison took another drag of the cigarette and thought about what to do next. He liked the investigation process. He felt comfortable in the linear discovery of unexpected clues, lining up the dominoes, the narrowing of attitudes and the eventual focus on a single suspect. He enjoyed the hunt, the suspended limbo of surveillance and logic and thought, always interrupted by the explosive action of knowledge, of parking-lot shootouts and satisfying arrests. He was no scientist. He learned more from interviews than from poring over tangible chunks of evidence. Leave that to the forensic guys. He learned more about motive and opportunity from listening than the forensic wizards did with all their technical tricks and magic potions. DNA might corroborate guilt, but it wasn't a genome of the guilty. There wasn't a motive gene, at least not one yet discovered. In the answers to his carefully considered questions, and more often in their asides and body language, people showed their true selves and revealed their innermost opinions and passions, whether they meant to or not. Even the dead pointed at their killers if you knew how to listen to them. That's what was bothering him. Kneisser and the girl were trying to tell him something and he couldn't hear what they were saying.

He heard the Kitchen Tent door squeak open and watched the Monk boy exit and walk to the yellow tent in the middle. He was carrying a domed object, like a birthday cake, at arm's length. By the distortion of the air and steam around it, Kennison guessed it was a heater of some kind. He'd talk to Kenneth Monk first. Why not? He was available.

When Kennison stepped out of the shadows the boy looked frightened, but he shrugged at Kennison's request, placed the cake carefully in his tent and zipped it closed. Inside, he followed Kennison to the Salon Tent, where he helped unfold a futon, carry a chair from the Mess Tent and move some of the boxes to form a small sitting area. Kennison sat in the chair.

Monk smelled fresh, as if he had showered and washed his hair. His Calgary Flames T-shirt was washed, if not pressed, and the tattoos peaking above it looked more professional than Kennison had thought earlier. Monk's khakis sat low on his hips, exposing the thick elastic white waistband of blue-and-green-patterned boxer shorts. He wore startlingly clean white sneakers and a flat-brimmed Detroit Lions baseball hat that sat square on his head, the peak angled to one-thirty on the clock, between his brow and his right ear. He seemed dressed to go bar-hopping, dressed for a downtown date. Still, his face was sad and his eyes still reddened from crying.

"Kenneth Monk. Right?" The boy nodded. He took off his cap and held it in his left hand, twirling it. "I'm Sergeant Booker

Kennison, Kenneth—they call you Ken? Kenneth?" The boy sat on the couch when Kennison pointed to it. He sank into the cushions, forced back by the angle of the seat and softness of the futon.

"Kenny," he said.

"Where you from, Kenny?"

"Calgary . . . Okotoks, really." Kennison didn't know where Okotoks was.

"Your parents there?"

"Mother. Old man left when I was nine."

"Brothers? Sisters?" The boy nodded his head.

"Sister. Stepsister. Just a kid."

"So what brings you from Okotoks to Victory Point, Kenny?" The boy looked uncomfortable, his mouth tense. Kennison could see the edge of his upper teeth biting his bottom lip. Was it guilt, or just general cop-related discomfort? Monk acted like he expected the worst from the conversation, which meant he'd been through it with cops before and come out a loser. He shrugged and spoke to his knees.

"I was in trouble downtown. On the street, eh? Drugs 'n' stuff, eh? Janey said it'd be good for me up here, right?"

"Who's Janey, Kenny?

"Janey Creighton," said Monk as if everyone should know. "The house mom . . . the social worker where I was—"

"You have a record, Kenny?" The boy hesitated and confirmed it by nodding. "And you were in some kind of institution down there? A rehab? A halfway house?" Monk nodded again, chewing his lip, not wanting to go back there in thought or conversation. Or maybe he was worried about a joint tucked in his backpack. Kennison liked the kid. He didn't know why.

"I spent time in a home, too, Kenny. Orphan. No shame in

that, is there? And no shame in trying to get yourself straight, either. The opposite, I'd say." The boy looked up. His eyes and lips softened slightly and he nodded agreement.

"So Janey thought it'd help you get even healthier to come up here for the summer and work in the kitchen?" Monk nodded again and smiled thinly, relieved that Kennison hadn't gone farther down the road he thought they were going. "Are you clean, Kenny?"

"I am, sir. Mostly. The crack and stuff, for sure. Clean since June twelfth. I get paid here. Don't get the money till I get home clean. Don't need it here anyways. They send it right to Halliwell—"

"Don't call me sir, Kenny. Sergeant's good enough. That's the, uh . . . the place you were? Halliwell?" The boy nodded again. He stared at his hat and brushed some imaginary dirt off the brim.

"They put it in the bank for me so when I get home I'll have some money to live on." He looked towards the Mess Tent, where someone was clattering pans. "I usually don't do kitchen stuff anymore—'cept Wayne hasn't been showing up regular lately and Lillian needs the help. I'm a boulder gopher now." He said it with pride.

"What's that, Kenny?"

"Helping out on the dig, y'know? Haulin' stuff. Doin' whatever they tell you to do." His eyes brightened when he spoke of it, his face became animated. "It's not as easy as it sounds, or looks. You lug stuff they find on the beach into the photo shack and tag it with the grid numbers so they know exactly where it came from. After it's shot and recorded, you haul it back and they place it back exactly where they found it, as if it never was moved."

"Shot?"

"Like, photographed, eh? That's what . . . that's what MC . . . that's what Marie-Claire did." Kennison nodded. "She . . . she took the photographs, recorded the grid numbers . . . like that." The boy seemed close to tears.

"You like that work, Kenny? The dig work?" Monk had blue eyes, like Kennison's, but lighter, paler, less certain. He opened them wide and his face softened at the question. Kennison thought he was about to make a long speech, but he held it back.

"Yeah," he said. "I really like it a lot." He thought for a beat. "Really a lot. Anne said she'd write me a letter, maybe help me get into school and study it maybe. When I get back. When I get paid."

"Good for you, Kenny. It's pretty special when you find something you want to do, isn't it? Doesn't happen to everyone. Some people go their whole lives and don't find it."

"You find it?"

"Yeah, I did," said Kennison, surprised at the question. "After school I came close to screwing up my life, too. Like you. Got in some trouble like you. Just like you. A friend of mine—a better friend than I understood back then—told me I was either headed for jail or should join the army. I chose the army, went over to Bosnia as an army peacekeeper, and saw some stuff no one should see."

"How did you become a cop—a Mountie, I mean."

"I'm a cop. At the end of the war, a bunch of police and Mounties came over to do forensic work, to study what happened, to collect evidence of war crimes and so on, eh?" Monk nodded, his eyes fixed on Kennison. "I knew as soon as I saw them that that's what I wanted to do, like you with the rocks and bones and stuff." Kenneth Monk nodded, understanding, an agreement of mature men with shared experience.

"Tell me about Dr. Kneisser, Kenny."

"Not much to tell, really. Strange geezer. We all called him the geezer—not to his face, just between us, y'know? Like they call me Piercey as if I don't hear. Kept to himself most of the time. Loner kinda guy. Shy—that's what MC said, even though he was sort of a giant in her world. She had a book of his—a schoolbook she wanted him to autograph. He acted all gruff and mean about it, but she figured he was just embarrassed."

"Was she . . . did she . . . did she hold him in high regard, Kenny?"

"Yeah. I guess so. Not like he was some pop star or something. MC wasn't like that . . ."

"Like what? What was Marie-Claire like?"

"She was special. She was beautiful and really smart. She liked what she did and worried that her dad thought her work was just, you know, a passing thing, a school thing. But she was very serious about it, wanted to be a full-fledged archaeologist, work in the North here—"

"Did she have trouble with her father, Kenny?" The boy looked uncomfortable.

"Not really. Not yet."

"What's that mean? Not yet?" Monk stared at the knees of his khakis. His eyes were swelling up. "Was she about to have trouble when she went home?" Monk nodded.

"She was . . . she was going to tell her dad a few things . . ."

"What kind of things?"

"Things like about how she . . . how she wanted to keep going to school, maybe in B.C. Stuff like that."

"Stuff like what, Kenny?"

"She wasn't going to marry a guy. A Québec guy. A politician. Big shot. She was going to tell her dad when she got home. Tell him that she wasn't going to marry that guy, that she wasn't going to do what he said anymore. She loved her dad a lot—don't get me wrong. It's just that . . . it's just that, like, he'd always been running her life, y'know? She . . . she felt it was time to run her own."

"With you, Kenny?" The boy looked up quickly.

"Eh?"

"Did she want to run her own life with you as part of it? Were you going back to school to be with her? To work with her?" The tears that fell on the boy's thighs were huge, growing quickly bigger as they hit the material and blossomed into toonie-sized circles. Kennison exhaled slowly, wishing he could smoke in here.

"She liked me . . . loved me. I loved her, too. We told each other. We . . ."

"I'm sorry, Kenny. Her death would have hit you pretty hard. Did others know?" Monk sniffed and wiped his eyes with the back of his arm.

"We . . . we never told anyone. Kept it private, like."

"What about Dr. Kneisser? Did he know about you and Marie-Claire?"

The boy shook his head. "No. At least I don't think so. Anyway he . . . he didn't care about stuff like that. He was into his work. Never talked about anything else. Never talked much at all, until a couple of days ago."

"Did people like him? Dislike him?" Monk looked trapped.

"I liked him all right. Let me help him out sometimes. I think he liked that I enjoyed it and wasn't lazy, y'know? I don't think Anne liked him much—she's always dissin' him. Trevor Patel is always goin' on about the geezer selling out. He acts as if he's smarter and louder and righter than anyone else, but I think he's a blowhard. Always playin' cards with Poncey. Always losin,' too." The boy shrugged. "I never paid much attention to the gossip—besides, they usually shut up when I came in the room."

"Can you tell me anything else about Dr. Kneisser?"

"MC was sure he'd found something important."

"Why did she think that?"

"I dunno exactly. But anyone could tell he was excited about something, eh? I mean, he was the one who discovered Hell, wasn't he? So, like, it didn't interest him much anymore and he never even went by. That's what pissed off Anne, I think. She felt like her job was cleaning up the mess Kneisser left to look for other things."

"What kind of other things?" Monk shrugged and looked away. "What do you think Dr. Kneisser found?"

"I dunno. Don't know even what he was looking for, really. These people don't think like normal people, y'know? What's important to them seems kinda weird to regular people. Like bones and stuff . . . marks on them. That kinda thing." The boy knew more than he was saying.

"You put a dome-shaped object in your tent earlier."

"The catalytic? Yeah."

"Heats the tent?"

"Yeah. Gets too hot to touch, but lasts the night if you keep it low and bundle up. Depends on the wind. Sometimes you just need to get away from the others, y'know? So sometimes I still sleep out, even in the cold."

"Whose are the other tents?"

"The three yellow ones are Wayne's near the kitchen door—the Inuit guy?—mine in the middle and Poncey's out near the wall."

"The other tents?"

"MC's is the blue one right behind mine . . ." Monk lost it for a moment. Memories of their first night in one of their tents, guessed Kennison. He waited it out. "Trevor's is brown, sorta beige, I guess, behind Penilik's. And . . . and Anne's is the orange one in back of Poncey's. Dr. Kneisser's is the green one out on the end. By itself, although he spent most nights up at his dig."

"Thanks, Kenny. Can you get me one?"

"What?"

"One of those heater things."

"Sure? You wanna sleep out? Where?"

"In Dr. Kneisser's tent. Would you put a heater in there for me? Don't worry about the yellow tape. Just don't touch anything inside, okay?"

"Sure. No problem." Monk nodded and stood up. Self-consciously he wiped his hand on his jeans and thrust it forward. Kennison didn't understand for a moment, then reached out and shook his hand.

October 1845

It has been some time since I wrote. The days on board seem to consume time as we consume our tinned meals, without thought, without measurement. We are bound westward at last on a bearing of 273 degrees, moving through increasing ice from Baffin Bay through Lancaster Sound and Parry's Channel. Both ships move forward with relative ease, the seas no match for them. Below decks I have seen the massive ribs and beams arching like the vaults of ancient cathedrals. The brawny bows of both ships are further strengthened with extra beams and cross-beams and the decks reinforced to withstand the crush of ice. The ships, through chine to keel, are ten inches thick, good English oak under two applications of impenetrable African hardwood overlaid with a further two layers of Canadian elm. Thick plates of sheet iron run 20 feet back on each side from the bow. The Terror*'s lead stoker is Petty Officer John Torrington, who, at 19 years, seems a mature chap, quiet but thoughtful, keeping to himself (and asked after my lessons this morning). He showed me the 20-horsepower, 15-ton steam locomotive from the London and Greenwich Railway, one installed in each hold, attached to screw propellers taller than a man.*

These are to be used to overcome dams of ice in emergency situations. They demand copious amounts of fuel that we have had to transport. The boy (for by his slight frame and tenor voice he seems not yet a man) coughs often, a factor, I'm certain, of working in the furnaces.

Despite T.'s youthful kindness, I am newly aware of residing in a community restricted in size and quality of companionship. Others here have had the experience or preparatory period to muse on such things, whereas I have had isolation and colleagues thrust upon me. This was made apparent to me in Davis Strait a month since. We were anchored to an iceberg (or rather attached, as these Behemoths move with the current), and some of the men were taking readings on the top of the floe when we were hailed by a pair of whaling ships identifying themselves as the Prince of Wales *and the* Enterprise.

A Captain Dannet of the Prince of Wales—*Prince of Whales? I said to F., the Purser's Steward, who ignored me and continued his Accounts—invited Commander Franklin aboard, but in the end weather and waves prevented their formal meeting. Our officers sent messages to Dannet and Captain Martin of the* Enterprise *for conveyance to England. The signalman, begrudgingly I thought, told me the messages reported all men were well and in high spirits. Commander Franklin added that we were provisioned for five years that, with care, could be stretched to seven. It struck me the messages were what the Admiralty and Britons wished to hear rather than fair reporting. There was no mention of G.'s illness, nor that of others who seem to be coughing and spitting excessively on all decks of the* Terror. *My unsummoned sense of utter isolation results from a feeling that those men we saw distantly on the decks of the whalers were the last Europeans we'll see for some months as we enter the frozen lands of the Esquimaux.*

On deck, the cold is intolerable, especially in the westerly winds that seem to blow uninhibited and horizontally into our faces, freezing the lashes together and obscuring sight so that the helmsmen have been known to pluck theirs out with Dr. Peddie's forceps or shorten them with knives. As we sail towards Melville Island, the dark increases like a cold hand on the heart and the ice shrinks our passage each hour. Yet these are not unknown seas, I'm told. Bealls, who all say has sailed here before, but the specifics are muddied to me, insists that Parry traversed them four times, and now whaling ships ply them like the London coach road. If that were true, I should think we would be seeing more of them, yet only mammoth barques of ice sail by, presumptuous in their majesty and rite of passage.

Yellowknife, Northwest Territories

Fifteen hundred miles southwest of King William Island, a diamond cluster of electric lights set in a Yellowknife dusk welcomed Ricky Monteith and three corpses as he landed on Great Slave Lake and taxied to the dock. This far south, the sun never completely disappeared in the winter. Even the shortest day of the year provided two hours of daylight before the days started getting longer. Everyone counted the days. Counting the days was how you made it through the winter here, other than work for those who had it, or booze and making babies for those who didn't.

Monteith pulled back the sliding window to let the outside air into the cockpit. He'd kept the heat as low as possible, as Jenny Giles had advised by radio, to ensure his passengers didn't thaw before she had them on her table.

Other than the frigid temperature, the flight had been uneventful. Monteith loved flying alone, humming pop songs to himself and watching the tundra roll out for miles while he thought about the night's dance. He'd flown the route enough now that he had his own landmarks, mounds and puddles in the shapes of animals that he recognized from the air. The sky was his domain. At ground level, he'd be as lost as anyone else.

As he taxied into the dock, he glanced back at the cargo area. The blue tarp on the floor held the soldier-stiff corpse of the sniper shot by the Inuit kid. On top of him, crammed as far back in the cargo hold as possible, was the black, zippered plastic bag containing the curled body of the professor. Forward of Kneisser, the matching bag holding the young girl was all elbows, knees and angles, stuffed between the folded webbed seats, jammed between stacked and labelled boxes like a badly wrapped gift. All three bodies looked and smelled the way they had three hours earlier, so the thawing, he hoped, had been minimal.

The welcoming party was larger than expected—a good thing, as Monteith found no joy in hefting dead weight by himself. He didn't envy cops and firefighters—too much waiting, too much danger, too much gore. He'd never harboured any desire to be anything other than a pilot.

The random red and white rack lights of the ambulance careered senselessly off the buildings and pier pilings of the harbour, flickering patriotically on faces emerging from idling steamed-windowed vehicles. Accompanying the new Leclerc kid who handled the mooring lines, Monteith made out the round form of Jennifer Giles and the imposing frame of Dutch Duchesne. Two EMT staff—Benjy and Diane, most likely—stood like sentinels on either side of a gurney, only breaking rank when Monteith jumped to the dock and opened an arm to the loading door.

"All yours, folks," said Monteith.

"Good flight, Ricky?" said Jen Giles. "Manage to freeze your butt off so my clients didn't thaw?"

"Think so, Doctor Jen. They look the same to my eye, anyway. One more than you expected, though. Hope you have the big van, Benjy." Monteith liked Jen Giles. Almost everyone did, although some were offended when she didn't mince words, called a spade a shovel. Since her husband's death she'd become more acerbic, as if she had earned a licence to offend. She worked long hours at the free clinic and the hospital as a GP, raised the three kids Tim had left behind, and was on the professional morgue A-list for surprises like this one. She didn't have time for bullshit.

Inspector Duchesne frowned and fiddled with his cell phone as if someone had called and he'd missed it. He looked pale, Monteith thought, ill maybe. Dr. Giles directed the ambulance crew to ease the body bags and the rolled tarpaulin out of the plane. There was a small amount of unidentifiable liquid on the floor beneath where Kneisser's body had been, and a damp stain on the seatback where the Fortier girl's bag had rested.

"Just water, probably," said Jennifer Giles. "Meltwater. If it starts to stink, come see me. I've got some stuff'll kill the smell. Course, it'll probably eat the upholstery as well."

Dutch Duchesne broke in to the conversation. He looked concerned.

"Rick? You see anything of Ivan? He came your way."

"Krevaluk? No. What about him?"

"Missing. No contact. Flew off to Victory Point with an American woman and some guy with fishing equipment. Imagine. Fishing here in November. Must be a Yankee. Mim's going crazy."

"Jeez. That's who it was. Yeah. The American woman arrived, not too long after we did at Victory Point. We were in the Mess Tent, too far away to see the landing. Thought it sounded like Ivan's Cessna. It took off right away. . . Wait a minute. This guy, the one there, in the blue tarp. He tried to kill Sergeant Kennison. Shoot him in the back."

"What?" said Duchesne. "Are you sure?" He paled even further, his concern dissolving to something that Rick Monteith thought resembled fear.

"Really. Kennison was working at the shack where the two were killed. The Inuit kid saw the sniper aiming and killed him first. Kennison kept his gun and backpack. American woman ID'd the guy as some fisherman that was with her on Ivan's plane. That means—"

"That Ivan is somewhere around Victory Point in his Cessna," said Jen Giles.

"Alive or dead. We'd better tell Kennison," said Monteith.

"Can't. No one's answering the satphone," said Duchesne. "I've been trying to call him all afternoon, tell him . . . tell him some stuff he should know."

"Like that there's someone gunning for him? To shoot him in the back? What's that about?" Duchesne shook his head, lost in thought. Giles looked at Monteith and signalled him to join her as she walked to her car.

"Dutch is really upset, Rick. I've never seen him like this. Something's going on. Keep your eye on him, okay? I'm worried about him." She looked up to the waiting ambulance. "That's it, troops. Let's go." Benjy Rosen waved at Monteith and made a let's-have-a-beer-later sign as he slammed the rear doors of the ambulance. Diane Casper jumped in the driver's seat and had the siren wailing even though here was little traffic and Grantley Regional was only three blocks away. Jennifer Giles tooted the horn of her dented Corolla as she pulled a U-turn and sped after the ambulance. Her car had one hubcap, and the windshield was starred by stones in three places.

Yellowknife, Northwest Territories

Within twenty minutes, Rick Monteith had cleaned up the Otter and jumped in his car to head home for a shower before the dance. He'd kept his eye on Dutch, who had tried to make a call from the driver's seat of his SUV, before angrily slamming down his cell phone and marching to the pay phone at the end of the dock. He was still there.

The dock boards rattled under the truck tires as Monteith passed the Inspector. Dutch looked serious. Cold—or angry. His broad shoulders shook and his heavily mittened hands switched the receiver from left to right to left again. Maybe he was trying to raise Kennison on that dead satphone. If Monteith had had his window rolled down, he might have heard the man screaming on the other end of the call.

"I expected you to contain this, Duchesne. *Contain* it. You understand? This is not remotely what you swore to me you'd do." Superintendent Gino Cosentino's voice was increasing in volume and pitch. "Not remotely what you promised. Sure, you got Kennison out of town like I asked. I've told you what he can do to us, Duchesne. How he can ruin our careers. Your pension is the least of it, for gosh sake. If Kennison testifies, we can start lining up now for night-shift security jobs—those of us who aren't in prison. That includes you if I want it to, in case you've forgotten,

Inspector." He spat out the title as if it had been stuck between his teeth and causing him annoyance for some time.

"But sir, I was not part of—"

"We're all a part of it, Duchesne, every single one of us, every officer in the force, darn it. And some people not on the force as well. And if we think we're not involved now, we sure as heck will be if Kennison sings."

Duchesne could imagine Cosentino's face, crimson with anger, nostrils dilated, the pulse in his pale temples throbbing in the dark room. He'd be standing by now, one hand on the telephone, the other propping himself up on the desk. His hand would be so hot he'd leave a damp palm print on the polished top. He'd be sticking his finger into his tight collar, pulling at it, trying to let the steam escape from his chest.

"But why the jeez do you send the one man I want to control to a crime scene that now looks like it will make news of the jeezing world?" Jeez was a dirty word in Cosentino's book. He paused before continuing in a more modulated tone, speaking each word slowly, one at a time, as if his listener had difficulty with comprehension.

"This. Must. Be. Contained. Inspector. Now. Understand? Sealed up like a tomb. Kolchak almost hung us out to dry with his testimony until we discredited him enough so he offed himself. Kennison has ten times . . . *twenty* times the knowledge, and none of the suicidal tendencies. Cavan was his baby, remember. He knows a hundred times the dirt—names, phone numbers . . . everything."

Your name and your phone numbers, Duchesne thought. Not mine, boyo. He was struck with an odd sense of ambivalence—you don't abandon your team in its hour of need, even if the team is corrupt. Or do you? You don't abandon your men, that's for sure.

Cosentino paused before speaking in an almost inaudible, mewling tone. "Listen to me, Dutch, and listen to me carefully. I've told you that your . . . your lapse, shall we call it? Yes . . . your lapse . . . is buried as long as you help me out with this. Only you and I know the truth behind that kid's death, Inspector. Let's keep it that way, eh? And be aware that this particular situation is life or death, Dutch, not some parking-ticket favour for a fellow officer."

His voice grew loud again, as if he was standing now, pacing in his cavernous office. "Don't think that you're somehow immune, Duchesne. This isn't an Ottawa issue, not by a long shot. If this blows, the force is going to have a hole in it nothing can fix. Others smarter than you have imagined that because they didn't personally sign the cheques or fill out the forms or move the money or hire the car pool that they're clean. Look at Kowaleski and Stratton. Where are they now? Look at the Commissioner himself, for gosh sake. Ormerod can pull the rug out from any one of us in a heartbeat, my friend. I know the man—know him better than most—and I know what he's capable of, and that's anything."

"Murder?" said Duchesne. He switched the telephone receiver to his warm hand and shivered uncontrollably.

"I beg your pardon?"

"Murder. Is he capable of murder? Or you? Of ordering the killing of one of his own men?" The silence at the other end of the line was thick. The landline was good—it had been Cosentino who'd refused to speak with Duchesne on his cell phone in the truck, who insisted he call back from the dock pay phone. No, the silence wasn't from a bad signal or any misunderstanding. Cosentino was either surprised or exposed.

Duchesne again pictured the Superintendent in his office. He'd only visited it once, when he and Margit visited Ottawa on a vacation and dropped in for a duty call. He could see the small man in his mind, close-shaven and tight-collared even at this late hour, his pink face stained green by the glass shade of the banker's light on his empty, polished desk, his thin hair plastered across his brow like a schoolboy. Margit said he looked like a rat groomed like a man, kept in the office by Assistant Commissioner Ormerod and fed under the door, a man with no home or life outside that high-ceilinged waxed room. Maybe she was right. Duchesne had never asked Cosentino about family. He had felt bad about that.

"I asked you a question, Duchesne. What's happened? What's this about murder?" Duchesne wondered how long he'd been asking.

"A marksman—rifleman, sniper . . . whatever you call him—hitched a ride with an American woman sent to the crime scene to deal with the effects of one of the dead . . ."

"And?"

"And what?"

"What happened? Is Kennison dead?"

"You don't sound surprised, Superintendent."

"Don't be stupid. I take it the Sergeant's all right."

"Yeah. Yeah, he's all right, as all right as a targeted guy can be. It was luck, Superintendent. Just luck or he'd be dead. The sniper's dead and the pilot who flew him is missing . . ."

"I'm glad he's okay. Kennison, I mean. Who's this American woman? Who sent her?"

"Her company, I think."

"What company?"

"I don't know its name, sir. American company based in Washington—D.C., not state—maybe Maryland or Virginia. They're all cheek by jowl down there . . ."

"Find that out, Inspector. Fast. I need that name. Yesterday. Jeez, I can't believe you let an outsider into a crime scene . . ."

"When she went in, it wasn't a crime scene, sir. Just a shack fire with two people reported accidentally dead. It's only now we think something might be amiss."

"Amiss? *Might* be *amiss?* You think something *might* be *amiss* when a prominent foreign scientist lies dead on sovereign Canadian territory with a bullet hole in his head and the only daughter of a doting Ottawa political mandarin—and the fiancée of the most up-and-coming politician in French Canada—is found dead beside him?"

"Sir, we couldn't know—"

"And that some idiot on the site called Declan Fortier at his Montreal office and left a message on his office answering machine that his only daughter was dead? On his—"

"Sir, the man was probably just trying—"

"On his *answering machine,* Duchesne. On his darned answering machine. Look, Duchesne, if this thing blows up, you blow up with it. We never talked here. I know nothing of this other than the simple fact that I now have to go to Declan Fortier's home and explain why you are so freaking incompetent that—"

"I didn't know about the girl, Superintendent. This is the first I've heard of it. You say she's the daughter of someone you know?"

"Someone *everybody* knows, Duchesne. Everybody who knows anything knows Declan Fortier is a political kingmaker, Inspector, not a man to be toyed with. Having him upset with us is one thing, but worse is his daughter's fiancé—this Raymond. He's the one threatening to take the Force to hearings. He's the one trying to bring us down—the one who got Kolchak to talk, the one who's after Kennison to spill the beans. He's poison, Duchesne, a smart aleck young pol who sees destroying our organization as a way to advance his career in his province, and you can bet in the rest of the country. He'll ride us all the way to Sussex Drive if we let him."

"There's no suggestion yet the girl was murdered, sir."

"And there better not be. Understand me? Put a clamp on this, Duchesne, the biggest clamp you can find. Get Kennison out of there and send him up to the darned diamond mines, anywhere but in the face of Raymond and Fortier. He must not speak. To anyone. Do you understand me?"

"Yes, sir."

"Good. Get on with it." Duchesne listened for a full minute before he was sure Cosentino had hung up the telephone. He slowly put the receiver on the hook, pushed open the stiff folding door and walked back to his idling truck. Poor damned Kennison. Faced with a murder instead of an accident. Stalked by a killer probably sent by his superiors, or people they knew. The poor bugger seemed to have no sense of how many people wished him dead for what he knew. And he was stuck without communication in a place even the Inuit thought barren. He pulled open the truck door and climbed into the warm cab. He sat, staring out the window at the dock and the lake. Across the inlet, a few lights said people were still awake in Detah.

Kennison had a lot on his plate, and he didn't even know that Turqavik was headed his way. Duchesne groped around the cab floor to retrieve his cell phone, looked up a number on the screen and dialled Constable Jensen in Ross Haven.

December 1845
Beechey Island (Lat: 74 deg, 43 min, 28 sec N; Long: 91 deg, 39 min, 15 sec W)

We are icebound on a dot of land called Beechey Island. C. says we shall remain here until spring, when the ice breaks up. He says it as if it's his decision and not inevitable, like the encroaching ice and immeasurable darkness. As friendly as he seemed in Davis Strait when he replaced G. with me, the Captain has not been so since, responding curtly when I asked him to announce the beginning of classes, promising writing implements and, to date, not providing them. Perhaps he has more on his mind than I know, despite our being stranded here with nothing more to do than what officers invent to combat boredom and ennui.

The last month has been difficult. We sailed north up Wellington's Channel as far as the 77th parallel before being blocked by ice. On the way, we gave a name—I say "we," but those of us below decks were only informed after the fact—to Barrow Island after Sir John. We also named Des Voeux Island after V., a Mate on the Erebus, *A foppish Frenchman—there are a few of them with us. One wag said Voeux means "wishes" in French, and that the Mate always wished he had an island named after him. Bealls laughed long and hard. So did I, as it seems to make them more comfortable when I join in their fun. To that end, I proposed that Sir John Barrow was probably having tiffin with Lady Franklin as we spoke, and the men seemed to enjoy that ribald thought. There seems little affection for Sir John below decks.*

Together, we noted that no straits or islands are named for the men who are not officers yet work to propel these ships forward. On turning back to the south, they named an island for our Captain C., and steered through McDougall Sound to our present location, thereby circumnavigating the island named for Cornwallis. Beechey Island, one should note, is only an island at high tide, more an extension of Devon Island from which it droops like a nipple on a newly birthed bitch. (It strikes me that Miss Lort may this moment be a-birthing, bringing into being her bloodied child, demanding through the sweat and pain and exhaustion its health and gender.)

From the land, our ships look mighty, rising above the ice like bell towers in the Catholic cities on the continent. The ice pinnacles grow daily, cathedrals of blue and green glass capped with impossibly white snow. Canyons of ice appear overnight, as if waves had been paralyzed in mid-crash as we slept. The frosty sketches on early morning windowpanes we enjoyed as children are here gigantic three-dimensional fantasies, beyond anything Mr. Coleridge could summon from addled Porlockian wits. As I have noted, we have a photo-graphic camera with us—I believe it is the first one transported to this part of the world—and E. the operator prays the ice sculptures will remain when light returns, as exposure is impossible in these all-dark days.

Even as a man with an immense respect for language and a sworn duty to report the truths, I am hard put to describe the utter and unworldly beauty of these things that surround us. Yet, in the bilges, this awe sublimates into fear, as we hear the pressure of that very same ice groaning and grinding, gnawing and gnarling at staunch English oak.

My classes are ill attended, but not without their gratifications. A few men are willing to admit they cannot read or write and are using these idle days to improve their lot. I encourage those who appear in my classroom, including young T., who is an exemplary student, to cajole others into attending, but I am met by blank stares and averted eyes, as if the act of learning carries some stigma of which I am not aware.

Below decks, Bealls and his coterie seem to feel illiteracy is some natural state bestowed upon man by God and hence superior in its purity to scholarship. I miss young Stoker T. of late, as he has been taken to sick bay to have his pestering cough treated. I am told he will return next week. Despite the lack of learners, I apply myself to the education of those who appear, despite coughs and complaints of illnesses ranging from nausea to pissing purple, from diarrhoea to constipation, seemingly in one gut in the same moment. I wonder, in fact, if these complaints are not the result of extreme boredom, the common hypochondria of the upper classes now exposed in lesser mortals due to ice-bound inactivity and permanent dark. Yet my own symptoms, if that is what I should call them, vouchsafe an illness we may share. I have noticed in the glass an odd bluish line on my upper gums, inexplicable to me. I have neither the gall nor the friendship of others to ask if they share this sign, or what indeed it signals, if anything at all. Perhaps my symptoms, too, are the product of little else to occupy the mind.

I think we all expected that, once we were unified by our wintering position, the crews from both ships would intermingle often, if not at will. In fact, I anticipated long conversations with L., my peer on Erebus, *perhaps discussions on instruction and learning methods, a shared sherry and a few games of whist, at which I consider myself quite proficient. (G. was unable to pay his debt before he was shipped home. I may forgive it, as money is of no value here. Or I may not, even though my own father said debt is better collected than paid.) It was also in my mind that the men on* Erebus *might be friendlier, more accessible than my present colleagues, more accepting of an inexperienced newcomer, less repelled by a non-sailor and a reader of books. I fear my lack of both seaworthiness and stomach for the lesser spectator sports such as bullock murdering have labelled me a pariah to the men.*

Alas, new friends from Erebus *are not to be found. Rather than the collegial blending of 129 men from two ships, there is a formal separation between the crews, a disconnection decreed, we're told, by Franklin himself. Inside the hull, lit by candles that cast the hard edges of enlarged shadows on the groaning oak, Bealls tells us that this is Franklin's way, his regular method of maintaining authority, by dividing an unmanageable whole into its parts. He tells tales of Franklin's past Arctic expeditions, one 24 years ago in which inexperience led to a lack of food supplies. Franklin split the group in two, each of which sought sustenance. In the end, 11 men were lost. Rumours of madness and eating the flesh of men were staunched and Franklin's ineptitude overlooked as the tales of him as "The man who ate shoe leather" delighted the British press and its readers. Bealls tells the stories well, as if he was there—and perhaps he was—with a quiet croaking voice and a rhythm of low-country speech that have you believing you were present as well. Franklin's second Arctic foray was a mapping expedition, says Bealls. With the taste of popularity, if only from eating his footwear, Franklin seemed intent on becoming a British hero, and the Admiralty, as we all know, sees its heroes as political currency. Despite a wife—his first wife, not Lady Jane—ailing with advanced tuberculosis and his ignorance of an ill-conceived budget, he accepted the task. The wife died six days after he sailed. Again, he split the men under his command. Yet, this time, no lives were lost, and the Captain won his knighthood.*

I have some thoughts on why the Commander chooses this divisive strategy, but I shall keep them to myself and observe further. Right or wrong, I am without options and, given the length of the journey, I had best make do with the potential friends on the Terror *and move to ingratiate myself with them further. I shall keep an ear cocked for challenges that may grow my stature in their eyes. One only needs Bealls' approval, it seems, and the others fall in line.*

Christmastide: We are cozy and warm, well fed and entertained by charades and even coarse theatrical productions the men act out when the officers are not present. One such skit had a man I shall not name playing Sir J.F., pillow stuffed in his trouser front, cocked hat athwartships on his head, his walk alone enough to identify the man. From one side of the mess to the other he waddles, tugging at some imaginary jewel 'round his neck, instructed by another in a dress and wearing a swab mop as a wig. He-she speaks in a contralto, telling the man what he must do as he orders the few under his command to go in different directions, all the while licking the upper leathers of a pair of boots he wears on his hands. The men were prostrate with laughter, banging on the tables, slapping their knees and holding their stomachs in pain. I watched a river of rheumy tears run down the ditch of Bealls' scar and soak his roll-neck sweater through the flume of his cleft chin. Shakespeare it is not, however, and, given their obvious enjoyment of ribaldry as theatre, I am of a mind to introduce them to the Bard and coach them to produce one of his lighter works. Perhaps that will establish bonds of friendship and collegiality that what seems to be the censorious yoke of literacy cannot. There seems a unity in shared insubordination, an attitude for which no great experience is required. I shall succeed in this. Love's Labour's Lost, *perhaps.*

Victory Point, King William Island, Nunavut

Kennison found Anne Ferguson-Crewe in the Dormitory Tent with an intense-looking Ruby Cruz. Ferguson-Crewe perched on the edge of her bed, a paperback book placed pages down to keep her place as if she'd been reading when Ms. Cruz had entered. The American woman sat on a folding chair, pulled up close to the bed. Heads close together, she was whispering, hissing at the archaeologist until Kennison stuck his head around the corner. Ferguson-Crewe looked up as if he was a wasp. Cruz looked cowed, as if she'd been caught shoplifting.

"Dr. Ferguson-Crewe. If I could see you in the Salon Tent, please," said Kennison. The woman didn't move. "*Now,* please." Her reaction was sullen, petulance contained in an overstated sigh as she bent to pull on her slippers. Ruby had to stand and move back to allow her room to leave. Grey Anne brushed past Kennison on her way to the other tent, hesitating when he didn't follow. "Go ahead, Doctor. I'll join you in a moment." Another stage sigh and she stomped out of the Dormitory Tent. Maybe she'd taken a minor degree in drama, thought Kennison. He heard the sound of her feet on the plywood floors of the Mess Tent as she crossed it. He turned to Ruby, who had sat back in her chair.

"Ms. Cruz. Whether or not you're a trained investigator or

just a fan of police work, I'm sure you understand I am in the middle of a professional examination of two deaths—"

"I'm not a 'fan,' as you put it, of police work, Sergeant. I'm a trained FBI operative with field experience."

"Are you presently an FBI operative?" She hesitated before shaking her head. "Even if you were, you have absolutely no jurisdiction here. You know that?" Ms. Cruz nodded reluctantly. "Good. What you may not know is that at least one of the dead—your colleague, Dr. Kneisser—is possibly a case of murder." Kennison waited until the woman nodded her understanding. To her credit, she seemed shocked at the news, yet there was something in her eyes that hinted she wasn't entirely surprised.

"You have no status here. I would ask you to avoid talking with any of the people here without clearing it with me first. Perhaps you could tell me why you're here in the first place." Kennison stood over her, close enough to make it difficult for her to stand. She looked up at him from the chair. Her eyes were tired. From this angle, her nose was a greasy blob of brown putty in the middle of her face.

"I . . . I was sent here by my employer—also Dr. Kneisser's employer—to escort the doctor home—"

"Who is your employer, please?"

"They're called AEI, for Arctic Exploration Institute. They represent companies' interests in the North—"

"American companies?"

She nodded. "I can't tell you what companies. I've only been with them a week. I'm a paralegal there. I came to get Dr. Kneisser. Take him home. I didn't know he was—I have things I have to—"

"I understand, Ms. Cruz, and I believe you had no idea Dr. Kneisser was dead until you arrived. But now the doctor's body is in the morgue in Yellowknife, and you're still here. Why?"

"Well, I—there was no—I need to call my office and ask them what they want me to do next. The phone isn't working. I can't very well leave if they want me to—" The more she spoke, the more aggressive she became, shifting from a defensive shoplifter to a frustrated tourist yelling at the locals because she can't communicate. "It was not my idea to come here, and it's not my choice to remain here, Sergeant Kennison."

"But why are you here, Ms. Cruz? What are you looking for? Why are you running around in the dark, bothering people in their rooms? Mr. Masterson says you're peeking into people's tents. Snooping around. What's going on?" She pressed her lips together, emitted an impatient breath and shook her head. Still embarrassed at being caught out, thought Kennison.

"I was instructed to accompany Dr. Kneisser and his possessions home. Dr. Kneisser's death is unfortunate—terribly unfortunate. Still, my job is to return to my employers with him and his possessions. I shall do my job and leave, Sergeant."

"Not if it interferes with mine, Ms. Cruz, and please do not forget that. When and if this crime is solved, your company, as registered next of kin according to Masterson, will receive Dr. Kneisser's body and possessions, such as they are. Until that time, I will ask you to confine yourself to this building and avoid speaking with anyone who might be considered as suspect, no matter how unlikely it may seem. Presently, that includes everyone on the site. Got it?" Ruby Cruz was silent. Her face was flushed, thought Kennison. Hard to tell in the weak light. "Got it, Ms. Cruz?"

"Yes, Sergeant."

"Thank you. Mr. Masterson will see you have a place to sleep." Kennison turned and walked out of the room. He was tired, but anger had given him a second wind.

Anne Ferguson-Crewe waited in the Salon Tent on a futon couch with her hands, palms up, under her thighs. When Kennison entered she smiled painfully, falsely. She removed her hands and pressed the tips of her fingers together. She crossed her legs slowly, almost languorously, as if, under her thick woollen tights, her legs were good legs. She pursed her lips, sucked in her thin cheeks and brushed grey hair from her eyes with quick, impatient movements. To Kennison, it was as if she'd decided to be someone different.

Her slippers were fluffy, girlish, and seemed out of character. She wore no visible makeup. In the warm yellow light of the two kerosene lamps, he could see her face was covered with tiny golden hairs. There was a groove on the bridge of her nose from wearing glasses, but she wasn't wearing them now. She seemed to have gathered herself, decided to replace the whimpering woman with a more forceful mien. Kennison made notes around the poems in the Heaney book.

"Your name is Anne Ferguson-Crewe—"

"*Doctor* Anne Ferguson-Crewe. We've been through this, Sergeant."

"You would be a doctor of . . . ?"

"I have a doctoral degree in archaeology?" Kennison still

found her querying speech pattern annoying and found himself countering it by asking terse questions.

"From what school?" Not that it mattered, but he liked to loosen people up by talking about what they knew before he asked them to speculate. He suspected that Dr. Ferguson-Crewe did not value speculation.

"Undergraduate from Leicester, master's at Southampton, doctorate at Cardiff? I now teach at Sheffield, from which school I am on a six-month sabbatical for this project."

"You grew up in England?"

"All over, really. Navy brat. My father went where he was posted, and so went my mother and me. The church held her interest . . ." She blushed as if she'd offered more than she'd been asked and had sworn to avoid that.

"And this project here is—"

"As I told you this morning at the shore, at Hell, Sergeant, this project is an ongoing examination and cataloguing of the remains of the crew members of Her Majesty's Ships *Terror* and *Erebus,* the vessels of the expedition to find the Northwest Passage led by Sir John Franklin." She sounded as though she'd said it a thousand times, and probably had.

Kennison slid back in his chair to get a different perspective of her. She slouched, shoulders forward, bony hands now clasped on her knees. She wouldn't smile, and looked like she never had. She was tense about something, as if she had much to do somewhere else. Or maybe the futon was uncomfortable.

"When was that expedition?"

"The ships left England in, I believe, April or May 1845. Trevor Patel is a better historian than I, if you can tear him away from his poker games with the staff. I'm sure he'll know the exact date?"

"And they were never seen again?"

"No. I mean, no, that's incorrect, Sergeant. They were last seen in the Davis Strait, I believe, off Greenland, shortly after they were resupplied by an accompanying ship. "Though I fail to see what the detailed history of the Franklin Expedition has to do with the unfortunate deaths of two members of—"

"Me neither, Dr. Ferguson-Crewe," said Kennison. "But it seems relevant to explore something that binds together the members of this group and brings them to this place. Don't you think?"

"Perhaps, Sergeant. If ignorance is a bond? That's what we're doing here at Victory Point, isn't it? Trying to draw solid conclusions with real evidence rather than continue crediting amateur hearsay. Are you a trained detective?" Kennison fixed her with a glare. "Then, as even you may be able to imagine, it is the unknown that makes science a passionate thing?"

"I think I understand, ma'am. Just as it makes the investigation of murder an obsession with me."

"*Touché,* Sergeant. You do speak French, of course. This is a bilingual country, *n'est-ce pas?*" Kennison couldn't figure her out. Her personality changed with every sentence. Now she was flirting, then she was angry. Here she was embarrassed, there she was pouting.

"Tell me what you're digging for here."

She looked at him as if he couldn't possibly understand. She sat back, secure on her own turf, spreading her arms to the sides, shoulders back.

"We're looking for irrefutable evidence of cannibalism, Sergeant. Until twenty years ago, there was only 130 years of conjecture, of unsubstantiated rumour, much of it—all of it, actually—from native . . . from *Inuit* sources. It's only been since the 1980s that scientific proof of Franklin Expedition cannibalism has been established."

"What kind of proof? What scientifically proves that men ate other men?"

"Well, murder for a start, Sergeant. You're familiar with that. An anthropologist named Beattie—a Canadian, if you can imagine; Albertan, to compound the wonder—discovered cut marks on a right femur on the south shore of this island. That's a thigh bone, Sergeant." Kennison clenched his teeth. "The skull of the man whose leg it was had been intentionally broken. He'd been killed by another."

"That's it?"

She looked offended, turned her head to the side like a dog that doesn't know what you're asking, wary of where you're leading him.

"An inordinate number of other bones on the site were similar bones, Sergeant—limb bones, which have the most flesh and marrow. Your Beattie suspected they might be tantamount to a transportable food supply for starving men."

"You say he only 'suspected' they might be food. Plus the so-called cut marks could have been animal teeth—"

"We're scientists, Sergeant, not novelists, not storytellers," she said, a bark more than a reasoned response. "I would have thought your vocation would respect evidence over conjecture. A high percentage of the cut marks are at or close to articular surfaces—joints to you. This is consistent with a conscious process of intentional disarticulation, the dismembering of a body for its meat? The cut marks—made by sharp blades, Sergeant, not animal teeth—further suggest the removal of flesh. I can be more specific if you're cognizant of Latin terms for skeletal components."

"You've made your point, Doctor—"

"Further, the breaking in half of what we might classify as the long bones, the femurs and the ulnae, strongly suggests cannibalism, as such ruptures allow access to the marrow inside those bones—"

"Who pays for all this?" Kennison waved his arms widely, changing the subject, trying to take back the interview. "The camp, the food, the staff . . ." The scientist smiled, knowing she'd won a point, pleased at his surrender.

"A group of like-minded institutions at home—in the United Kingdom—under an umbrella called the International Franklin Expedition Consortium—IFEC?" She brought her arms forward, crossed her legs and clasped her hands over her knees. "It's comprised of people, of members, scholars like myself and administrators from archaeologically oriented universities and colleges like mine that could not afford such explorations on their own? We share resources. One applies to attend the dig here. I applied four times before being accepted this summer . . . this year."

"If this is a British project, why are there Canadians and Americans here?"

"Good manners where the Canadians are concerned? This is their country—your country—after all. As presumptuous as we British have been throughout our history—including Commander Franklin and his superiors, I might add—we can no longer afford, figuratively or literally, to presume sovereignty over territory we cannot defend? We can barely defend our own should it come to that. The Canadian government allows us to do our little research and we provide a limited opportunity for a few students, scholars and support staff to accompany us."

"And this Marie-Claire Fortier was one of those students?"

Anne Ferguson-Crewe nodded. "I believe she is also well connected? Was. Usually the graduate students, like Trevor Patel, for example—although I question his manner and most of his youthful opinions—are exceptional scholars, chosen for their thesis orientation or erudition—"

"I don't understand. You're saying that Ms. Fortier was not of that calibre?"

"Yes, I am." The archaeologist shrugged. "She is—was—a young woman. What can one say? Pretty thing, but still unfocused, not to speak ill of the dead. Immature, perhaps? Certainly not, ah, emotionally mature? She had not yet tasted life, I'd say. Polite, hard-working perhaps, but certainly less advanced than I expected? Although I must admit she was passionate about it all, even the tedious jobs of photographing and recording scapula and metacarpals."

She exposed her grey teeth in what Kennison thought might be a smile, offering a confidence. She arched her unplucked brows. "One's twenties, Sergeant, are an emotional age for any woman, no less for a female academic. There are choices one must make, choices between one's . . ." Her mind seemed to wander, perhaps to the decisions she'd made when she was Fortier's age. Or regrets. Was she thinking of the girl? Had there been something between them, or was it only a thought of what might have been? After a moment, she tossed her grey hair, shaking her head as if to clear it of history.

"At first the girl prattled incessantly about her father and boyfriend—her fiancé, she insisted on calling him at first, and not kindly. Some up-and-coming French politician, name of Raymond, but I don't know whether that was a Christian name or a surname. After a week or two, she did stop mentioning him every five seconds, I must admit. Stopped complaining about her father. But she was not focused on her job."

"The young man, the one with the pierced—"

"Kenny. Kenneth Monk. Had some problems, I believe, with

illegal drugs. Sent here from one of those large cities in Alberta—there are two of them, I get them mixed up—to help in the kitchen. Nice young chap behind all the unfortunate and possibly painful jewellery. Worked hard, volunteered for the dig work in his off hours as kitchen help. Seemed to understand our challenges. Borrowed books, even asked me for a letter to get him back into school. Of course, he was besotted with the Fortier girl. It may have all been as shallow as that." She slumped again. Kennison thought she looked hurt, perhaps betrayed.

"The Americans. What do they bring to the table?"

Anne Ferguson-Crewe raised her shoulders and turned her palms upwards, open. "Money, I imagine. Isn't that usually the case? Certainly not foreign policy. Sorry, that was petty of me. The Americans always pay their way. It's that simple? In fact, I suspect they pay more than their way, and that alleviates some of the expenses suffered by the IFEC, which does not have very deep pockets. This specific project has been going on for eight years? Since Dr. Kneisser discovered the sites to the south and has taken credit for the rest."

"What do you know about Dr. Kneisser, Doctor?"

"He's a well-published scholar, German originally, attached to a small American college in Dakota or Montana or some northern state? Probably emeritus by now, I should think?" Her speech pattern made all statements supposition.

"Emeritus?"

"An academic kindness, Sergeant, meaning retired? It doesn't mean you're better, just that you're no longer a thorn in the side of administration. It's the necropolis to which we're all condemned."

"I'm hearing a tone that suggests you weren't a fan of Dr. Kneisser."

"Oh no, Sergeant. Well, perhaps not a fan, as you say. He was a gifted scientist, but an egocentrist. A man who held himself in the highest possible regard and shared his opinions accordingly. In truth, before we arrived I expected to have him underfoot, in the way, but he ignored us and our efforts—"

"How do you mean, ignored?"

"Exactly that. He never came by Hell, or usually only in passing as he came in from his ever-so-secret site to eat or load up the ATV with food so he could stay at his new project. I felt—I think we all felt—a little, how shall I say, slighted by the master? I know I did. As if having made the discovery at Hell here, he had moved on and we were left to do the dog work that would record the facts and further secure his place in the firmament with all of us as journal footnotes."

"You sound bitter."

"I suppose I am—was. I expected more, I suppose. I worked hard to get this assignment, only to discover it was of a secondary capacity? Of course, there's always the chance that we'll discover something smashing that will rewrite known history, isn't there? Something Dr. Karl Conrad Kneisser overlooked in his hurry to discover the next best thing?"

"Dr. Kneisser was murdered," said Kennison.

"Oh. Dear me. I'm not . . . I'm sorry. I didn't know."

"Did you have any confrontations with Dr. Kneisser?"

"Not really. No. I never addressed my disappointments with him, if that's what you mean . . ." She turned to the door, lost in thought for a moment, and shook her head again. When she turned back to Kennison, her eyes were wide, as if lit from within.

"You cannot possibly understand the importance we attach to discovery, Sergeant. It can make a career for one in this business. Give one a life. Like a botanist having a plant named for them, an astrophysicist forever joined to a star. The world becomes inordinately straightforward for an academic with such success in the field, a series of appearances well attended by one's peers, institutions lining up to have your name on their faculty and discovering their purse strings aren't so terribly tight in your special instance. Publishers clamouring, conferences in exotic places, even possibly becoming a noun, as in 'Have you read the Blishen—or the Ferguson-Crewe?'" She dropped her head, her thin shoulders folding forward again. Kennison stayed silent. She looked up. The light was gone, replaced by contrition.

"These are, of course, every scientist's not-so-secret dreams, Sergeant Kennison. Perhaps Dr. Kneisser deserved his accolades. I imagine he had, as you Americans say, 'paid his dues.'"

"Canadian."

"I beg your pardon?"

"I'm Canadian, not American."

"North American, surely." Ferguson-Crewe shrugged and her lank hair shifted.

"If Dr. Kneisser wasn't of help to the project, why was he included here?" asked Kennison.

"He *was* the project. The reason we had funding. The aura of the great man and his discoveries. He himself was funded separately by an organization out of Washington? Probably a group like IFEC? A consortium of sorts? Has initials, like they all do. Confusing. No one quite knows what it does. This Ms. Cruz works for them, too, as you probably know, unless she's lying. I don't trust that woman, don't know what she's doing here . . ."

"Dr. Kneisser. His role?"

"The Americans sometimes have more trouble gaining scientific permissions in Canada than we British, so I suspect he piggybacked on our agreement. As I suggested, I wouldn't be surprised if his organization paid the larger meat of the nut for us to be here.

Some last-minute cash input allowed us to come, however late, and Dr. Kneisser as a necessary part of the deal? I don't know."

"Do you think there was a . . . a relationship of any kind between Dr. Kneisser and Ms. Fortier, anything—"

"Oh my God, no." She snorted loudly, then blushed, covering her mouth with her hand. Her nails were bitten and the flesh around them red. "The hoary old bugger and the sweet young thing? The mind boggles. I mean, she was properly impressed to meet him—all the young ones are because they've had to read his dated, stuffy old books as undergraduates. But a relationship? No. No. I would say not. He wasn't a . . . a sexual man in my opinion."

What an oddly British thing to say, thought Kennison. He wondered what a sexual man was, and if *he* was one. He'd like to be, if only for an hour or two. He needed a smoke.

"Do you have any idea what he was searching for?"

"Of course. No question. Same as all of us. Franklin's grave. It's our grail, Sergeant, the gold for those of us who moil in the north country, as Service might say? Just as Franklin's grail was the Northwest Passage, so ours is his final resting place."

"Do you think he found it? Is that why he was killed?"

"Franklin, or Kneisser?"

"Kneisser." She looked at her hands for a moment, realized they were uncared for and put them back under her thighs before she spoke.

"Good question. Up to a week or two ago, judging by temper and circumstance, I would say no. But in the last days he had been highly excitable? He asked me if he could use the Monk boy as a helper, if he could take—'borrow,' he said—the Fortier girl's photographic skills when she wasn't working for me. I never learned why."

"Do you know, or do you suspect any reason, why Dr. Kneisser or Marie-Claire Fortier would want to harm each other, or why any third party would want to harm either of them?"

"No, I can't think of a single thing," she said. "In small and remote communities like this one and other digs, there occurs an 'intensity of relationships'? Like some summer camp for hormonally raging teens, I would imagine. Interpersonal trouble is always in the air." She batted her sparse eyelashes. "People share each other's passions, and sometimes each other." Her mind drifted again and she shook it back. "I'm not speaking from personal experience, of course, but it's a natural thing in this business—and, I imagine, others? Perhaps not the police force, although I'm sure such things occur . . ."

Kennison watched her, waiting.

"But not those two. No. Karl Kneisser was a loner, a professional man consumed with his occupation, and to tell you the truth, all I can remember young Fortier going on about was her coming nuptials with her dread fiancé and her father, to whom she referred persistently as 'Daddy'? Neither of them were targets for criminal minds, Sergeant. And to my knowledge, there are no real criminals here. The worst that happens in places like this is petty theft, and I hardly think that whoever stole my money—although it's not petty to me—would be likely to have committed a more heinous crime—"

"What money, Doctor?"

"I had three hundred pounds sterling in my toiletries case. In a wallet, a tweed and leather-trimmed wallet that a good friend—a close associate—gave to me before I left England. It was there as late as two days ago. I know that because I'd decided to buy her an Inuit soapstone carving to take back to England, and I checked the amount. The money—the wallet—is no longer there."

"That's about six hundred dollars." Anne Ferguson-Crewe shrugged as if she didn't care how much it was in Canadian funds.

"I suspect it was taken during the hullabaloo surrounding the fire. That's it. That's all I can tell you."

"We'll probably chat again, Doctor. Do not, under any circumstances, share this interview or anything else with the others, including Ms. Cruz, who has no role in this investigation." Kennison waited for her to raise her chin and look at him. Her brow creased at the request, but she nodded agreement and frowned as Kennison stood and removed his cigarettes from his pocket.

"One question, Sergeant. Who was that other man? The one who was just killed. Should we be worried for our safety here? Are there others?"

Kennison paused. "I don't know. There could be."

The doctor fixed him with a grey stare. "I must say, Sergeant, I do hope your detective skills improve with the hour."

Yellowknife, Northwest Territories

Grantley Regional Hospital was only four years old, and looked it. A white post-construction efflorescence mottled the red bricks near the eaves and inside corners on the entry side, and the surrounding grounds awaited some heavy landscaping come spring. Like a few of the buildings in town, including the new hotel and the high school, it seemed ahead of its time, the leading edge of some urban plan that is invisible to most and makes sense on paper to a select few.

The predominant odour in the spacious lobby of the emergency facility was not of acrid ether or industrial floor polish or that mysterious cocktail of medicine and alcohol solutions found in southern medical facilities. Here it was sweetgrass, the pungent native herb burned regularly in ceremonial native healings with permission of the medical staff.

The 121-bed Grantley was the primary medical facility for the whole of the Northwest Territories, providing health care from birth to death for local patients and a travelling medical outreach treatment and educational program to service those who lived in remote cabins and hunting camps. A helicopter pad on top of the four-storey building provided access to those flown in with a need for emergency treatment, often involving limbs and chainsaws, exposure or frostbite. Locally, the unit provided services 24/7 in response to the accidents of work and home, efficiently treating scalds and imagined heart attacks, fat lips from bar fights and the occasional family stabbing.

The doors to Emergency slid open automatically, silently, to face a curved triage desk made of laminated blond wood perched on a kick plate of stainless steel. To the right was a large waiting room in which, architecturally reminiscent of Canada geese in flight, rows of soft green cloth chairs with arms were mounted on forward-leaning steel legs. To the left was an industrial metal door with a small glass-and-wire window under a red warning light. An adhesive label on the push bar warned that lights would flash and sirens wail with unauthorized entry.

Jennifer Giles ignored the warnings. In her down parka with the hood up against the cold, she knew she looked like a round snowman on surprisingly skinny legs. She trotted quickly through the automatic slider, waved her fingertips at the triage receptionist and turned left through the metal door. No alarms sounded, and the heavy door slammed loudly behind her. Inside, she walked quickly down a polished white-tiled corridor that reflected the green tint of fluorescent lights high above. One of the lights flickered sporadically, and a ballast buzzed as if a wasp was trapped inside. Dr. Giles pulled off her coat as she walked to a doorway at the end of the corridor, tossing it on a hook inside the door, where a gowned assistant sat at a desk typing in front of a computer screen.

"Hi Bev."

"Hi Dr. Giles . . . Jen. Didn't expect to see you here tonight. At least not until Benjy and Diane showed up."

"No rest for the wicked. Marg Duchesne took the kids to the Dog Derby, thank God, or I'd have a revolution at home. Ricky Monteith fed Dutch some sob story about wanting only me to do the postmortem."

"Always a sucker for a sob story, eh, Jen?" Bev Williamson wore dark purple scrubs. As loose as they were, they couldn't disguise a body that her male high school classmates still fantasized about five years after she'd graduated and gone south to attend a community college. She was twenty-three, with severely plucked eyebrows and blonde hair from a bottle. Her face had inherited the flat Slavic features of her mother. She'd go out with Benjy Rosen if he ever asked her, but he never look her in the eyes, just stared at her breasts like she was a hypnotist and they were pendulums.

Dr. Giles washed her hands in the large, deep sink on the wall opposite the coat rack. Through a large tinted window she could see the EMT staff putting the two body bags on separate stainless-steel tables and leaning over them as they tugged at the zippers to expose the contents. A third shape, covered in a blue plastic tarpaulin, was wheeled into the cold-storage room and left on the gurney.

"Well, I gotta admit that this is an interesting one, Bev. You ready to go?" The assistant nodded and handed Giles a sheaf of pages taken from the printer tray. Giles scanned them. "So this new guy, Kennison, says the male has a bullet hole in his head. The other one, a young woman, had no obvious external wounds he could find. Anything else?"

"The bodies are still frozen, the man's less than the girl's." Maybe the position on the Otter, thought Giles, maybe there was more heat down near the floorboards. Poor Ricky Monteith half froze himself to preserve the integrity of the corpses. Beyond the call of duty, but then most of what those young pilots did was exactly that.

"Feelin' strong, Bev? Wish those EMTs hadn't split so quickly. Thought Benjy Rosen would hang around and drool for you, or on you. He'll be on his second beer over at The Sly by now. Let's hump this young lady over to the drain table so she can thaw without making a mess. I think we can begin on the male here before too long. Sooner we cut him, the sooner he'll thaw." The two women grabbed the ends of the body bag containing Marie-Claire Fortier and hefted it over to a long, corrugated stainless-steel platform that drained into a deep sink. Jen Giles carefully cut the bag away from Marie-Claire's body while Bev did the same at the table that held Kneisser's corpse.

"Where's that paper, Bev?" The assistant handed Giles the printout. "Ooookay. Who do we have here?" She shuffled the pages and looked down at the charred fetal form of Dr. Kneisser. "Karl Conrad Kneisser. Doctor," she muttered to herself. "Wonder if you pronounce the K. Professor Emeritus of Anthropology at Marshall University, South Dakota. Author of *A Guide to Basic Anthropology*—jeez, I think I used that book in school. First year." Giles reached into a long metal container with high sides, crammed with implements soaking in a blue-tinted liquid. "Here, shove this up his you-know-where and we'll see how cold he is at the core." She turned back to the information Kennison had supplied.

"Found on November 8 at approximately 2 p.m. by a Paul Stewart Masterson in a small shed destroyed by fire at Victory Point, King William Island, Nunavut." She looked over at Bev, who was examining Kneisser's body. "Why the hell are our boys doing Nunavut's cases?" Bev shrugged, removing the thermometer from the corpse's rectum and turning it slowly to read the temperature in the light.

"You hear 'bout the new Wal-Mart, Jen? Over by that swamp lot up the Proctor Lake Road they said was gonna be a Home Depot, eh? Now it's gonna be a Wal-Mart apparently. Sam's Club and everything."

"What've you got, Bev?"

"Still too cold to cut, I figure." She wrapped her rubber-gloved hand around the charred right wrist of the victim and moved the arm slightly with ease. She raised her eyebrows. "Maybe not?"

"Better let him warm up for half an hour. Make life easier when we get in there. So what about the Home Depot? Does the Wal-Mart mean there won't be a Home Depot coming at all?"

Bev shrugged. "Who knows? Have to ask Mario at Canadian Tire. You can bet he knows. Must be scared shitless. Should be."

May 1846

I weary of this writing. I apply myself less and less without good reason, perhaps an increasing, indefinable despair, perhaps a laziness, a torpor that seems to infect us all of late. Yet, one year since we left England's shores, we sail again. Yesterday, with a cracking heave and an expulsion of air Bealls deemed "the fart of a fruit-fed African hippopotamus," the Terror *was freed from its icy grasp. Nearly six months after our capture by ice, we are again free, although the way ahead looks impossible to navigate. Thomas Blanky, our Ice Master, stands at the bow with C., both staring first into the water, then far ahead like synchronized ducks dapping at pond's edge.*

With our cautious, quiet progress, the masts of the Erebus *soon disappeared behind us. That ship remains icebound, and agreements have been made that it will follow, meeting up with us at a latitude and longitude of which we lesser mortals have not been informed. There is disquiet about this—the cream of a winter's harmless mocking of officers has curdled somewhat into what I can only call a mistrust, less focused on our own Captain C., who seems a forthright, albeit a terse and unapproachable, man, than Commander Franklin and the officers of the* Erebus.

(I must comment here that my attempts at staging a Shakespearean play while on Beechey were disastrous. The sight of a besotted and rude King of Navarre trading lewd lines never imagined by the Bard with his three supposedly celibate companions had the audience hissing. Before the end of Act I, I removed myself to the quiet of the library, where, I must admit, I wept, both for the ignorance of man and my increasingly intolerable loneliness. I am further ostracized for my miscalculation, exiled for my pains to become one of those who disparage me.)

Our collective sense of comfort—if that is not awarding it undeserved stature—has been qualified, if not shattered, by the deaths of three of us. Sadly we have buried young Torrington, 19 years old and a boy with such grand promise. With him on Beechey lie Royal Marine Private William Braine, who was 31, and Able Seaman John Hartnell, 25. I knew these men and all served well on the Terror. *With C. presiding, we buried them with ceremony near the pit where we buried the empty Goldner's food tins used to date. The rocks are smaller there, more manageable, more conducive to opening the dry pit required for an Arctic grave and covering the corpse with rocks that animals cannot remove. God rest their souls and the hearts of all those who shall grieve them. Dr. M. tucked a note into the rocks—a diagnosis perhaps—and men wept when Tom Evans, the boy, placed on the grave a painted ashtray Hartnell often used for his cigar ashes. Neither the Commander, Captain F., nor any men of the* Erebus *were present, nor did any men on that ship expire.*

I took Doctor M. aside and queried him as to porphyria, the sickness that gripped our King George III fifty years since. The symptoms, as I remember reading somewhere, were blue-tinted bodily fluids and an appearance of mental disorder. He dismissed me abruptly—rudely, I thought—compounding the offence by warning me in his thick brogue to not be spreading rumours below decks. As if I had the ears of the men who toil there.

What is perhaps as distressing as the deaths of these fine men is that the bond of playfulness the men shared died with them. The camaraderie of poking fun at one's symbols of authority—a joy all lesser men surely share—has evolved over the winter into a collective resentment, an ugly suspicion, at worst a fear, of the divisive tactics of Sir John Franklin. Rumours—as ever the faggots that feed fires of frustration—are rife, the most insidious of them regarding an odd exchange of men between Terror *and* Erebus *immediately following the funerals. C. stood silently—stoically, I thought—alone at the top of a wooden-runged ladder leading from the ice surface, his forehead creased with what I cannot but imagine was private concern as he watched loyal men in his command depart and strangers from the* Erebus *climb to take their place. Not unnaturally, those of us remaining on the* Terror *sought explanations that only conjecture could supply. Such speculation is, I know, dangerous if not foolhardy, as those in command are charged with decisions we cannot expect to share or understand. Nonetheless, Bealls' muttered proposition that the exchange was of our hale for their sick struck us with force. The refusal of Drs. P. and M. to address the issue did nothing to defuse it. Rather, the opposite. Hourly, I see men stifle coughs and walk the decks, ducking to expectorate overboard, to avoid notice and confrontation.*

As we sail again, leaving the Erebus *behind, there are many questions, most yet unformed by words. Perhaps they are only my questions: Are we a death ship, a drifting bier of disposable sick men released to the elements by Franklin as floating sanatorium? Did the men buried on Beechey die of consumption, of the scrofula lately called tuberculosis? (They say Franklin's first wife died of it—did I write that? I am becoming forgetful, even of my dreams.) Perhaps he refused to attend the funeral of his men for fear of contracting the disease. Perhaps he suffers an inordinate fear of the contagion and lags behind to distance himself from it—from us. He is not a young man, and may not survive such a sickness. Younger men, like T., did not. Still, a leader, to my way of thinking, does not lead from behind.*

I, for one, am willing to wait for answers. Others, increasing daily in number, are not. They regard me with resentment as we pick our way southwest, into Parry Channel once again, thence to Viscount Melville Sound, as if my reticence, my inability to subscribe to their simple theories, marks me as untrustworthy. I must do something to reverse this, to become a trusted member of this crew, if not a confidant of its real leaders, like Bealls and others who attract the ears and hearts of men. I have dreams now, ones that wake me, silly dreams in which Lady Franklin, diva on an ice-covered stage surrounded by a pelt-laden chorus of Esquimaux admonishes me from an iceberg, frowning, shaking her finger as if I have done something terribly wrong. My words come with more difficulty and sometimes will not come at all. I spend too much time staring at these pages, willing the simplest of phrases to step forward.

Rumour says we are heading for Cape Dundas, on the western coast of Melville Island, which is as far as Englishmen have sailed in these climes. From there, Bealls says it is a mere 900 miles to known waters and we will have accomplished our task. Nine hundred miles is nothing compared to what we've travelled to date. But even hopes of expeditionary success are eroded with a distrust of leadership. Perhaps we're simply suffering from a winter of darkness, fevers brought on by limited activity in limited light. Perhaps we'll soon be wearing sarongs, being tattooed by similarly clad men whose wives demand we share their beds under wafting palms.

Addendum: Three days later. For all the forecasting about forging west to Cape Dundas, it seems we are turning south, dodging castles of ice in what is being dubbed Victoria Strait. My dreams continue, each more frightening than before. I wake wasted, unable to remember what I fear. I wonder if the child lived, if it's a boy playing with carriages on the hearth or a girl plaiting the hair of her own doll-child.

Victory Point, King William Island, Nunavut

Kennison lit another smoke and held it in his fingers, pulling up his sleeve out of the incessant wind, not smoking but holding it like it was incense. It's how he did some of his best thinking. In the old days, when you could light up in your office whenever you felt the urge, much of his smoking involved lighting cigarettes and letting them burn down. That didn't make them—or him—smell any better, as Ginny regularly observed, but the mess at the end of the day belied his actual nicotine intake.

Kennison could hear bumping and banging in the kitchen as Lillian and either Masterson or Monk cleaned up. He took a deep breath of the fresh, cold air. It felt good to breathe air up here, air no one had breathed before, maybe stand where no non-native had ever stood. There was a sense of newness, of being the first. The cattle drivers in the old west must have had this feeling. Explorers everywhere.

Raising the cigarette, Kennison puffed and inhaled deeply, coughing hard from the impurity of it, tossing the unfinished cigarette into the snow as if it had betrayed him.

Thousands of stars hung in the sky. The hard photoelectric yard light that normally lit up the compound's immediate surroundings had become a victim of low fuel, stepsister to the generator and the satphone. Without the electric lamp, the sky was a pool of its own light, a three-dimensional black dome through which pinpoints had been pricked, like the Mexican candle shades Ginny bought in Cancun—tin with a connect-the-dots pattern of nail holes in the shape of angels. It must be terrifying to lie here on your back stoned and look up at the sky, Kennison thought, shaking his head at a memory of those experimental days sandwiched between the nuns and the army.

Monteith and Kniesser should be in Yellowknife by now. Maybe Dr. Giles was already opening the corpses. He was at a loss without that report, but was likely to be home before it was ready. This case was interesting. It had possibilities. It had his attention despite the bloody freezing location. Two people dead in an isolated community of eight. Leaving six. Did Fortier kill Kneisser, then burn herself with the evidence? Did someone else kill both of them? Was there one killer or two? Or more? Was there a motive beyond the personal? He was no closer to the basic answers, though he was developing a sense about some of the parties involved.

He knew he was avoiding the real issue. He was good at that, as he had been told many times. He shook his head as if to jumble its contents. Did they really think he was so stupid that he couldn't see what they were doing? Maybe he was—he found it almost impossible to believe that someone had sent a professional hit man to shut him up, especially when he hadn't decided whether or not to talk. He smiled grimly. How deeply in denial can you be, Kennison? He was perhaps the only one who could name the names.

He knew exactly what those who wanted him to blow the whistle needed him to say. He knew they wanted his hard evidence that high-level—very high-level—RCMP officers and bureaucrats had manipulated the pension fund with the help of non-governmental bureaucrats. They had filled office buildings and car pools with their relatives and others who would support their games and willingly protect their benefactors. The Cavan Commission was supposed to blow it wide open, name names, point fingers. The evidence was all there. But the findings were buried by the very people who had been accused, and nothing had happened. Well, not much, until Kolchak blew the whistle.

Eddie Kolchak was Kennison's friend—maybe his best friend, if either of them stopped to think about it. Nether of them did: they were cops. They'd both been army peacekeepers in the Balkans—Kennison in Srebrenica, Kolchak in the Medak Pocket. They'd first met as Mounties in the post-war cleanup in Kosovo. As a team, they'd entered houses, found women raped and slaughtered, seen gutted children hung on coat hooks, classrooms bombed and infants tossed on the tall, burning haystacks that dotted the countryside like illustrations from Grimm's fairy tales. The two of them had seen more death in that six-month tour than frontline soldiers in war see in a lifetime. None were from natural causes, unless being murdered by neighbours can be considered natural.

Each reacted differently on their return. Kennison opted to stay in plainclothes, stay on the streets. Kolchak craved a desk job in the Human Resources office. They kept in touch, less and less over the years, but they still shared the intensity of their experience and an inability to talk about it with those who weren't there. Soon after their return to Ottawa, each had been approached to join what was dubbed "The Price Club"—after the discount department store—a privileged group that shared fraternal spoils on the QT. Both had refused, and both were ostracized for it.

His isolation and work ethic made Kennison a natural choice to head up the investigation for the Cavan Commission. Kolchak agreed to become one of Kennison's chief witnesses and the prosecution's wedge. From his seat inside Human Resources, the man knew every hiring, every procedural bypass, every nudge and wink that passed for carefully considered judgment. When the Commission's findings were buried by those same people, Kolchak steamed until he blew, and he blew long and hard—and publicly. He told the press what had been going on, and he served on every internal committee cast to clean up the mess. He named names, and told them who knew what, including the good guys like Kennison who could back up his information but had yet to speak.

The result was a split camp in which no one knew whose side their office mates were on. Kennison and others were removed from their posts and stashed in places where they were difficult to find, where they were impossible to interview or neutralize. But had they been hidden away by the good guys or the bad guys? Not even Kennison knew for certain—until now. It wasn't the good guys who knew he was here and had sent a contract killer. Kennison thought he saw a movement on the horizon. Since the bullet meant for him had ripped into Marie-Claire Fortier's body, he saw movement everywhere. It was driving him crazy.

He inhaled the fresh air through his nose. He was tired, his neck and back stiff. He lit another Rothman's and counted those in the pack. Eight left. He hadn't brought enough for a long visit. He'd have to start budgeting them. He took a drag and tucked the cigarette up his sleeve, then coughed hard as it hit him, hurting his throat, forcing him to spit brown smoke into the fresh air.

He'd been about to join the Commission whistle-blowers after the Patsy Prévost killing. It was a natural reaction to what he felt was an utter lack of support for police work. Kolchak had been onto him immediately, telling him to stand up, to say his piece for the good of the force. It was an attractive argument, but look what it had done to Kolchak. The public profile and peer pressure had ruined his life, cost him his job and his marriage. His kids looked at him, he'd said, like he was a traitor, and his neighbours were polite but no longer stopped to chat when they saw him trimming the lawn. Word of Eddie's own roles in some suspicious activities began to spread—sourceless rumours that escalated until he killed himself, by ordering a cylinder of hydrogen sent to his hotel room and inhaling it until it replaced his oxygen and death replaced his sorry life.

Was that what had made Kennison back off? He wasn't sure. Maybe it was the ethos of not ratting on your colleagues, even the ones with a contract out on you. Maybe the ignorance and avoidance factor—if he just kept policing the best he could, the rest of the political bullshit would go away. On one hand, unlike Kolchak, he had nothing to lose—no wife, no kids, no lawn, no neighbours. On the other hand, he was a Mountie, and Mounties didn't rat on Mounties. Though maybe that was the long, deep root of what was wrong.

Then it came to him. While the front of his brain had been thinking about being hunted, the back end had been processing data. As suddenly as if someone had told him, he knew what it was that had been eluding him about the bodies in the fire. By not focusing on it, the answer had appeared, exposing itself like a tapeworm in the night.

It was the stiffness of the bodies. The rigor mortis. The state of rigor in both bodies was different. A lot different. It was different because the bodies hadn't died at the same time. If he remembered correctly, rigor set in about three or four hours after death and lasted thirty-six to forty-eight hours—maybe shorter or longer in the damned cold or the intense heat of the fire. Kneisser's arm had flopped down when Kennison had lifted it. Rigor mortis was over in him—*his* stiffness was from being frozen. The girl was in mid-rigor. Her head and arms were locked. Kennison did the math.

If Kneisser was on the far side of rigor, he could have been killed up to two days before. Kennison had examined the bodies at eleven this morning, about twenty-three hours after the fire on Sunday. Thirty-six hours before that would have been midnight Friday or early Saturday morning. Kneisser could have been killed by the bullet on Friday night or even earlier. Had anyone seen him since then? Had he asked? He didn't think so.

When exactly did he call his employers? Was that on Friday, before he was killed? Did someone overhear that call and kill him? For what? What the hell was at stake here?

The girl's death came after Kneisser's, as much as sixteen or maybe twenty-four hours after. If she'd died in the fire, that would make her twenty-three hours dead before Kennison had examined her. Rigor would still be in place, and it was. He couldn't move her neck when he tried to take her pulse after the sniper shot or check her burned body for bullet wounds. So, they didn't die together. Kneisser had died first by a day or more. Had she killed him and gone back to the scene to burn the evidence and killed herself in the fire? Was it an accident? Was it suicide? Did she do a Joan of Arc out of her own guilt? Why go back at all? Did Kneisser have something she wanted? Or know something that she needed to know?

Kennison paced the ground. Kenny Monk had suggested the girl was in love with him, enough to give up her pending marriage and seriously dent her relationship with a doting father. It didn't sound as though Fortier had any deep agendas where Kneisser was concerned, nothing deeper than obtaining an autograph, nothing more complicated than being an anthropology groupie.

Until the autopsy report, he could only guess at things. Other than the fact that they hadn't died at the same time, what did he know for sure? Kennison burned his fingers with his cigarette and tossed it angrily aside. Giles would tell him what he didn't know. Monteith said she was a hard worker, solid, without bullshit or ego. A lot of cops married nurses or doctors. They had similar lives. Both lived on the dark side. Both experienced death as a common event. Both worked strange shifts and spent a lot of time watching and waiting between sporadic bits of intense activity. And neither was quite sure why they sacrificed so much to do what they did. Except that Ginny was a nurse and turned out to have nothing in common with Kennison. Why was he always the goddamned exception to the rule?

He heard the ATV roar to life by the Kitchen Tent door and watched, motionless, as Ruby Cruz revved the machine and drove jerkily out of the compound despite his orders. Kennison stepped quickly to the side, putting Kneisser's tent between himself and the kitchen door. He watched the red taillight as she hit rocks and swerved dangerously, unused to the vehicle and the terrain. He saw Masterson's yellow tent shake, heard the rip of a zipper and the Factor stepping outside and swearing.

Both men, unseen by the other, watched the ATV brakes flicker on and off intermittently as the driver moved down the rough road to Hell. Masterson went back into his tent, mumbling to himself. Kennison cursed as he watched the rear lights of Ruby Cruz reach Hell and turn north beyond it, following the shore to Karl Kneisser's dig site.

Yellowknife, Northwest Territories

"Easy, Bev. Move around to the end there and hold his shoulders. Want some Aqua Velva?" Jennifer Giles's voice was muffled through her mask. The upside of waiting for the Kneisser corpse to thaw was its flexibility. The downside was its smell, a cloud of blistered charcoal and roast pork well past its best-before date. Giles kept a bottle of Tim's old aftershave in the medicine cabinet of the morgue washroom. The kids had given it to him for Christmas, a month before he was killed. In three years, she still hadn't used half of it. It only took two or three drops on the top of the mask near the nose to fight the odours of death. Besides, it reminded her of him, clean from a shower and shaven. Bev Williamson shook her head. The reek of Aqua Velva made her even more nauseous than the cooked flesh of Dr. Kneisser.

"Damn. It's a tough one. Damned flesh keeps peeling off when you try to get a grip. Press down, Bev. If you press down on his shoulders, I'll try to straighten him out." The assistant nodded and pushed down on the bearlike shoulders. Slowly, with some force, Giles was able to bring the corpse's knees and legs down to the level of the table. The fetal curvature of the spine wouldn't completely unwind, and the upper body rocked slightly.

"Have to cut him. Vertebrae fused in the fire, maybe. Check his temperature again, Bev. Maybe he's still frozen solid inside." Giles walked into the next room and searched through the tall beige office cabinet for the electric bone saw. It was a circular grinder Tim had bought at Canadian Tire, to which he'd attached a five-inch blade designed to cut plywood. It worked like a charm.

"Mario at the Tire'll be happy," she shouted into the operating room. "About the Home Depot not coming in, I mean."

"Temperature's fine, yeah?" said Bev. "Must have been the fire fused the spine like you said, Jen. Yeah, 'cept the Wal-Mart'll give him a run for his money anyway. He's got more Christmas decorations and lawn ornaments in there than tools and fishing gear. Used to be a hardware store in the old days. Now they've even got a bridal registry if you can believe it, eh? Pete Dexter and Pearly Gagnon signed up. Imagine getting a radial arm saw for your wedding present? Jeez. Anybody got me that, I'd cut 'em up with it." Giles walked into the operating room uncurling the cord on the saw.

"Better than an ugly lamp or another damned punch bowl. We got three punch bowls. Ever used a punch bowl? Right. Let's flip him for a sec." The two women rolled the body onto its side, and Giles deftly made two cuts at forty-five-degree angles to the spine. "That'll loosen him up at bit. Ooookay. Back over?" Bev nodded.

"No, wait. Let's get him on his belly, clean up the back of his head and see if there's an exit wound." They worked, but found none. "Still, the way a bullet can crang around inside, it could go in his mouth and come out his you-know-where. Ooookay. Over he goes."

"One, two, hmmppph." They flipped the Kneisser corpse on its back, where it settled solidly on the table. Giles jiggled the corpse's shoulder and seemed satisfied with the stability.

"So, let's have a look at this bullet hole," said Giles, moving around the table. "Better get your book, Bev." The assistant went to her desk and returned with a spiral-bound school notebook. Attached to the spiral with a paper clip was a cord. At the other end, with once-white adhesive tape, was fastened a ballpoint pen. She gathered the pen, opened the book and wrote the date.

"Neisser?"

"Yeah. With a K. Kneisser."

"German name?"

Giles shrugged. "Could be," she muttered, her mask up and her eye within an inch of the wound in the skull. "Gimme a swab, Bev. And some tweezers or something. The skin is like those red peppers you roast on the gas ring. I could use those sausage tongs at home to peel this black stuff off. Otherwise it cracks and breaks into little flecks and gets all over and into everything. Biggest tweezers we got, please. Thanks."

Giles cleared the burned flesh from around the bullet hole. "No visible burns or deposits," she said, "though it's hard to tell if any would have stuck with all this heat and skin loss. Still, I don't think he was shot from close range. Didn't shoot himself, that's for sure. Looks like it entered pretty much straight in. Gimme that metal probe thingee. Thanks." Giles inserted a thin metal rod that looked like a kebab skewer. "Goes in about three centimetres and a bit. Must've hit bone then and diverted. Grab the saw and let's see what we can see." Bev made notes and watched, writing with a clenched hand, her tongue stuck out the side of her mouth between her teeth. When the saw noise stopped, she sniffed with wrinkled lips at the burned-bone smell as Giles pulled the top of the skull away.

"Yukko. Heat must've boiled his brains, Bev. Sloppy seconds in here, that's for sure." Giles moved her hand in under the soft mass of brain tissue, feeling for a small, hard object. "You been to that new bakery at all, Bev?"

Bev wrinkled her nose, reacting either to the situation or the bakery. "Twice so far. They open early, like in France, the guy told me, eh? First time I just got some croissants—"

"Ahhh. What's this? Get me a steel bowl, will you, Bev? Big one." Giles drew out the brains of Dr. Kneisser and placed them in the bowl. Some phlegmy, noodle-like tendrils spilled over the edge.

"—real buttery and everything. Thought I'd make a treat of it once a week, y'know, get up early on a Sunday, get a couple croissants—they got good coffee there, too—come home, have a shower, wrap up in that terrycloth robe from the Holiday Inn in Lethbridge and just read the weekend *Sun* all morning long."

"Sounds good. 'Nother bowl, please. Small one. Thanks, Bev."

"Second time I went in, they had all these little round cakes behind the glass, eh?"

"Tortes?"

"Eh?"

"Tortes, I think they're called?"

Bev shrugged and moved around to see what Giles was digging at the back of the face for. "Maybe. Anyway. I go in and wait 'cause the place is crowded, order the croissants and ask the guy behind the counter—he's got one of those tall chef's hats on and an apron with blue stripes on it, *très français,* if you know what I mean—I ask him if one of these cakes is a cheesecake . . ." Giles extracted her hand slowly, making a small slurping noise, then a clang as a small, hard object rattled in the small steel bowl.

"Bingo."

"Yeah, so he stands up real tall behind the counter like, and puts his fingertips together like this, and with this little pursy-lipped look on his face, says in front of absolutely everyone there,

'*Fromage? Fromage? Mademoiselle.* In la Frawnce we eat our *fromage avant* the daysairt. Not *for* the daysairt.'" Giles moved over to the microscope on the countertop opposite the sink. "You believe it? I could have died right there, eh? I must've went red in the face. I walked out and forgot the damn croissants."

"So, 5.65 mil. That's interesting. Rifle. From the markings. So you don't think you'll go back?"

"Not on your life. After I left, I thought of a million things to say, most of them about him taking his effing *fromage* and effing retournaying to effing la Frawnce. What is it again? Sorry."

"It's a 5.65 millimetre. Found behind the sphenoid sinus cavity, just above and behind the front teeth." Bev wrote down the information in her notebook as Giles stuffed the skull contents back where she found them, washed her hands and changed gloves.

"We'll need to staple this skull cap back on, Bev."

"Sure. You gonna cut the chest now?" Giles nodded and Bev Williamson went to the sink and began washing the saw blade. "This one's thawing out," she said, pointing to colourless liquid running into the sink from the black corpse of Marie-Claire Fortier.

"I guess we'll have to pick up the pace here." Giles pulled crisp, black blisters of skin from Kneisser's chest, cleaning him up for the Y incision. There seemed to be an inordinate amount of crust near his chin where it rested hard against his breastbone. Bev came over, drying the saw blade and plugging the cord back into the three-pronged orange extension. Giles placed her finger under the chin to lift it away from the body and give herself some room for the blade entry at the collarbone. The head almost fell off.

"Sweet Jesus on a pony!" said Giles.

"Ewwww."

"This crusty stuff around the chin is burned blood, Bev. Lots of it. He's had his throat slit, almost ear to ear. Look at that cut. Jeez. Almost took his head right off."

"Slow down, Jen." Bev Williamson scribbled in her notebook. Giles leaned closer and prodded the man's neck, tilting his head back to see the extent of the damage.

"Jesus wept. A very sharp knife. See how it's shallower over here on his throat under the left ear?"

"Yeah. So?"

"That's where the cut started. I'd guess it could only have happened from behind, so whoever did it could use the body as leverage to cut this deep." Giles mimed the action, reaching from behind an imaginary body with her left arm and drawing a knife across a throat from left to right. "See how it's deep here on the other side? It only stopped when it hit the jawbone here." Bev nodded and made a snapping noise. Giles hadn't realized she was chewing gum.

"So whoever did it had to be right-handed, eh? That what you're saying?"

"Guessing, Bev. Probably."

"Anything else?"

"I'll bet this cut is the cause of death. Look at all the blood. The bullet entered his head after he was already dead . . ."

"Why would anyone want to shoot a dead man in the head, eh?" Bev put her notebook down and began removing her rubber gloves at the sink.

"Good question, Beverly. We'd better tell this Kennison about this right away. He's got a problem on his hands."

"You want me to call Dutch and get a number?"

"Yeah. This guy needs to know about the real cause of death here. Dutch won't mind the call. Margit'll be fast asleep. She'll deserve it after sitting my kids. Can you come back? I know it's your day—"

"Sure, but right now I gotta eat something or I'm gonna pass out."

"Me three. What's the soup, d'you know?" Giles headed for her purse.

"Minestrone. I got it. I owe you, Jen. No worries, eh?"

Victory Point, King William Island, Nunavut

The last tint of twilight was dissolving to black as Ruby negotiated the ATV north along the rough shore. It had been difficult enough on the so-called summer road, but here, off track on the beach, without guidance other than the black water on her left, it was tougher than Patel had described—or maybe he was stronger than she was. Her arms ached from wrestling with the handlebars as rocks and pockets of deep sand wrenched the wheels wherever they wished, threatening to break her wrists, twice ripping the grips out of her hands.

With the dark came the cold, or so it seemed. In this place, they were permanent partners. The ATV slewed suddenly, sharply, to the left, into the water. The seawater splashed on her leg, and she could feel the cold through the quilted pants of her ski suit. Her foot felt wet, but it might have been her imagination. She cranked the steering wheel to the right and struck a rock, stopping dead, stalling the machine. Her teeth hurt from the impact. It was an eternity before the engine started again. She could smell the gas fumes.

This was doubly a fool's errand, as she was both the fool who had initiated it and the fool who had gone. If it hadn't been for the tent, she would have missed it entirely and driven far to the north. The tent—probably Kneisser's, she thought, as Patel was anxious to leave the place and would have packed up already—was white or beige, light enough to attract what ambient light was in the air and make itself known. It seemed to have torn itself from its foundation and flapped noisily in the wind like a ghost beckoning her closer. There was no path visible from the shore to the tent, so Ruby dismounted, thankfully rid of the ride. Her biceps and shoulders ached, her thighs were sore and her butt had been less pummelled on a long weekend with a mean horse.

The small flashlight didn't have a wide beam, but it was enough to see the rocks lying in wait to trip her. There was no path that she could see. Every few steps, she looked up for the tent, making sure she hadn't wandered off track while staring at the ground. Her mind wandered to the cobbled streets of Ridgley's Delight. On closer inspection, the tent was ruined, left to flap like a tattered flag in the wind, more a site marker than shelter. It was nylon, not canvas, so it couldn't be that old, and the material was attached to black fibreglass poles bent over each other and firmly secured at each corner between rocks. A rough wooden pallet—where on earth did the wood come from?—served as a sleeping platform, and a tattered polyester sleeping bag was rolled at one end and weighted down by rocks.

Ruby was tired. She sat down heavily on a waist-high boulder in front of the tent, a rock that was depressed on top like a barstool. A sitting rock, she thought, like the one on the shore she'd crept to secretly between waiting tables in Maine, a place to think about boys and the way they made her feel. It struck her suddenly. This was Kneisser's seat, she thought. This was where the old man sat and stared out to sea, seeing the ghosts of the tall ships that had been frozen here, watching the wraiths of men approach across the ice cap, confident that survival was to be found ashore.

For a moment, the wind died. The tent stopped flapping and the small waves at the shore were muted by the viscosity of the water. The silence was somehow louder than sound, more powerful than noise. A calm came over her, a feeling of being somewhere safe, somewhere quiet and beautiful, like a cathedral, but without the artifice of architecture or the organization of adoration.

Just as suddenly, she wanted someone. A man. Harry. Someone. Maybe anyone. Her mother had embarrassed her as a teen by braying, usually in front of her father, that orgasm relieved stress better than most women knew. The tent flapped again as the wind came up, and she shivered in the seat. For a moment, she'd had something, tasted something perfect, wanted something specific, but now it was gone.

As she slid down from the seat, the flashlight picked up an unnatural reflection from the ground. By kneeling down and shining the light from angles between boulders, she saw a tool of some kind—a rough native tool, it seemed, that had either fallen between the rocks or hidden there. A flat piece of metal was inset on one end into a handle. The blade, if it was a blade, was stained black as if dipped in pitch and curved in a shallow arc at the end opposite the bone grip. It was as if it might be used to scrape hides or smooth wood.

She tried to move the rock that trapped it, but the stones were large and wedged together. Probably one of Kneisser's archaeology finds, she thought, maybe so common it was overlooked. Or maybe she'd found something he hadn't. For a moment, she felt the thrill of the find, a sense of how exciting it must be to be the explorer, to be the first, to be the one whose work or discovery changed history or opinion. It didn't last. The cynical Ruby returned quickly. If it was stashed at the foot of someone's regular seat, it was probably tossed there as an unremarkable artifact.

As her eyes became used to the dark, she saw a pile of rocks about fifty yards to the north, part of a ridge that ran inland from the strait and prevented those not on foot from progressing farther up the shore. She could hear, rather than see, small flags flapping on top of it, like the markers at Hell. She stumbled towards the ridge without using her flashlight, trying to preserve her night vision, staring into the dark. Her shins struck small boulders, and her ankle twisted when a rock rolled from under her foot. The cold made her shiver.

It was more tiring to reach the top of the ridge than she'd expected. Kneisser and Patel, she imagined, had laid out this grid and recorded the contents in each sector. This must be where the oak lifeboat remains were found. To the east was a pile of rock, heaped like a cairn. Closer, she saw that the rocks had markings on them—chalk or some other implement had named each one with letter and numbers, as if they were part of a three-dimensional puzzle waiting to be solved on a rainy afternoon. Beyond the pile was a depression in the ground, most likely the hole from which they'd been removed. Ruby shone her flashlight into the hole and gasped.

A perfectly formed skeleton filled the bottom of the hole—a man, she guessed, laid out on the rocks as if sleeping on his back. His arms were extended and away from his sides, palms down, as if he had fallen in backwards and reached out to protect himself. One leg was slightly bent at the knee, the foot turned outwards, suggesting he was about to roll over and sleep until late. Skin and even hair still clung to his bones. Ruby shuddered from the cold wind and from apprehension.

She knelt down and leaned forward, over the grave, wishing for a better flashlight. The body's clothes were peeled back from his body, probably by Kneisser or Patel. Was this the man who wrote the journal Kneisser found? Was this the grave he took it to? Ruby moved carefully down into the grave, lowering herself onto the boulders lining the crypt. It was warmer down here, out of the wind, as if the rocks had absorbed heat during the twilight. She trained the flashlight beam on the skull, trying to imagine what he must have looked like with living flesh and young man's hair, how he spoke with his shipmates and rode the seas, toasted the King or Queen at meals at cramped tables below decks, with pints of rum. She imagined he had been a good-looking young man who had broken girls' hearts, perhaps left someone pregnant or a widow, young children fatherless.

A side pocket of what must have been his coat or jacket had been sliced with a sharp knife or razor blade and folded back so that its contents could be removed without affecting the skeleton or its common shroud. This must have been the pocket that held the journal. Kneisser had cut it out and run to the satphone to call Dickerson in D.C. Was Patel here at the time? Did he know about this? He must. Ruby could decipher the events, and she was no scientist. Or, on finding it, did Kneisser sit in his rock chair reading, entry by entry, the story no one had heard before, imagining its author as a colleague, sighing at his innermost thoughts and frustrations put to paper? Did it say what Dickerson wanted it to say? Did it expose success? Or divulge failure that must be concealed? Most important, where was it now?

Ruby leaned closer. She pulled off her mitts and lightly touched the pockets of the clothes with her freezing fingers, knowing she'd find nothing but wanting to connect with this 150-year-old thing. She moved her index finger over what was once the cheek of a man with a gesture an observer might think a caress.

Her legs ached in the crouching position, and she leaned back against the tiered rocks on the side of the grave. She shivered again. The temperature seemed to be plummeting. She could hear the wind above picking up and looked to the black sky. There was no luminescence tonight from stars, no glow that would light her way to Heaven.

The climb out of the grave was tough-going. The rocks were untrustworthy, and she had to rock each with her foot before trusting it with her weight—a runner's fear of sprained ankles. She made a cursory search of the ruined tent, checking for inside pockets, pressing her hands on the rolled sleeping bag, feeling for something, anything, under the rough wooden platform in the dark.

There was no journal here. If this is where it was found, Kneisser or Patel had removed it, of course, not left it like the bones of its author. It seemed strange to leave the skeleton, the body, where it was, alone in the dark. She moved down the ridge as quickly as she could, almost running when she came to the shore and the ATV. The gravesite was pressing on her now, frightening her, making her feel like a small girl, alone and out of her depth. A fool's errand from the outset.

Throwing her leg over the ATV seat, she felt for the key and turned it. The machine roared to life, and she engaged the gears to head south. She'd forgotten how her biceps ached. Less than five hundred yards down the shore, the engine sputtered and died. The starter whined in the vast silence. She shivered and waited impatiently, tapping her foot, knowing she'd flooded the engine again. She tried again. Nothing. Just the screech of the starter bouncing off the rocks, disappearing into the sky like smoke. Ruby checked the gauges. The battery was good. The lights worked, and in their glow the gas gauge read empty.

It has been some time since I wrote, less a factor of nothing to report than a ~~grevious~~ grave hesitancy to write down what has occurred over the short months of summer. Even now, I am uncertain of my motives in writing this on paper, as it condemns me and others should this ever be read. I sit at a ~~mohagany~~ wooden desk in my library, mine because no one appears here but me anymore. I hold my pen, nib dripping black ink, yet my hand has no natural tendency to move it to paper. I must force the writing, as I must force myself to tell the tale. Even now, I wallow in the preamble, unwilling to begin. My friendship with the men, so recently a concern, is secured for all time, established beyond doubt, yet at the cost of my becoming an ~~anethema~~ anaethema to myself.

We are alone here, the Terror *seized again in the ice, this time ~~is~~ in a stretch of water named Victoria Strait after our Queen, bound earlier than expected in an autumn of extreme cold according to those who have been here before. Even my own memory, ever decreasing, reminds me that last year at this time we were circumnavigating Cornwallis Island, farther to the north, and, one would think, in colder climes.*

The massive locomotive engines designed to propel us through the ice have failed to do so, and we are too low on fuel to operate them with any degree of power. The Erebus, *if her intent was ever to join us, has not appeared. Speculation is the only topic of conversation below decks. Even the officers are silent and speak only to each other without smiles, through tight lips and with terse words that cannot be overheard. The kindest opinions suggest the* Erebus *was unable to free itself from the Beechey Island ice even during the summer months. The more malicious, Bealls included, if he is not indeed the sole source, insist we have been abandoned, that we are a death ship of sick men sent to die while* Erebus *and Franklin sail in another direction to conquer the Passage, perhaps to Melville Island.*

We are sick, each one of us to some degree, ~~Lathargic~~ Lazy and unable to concentrate. Already we have lost men to consumption. I have been unable, despite the terse instructions from Dr. M., to keep my thoughts of self-poisoning from the men. In fact, I believe we suffer from plumbism, that this insidious internal poisoning is from the ingestion of lead, whether from the pipes through which our water flows or the gobs of ~~soldier~~ solder sealing Goldner's tins, affects our bodies and our minds, although measuring the extent of damage of the latter is difficult, if not impossible. How does a madman judge the actions of another? The physical damage is obvious. That blue line I mentioned, now visible on the inflamed gums of many others, has, in fact, a name. One that escapes me for the moment. Is a symptom of lead in the bloodstream. Other symptoms include the nausea we experience, the insomnia and irritability that has us too often at each other's throats. One can only surmise at the extent of mental damage of men whose food supplies are killing them. Burton's Line is the name. Dr. Henry (I believe) Burton's discovery only a few years past. I suspect the food to contain parasites as well. Whether or not that is true, one cannot convince the men it is not. To compound this idiocy, we inhabit this death ship, designed by Barrow and Franklin and God knows what other fools, who experiment with real men as if they were mere rats in a scientific laboratory. The gallons of lemon juice we imbibe to prevent scurvy seem to have a limited life. Our teeth and tongues begin to blacken from the disease as our lips and gums pale from the anemia associated with poisoned blood. I am tired, always tired, and this writing saps me so that I continue only by habit. By lack of other exercise for my mind.

I dreamed last night, or perhaps I dreamed awake, of men and women with small children gathered on the edges of Pall Mall, dressed in the city finery of a Sunday afternoon. As we proudly passed, waving gaily from a ship mounted on wheels and drawn by horses. They stood as one to applaud brave sailing men, and only when they smiled did I see their toothless heads. Alice Lort or perhaps Lady Franklin bent to a female child, and called her Daisy and pointed at me in the parade. Hiding my blue-black mouth, I waved, and the dear child smiled with bloody gums and blackened tongue. I saw that it was the crowd that passed in motion, and we were static, frozen in ~~terror~~ Terror like remnants of their dreams.

Our anger is palpable, expressed more often and louder each day and with each new symptom. And who can blame us? We feel tricked and abandoned by our leader, if ever he was a leader. There is hate in the air, thickened each day by the bile and blood of the diseases that will kill us all. Still, in the manner of men either too brave or too blind to accept their fate—heroes by any other name—we attempt to adapt, to mend our ways, to survive 'til the ice melts and frees us, if only to return home toothless and aged, destroyed by an Admiralty who heaps praise on undeserving men. Men who should be charged with the abandonment and attempted murder of their crew.

Still, we try. (I am avoiding the tale, I know I am.) We do not drink the water from the tanks now, even that disabused of brine. We no longer sip the foul lemon juice. Expeditions collect piles of the surprisingly small amount of snow here and break off small chunks of the ice itself to melt for water. As for food . . . let me say that some insist, despite the obvious warnings, to eat from Goldner's tins. I am among them. It's that or try to live off chocolate and sips of port.

Or . . . Others have seen wild animals on the horizon~~, large po~~lar bears, foxes, hares, all white, all in nature's northern camofla camouflage. We have neither the clothing nor the weapons to kill game. We have tea. We have sherry. We have candles. We have books.

And we have company.

They hover on the horizon, closer one minute, farther now, as if the gusts of wind alone provide them cover to move inexorably forward. By the manner of their standing and walking, they are men, Esquimaux we surmise, drawn by the tall masts of the Terror, *a magnet to aboriginals desirous of barter, yet however wealthy we are with books and buttons, we have no food to trade, and nor do they.*

It was Bealls who suggested I kill one—who else? Bealls, who has presented me with the terrible opportunity to become one of his gang by dint of a hazing ritual unheard of in the meanest halls of Eton or Portsmouth. To them, murder is only sport.

Kneisser's tent at Heaven was made of green ripstop parachute material, or something like it. It stood apart from the other tents, zipper threaded with the yellow swatches of police tape he'd found in the crime bag. Ten feet away, he could hear the wind snapping the tape he had draped around Marie-Claire Fortier's tent. Dim light glowed through the yellow tent walls Kennison knew were Monk's and Masterson's, both taking advantage of the opportunity to be alone. Masterson had been angry at the delay in leaving.

The rest of the tents were dark. Kennison guessed that Anne Ferguson-Crewe would stay in the comfort of the Dorm Tent. Penilik was missing again, as if he wanted to bring his guilt to everyone's attention. All Kennison had to do was match the bullet in Kneisser's head—if it was still in there and he hadn't found an exit wound—to Penilik's rifle, and bingo, one death explained and the other probably an accident. For a moment, he wished he'd gone to Yellowknife for the autopsies. Followed the bodies. He needed to communicate with the coronoer as soon as that satphone could bear use.

It smelled like old man inside the tent, a combination of night sweat and stale farts, unbrushed teeth and foul breath that had leached into the bedclothes and tent fabric. Monk had delivered the catalytic heater as promised, so it was warm, but that only exacerbated the odour. Outside, the wind had shifted to the northwest, and even though the snow wall interrupted its direct force and the tent had its back turned to the constant western gusts, the temperature was well below freezing.

The tent seemed relatively windproof, and the sleeping bag, despite its smell, was a puffy, down-filled tube version you could snuggle into and zip tightly around your head. Top-quality stuff. You couldn't bring less to this climate. Kneisser had brought a few comforts of home, including an analogue travel alarm in a scuffed red case with gold trim and a thick foam pillow covered with a rough cotton pillowcase that looked unwashed even in the forgiving glow of Kennison's flashlight. Did he have another sleeping bag at his dig? Another tent? Ruby Cruz would know before he did. Kennison hoped she'd at least respect the rules of evidence and not mess up the site. He would grill her about Kneisser's long phone call first thing in the morning. He wondered what she'd done for the FBI.

The tent was reduced to two metres in diameter by the circle of smooth rocks that weighed it down. On the right side was the sleeping bag discarded on a thin camping mattress. The tent's left side was taken up with a substantial, brass-trimmed, blue metal trunk, two feet by four feet and a maybe a foot and a half high. On top of the trunk, suspended on insulated spider legs and encased in a metal basket, sat the heater. Kennison lifted it carefully by the legs and placed it on the floor at the bottom of the sleeping bag.

Despite the camouflage of bright brass corners, hinges and the large keyhole on its face, the trunk was unlocked. Kneisser had been a big man from the look of his curled, burned body, and the unlaundered XXL sweaters and turtlenecks in the trunk corroborated that. The trunk's interior smelled worse than the sleeping bag.

Kennison ran his hands under the clothes and into the corners of the trunk, but felt nothing out of the ordinary. No weapons, no secrets, no clues. The chest was lined with thin sheets of some inexpensive composite wood, and he rapped at the bottom, sides and back to expose hidden compartments, but found nothing. He'd need more light than the small flashlight provided to do a proper check. Daylight would be nice, but there'd be none of that until April.

He closed the trunk, gently lifted the heater and placed it back on top. Sweating now, he pulled off his coat. It was hot in here, verging on claustrophobic. There was no middle to the North, no comfortable average, only extremes: hot or cold, windy or still, alive or dead.

Kennison thought he heard a crunch outside, the squeak of a boot on cold, dry snow. He doused the flashlight quickly, flattened himself on the ground intuitively, and listened again. Twenty feet away, the crime tape on Fortier's tent flapped in the wind like plastic pennants at a used car dealership. Was that another squeak of foot on snow? Maybe it was Monk or Masterson moving back into the compound. Maybe Penilik had finally returned.

It could be anything, but he hoped it was human. He didn't need a confrontation in a flimsy tent with a polar bear. The great symbol of the Far North didn't discriminate between seals or hares or humans, or even other bears. Last week, the Yellowknife papers had run headlines about two female polar bears in Alaska devoured by a male. Maybe cannibalism was a Northern thing, thought Kennison, and the indigenous fauna were taking survival cues from the British Admiralty. He raised his head and listened, but could hear nothing inside the wind.

He turned the flashlight back on and resumed his search. Near the stained foam pillow was a soft-sided bag—a small backpack, modern, with Velcroed pockets designed for cell phones and iPods. They contained neither of those, but a cursory search inside the largest compartment turned up a worn hardcover copy of *A Guide to Basic Anthropology,* edited by Karl C. Kneisser, Ph.D.

He opened it to the title page to see when it had been published, but his eye was drawn instead to a scrawled dedication. "To Marie-Claire," it read, "With kind regards and best wishes for a successful future in the exciting world of anthropology." It was signed "Dr. Karl Kneisser" in a loopy, oddly pretty and well-formed hand. Not "Karl" or "Thanks for the roll in the hay, Karl," or "Love, Karl." What kind of a lover signed his name as "Doctor"? Most likely, there had been nothing between them. So why were they together in Purgatory? Not to give her this book—he didn't have it with him. Besides, he was thirty-six hours dead. Perhaps he was waiting until they departed to present it. Maybe he was too shy to give it. Maybe . . .

The sounds came as one, a unity of noises, a score for violence that defied sequence and amounted to death. Later, Kennison wouldn't be able to clarify their order, no matter how often he retraced the events. He had only sounds as a record. Being trapped inside the green tent made for a sightless experience, and a more terrifying one for it.

Running footsteps on squeaking snow. A rough deep voice yelled "Mountie," cuing a triple burst of rifle fire that ripped tent walls in counterpoint to a deep groan.

The treble tearing of nylon cued a dissonant dead weight that crushed the tent and triggered the percussive snaps of crushed plastic poles.

Shattered fibreglass batons whipped Kennison's forehead and neck. His own blood rained into his eyes. He dropped the flashlight, scrambling to find it, waving his hands crazily above his head like a blind conductor led by his band.

He burned his palm on the heater, knocking it off the trunk in a staccato of bullets.

Treble spits rang off the metal trunk.

Bass missiles buried themselves with anechoic thuds deep in something falling on top of him—something large, something already dead.

Kennison was knocked face down, twisting quickly, knowing he had died, wishing himself beneath the tent floor, smashing his right temple on a brass-clad corner of the trunk, his last conscious coda the segue between the high soprano keening of the wind and the thrumming plainsong pain of Lillian Ooqlooq.

I must tell it. I must tell what I did. In the name of my Child, I must tell it. To my shame. To my disbelief. Three of them, two inside a small snow house they call "iglu," one in front of the entry hole bending over a table of ice, scraping at animal hide with a curved knife. We wait behind a plate of frozen snow, tossed up by the compression of the sea below. We watch. The one outside yells something guttural, a summons, as the other two emerge, pushing long poles before them. Behind us, the tips of the Terror*'s masts angle north. Heaving ice has skewed the ship to port.*

My two companions stay back, Bealls' witnesses, I thought. One, called Scurvy by his mates long before it blackened his mouth, shivers in light clothes. The other calls himself Billy, crosses his arms for warmth and nudges me forward with his elbows until I growl.

My boots are thin, teacher's boots, not sewn for snow and ice. My uniform is made of thin felt, and even the greatcoat I borrowed was of little protection against the wind. My pistol, too, is borrowed, and I am not ashamed to say it shook in my hand as I watched the two who emerged with spears with sharp tips carved from bone affixed to the poles with sinew. They mutter to the scraper of hides and walk away in the direction opposite our hiding place. Billy's nudging is painful and tedious.

I move from behind the ice, goaded by Billy's elbow and the sound of Scurvy's few teeth chattering in the cold. The hide scraper maintains a rhythm of movement, back and forth, arms outstretched, hands crossed over the tool. I creep closer, the squeak of feet on snow masked by howling winds. I see the hide is of a large animal, a seal or a bear. My stomach aches with hunger, but the lack of blood on the ice says this is not recent kill. Perhaps some odd ritual where scraping brought luck to the hunt, or some aboriginal mumbo-jumbo such as British explorers discovered in African heat. Closer, pistol raised in the cold dark air, my hand shakes from the strain or cold or the moment.

I hear a song, a chant, a repetitive mumble, a rhythmic incantation in time with the rocking motion. Perhaps a prayer, if natives pray. I look back to see Scurvy and Billy nodding, motioning to me with their heads, arms wrapped around their bodies for warmth. Scurvy smiling, top tooth shining in light that seemed to come from the ice ~~on that~~ he leaned ~~which~~ on. The hunting Esquimaux are dots in the dark distance. The scraper senses me, smells my fear. Chanting stops and scraper begins a slow turn to me. Rather than look on his face, I shoot him in the side of the head. He falls to the ice, shudders once, and again, convulsed in death.

Hunters turn, drawn by the shot. I see them—or imagine them, I cannot tell the difference here—run over the ice, run in an odd side-to-side motion that seemed to absorb terrain and cover ground quickly. Too quickly. I run towards Terror, *slip on the ice and snow in thin leather boots,* tossing *the pistol away on the frozen tundra as if it ties me to the murder and I am absolved without it.*

The air I gulp is cold inside my chest. I hear Billy and Scurvy follow, grunt with effort. I look back; the hunter dots seem larger now, moving more quickly than we over a land of their blood. To my horror, Bealls' men drag the body of the Esquimaux by the neck of its hide cloak. It slips over the snow as if it has sharp runners. Evidence for Bealls, I supposed. But where is the seal? I might have known better. By the time we are hailing the Terror, *the hunters reach their iglu, where they stop, seeing the blood on the ice where their friend died. The brother? Their son? Bealls and his gang of perhaps twenty come down the ladders, Brandishing pistols and sticks and shouting to keep the hunters where they stand. My guts scream with a lack of breath and I collapsed on the ice at the bottom of the ladder to the deck. I was unconscious, or perhaps semi-conscious. For only minutes—any longer, I die from frostbite. Men were pulling me to my feet, patting me on the back, hugging me and whooping loudly. I cannot feel my toes. Above, on the deck, I see an officer look down briefly before averting eyes and moving out of sight. The body of the Esquimau is obscured by the group surrounding it, bending over it like at a Rugby scrummage, rearing back and cheering every time someone—Bealls, by his coarse voice—accomplishes some small task. I move closer, still winded from the run, still woozy from the faint. Men look up angrily, then change their sneers to smiles, part for me to pass, bang me on the back with their open palms, hero of the day. Welcoming me to their disgusting company.*

I was not sick. I did not vomit and I do not know why. I looked down through the crowd to where Bealls knelt over the body. It was a woman I saw, flabby brown breasts exposed, black nipples pointing to the black sky, dark skin steamed in the cold as Bealls cut strips of bloody brown flesh from her arms and thighs. Gently, proudly, placing each fillet of flesh on the ice, the men cheered, as if this was a white bear and not a woman. I did not vomit. God forgive me, but I was not ill.

TUESDAY, NOVEMBER 10

Yellowknife, Northwest Territories

Bev Williamson poured her coffee from the Tim Hortons cardboard container into a stained white mug with a photograph of a German shepherd on the side. "You want yours in a mug, Jen?"

Jennifer Giles was on her cell phone. They were almost finished with the body of Marie-Claire Fortier. The charred corpse was lying on its back on a stainless-steel table in the middle of the room. Dr. Giles hung up her phone.

"Bev, I have a feeling our Sergeant Kennison needs whatever we can give him as fast as we can find it, so let's finish up quick, okay?" Bev took a sip of coffee, checked her makeup in a small wall mirror, popped a sour cream–glazed Timbit into her mouth and joined Giles in the theatre.

"How went the Dog Derby, Jen?"

"Little Jen woke up to say she had her picture taken with a Mountie. 'Like Daddy all dressed up in his uniform,' she said, but she didn't seem upset about it. Maybe she thinks he's in Mountie Heaven, where they all wear dress reds and own black horses. No idea about the older ones. They were passed out when I got home and still asleep when I left. Same as always lately. Must've had a good time."

"Wonder how Marg Duchesne survived."

"Yeah, me too. That was Dutch on the phone. Wants to meet.

For breakfast. Can't sleep, I guess. He's worrying me. Looked like death at the dock last night."

"Maybe he'll buy."

"Fat chance, Bev. I know Mountie budgets. I want to be able to tell him our results, far as they go."

"So you want to cut now?" Jen Giles nodded as Bev went to fetch the saw. She'd already decided the girl hadn't been shot. And her throat wasn't slit, either. So far, it looked like she'd been literally burned to death. Bev licked the sugar glaze from her fingers, washed her hands in the sink and carried in the saw. Jen adjusted the overhead light and bent low to the table, bending the dead girl's head back. She ran her hands gently over the charred skull.

"Bev, hand me those tongs on the edge of the sink there."

"These things?"

"Yeah."

"Never seen these before."

"Brought 'em from home."

Bev handed Giles the sprung salad tongs, which she used to capture the edges of burned skin pieces and peel them back from the chest. She wanted to remove as much burned skin as possible as the charred flakes inside the body cavity just made the job harder.

"Work pretty well, Jen. We should get some for here."

"Dollar and a half at Kitchen Stuff. I'll donate them. Otherwise, it'd take three months and a dumpster load of paperwork."

"Plus they'd pay some scammer twenty bucks a pair, eh? Call it medical equipment." Jen made the Y incision, and the two women worked over the body silently for some time.

"Rigor's right out of her now. Let's take the lungs and see what's cookin.'"

"Bad joke, Jen."

"Sorry, Bev. Get that coffee for me now, will you."

"Milk today?"

"No. Black for me. Didn't get much sleep."

"Mug?"

"Sure. Thanks." Dr. Giles continued to probe the body, placing organs in stainless-steel bowls. She hummed to herself. The same tune over and over, leaning over at one point and calling, "Bev."

"Magnifier, please. Take a look at this." Bev came over with a rectangular magnifying glass and bent down to see what Dr. Giles meant.

"Holy cow," she said. "Bad girl. Wait'll the Sergeant hears this one."

"You seen him yet?" said Giles.

"Who?" Bev shook her head.

"Kennison."

"No. You?"

"No, but I heard he's sorta cute. Single, too. Might be worth one of the famous Williamson wiggles, Bev."

"Go on, Jen. I don't do that."

Jen Giles winked at her. "Yes you do, girl, and you do it well."

"Well, we won't be seeing him today. Not in this weather."

"Oh, here's Dutch. Can you handle this?"

Bev Williamson nodded and yawned. "Be back as soon as I can. You'd better try calling that satphone again after this."

"What's up, Dutch? You look like you lost your job." Inspector Duchesne raised his eyebrows. Jennifer Giles didn't know how close she was to the target.

"Thanks, Sue." He took the oversized menus and handed one to Dr. Giles and buried his face in the other. "All-day breakfast for me. Bacon. Over easy. Brown."

"'N' for you, Doc?"

"Benedict. And some more coffee please, Sue." The waitress scribbled and left. "Best Hollandaise in town. Including my house. Why so glum, Dutch?"

The Inspector toyed with his car keys on the hard tabletop. "Complications. Couldn't sleep. Worried about Ivan, about how some killer could get within thirty feet of my sergeant, about who would want Kennison dead . . ."

"Is that all?" said Jen Giles. Then, seeing his face, she added, "Sorry." Sometimes the doctor's timing was wrong, even if her intent was good. "Sorry, Dutch. I know it's difficult for you, 'specially because we can't raise him on the satphone. We've been trying all night."

"You have anything to tell him?"

"Yeah. The professor was killed by a slit throat with a sharp knife from behind by a right-handed person."

"But the bullet hole?"

"Shot after he was dead, if you can imagine. Definitely not the cause of death."

"He missed this at the scene?"

"He couldn't tell. Kneisser's chin was pinned to his chest, frozen solid. Plus his spine was fused, so he couldn't stretch him out. Not his fault. Amazing he found the bullet hole in the damned dark." Duchesne nodded and picked up a piece of crisp bacon with his fingers.

"Anything on the young lady?"

"Bev's cleaning her up now. Not shot. Lungs clean—like, no smoke inhalation, I mean, but best guess is she died in the fire.

Boiled to death rather than the normal smoke death. Not pretty. Oh yeah, and she's pregnant, for what it's worth."

"How pregnant?"

"A month, maybe a little more."

"So it happened while she was here?"

"You're the detective, Dutch. I'm just the pathologist. You have anything from your boy up there?" Duchesne felt his shoulders slump, the weight of his uniform suddenly too much to bear.

"A bit of background on some of the people there. Minor stuff. Nothing that points at a killer. At least not the killer of the people in the fire."

"Why do you say that? What do you mean?"

Duchesne shrugged. He wished he could talk to someone about all this, but that way led to disaster. "Lot on his plate. Two bodies. Being sniped at. Ivan's plane must be there somewhere, and so, I guess, must Ivan. No backup. No communication, and now Turqavik . . ."

"Turkey what?"

"Turqavik. It's a fringe native group—at least it started out that way. Sort of developed as a kind of political group about the same time Nunavut was formalized. Inuit pride. Lords of the barren lands, that sort of thing. Since then, it's become more focused on land claims and Northern sovereignty—"

"Isn't everyone? If we get one more Ottawa politician up here jabbering about the ice cap melting, palms trees around Frame Lake and Canadian sovereignty in the North, I'll throw up." Dutch wasn't smiling.

"Turqavik—means homeland, or something like it—has become a real threat."

"How d'ya mean?"

"Lise Jensen, the Constable in Ross? Called her cell last night but didn't get an answer. Called again, and a nurse at the clinic there finally picked it up. Jensen is in hospital. Knifed. Life-threatening injuries. Moment to moment, they say." Jensen had visited Yellowknife, been to Dutch's house, and Tim and Jen had been invited. She was young and a Scandinavian beauty, with long, white-blonde, blunt-cut hair wrapped in a ponytail and a smile that made her pale blue eyes sparkle like a Scanian sky.

"I'm sorry, Dutch. Anything I can do?"

"Not in this weather, or I'd ask you to go to Ross with me."

"This Turqavik. Did they do it?"

Duchesne nodded wearily and sighed before looking up at her. He pushed a plate of congealed egg yolks to the side, his hunger muted. "Seems so. Seems their tactics have shifted from speech making to harder-edged activities, most of them far below our radar. They're still about native pride and noble history, but it's much more in your face now, as if they'd undergone training—you know, like the terrorists taught by Cubans in Africa . . . that sort of thing. There are small cells, some of them public, some secret, in just about every Northern community in the Territories and Nunavut. Two, three, four people who go about their daily business in the community but who meet at night and plot things."

"Like what?"

"Like violent takeovers of local political organizations. Like replacing land claim conferences with confrontational acts, like replacing discourse with armed standoffs. Rumours are that they're tied in with some FLQ nationalist resurgence in Québec and maybe with some Akwesasne-type Mohawk radicals who wrote the book on getting attention on the Mercier Bridge in the '90s."

"Jeez. So why did they hurt Jensen?"

"I sent Kennison to cover at Victory Point because Jensen is expecting an Ottawa minister to fly in this afternoon and—"

"Another one of the sovereignty speechifiers?"

Duchesne nodded. "She also heard from sources that there would be a confrontation at Ross Haven by the local Turqavik cell—"

"Tossing tomatoes? Or seal blubber?"

"This isn't so funny, Jennifer." Giles winced and gave an apologetic smile. "Jensen's a good cop. Head on her shoulders. Does her job well. She heard that Turqavik were planning to target, maybe even assassinate, the Ottawa pol. Get some attention for their cause."

"Jeez. Up here?" Duchesne nodded. "Sounds like the States. Or South America. Or Québec maybe. Not here." Giles had only finished one of her eggs. The Hollandaise sauce curdled on the other. She pushed them away and sipped her coffee. "Is this secret stuff you're telling me, Dutch?"

Duchesne smiled wanly. "Not generally known. We've been watching Turqavik here for some time—the Northern divisions, I mean. It's real and it's operating, but most people don't know about it. If they'd killed the pol in Ross, it would be known around the world."

"But they almost killed Jensen instead. Why, do you think?"

Duchesne shrugged again. "She's unconscious. The nurse doesn't know. Someone found her on the edge of the village. A trapper, I think. He saw three people in the distance, heading north."

"For where? It's the middle of nowhere. There is nothing north of there."

"Victory Point."

"What? Why?" People at other tables looked up. Duchesne leaned forward and lowered his voice.

"Because there's something there that is more important to them than a major strike at a high-profile politician."

"What is it?"

"I don't know. And if Kennison knows what it is, he doesn't yet know they're coming for it."

Victory Point, King William Island. Nunavut

Kennison regained consciousness on the folded-out futon in the Salon Tent. Boxes and bookcases had been re-stacked or moved to give him room. Beyond the canvas roof it was dark, but it was always dark, so it was impossible to guess what the time was. His watch was on his wrist, but he felt too tired to raise it to his eyes. Besides, his left hand was freshly bandaged to the wrist and his forehead felt constricted by something. He raised his right hand to feel a bandage around his head as if to confine the memory of what had happened. When he tried to sit up, the futon cover slipped beneath him, forcing him to put his bandaged hand down for balance and making him wince with pain.

He must have called out, because Lillian Ooqlooq opened the door from the Mess Tent and shuffled into the room, wearing the smell of food on her cotton dress and the weight of the world in her face.

"You feel better, *pukitalik?*" Kennison nodded. Better, if conscious was better than unconscious. She was a short woman, as wide as she was tall, with a face the colour of nicotine and a manner of holding her mouth so you thought she was smiling. She'd called him by the Inuit name for Mountie. Literally translated, it meant "stripes," like those on the breeches of the original North West Mounted Police a century before. The Inuit had long memories.

"I think so, Lillian. What happened?" Tears welled in her eyes but seemed suspended, as if too viscous with grief to run down her cheeks.

"Sad time, Mr. Mountie. My fault. I brought Wayne here with me to take him away from bad friends, from bad drugs. Not just glue and gasoline in Ross now, Mountie. Drugs from the south. Pills. Bad friends followed him here, and now he is dead."

"He's who fell on the tent? Wayne fell on me? Wayne is dead?" She nodded and sighed, the persistent bend of her face making her seem happy despite her pain.

"Turqavik shoot him. Shoot you. Mr. Poncey in his tent, Mr. Kenny, too, ran out and helped me bring you here. Put you to rest here, *pukitalik*."

There was something niggling again, something nibbling at the edge of his mind like the rigor mortis thing. Something that had happened before he lost consciousness, something in the sound sequence of Wayne Penilik's shooting that bothered him. It wouldn't come, and his head ached from the effort.

"The men who followed him here. Is that who I've been seeing in the distance? The ghosts on the horizon. Men hunting Wayne?"

"They killed him. But they were not here to hunt him. They were here because he called them here." Kennison was confused. Things didn't make sense. Kennison gave up propping himself up on his elbow and sunk back to the mattress. Lillian adjusted the blankets and the slippery comforter that covered him.

"Let's start again. Who are these men, Lillian?"

"Turqavik."

"What's Turqavik?"

Lillian sat on the chair Kennison had used for the interviews, her hands limp in her lap, her eyes down, reticent even in mourning.

"Men who think the North is for them to own or trade for money. Turqavik gangs are across North in villages, like secret clubs. They plan to take Nunavut for themselves, and more. These three from Ross Harbour, our village."

"What does 'Turqavik' mean? Anything?" The woman nodded, staring at the end of the futon rather than looking at Kennison.

"Inuit words mean many things. *Turqavik* is where a man feels at home with no thought of going anywhere else. It is a place of birth, a—"

"Native land?"

Lillian looked at Kennison, all her years in her eyes, and nodded.

"Yes. A land you love. They make this a joke, I think."

"I'm sorry about Wayne."

Lillian shrugged stoically. "Wayne was young. Not smart. Wayne wanted to be Turqavik. Thought them big heroes, saving the North for Inuit, not for Canada. But they are lazy men. Drinkers. Talkers. Troublemakers. I brought Wayne here to be away from that, to hunt on the land like his fathers, to understand what this place is to us, to live off the land like we have for generations, since before the Englishmen came and died here."

Kennison swung his legs to the floor and sat up. He felt woozy for a moment, dizzy, but not sick or in much pain. His burned palm hurt, and his forehead itched when he furrowed his brow. He had a headache, but a superficial one, not as deep as a hangover.

"Where is Turqavik now?"

The Inuit woman threw her short arm vaguely to the north.

"Out there. On the edge of sight. They have guns. They will be back here for what they want." Was it *him* they wanted, wondered Kennison? Had the men who hired the sniper co-opted these Inuit rebels with some promise of reward?

"Why did they kill Wayne, Lillian?" Kennison didn't expect the mere question to break the dam, but Lillian wept instantly. Tears poured down her face, and yet she made no sound or attempt to stem the water that dripped from her round cheeks and nose to her dress. She stopped weeping as abruptly as she began, as if there were a finite amount of water allowed to pass through her eyes, as if she must conserve the resource for later use. She sniffed once.

"He was coming to you. Wayne was coming to tell you things. That's why. They killed him for that."

"What things?" The woman sniffed again and wiped her sleeve across her broad nose. She didn't answer, but she may have shrugged. "Where is Wayne—Wayne's body?"

"Wrapped in a tent—professor man's tent. His soul is gone. Reborn in a child, we say, maybe this day. I will take him home to his mother, my daughter. She'll bury his body at her church." She stood quickly, called by a smell of spitting bacon that made Kennison's mouth fill with saliva and his mind with memory, the smoky comfort of the kitchen after Sunday mass when the nuns let him help cook breakfast. The solace wasn't really about the bacon—Sundays were holy days, meaning no visitors, no foster parents shopping for lost boys, no leaving. He shook himself back to the present.

Had this Turqavik shot and killed Kneisser? What did the old anthropologist have that they wanted? And how would they know he had it? Penilik. That must be it. That must be what Lillian meant. Wayne Penilik had told them something was here that would interest them or support their agenda. The thought process scraped the inside of his skull. He forced his thoughts forward, squinting with the effort. Penilik had known what they wanted, but he was killed trying to tell Kennison. The boy must have suffered a change of heart. But why? Whatever it was, whatever they sought, they hadn't found it or they'd be gone, not out there watching, like Lillian said.

In one of the other compound tents someone sang a song—a child's song, or a hymn, perhaps—but the melody was hidden in the wind.

Victoria Strait is our prison. Surrounded by miles of ice ~~indistinguis~~ same as ~~from~~ land, coldest anyone remembers, yet who remembers. Wild game gone, ice too thick to hunt for seals or fish. Idiocy of libraries and high teas. I've lost what the V. calls "élan" and with it any joy in writing this. Dreams of fame from words are foolish dreams. I write more by habit than reason or desire. We sad representatives of Victoria's Navy, trapped unprepared in a land that cannot support itself, let alone we foreigners, nor those out there on the land who rely on its meagre offerings. Still they hover there, watching. Do they wait for us to die? Do they plot our sorry deaths? Are we a solution for their dark, cold winter? I shiver when I glimpse them, or think I do, and not a shudder from the cold.

Winter passes slow alone, hidden in my library, sitting daily at my bile-stained desk, reading adventures that pale beside my own. What will the child think, my Daisy, when stories of her father's survival reach her pretty ears? And what of Alice? How might she suffer as mate of a murderer? I daydream walks to Old Wives Lees along the Chilham path, Alice smiling from behind as I hold Daisy's impossibly tiny hand, both wary of the brambles that might scratch her perfect skin.

My inclusion in Bealls' group pales beside the murder of the Esquimau woman and witnessing the harvest of her flesh. The habit has expanded, I am sick to say. I have heard rumours it is not only lone Esquimaux preyed upon but crewmates near death or recently passed, targets for meat eaters who refuse the tinned food they insist is killing us. Eat the poisoned flesh of men, think it purer than the food that killed them. A man devours a poisoned man, adds his toxins to his own. Bealls' argument that human flesh is safer to eat than Goldner's pies is a spurious one, at least where the men of this ship are concerned. The Esquimaux are, perhaps, a healthier option. They do not run away. Where would they go? I think I see them in small groups, on the horizon, obscured by dark and blowing snow, staring towards the Terror. *What are they thinking? What do they think about? Are they simple, tribal people? Perhaps survival is their single role. Perhaps the murder of one of their women is a more natural event to them than it can ever be to me. Man is hungry. Hunger kills. Man must eat to live. Perhaps they are watching us now, stomachs retching with hunger, waiting to cull the weakest from our herd for their own supper, their own survival.*

I wonder if they taste differently than we. Oilier, I think. Fishier, given greasy skin and diet, reliance on blubber and fish. Perhaps we taste like sweet tea and scones or sherry and biscuits.

Dreams continue, although to call them dreams is to suggest they occur at night when I sleep. I do not sleep, and it is always night. They occur when they will, even awake and walking the ship. Lady Franklin less and less, her admonitions pale beside my actions, still floats above the ice, wagging her finger, rebuking me for things I have not done. She's not alone. I have seen Miss Alice Lort, her naked breasts taut with mother's milk, gnawing like an animal on red meat. She turns to me slowly, smiling like a whore, hair matted and teeth stained red. Blood runs down her chin onto her pure white shoulders, and splits like a field stream to make its way around her heavy teets. She waves her meat to me and I see with terror it is my child, as a chorus of Esquimaux prevent my approach, chanting, applauding survival at any price.

We wonder aloud about Erebus. *Are they are freed from Beechey's ice? Or if they sailed west, have they conquered the Passage to laze on Island beaches wearing little? Laughing in the light and warmth, fat with fresh food as they beg smiling brown women to let them sleep in the shade of tropical trees.*

I cannot say the officers know what is happening below, if they are turning a blind eye. Perhaps some of them too are tempted by the taste of men, or perhaps they live in ignorance. To tell them would be to demand they act, an unwelcome call to action. Informing would be at the cost of one's life. Survival takes on many unexpected forms; the Cerberus between ourselves and Hell wears many different heads. I have little energy. I am losing weight, by diet or disease I cannot tell. My stomach aches and my bowels cannot decide on solid or liquid waste. The entire ship smells a pisser, perhaps an abattoir. Even in my library the stink seeps, unqualified by the once favoured smells of books or furniture. I open tins with difficulty, with tools designed for other purpose and fool myself ~~into believeing~~ that, by leaving the portions soaked in solder, I do not contaminate my guts. A conceit preferable to the inevitability of death, I think. I no longer drink the lemonade, and the shadow of scurvy shows on the back of the tongue, a macabre complement to Burton lines.

Sleep is the cosmos of new demons to be battled until blessed oblivion scours it of dreams.

Kennison walked into the Kitchen Tent with purpose. Lillian was pulling fatty bacon off the grill with tongs and laying it on layers of paper towel. Eggs were already broken into a large metal bowl with a question mark of ersatz milk and grains of black pepper on the surface. The coffee urn belched like an incontinent dog. It was pitch black outside the door, but that could mean anytime from late morning to early afternoon. In the light spilling from the kitchen, Kennison could see the green-wrapped body of Wayne Penilik lying on the snow.

The Turqavik group were out there waiting for something, something that was important enough to them to kill one of their own. He shuddered. Maybe *he* was the something. The people Ormerod and others had conspired with had a long reach. Maybe their arms stretched to the Arctic, mustering forces unknown to most. Like Turqavik. It seemed unlikely, but the threat, whatever it was, was real. Time to circle the wagons if it wasn't already too late.

"Where are the others, Lillian?"

"Mr. Poncey and Mr. Kenny are in the bunkroom. Mrs. Doctor Anne sings songs in the other. Mr. Trevor is asleep there, too. Not with Mrs. Anne." Kennison couldn't tell if she was being funny or not, which seemed unlikely in her grief. Her face was passive except for the permanent smile of her mouth. Kennison hadn't been the first schoolboy who thought Sister Elizabeth's twisted grimace was a smile, but when he'd wrongly answered her geometry question and smiled back in collusion, she'd hit him with a yardstick and a "Don't you grin at me, young man."

"And Ms. Cruz?"

Lillian's face fell, shocked, as if she'd forgotten the American woman. She shook her head and her eyes darted as if embarrassed, panicked.

"I haven't seen her. Long time now. Sorry, Mountie."

"I saw her leave the camp on the ATV." He held his arms wide, palms down, and twisted his wrists back and forth. "Yesterday? End of twilight? Is the machine here? Is she missing?" Lillian shuffled across the Kitchen Tent and opened the door. A fierce, cold wind, carrying snow and ice pellets, filled the tent with air, pushing the roof upward. Visibility outside was zero. Lillian fought against the wind and slammed the door closed. The roof sank in again.

"No ATV. No American lady. It's a bad storm." She moved towards the Mess Tent door, then a step back, a dance of indecision.

"We'd better find her, Lillian. Fast," said Kennison. "And we have to get in touch with Yellowknife right away. Whatever it takes. Maybe they know things we don't. If these Turqavik are out there and want something we have, or they think we have, we need some help. I'll wake up Masterson and Kenny. You get Patel and Dr. Anne."

In the Salon Tent, Kennison quickly pulled on dry socks and his boots. He felt better than expected. What little sleep he'd had was intensified by the density of unconsciousness, and he felt more rested than since he arrived yesterday. Still, the lights had coloured haloes around them and no amount of blinking would clear his vision. His head still ached, although he'd removed the bandage. He banged on the frame of the bunkroom door, shattering the dark quiet.

"What the fuck is it? Jesus, it's like fuckin' Piccadilly in here." Masterson sounded more frightened than angry. Panicky, even. After what had happened to Kennison and Penilik, who could blame him? "Who the fuck's there?"

"Kenny. Masterson. I need you in the Kitchen Tent. Now." Kennison turned away. Not ten seconds went by before a disgruntled Masterson and a sleepy Monk entered, pulling on their jackets for warmth.

Lillian came in from the Dorm Tent, followed by a yawning Patel and Dr. Ferguson-Crewe in a surprisingly soft, feminine robe and girly slippers. Nobody looked happy, and Kennison was about to make it worse. In the kitchen, the bacon congealed on the paper towel and the eggs in the bowl, mixed now, remained uncooked.

"I know we've all had a shock with Wayne's death, but we have an emergency. Two, in fact. Big ones," said Kennison. Lillian banged thick cups and saucers together and poured coffee for all of them. Anne Ferguson-Crewe seemed oddly detached, humming to herself. Playing another role, perhaps. Kennison couldn't tell whether she was listening or not. They sat loosely around the table that only forty-eight hours ago had included a newly garrulous Kneisser, a pert Marie-Claire Fortier and young Wayne Penilik.

"Listen carefully. All of you." He waited until Anne Ferguson-Crewe stopped humming and made eye contact with him. "I have to contact Yellowknife as soon as possible. Emergency number one is that the people who killed Wayne Penilik are an arm of an organization determined to get something they believe is in this compound—"

"Oh, hell, that—"

"Quiet Masterson. Listen to me. They call themselves Turqavik and are an offshoot of violent Inuit. In any other country, they'd be called terrorists. Wayne Penilik was an aspiring junior member, until tonight—last night." It was always night. Only the residual bacon smell made it morning. Kennison was starving. "For reasons we don't know, he broke from them and was shot dead when he came to tell me something. It's not a great leap to suspect they killed Dr. Kneisser as well. What we don't know is why. What it is they want. If you know, now's the time to spill it."

There was that something he couldn't pin down, nagging him again. Each time he mentioned Penilik dying, it got nearer, but it wouldn't come close enough to make sense.

No one spoke. Ann Ferguson-Crewe was quiet—oddly so, thought Kennison, her sharp pink tongue pressed between thin blue lips. She looked towards the Kitchen Tent door as if waiting for someone. Monk looked stricken and stared at the chair where Fortier used to sit. Kennison thought he saw Patel glance quickly at Masterson and look away, but the Englishman ignored him, staring down at his boots, arms folded across his chest, still angry. Or was it something other than anger? Was he scared? He should be.

"Masterson, I need to talk to Yellowknife right away. In any context, these Turqavik people are dangerous and we need backup. Fast. Whatever they're after here is valuable to them. They're not against killing any one of us for it—remember that Penilik was one of their own."

"Well, whatever they are and whatever they want, there's no way we can communicate with anyone beyond flying out of here, and that's not happening in this bloody storm. I've said it a thousand times—when are you people going to get it? You can't charge a solar phone with no bloody sun. We shouldn't even be here now, for Christ's sakes."

Patel nodded to emphasize agreement with every point Masterson made. He seemed relaxed, less tense now for some reason, his superior, sardonic smile back in place.

"There has to be some way to charge the phone," said Kennison.

"Yeah, sure there is, mate. The generator—the fucking generator you used at Purgatory and burned up all the bloody petrol for."

"Is there any other source of fuel?"

"There were emergency backup containers stashed in Purgatory, but they went up like fireworks.

"The ATV," said Monk.

"What about it?" asked Kennison.

"If the ATV has gas, we could put it in the generator and use it to charge the satphone." Kennison looked at Masterson, who nodded, then stared daggers at Monk for being such a smartass.

"There's another bloody problem," he said. "Where's my ATV?"

"That's emergency number two," said Kennison. "Ms. Cruz took the ATV last night and hasn't returned." Then it hit him. "The plane. The little plane."

"What little plane?" said Masterson.

"The plane the sniper flew in on. With Ms. Cruz. The pilot must have faked the takeoff, or been told to. The shooter came overland to target me, and Wayne Penilik shot him—killed him. So there must be a plane stashed down there somewhere, and planes have gas, right? Petrol, right?"

Patel stood up, nodding, eyes wide. Masterson nodded to himself, twisting his mouth, dropping his chin as if surprised he didn't have the only brain in the building. Grey Anne stared at the floor, moving something across it with her slipper.

"Krevaluk's plane. Ivan's Cessna 185," said Masterson. "Auxiliary tanks, too . . ." A thought struck him. "Christ Almighty. Ivan could be in it. Could be freezing to death."

"And he could be dead. Face it, Paul, this is important. I need you on this right away. You and Kenny here go and find that plane. Suck some gas out of it into whatever you can find. There's no time. Get that generator cranked and that phone working, whatever it takes. Got it?"

"What about Patel?" said Masterson.

"Take him with you. Dr. Ferguson-Crewe?" Grey Anne looked up. She smiled at Kennison, raised one eyebrow. Working on being an enigma, thought Kennison. "You remain here and keep watch for this Turqavik. Set up a warning system. Do you have a weapon?"

"Good Lord, no. What would I do with a—"

"Masterson? Give her yours."

"How did you know—"

"Just do it. Lillian and I will go after Ms. Cruz."

"Lillian? I don't think—" Masterson was frowning.

"Lillian knows more about survival in this damned place than all the rest of us put together," said Kennison. "It's her land. If the poor bastards who died out there on the shore had half an ounce of Inuit intelligence, they'd be alive and heroes of their time, and we'd all be home in warm beds."

Kennison hunched low behind Lillian Ooqlooq, trying to make himself as small as she was. In the winds that whipped them, he saw the advantage to her physiology—a low, rollicking profile hugging the ground so that the bitter knife's edge of the weather passed above her rather than biting her in the face.

It must have been like this when the Fortier girl was trapped, he thought. He tried to emulate Lillian's rolling waddle, her side-to-side motion as she moved persistently forward. Kennison didn't know whether it was Inuit technique or just the way she was built, although her grandson had walked like that, too.

They decided to hike the northwest hypotenuse of the triangle rather than walk the longer distance west to Hell, then north on the shore to Kneisser's site. The upside was reduced distance; the downside was heading directly into a fierce wind. Kennison didn't think it was snowing, but in the dark it was difficult to tell. There was ice and snow on the wind—he knew that. He just didn't know if it was being recycled from that fallen on the ground. What did it matter? Lillian was only fifteen feet ahead of him in the dark, but he watched her carefully as every few minutes her squat form would be veiled by the gusts of snow. They didn't speak. The wind was too loud and there was nothing to say.

He didn't envy Masterson, Monk and Patel trying to find

the Cessna in this weather, although Masterson should know the few places where it might have been stashed. At first, they'd have the wind behind them, but carrying the large red gas cans back to camp would be painful. Kennison sang to himself, under his breath, the song Father Fahey had taught them all on the hikes to the quarry. *Valderee. Valderaah.* He couldn't remember the name of it. Something Swiss or alpine. It seemed to fit the pace, even in this damned place with its wind that pushed you backwards if you stood up in it.

Kennison bumped into Lillian's back. The Inuit woman had stopped suddenly and raised her hand, pointing to her ear for Kennison to listen. With the song in his head and the keening of the wind, he heard nothing at first; then a snapping, a cracking of a whip, like gunshots in a city alleyway. Was it Turqavik? Had they come here, to Kneisser's site, to find what they were after? Had they harmed Ruby Cruz? Killed her too? Kennison moved forward, following the sound until he saw the torn white tent flapping, snapping in the wind. He felt Lillian behind him.

While they stood there, the wind, as if furious at their arrival, ripped the final shreds of nylon from the poles, tossing them high and far into the void of its own storm, exposing the wooden platform and forlorn bedroll weighted with large rocks. Kennison saw Lillian cross herself out of the corner of his eye. He sensed there were spirits here he could not supplicate. He pointed Lillian towards a rock ridge barely visible to the east, then to his chest and to where he thought the shore might be. She would search there. He would search the shore.

The wind was colder here, near the water, than inland—if that were possible—as if it absorbed the sub-zero frigidity of the black sea as it frothed the water into gooey whitecaps that seemed frozen in movement. Kennison fought his way to the shore, knowing he was there only when he walked into the icewater. He turned south and finally made out the shape of the ATV, snow and ice crusted on its seat, frozen sea spray trailing inland from its handlebars like streamers on a child's bike. Ruby Cruz was not here.

Kennison returned, finding the walking easier with his back to the wind. Lillian waited for him, agitated, uncommonly panicked. She held the bedroll in her arms, the wind ripping at it as if to claim it back. She motioned for Kennison to follow quickly and climbed the slippery rocks to the ridge. Both peered down into a pit that reminded Kennison again of the quarry. But this was no industrial necropolis. This was the grave of a man. Through the horizontal snow and ice, Kennison made out the outline of a skeleton, and beside it, hunched like a hedgehog, like the corpses he found waiting at Purgatory, was the ski suit and hot pink accessories of Ruby Cruz.

Kennison held his arm out and lowered Lillian into the pit. He followed, slipping on rocks made slick with blowing ice. It was warmer in the grave, out of the wind, below the rage of the storm. Lillian already had Ruby Cruz lying on her side, hand inside her jacket, feeling her breast for a pulse. She nodded to Kennison as Ruby opened her eyes for a moment. She was alive, but barely. Lillian took Kennison's hand and guided it inside Ruby's clothes. Kennison felt the pulse, slow but still pumping. Her flesh was cold, the goosebumps large on her breast; her skin was puffy, tan tissue tinted blue in the flashlight beam.

Kennison searched the files in his brain, trying to recall a hundred courses in a hundred smelly church basement classrooms, falling asleep in stifling summer heat as instructors droned on about hypothermia while green flies hit their fat heads on spotted window glass. He knew it was a condition that set in when the body temperature fell below normal, when the cold was such that the body itself could not replenish its own heat. Eventually, the organs shut down. Shivering would help—goosebumps would form to raise body hair and provide an insulating layer. But hypothermia still killed.

Ruby smiled, as if in a dream. She shivered suddenly, violently, without control. She tried to speak, but her words were as cold and sluggish, as thick and inaudible, as the roiling sea. Kennison began to rub her arms.

"No," barked Lillian. "Don't rub. Take the clothes off." Kennison stared. It was thirty-five degrees below zero. Lillian was stripping the clothes from Ruby, rolling her onto the bedroll laid out on the flat platform shared by the skeleton. "*Your* clothes off. Fast, Mountie," she said. "No time. No time." Kennison had a vague memory of why she was demanding this, but he couldn't place it, couldn't bring the logic forward.

"Now, goddamn. Now, goddamn." Lillian was angry, shouting at him, pulling at his coat. Quickly, he ripped it off, then his sweater and turtleneck and undershirt. "More," she said. "All clothes off." The cold was so intense he couldn't feel it. He undid his belt and dropped his trousers, lying down beside the now-naked Ruby as Lillian wrapped them both in the cold bedroll and piled blankets and their clothes on top of them, covering them from head to toe.

Kennison shivered uncontrollably at first, but his body felt hot compared to the deathly cold that came from Ruby. Heat transfer—that's what Lillian inherently understood. Use his heat to bring Ruby's up to a state where she could be moved somewhere warm, somewhere safe, to complete her recovery. Lillian was muttering to herself in Inuktitut. A prayer, perhaps. Kennison could smell Ruby's hair, feel her head on his chest, her breasts against his belly. He felt a stirring, utterly unexpected in a grave with a near-frozen corpse. Oh Jesus, he thought. Am I some kind of necrophiliac? Do cold, dead people turn me on?

He felt her breath growing warmer on his chest, then the press of her breasts as she shifted, moving her hips against him, feeling his heat as he felt hers.

Spring.
Warmth of the sun, with life-renewing powers. Lost two fingers on right hand, frostbite, one on left, with another due for Dr. P.'s snips. Three toes on my left foot.

Write on foredeck coil of rope, one day hauled to raise a sail To catch a wind and take us home. Pain of a removed digit is unspeakable. Times six agony. Toes affects balance out of all proportion. Only the plan keeps me sane.

I look northeastwards to where the Erebus *lies, less bound by ice as we on the* Terror, *But trapped just the same. Arrived five days ago, upon us before any raised alarm. Her Officers already walked to land, built a cairn, left a note, the conceit that others will find it or care. The presence of* Erebus *puts the lie to all of Bealls' talk. An evil man, incarnate. He watches me always, smirk on his lips, as if he has some purpose yet unshared.*

News seeps that Erebus *was trapped at Beechey. Not abandoned us as a ship of death, followed as soon as she was able.* Erebus *crew as ill (and angry) as we. L. looks ghastly, emaciated and black-faced with scurvy. Most wear blue gums like toxic identifiers, pain and sickness more obvious by the way they move, rolling their shoulders, hunched like old men they have yet to become. We resemble prisoners freed after years of captivity, with nowhere to go, no sense of haven, but back inside the gaol cells we ached for so long to escape. Those to whom freedom is a curse and a confusion.*

We are 105 men and officers together, meeting on the ice between the ships. Twenty-one have died since the three we left on Beechey. Some say the deaths are natural, if death from poisoned food and quiescent lemon juice is natural. If young men dying is natural. I followed Bealls and his men with my eyes, whispers to their peers, separating with nods of agreement and grim faces. I wonder if they share their terrible secret with their friends on Erebus, *proselytising their new diet with sneers, insinuations of weakness for those who don't concur. The Esquimaux are on the horizon—more of them now that the* Erebus *has come—constant reminders of my sin, watching without respite.*

Daisy dances with me, shiny patent shoes standing on my boot tops, as I hold her clenched hands high and move my feet to a new waltz, careful not to step too far. Her little legs move in time with mine and her laughter lifts my soul to heaven.

Bealls has a plan, revealed to us below decks after the sun set this afternoon. It's another contagion, I know, but despite my distaste for the man and his relentless quest for the hearts and minds of other men, his idea seems to be our only way home. A seizing from what Bealls calls this "mad old man." A mutiny.

It was for perhaps only an hour or two that Kennison and Ruby traded heat for cold, cold for heat, as the storm wore itself out over their heads. All the while, Lillian had chanted, an intelligible drone, an elegy for saving the living and respecting the dead. Now Ruby slept in the Dorm Tent, a hint of colour back in her face, snoring softly as Lillian sat at the end of the cot, adjusting blankets like the mother of a sick child, measuring every breath, transferring the power of her grief to the tending of the living.

Kennison slumped, exhausted, near sleep, on a table in the Mess Tent, arms forward, head resting on his arms. Carrying Ms. Cruz on his back from Kneisser's site to the compound had sapped the last of his energy. His head still ached where he'd struck Kneisser's brass-trimmed chest, and the blisters on his palm oozed clear liquid onto his sleeves as the bandage had fallen off somewhere along the trail.

Beside him on the plastic, flowered tablecloth was a thick cup of coffee gone cold and a saucer with the long ash of a forgotten cigarette leading like a spent fuse to a burned filter. In the centre of the table was an implement, a stained, rounded blade beaten from rough metal, a bone handle fitted opposite the blade.

Ruby had been conscious when they left Kneisser's site, conscious enough to mutter something Lillian understood as Kennison shivered uncontrollably while pulling on his clothes in the grave. Lillian had walked down the ridge towards the tent platform, glancing back often, guided by Ruby's weak hand signals. Finally, she'd bent down in front of a tall boulder, wrestled with some rocks and come up with an implement that, from where Kennison dressed, looked like a small plate.

Up close, it was some type of native implement, the metal rounded at the sharp end, the opposite end in a protective piece of antler or bone. It looked as if it could be designed to scrape the flesh from hides or chop blubber or vegetables with the rocking motion of a chef's knife.

"*Ulu,*" Lillian said, pointing at the blade. "*Ulu.*" Kennison guessed that was what it was called.

"*Ulu,*" he said. Lillian nodded, showing her teeth.

Cruz seemed all right. She was alive, which she wouldn't have been if they'd arrived an hour later. While they lay in the grave beside the skeleton, the storm had passed and, apart from the small drifts of snow left on the ground, the going was much easier on the return to Heaven. Kennison was beginning to understand why the camp's name was apt, compared to its surroundings. He had followed Lillian, whose rollicking waddle found paths between rocks that Kennison couldn't see with Cruz thrown over his shoulders.

Despite their bedroll intimacy, Ruby Cruz was shy on their return. Her physical movements, even those of her brown eyes and long black lashes, were still slowed as if she'd suffered a stroke. What few words she spoke were slurred. Kennison wondered if it would stay that way. There was no question it had been very close; she'd been in an advanced stage of hypothermia and, with possible cardiac damage and the interruption of blood flow and oxygen, could easily have suffered permanent brain damage. The only possible upside of the cold was that it had prevented some of the cellular damage that oxygen deprivation caused at warmer temperatures. Wait and see, said Lillian. Wait and see.

Kennison raised his head and stretched his neck from side to side, staring at the *ulu* on the table. The black stain on the untreated metal blade was blood, he was certain. But whose blood, and from how long ago? Was the knife modern, still used to scrape or cut? Or was it something people commonly found at Arctic archaeological sites, like lead Union bullets at Gettysburg? Kennison ran his thumb along the blade, mindful of his burned palm. The metal was extremely sharp, honed like the axe of a lumberjack.

He shook his head, less to clear his thoughts than to admit defeat. Without including the sniper, he had three murders with no known motive, and now a possible murder weapon with no damned victim. The sight of the long ash in the saucer made him want another cigarette. There were only three left and he closed the pack. He might need one later. He might be here forever. He already had been.

The sound of Lillian shuffling back to Ruby Cruz was drowned out by the sudden roar of a generator being started in the yard. The Kitchen Tent door flew open, ballooning the canvas roof, and Masterson, frost on his exposed hair and crusted on his mustache, stomped into the room, sneering at the makeshift ashtray on the table with the portentous malevolence of an ex-smoker. If he saw the *ulu,* he didn't comment.

"Bloody Cessna was in Couch Cove. Driven right up on the shore. Ivan Krevaluk still strapped in his seat with his throat slit like a farm chicken. Poor bugger. Wife's due any day now, I should think. Body was frozen solid. We left him there. Plenty of petrol. We got enough to fire the genny. Find the American woman?"

Kennison nodded. "Near frozen to death. At Kneisser's site. ATV ran out of gas, I think. She'll survive."

"We've enough petrol for the machine, too. More where it came from. Bloody brilliant idea of yours, Kennison. Don't know why I didn't think of it. I'll send Monk up to get the ATV going, shall I? Needs to get away, that boy—getting weirder every minute. Weeping and laughing, talking to himself—or to her, maybe . . ."

"Who?"

"The girl. The dead girl. Must have been his girlfriend, I think, going on about all kinds of mumbly-fumbly shit as to how they're going to change the world together. Damned shame. People should leave the fucking world alone. Stop saving it. Let it change at its own pace." Kennison hadn't heard Masterson say so much in one breath. He glanced outside, towards the road to Hell. Were there Turqavik out there, waiting?

"Yes? Lillian?" The Inuit woman was nudging him gently.

"She's awake, Mountie," she said, tossing her head towards the Dorm Tent. "Wants to talk." Kennison stood up.

"How long for the phone charging?" he asked Masterson.

"Half hour. Maybe a bit more. You can use it before it's fully charged, but it's hard to hear a bloody thing over the genny, and the cord's not long."

"As soon as it's working. Let me know. It's important."

"Better bloody be, after what we went through." Masterson stomped into the kitchen and banged cups and saucers under the coffee urn. He was the kind of man who, despite his average size, took up space, made rooms feel crowded when he was in them. Perhaps that's why he was in the North—there was enough room for him here. Kennison could hear the single shower running in the Wet Tent. Patel, maybe, or Grey Anne.

Ruby Cruz was sitting up in bed. Kennison pulled up Lillian's chair beside her, putting the *ulu* on the side table and motioning for the Inuit woman to sit by the door and monitor their privacy.

He checked behind the hanging blanket in case anyone was resting there. He didn't need Masterson, or whoever was in the shower, eavesdropping.

"You okay, Ms. Cruz?" said Kennison.

Cruz nodded. She looked pale, but the deathly blue tinge in her lips and the skin under her eyes had receded. "Thanks to you. That was . . ." She blushed, and the sudden flush of blood through her cheeks looked good on her. "That was an experience."

"Yeah, well . . . it was Lillian's idea. She—"

"I think you saved my life, Sergeant. I remember trying to get out of the wind. I remember being cold, but I don't remember . . ." Her eyes teared and she sniffed. Lillian appeared like a silent angel and handed her a tissue. It struck Kennison that these very different women had established an odd bond, a connection through cold. Then again, maybe they weren't so different. Ruby blew her nose. "Um . . . did you see the knife or whatever it is?"

Kennison nodded. "Covered in blood, but I don't know whose."

"It was right below a rock, sort of a seat that I'm guessing was Kneisser's, near his tent platform. Blood all over the rock, too." Kennison recalled the black bib on Kneisser's burned body, the unnatural fetal crouch with the chin pressed hard to the chest. Had he missed something? Had he missed *everything?* Had he been so taken by finding the bullet hole, by the death not being an accident, that he missed the actual cause of death? Was Kneisser the missing victim of the Inuit blade? Even if he'd been rattled by being the sniper's target, there was still no excuse for missing a cause of death, especially one so damned obvious. He felt the blood drain from his face and wondered if Cruz saw it.

"Why are you here, Ms. Cruz?"

"I think you can probably call me Ruby now."

"Why are you here, Ruby?"

She looked away. Under the blankets, her hands moved over each other as if she was washing them. When she looked back at Kennison, it seemed she'd made a decision. Kennison saw that she had black-olive eyes, nice eyes. Her hands went still.

"Kneisser found something—something he thought extremely valuable. He called Dickerson—Keith Dickerson, my employer, my boss—to tell him about it. They played me a tape of the call. Dickerson and a man named Fernandez—security type—sent me here to get Kneisser and whatever he found, to bring him back, make sure he brought his treasure to the people who paid him to find it. We didn't know—*I* didn't know he was dead until I got here. My people still don't know. I should call—"

"What was it, Ruby? What did Kneisser find?" Again, a hesitation followed by a decision.

"A book. '*Ein Buch*,' Kneisser said. A journal. A diary type of thing, huh? Kneisser was excited by it, and I got the impression he wasn't excited by much. My employer wants it back badly."

"Why?"

Ruby rubbed her hands again under the blankets.

"To do with the Northwest Passage, the sea lane through the ice up here."

Kennison nodded, saying nothing. Motive at last. His emotions were crashing into the inside of his head and each other, the recognizable pride of discovery in a three-car pile up with the shame of his ignorance and the embarrassment of others' betrayal.

"AEI wants to prove that the Passage was discovered before Canada was a country so that Canada can't claim ownership of a waterway established by international powers. Or . . ." She hesitated.

"Or what?"

"Or wants to destroy any evidence that proves otherwise," she said. Kennison looked at the blankets, seeking something neutral so his mind could massage the message without complication. His hand stung and felt wet with blister juice. He pressed it to his trousers, but they would not absorb the fluid.

"Who else knows about this . . . this journal?"

Ruby shrugged and looked to Lillian, who shook her head.

"You tell *me,* Sergeant. I don't know. I've been trying to find out. Maybe no one but Kneisser knew."

"And whoever slit his throat with this knife." Kennison picked up the *ulu* with his bad hand and touched the blackened blade lightly with his fingertips. It would be a simple matter to find out whose blood it was, but Kneisser's sounded like a safe bet.

"Someone here, you mean?" said Ruby.

Kennison nodded, playing with the *ulu,* turning it in his hands. "Someone here, or maybe Turqavik, if they've been here that long." He tossed the blade on the blanket. As if he'd cued an explosion, the tent ceilings billowed to their utmost as a door somewhere in the compound burst open and Masterson bellowed like a bull.

"All right, you fucking bloody low-life bastards. Who took my fucking book? Which one of you fucking bastards took my fucking book?"

Billy has not reappeared. Bealls says he is in chains on Erebus *for cannibalism, under orders from Commander Franklin, denied food other than Goldner's and liquid other than lemon juice. Sentenced to that which was provisioned to save our lives for years. It's said he will be hung by the neck from the second spar on the mainsail mast, unexpected use for the same coiled line we thought would raise the sail to take us home. We wait in fear to hear if Billy's brother gave names other than his to Franklin or to Captain F. or others on that ship.*

I do not sleep in expectation of a knock on the library door, and my dreams broken by those of Royal Marines binding my arms and marching me off to stand on trial.

We meet at night in the hold beside the impotent locomotive. Candles yellow-light the faces and cast hunched shadows on the hull's sooted oak as we sit cross-legged, listening to rough whispers of Bealls. Promises of escape, of heading home under free sail, running fast where no ice interferes, are punctuated by creakings of the hull, filling each of us with hope that ice is melting and will free us soon. There is no longer thought of going forward, only of returning home. We have pistols and some rifles, some cudgels and native spears traded in friendlier days that we have secreted (Lady Jane, forgive me) in the Library, as no one comes here. L. has used his classroom for like purpose on Erebus. *The plan is simple enough.*

On the 11th day of June—Charles O., the Erebus *Purser, has mapped the days—Officers from both ships are to gather on the ice after midday. Commander Franklin and the Captains have arranged to pose for a Daguerreotype image showing them and their ice-bound ships. They say Franklin has a heightened sense of recorded destiny since the shoe eating. After the photograph, as they are called, all officers will board* Erebus *for tea.*

While the officers are on the ice, posing in the cold to make history, we will disembark the Terror *on the starboard side. Out of their sight, we will make our way with arms, behind hummocks of ice and snow, to the* Erebus, *where her men will haul a few of us aboard. The rest will remain on the ice, hidden by the ship itself. Those on* Erebus *will gather armed on the main deck, hidden behind masts, lifeboats, rigging. When the officers have mounted the portside ladders, the men on the ice will round the ship and prevent them from reversing. Men on the deck above will move forward, trapping the officers on the long ladders, where they can be easily disarmed, flies in a web, with no option but to surrender.*

It's a plan that no one is capable of disputing, and Bealls is full of himself for that, even smiling which distorts his scar and turns his face into a grotesque mask in the candlelight. Tonight he called my name and that of Scurvy and Stockton. We three are to be hauled aboard the Erebus *before the mutiny. Scurvy and Stockton are to release Billy from the brig. I will have a major role as well. Bealls' broad wink and grotesque smile do not promise consolation, yet the larger promise of freedom outweighs my qualms.*

With God involved with other men than we,
I think on Daisy's dance to set me free.

Except for Ruby, who was confined to her bed, they entered the Mess Tent from three directions. Kennison and Lillian came from the Dorm Tent, where Lillian had tucked Ruby in and wished her sleep. The raging Masterson burst in from the Kitchen Tent and, wrapped in a striped towel with an armful of clothes and peeking through the connecting door to the Wet Tent, was a dripping and terrified Trevor Patel.

"Which one of you mealy bastards took my fucking book?" Masterson was red with fury, spitting his words, pounding a fist on the Mess Tent table so that the saucer ashtray rose high and flipped, salting the tabletop with ashes and smashing into pieces on the floor. "Was it you, Patel? You fucking Indian giver. You, Kennison? It's fucking theft, you know. Taking a man's private property. Where's that goddamned American bitch? Where's fucking Ferguson-Crewe? I want a meeting. Now. Everyone, goddammit."

"What book, Mr. Masterson?" Kennison's even tone was enough to counterpoint, if not defuse, Masterson's anger. His red face paled and his shoulders sagged suddenly, as if he was in pain from saying things he wished he hadn't. "Sit down, Mr. Masterson. Now, please." Kennison had his right hand on his holstered 9-millimetre Smith and Wesson and opened his jacket to show it. "Sit down, please, Mr. Masterson. Mr. Patel . . ." Trevor Patel moved towards the Dorm Tent. "Sit down, Mr. Patel."

"But . . . I'm not—"

"Sit down *now,* Mr. Patel. You can dress here. No one is leaving this room right now. Lillian, get Ms. Cruz please. Does anyone know where Dr. Ferguson-Crewe is?" Heads shook. Patel stared at the floor, where a puddle formed at his feet. "Check the Dorm Tent, please, Lillian. Kenny Monk?"

"ATV," muttered Masterson, almost inaudibly. The drone of the generator outside forced everyone to speak loudly. Patel tried to slip on his underwear under the towel, one leg, then the other, his dignity lost and his face unforgiving of that. Masterson breathed deeply, sitting at the table, calming himself, perhaps realizing his temper had caused another unthinking mistake in his life, senselessly brushing the loose cigarette ashes into a pile with the edges of his hands.

"What book, Mr. Masterson?"

Lillian came into the room slowly, leading Ruby, who had a blanket wrapped around her shoulders. Both took seats at the table. Kennison looked up and Lillian shook her head. No Grey Anne in the compound.

"A book I have. A book of mine. A book that's important to me. Someone's taken it. They have no right. They . . ." He looked up at Patel, who would not meet his stare. "Ask Mr. Fucking Patel what book, why don't you? He sold it to me."

Patel rose quickly, half wet, half dressed.

"Sit down now, Mr. Patel. Ms. Cruz, check these men for weapons, please." He watched while Ruby threw off her blanket and stood, shakily at first. She made Masterson and Patel stand and patted them down. She knew how it was done and did it thoroughly, shaking her head to say they were clean. The process seemed to give her strength, as if the source of her weakness was lack of purpose. Kennison signalled the men to sit. He stood. "Talk, Mr. Masterson. Tell me a story." Masterson looked up and turned his head slowly towards Patel, who stared back with trepidation mixed with hate.

"Sold it to me. Manner of speaking. As good as, eh? Owed me." Then, more to Patel than to Kennison, "Fair and fucking square, mate. It's mine. Fair and fucking square."

Through the Salon Tent door, Kennison thought he saw movement on the horizon. "Lillian? Check outside, please. Mr. Patel? Explain. *Now.*" Patel was in the midst of pulling on a heavy knit patterned sweater, fully dressed now except for his socks and shoes. The face that appeared through the sweater neck was one Kennison hadn't seen before, the face of a different man, a weak, sneering face without charm, bereft of the dazzling smile and flashing eyes, a face twisted into a pursed pout, whining like a trapped rat, shrinking against the tent wall.

"I didn't sell it. I traded it. I owed him money. Too much money. More than tuition, even. More than my parents—"

"So you gave him this missing book to cancel the debt?' Kennison looked from Masterson to Patel. Masterson said nothing. Patel hesitated before nodding yes. "Where did you get this book?"

"From the dig, of course." The boy was angry now that denial was taken from him. "Where the hell d'you think? At the site. The one Kneisser and I excavated—mostly me. Marked and piled rocks for weeks and weeks until we found the body, but it wasn't Franklin like he said it was. Just a nothing sailor, bones and skin and bits of hair. Another damned skull staring at the bloody dark. Book was in his pocket. Didn't matter a damn to the geezer that it wasn't Franklin. Still thought he'd found the big prize—"

Kennison tossed the *ulu* on the table. Patel stopped immediately, staring at it, stunned. Kennison squared his shoulders to Patel, who looked as frightened as he was angry.

"So where is it now, Mr. Patel?"

"I . . . I told Anne that Masterson had it. The book, I mean. She must have taken it. I told her to take it. That . . . that . . ." he pointed at the *ulu* as if it was a talisman.

"Thieving bastard," said Masterson, standing, fist raised at Patel.

"Sit down, Masterson. *Now.*" The man sank back into his chair. "Did you kill Dr. Kneisser, Mr. Patel?" Patel sprung to his feet in a leap, tossing the round tabletop over Kennison, Masterson and Cruz with one motion. Masterson's eyes were peppered with ashes. Cruz lost her balance and fell to the floor. Kennison reached for his pistol, but Patel was across the Mess Tent and out the Salon Tent door, bowling Lillian Ooqlooq over on the way, before he could unholster it.

"I'll get the thieving bastard," said Masterson, wiping his eyes as he rose to his feet.

"No. Not necessary to chase him, I think." Kennison held up Patel's socks and boots, then tossed them on the table Cruz had righted. Kennison went to help Lillian and whispered to her.

"Anything out there, Lillian?"

"Turqavik," she said, and held up three fingers. "Three here. I saw only one. By the Hell shore. Closer now."

June 11, 1847

The day of atrocity, the day I will never report, for I would rather die than carry such infamy in my soul. This is not a day that scars me with the brutality of killing bulls, or the gory senselessness of others. The horror is my own, and of me. I care not what happens now, care nothing about who leads, who follows, who favours me, dismisses me. This irrevocable guilt carries with it a strange freedom. For I have only the sovereignty of my soiled soul, liberation from attitudes and views of others for the first time in my life, for no one detests me more than I abhor myself.

I have killed Commander Franklin. In currying favour, in weakly becoming Bealls' Punch, clad in frosted motley, I have allowed him to use me as his weapon. My books do not help—they are preposterous in light of my reality. Friends, I have none. Those who think my actions heroic are fools. Those who despise me cannot match my self-revulsion. Perhaps by putting these words on this page, I exorcise them from my psyche, yet by leaving them to be read I condemn myself to a deserved death.
To write words no one will read, to confess to crimes no one will prosecute, to offer rationale no one (including me) will credit, is

to wallow in a slough of self-pity that need not be shared. By my script, I am tired and unwilling to write. And my supply of ink is mercifully low, as if that is what drives me to record as best I can with grater effort than of late.

The day saw the sun circle the southern half of our sky, darkening only slightly as it slipped to the horizon, yet never fell below it. The constant light, as the persistent dark of winter, gives an otherworldly feeling.

At midday, the officers descended the ladders to the ice. I had not realized—nor had others I overheard—that so many were ill, near death from the same toxins we had been ingesting. They descended slowly, legs cramped by inactivity, lips drawn back over gums with the effort of lowering themselves, exposing the blue lines and black scurvied mouths we thought were our private chattel. Any anger mustered to drive my purpose dissipated by the sight of a self-defeated enemy. It was not until we were safely unobserved and gathered behind the hull that we were informed that Commander Franklin had not disembarked, that he was ill and lying still in his stateroom. And it was not until we were hauled aboard that Bealls told me my job was to murder him.

I did not simply agree and get on with it. Though that will not save my soul. Bealls leaned close, face sweating, breath rank, whisper spraying my cheek with spittle, telling me my refusal would see me damned as a coward. I said I did not care. Closer he leaned, so close I could feel the bristle of his beard on my cheek and smell the tooth rot from his mouth, the urine on his clothes. I heard ladders creak as officers climbed aboard, the stronger pushing the weakest up before them. There was no banter, no quiet laughing or exchanges that men of similar station share after a group activity. I heard the rush of feet on ice as men circled the bow. I heard their shouts as they shook their fists and weapons, the dismayed and broken sighs of the officers trapped. Scurvy and Stockton had disappeared. Bealls' breath, thick as custard and rotten as a corpse, told me that failure to perform this simple task would result in my deserved death for killing the woman. I remember the precise moment. I am not lying. I remember the confusion of emotions, the horror of the task, the trap laid for not performing. With a pistol pressed into my palm by my tormentor, I stumbled towards the stern. I cannot remember my legs being directed by me, and cannot recall cutting my hand, re-opening the rough sewn stub on one of my removed fingers, ripping it on something that makes it bleed profusely still and drip on this page when I squeeze the pen. I cannot remember walking down the passageway to the ornately glassed door of the Commander's state-room, nor striking the loyal guard unconscious, nor opening the door and entering the room. I remember only the smell of camphor mixed with other medicines, reducing the opulence of the quarters to the meanness of a Hammersmith hospital cell. I believe I saw the Commander open his eyes, but I am not certain. He lay on his back under blankets. Bloated, incapable of standing or walking. His face was long unshaven and his finger nails long and twisted and dirty. His untrimmed hair hung forward, struck to his fore-head with his sweat, more a forgotten prisoner in a Spanish gaol than the Admiralty's pride, their chosen Commander to find the Northwest Passage.

I moved closer, feeling again the pistol in my left hand, on which I have enough digits remaining to hold it and still have finger for the trigger. As I approached the bed, he expectorated a toadlike gurgle of slime that dribbled from his bloodless lips and clotted on his hairy cheek. At that moment, his bowels released and he filled his bed with shit and piss, the viscid vacuity of his long life. Did he see me? I do not know. Did he fear me? I do not know. I did not fire a shot at him. I could not, whether or not he was dead. I cared not. I fired a bullet through the open stern porthole, masking the stink of medicine and viscera with burned sulphur. I approached him and, God forgive me, ripped the stone from his fat neck as evidence of my task. The thin gold chain broke easily. The gem is black and smooth, mottled in spots with translucent white and with a startling red centre. I put it in my pocket and I walked out the door, shutting it carefully behind me. Surprised by the unconscious body of a guard. I moved purposefully to the deck, where I could breathe the cool air before I filled my mouth with sick and understand what Lady Jane chastised.

"Hello?"

"Hello?" The voice at the other end was barley audible over the static. The drone of the generator didn't help, either. Kennison tried again, louder.

"Hello? Sergeant Kennison here."

"Sergeant Kennison?"

"Yes?"

"This is Inspector Duchesne, Kennison. About time we heard from you."

"Satphone's been down, sir. Low on sunlight and gas here. Had to siphon some from a Cessna."

"Ivan Krevaluk's?"

"Pardon, sir? Losing you, I think." Kennison walked around the compound with the phone, seeking a sweeter spot for the signal. He signalled Masterson to turn off the generator motor, which he did with an I-told-you-so purse to his lips.

"Ivan Krevaluk's Cessna 185?"

"Yes, sir. Pilot found dead in his seat. Throat slit—"

"My God. Poor Mims. . . The sniper, I'm guessing. Your sniper."

"Pardon, sir? Losing you. Sir, I need—"

"I understand we have more than an accident on our hands."

"Yes, sir. At least one of the two shack victims was killed before the fire occurred—"

"Better than that, Sergeant. Killed twice. Let me put Dr. Giles on." There was static and the sound of a clatter at the Yellowknife end.

"Sorry. Hello? Hello? Sergeant Kennison?" The weather above was clearing. In any other part of the world, it might have been a nice day. This place was all right when the weather was reasonable—beautiful, even. It was cold, but it didn't seem as cold as when he'd first arrived. Was it only yesterday? Surely not.

"Yes ma'am. I'm here. Heard of you, Dr. Giles. Glad you're on this."

"Thank you, Sergeant. Heard of you, too. We've completed the autopsy on this Dr. Kneisser and the Fortier woman." There was a swishing sound in Kennison's ear, annoying, like a radio mistuned.

"Yes? Sorry, you're breaking up."

"That better?" It wasn't, but he said yes. At least he could make out what she was saying. "The cause of death was not—repeat, *not*—the bullet fired into the left front quadrant of the skull, Sergeant. That bullet entered the skull after death. Repeat: after death." A cold sweat spread from Kennison's throat to his chest. Giles continued.

"A 5.65-mil bullet was retrieved inside the skill behind the sphenoid sinus cavity, just above and behind the front teeth." The 5.65 was military. He'd fired thousands of them from his army-issue C8, some into people. That thought raised another in his mind, but he couldn't move it forward.

"And that was not—repeat, *not*—the cause of death?" He knew what was coming, what he'd missed.

"Affirmative, Sergeant. The man's throat was slit—ear to

ear—with a very sharp knife. The cut was . . ." Static washed over the conversation like a wave.

"Hello? Hello? Sorry, Doctor. I lost you."

"Where?"

"The man's throat?"

"The man's throat was slit—ear to ear—with a very sharp knife. The cut was made from the left ear to the right. From behind, I'm thinking. Quite deep, almost severing the head. Not your fault you missed it. The head was tucked down in the fetal position and the body frozen solid. Didn't notice it ourselves until the body thawed."

"I have the weapon," he said.

"Beg pardon?"

"Tell Inspector Duchesne I have the weapon. An Eskimo—I mean, Inuit—knife. An *ulu,* it's called. Round. Extremely sharp." He heard her passing on the information to Duchesne before she came back on the phone. "From the direction and depth of the cut, I'm guessing it was made by a right-handed person."

"Strong person?"

"Sorry?"

"Was it done by a strong person?" Was that movement near the shore?

"Hard to say. Anyone with a sharp enough blade could have done this. The body itself would act as a sort of lever. Anyone of average height and weight could have done this—yes, even a woman. Dutch already asked that."

"I believe I have the perp."

"Sorry?"

"Tell the Inspector I know who killed Dr. Kneisser. I have him—or will have him. The man who slit his throat. His name is Trevor Patel. American of South Asian descent. Kneisser's assistant.

Can you tell if he was killed in the shack?" More off-mic mumbling before Dr. Giles came back on.

"Kneisser's body's in rough shape, as you know," she said. "So I can't tell by bruises whether or not it was dragged to the scene of the fire or killed there. Just that the bullet hole came after death." Kennison said nothing. "That's all I've got for Kneisser," said the doctor.

"What about the girl?"

"Died in the fire, we can say safely say. *Because of* the fire. No foul play, I don't think. Residue on her hands and bits of clothing suggesting some kind of fuel or oil. She may have set the fire, but I can't tell you whether it was on purpose or just a terrible accident. By my count, she died about twenty-four to thirty hours after Kneisser. There was one bullet in her right thigh, a Russian-made Wolf 7.90-millimetre, 125-grain weight, but we think that was from the rifle of the man who tried to kill you. Can't tell until you bring the rifle in. Do you copy?"

"I copy."

"You want the PM on the man who tried to kill you when we're finished with him?"

"Not really. Should be a thirty-ought-six in him from the Inuit boy's rifle. Any different, I need to know." Kennison had enough on his plate. "He's been killed, by the way. Shot."

"Who?"

"The Inuit boy. Wayne Penilik. The kid who saved my ass. I have a problem here, Doctor—I need to talk to Du . . . Inspector Duchesne."

"Okay. Over to Dutch—oh, one last thing though. For what it's worth, Marie-Claire Fortier was pregnant, Sergeant. Just pregnant—maybe a month or a bit more."

Kennison did the math. She'd been at Victory Point nearly two months. His heart sank for reasons he didn't have time to explore. Duchesne came on the line.

"Kennison?"

"Yes, sir."

"Good work nailing the perp on this. He in custody?"

"Not at the moment, sir, but he will be."

"Good. Secure him. Feather in your cap." Kennison saw a definite movement to the east, from the barren inland, from where the sniper had come. A bear, a musk ox, a rabbit—maybe a man. He hoped Lillian was watching.

"Sir, I think you should inform Kneisser's employer that he's dead and tell them that their Ms. Cruz is well . . . that we've been unable to communicate with them."

"Will do, Sergeant. Soon as we're through here. I have—"

"Sir, I have a problem here that—"

"—some information for you, Kennison. This Masterson? Bit of an adventurer, it seems. Drinker, or used to be. Opportunist. Good family, bad actor. Nothing violent, nothing dangerous, just low-level fraud-related, so far. High potential for criminal activity. Suspicion is that he's a low-level Farmer—"

"Thank you, sir. There's a group—"

"As for the rest, your Monk boy has a mild narcotics possession charge and a tossed shoplifting. Nothing serious. Been in rehab. Good reports. Everyone else there clean, at least in Canada . . ."

"Thank you, sir. I need some information on—"

"One more thing, Kennison. Important thing. 'Member I told you that Constable Jensen couldn't investigate this because she was busy with a DV in Ross Haven?"

"Yes, sir."

"She was expecting a whack of trouble—serious trouble, as in physical attack on the DV, weapon attack as in assassination.

That's why she had to stay in Ross—why you had to go to Victory Point—

"Turqavik, sir."

"Yes. They shot Jensen. We've sent a plane in for her. You knew this?"

"They're here, sir. Three of them, we think. Armed . . ." It hit Kennison hard, like an unexpected punch in the kidneys. Three. The triple burst. That was it. The shot cluster he'd heard in the chain of sounds when Penilik was killed. He knew that burst. He'd fired it a thousand times. Ten thousand times.

The weapon had to be a Canadian Army C7. It made sense. The ammo was 5.65-mil, same as the bullet that had been found in Kneisser's head. An identical bullet must be somewhere in Wayne Penilik's body. "They're here and they're heavily armed, sir. At least one of them with a military issue C7. They have already killed the Inuit boy—Wayne Penilik—apparently because he was coming to tell me something, maybe about them. He is the most likely one to have called them here. They're out there somewhere, Inspector, and they're after something we have, something even more important to them than their plans in Ross—"

"That what I was going to tell you. That's why they left. The leader is a Quebecer named Charbonneau. Réal Charbonneau. Long record. Half or quarter Inuit, maybe. Got it?"

"Got it, sir."

"Connected with some very bad people, Kennison—political guerilla training types out of Montréal."

"Got it, sir."

"What could they be after, Kennison?"

"No real idea, sir. Maybe a journal Kneisser found. That seems to be the motive for Kneisser's murder. So far. Everyone here seems to want it. But I don't yet know why. Haven't seen it. Haven't found it."

"Who do you have there, Kennison? And what weapons?"

"Me, sir, and my standard 9-mil. I also kept the sniper's AK-47, and his backpack. Maybe there are some extra clips in it. Haven't had a chance to check. I have Wayne Penilik's rifle—the dead boy's—a Winchester 70, I think. Masterson has a weapon here. I don't know what kind."

"Not legal, I'd bet. Personnel there?"

"Me, Ms. Cruz—the American woman who flew in with the . . . with the sniper and your friend the pilot. She's ex-FBI, she says. Don't know about her weapons expertise, if any. Lillian Ooqlooq, an Inuit woman who's the cook here, the dead Inuit boy's grandmother, sir. Let's see . . . Masterson, the Monk boy, a female scientist . . ."

"Anyone know weapons or strategy?"

"Maybe Ms. Cruz, sir. Just a maybe."

"What's the weather?"

"Seems to be clearing. Not bad now. Clear skies if you could see them, sir. Never know what's going to happen in half an hour, though."

"Welcome to the Arctic, Kennison. We've got that storm here now. Blizzard blind. Can't fly out now. I'll send people first chance." The static washed again. Kennison looked at the charge meter and realized he was about to lose contact.

"Anything else, sir?" Kennison expected to hear something about testifying, but Duchesne avoided it. Almost.

"One thing of interest, maybe. The Fortier girl's fiancé? The Québec politician she was set to marry?"

"Yes, sir?"

"Name of Raymond. Ring a bell?"

"No, sir."

"He's the up-and-comer who's stirring up the internal investigation, Kennison." The politics of the force was the last thing Kennison needed to think about. There was a definite movement to the north, more a shift of darkness than a shape.

"Interesting coincidence, sir."

"Maybe, Kennison. Maybe. That sniper was no coincidence."

"No sir. Losing power, sir."

"Last thing: do not confront this Turqavik group, Kennison. They're radical. They're very serious and will do anything to get what they want."

"I know, sir. They killed the Inuit boy, and I suspect he was one of theirs—for a while."

"Be very careful, Sergeant, until we can send a plane to reach you. Out."

"Out, Inspector." Kennison's ear hurt from the phone and his arm from holding it up to his ear. He stretched his arm, placed the satphone in its cradle and pulled the rope on the generator until it sprang back to life. He stepped back and lit a cigarette—two left—watching Trevor Patel hobble across the snow towards him, tears frozen on his face, bare feet bloody and cut with ice, toes blue-grey and dead with frostbite. Kennison followed his red footprints in the Kitchen Tent door.

Abandoned ships. No food. Ink frozen. I write with pencil taken from a dead man's hand. Erebus *on ice, two large door holes dug in her hull like caves in a limestone cliff. C. commands, as Bealls is in chains. Esquimaux on the horizon fill us daily with dread. Men have not returned. One found devoured. But no animal did it. Metal ripped from hulls, traded for rabbits, small birds. Esq. made the metal into weapons. A Fool traded gun for food. Yet we hold the ammunition. Guards of the key to our own death by rifle.*

Scurvy rages, lead poisoning creeps slowly, a host for death and not itself a killer. I think of F. awake and asleep. I imagine he lies in his bunk, expanding each day, icy maggots of arctic flies breeding in his frozen belly, flying throu holes in his chest dug by devouring gargoyles with the canted casts of women I once knew. Lady Jane or Lady Lort. The face of Daisy tells me 'tis a dream, for none so perfect would attend this rite.

C. decided to abandon ships three days ago. Erebus *will sink like a stone with the holes, Franklin to the grave he deserves beneath the ice. No reason to stay on board, no chance of survival if we do.*

We travel in groups. Ours is six. There are others of three or four, some already farther south along the shore, and a large contingent that insists on staying together. Bealls, of course. And his flesh-hungry men. C. insists we drag these damned lifeboats with supplies. Chocolate in boxes, metal curtain rods, to trade for food or for our lives. Books (Goldsmith I brought), ropes, buttons, stupid frippery. The oaken boat is heavy—difficult to push over the ice ridges. In three days we have covered only the five leagues to land. To the cairn built by Erebus *officers. Opened the paper they left.*

28 May 1847
H.M. Ships *Erebus* and *Terror* wintered in the ice in Lat. 70deg 05min N. Long. 98deg 23min W. Having wintered, in 1846–7, at Beechey Island, in Lat. 74deg 43min 28sec N., Long. 91deg 39min 15sec. W., after having ascended Wellington Channel to Lat. 77deg. and returned by the Westside of Cornwallis Island. Sir John Franklin commanding the expedition. All well. Party consisting of 2 officers and 6 men left the ships on Monday 24th May 1847.
Gm. Gore, Lieut.
Chas. F. DesVoeux, Mate

Written by officers for history. No deaths on Beechey, no poison food or scurvy. Such is the manner in which history is written, rot and failure ignored. C. ordered me to add a notation around the border of the note.I copy it as he said it.

April 25th 1848
H.M. Ships *Terror* and *Erebus* were deserted on 22nd April, 5 leagues N.N.W. of this, having been beset since 12th September 1846. The officers and crews, consisting of 105

souls, under the command of Captain F.R.M. Crozier, landed here in Lat. 37deg 42min N., Long 91deg 41min W. Sir John Franklin died on 11 June 1847; the total loss by deaths in the expedition has been, to this date, 9 officers and 15 men.
James Fitzjames, Captain of H.M.S. *Erebus*.
F.R.M. Crozier, Captain and Senior Officer
And start on to-morrow, 26th, for Back's Fish River.

First any of us heard a plan,
Or thought there was one . . .

The trek back to Kneisser's site was much easier in the calm weather. The dark made negotiating the rocks difficult, but the lack of wind and the bitter cold of its leading edge made for what amounted to a pleasant stroll in this world. Did that mean he was getting used to it? That worried him. With one ear listening to the trailing progress of Ruby Cruz, who had insisted on coming, he recalled his first days in the Balkans straight from the Combat Training Centre in Gagetown, New Brunswick, stunned that every second building in the Bosnian villages through which they drove was pockmarked with shell fire or levelled by mortars or land mines. Neighbours killing neighbours—that's not what puzzled him. It was that, after only a few days, he didn't see the damage anymore. He became too quickly inured to the domestic scars of mad wars between former friends, even relatives. Desensitized. Not good.

Kennison watched the horizon, nervous about Turqavik and about Lillian's belief that they were closing in, circling the camp like impatient, hungry bears. He'd feel better if he knew what they were looking for, what Penilik in his hero-worshipping naivety had told them was worth aborting their plans in Ross and travelling a hundred kilometres over land to come here. Was it the damned journal that everyone else wanted? Or was Kennison's life the cash prize? Were they the backup contract to the man who had failed to shoot him in the back? Leading Ruby Cruz between boulders, he scanned the shadows as he walked. He wore the sniper's AK-47 rifle on his back and had pocketed three extra clips that he'd found in the backpack. There had been no identification or anything that might suggest the killer's background. That was odd—the man had to have carried even minimal photo ID to travel. Even bogus ID would offer clues as to his origin.

Behind him, stumbling on stones, Ruby Cruz negotiated her way, complaining that Kennison always took the most difficult route. She seemed recovered, normal—if bad temper was her standard state. Hypothermia is a strange animal—the bitter cold that lowers your body temperature to the point it can kill you, also prevents extreme damage to your cells.

Kennison decided a movement on the rock ridge was a cloud of snow blown north by a rogue gust.

Patel's barefoot stroll on the permafrost had changed the man's mind about escaping. Where was there to go? He had been in severe pain when he returned to the tent, the thawing of his extremities more painful than the frostbite that would inevitably cost him toes. There was no choice—either amputate them or die when the gangrene entered the bloodstream. While Lillian had given him pans of cool water to coax his bleeding feet back to normal body temperature, his sarcasm had returned.

With a few stern questions, Kennison determined that Patel had been with Dr. Kneisser when they'd removed the last layer of rocks to find the remarkably preserved body, untouched by animals or insects.

"Rocks too damn heavy, even for bears," Patel had muttered as he lowered his feet into the pans.

"Who found the journal?" asked Kennison.

"He did. Kneisser. Geezer wouldn't let me near the skeleton. Wanted all the credit for himself." Patel winced and sucked in air noisily as Lillian added warmer water to the pan. "Cut the pockets with his knife. Found it inside the right one."

"And you killed him for it?"

Patel looked at his feet, playing for time.

"The question won't go away, Mr. Patel. Did you kill Dr. Kneisser for the journal?" Patel would not raise his head. He stared instead at his thawing feet, marked with blue splotches and red blood.

"That crazy old fool. Dancing on the rocks, waving his arms in the air like the fiddler on the fucking roof. I just wanted the book. All this is bullshit."

"Did you read it?"

"Not then. Later. Some of it. After—"

"Tell me how it happened."

Lillian moved between the Kitchen Tent and Salon Tent doors, eyes darting, watching, raising her hand when she thought she saw someone outside. Masterson sat backwards on a kitchen chair, legs spread, glaring at Patel, becoming slowly aware that, whatever happened here in Kennison's presence, he'd lost proprietary rights to his latest fortune, lost his winning lottery ticket to the wind. Ruby Cruz sipped tea, hands cupped for warmth, inhaling the steam with renewed sensitivity.

"He was crazy, the old coot. He'd sit on his damned rock at the end of every day—like, just sit there like some king on his throne and stare out to the strait. Told me sometimes he saw the ghosts of the Admiralty sailors, saw them on ladders and ropes climbing down from the ships, saw them waving at him across the open water, running back to the icebound *Erebus* and *Terror* when small groups of Inuit approached . . . that kind of thing. Bullshit, is what it was. Fantasy daydreams is all. Silly old bugger . . ."

"How did it happen?" asked Kennison.

Patel stared at his feet. "I just wanted the book."

"How did it happen?" Kennison asked again.

"I was in debt from playing cards. My parents would kill me. Only one semester left to get my degree. Besides, I was fed up. It was always dark, always cold, all the work—I was the one did all the work. The geezer just sat there jabbering away to his ghosts, reading bits of the journal out loud with a flashlight. Kept saying 'Oh dear, oh dear, oh my Lord' every time he read a fucking sentence." Kennison listened and frowned. Patel was lying.

Kennison walked towards Masterson and held out his palm. Masterson reached into his jacket pocket and pulled out a deck of cards in a torn box that he placed, like evidence, in Kennison's outstretched hand. Kennison opened the box and examined the worn backs of the cards, the subtle marks integrated into the swirl of blue lines. He looked at Masterson, who looked away as if to deny the marks were his.

"You owed Masterson money from playing cards." he said. Patel nodded. "How much?"

"Fifty-five hundred quid," said Masterson. "Give or take."

"What's that?" said Kennison. "Eleven, twelve thousand dollars?" Patel shrugged. "So in the end, you killed Dr. Kneisser for eleven thousand dollars?"

Patel stared at him, eyes welling, he nodded once.

"You cut his throat." Patel looked away. His feet were thawing slowly and the pain in his face twisted his jaw so that his teeth were offset and made his eyes squint. Kennison paced the small room, playing with the deck of cards, tossing the box from one hand to the other. Crime made him tick, made him think, but stupid criminals made him angry, and most criminals were stupid. Suddenly, he tossed the pack to Patel, who caught it deftly and stared at it, confused.

"Did you steal this book back from Mr. Masterson?" Patel shook his head. "Did Dr. Ferguson-Crewe?" A hesitation, then a shrug. Patel suspected as much, if he didn't know for sure. Kennison looked around the room. Lillian hovered by the Salon Tent door, eyes staring into the dark. Ruby Cruz sipped tea. Masterson watched Patel's every move. Only the Monk boy and Ferguson-Crewe were missing. Kennison turned to Patel quickly. "Why did you steal money from Dr. Ferguson-Crewe's luggage?" The question startled Patel and everyone in the room. Patel hesitated, sensing an opportunity.

"Look, I'm being co-operative, right? You'll tell people that? That I helped out? I needed to pay the damned debt. Don't you understand? I had to find money wherever I could. Masterson was being unreasonable—wanted it all before we left here. I didn't have the money. Where the hell was I going to get it? I gave the book to Masterson as payment and I took the money from Anne. I'll give it back to her. No big deal. It's not like I spent it at the local gift shop or anything."

Kennison felt disgust. How Kneisser came to be in the Purgatory shack could wait. There were more unanswered questions now than before. He stood and offered Masterson the butt of his Smith and Wesson. Masterson smiled, shook his head and pulled a 9-millimetre Beretta from his jacket pocket.

"So you *are* a Farmer," observed Kennison. Duchesne had mentioned the possibility on the satphone. Masterson hesitated, but only for a moment. He nodded. "Farmers," or sometimes

"MacDonalds," was cop talk for agents from the investigative wing of the European Union, primarily responsive to Arctic issues. The nickname was the obvious result of the acronym for the Euro-International Environmental Investigative Organization. Like the Americans, the EIEIO insisted the Northwest Passage was an international waterway. "You have ammo for that?" said Kennison, holstering his own gun. Masterson nodded.

"If he runs, shoot him," said Kennison.

"I hope the bastard runs," said Masterson. The room had fallen silent. The only sound was Kennison clumping across the plywood floor to the Kitchen Tent, where Lillian looked northward.

"It wasn't just me! I wasn't the only one who killed him," shouted Patel. Kennison stopped at the Kitchen Tent door and turned.

"What does that mean, Mr. Patel?" he asked.

"I . . . I cut him with the knife, from behind." He made a motion with his arms, one wrapped around a person, the other drawing a knife across a throat. "Sure I did. To shut him up. I admit that, okay? Left him sitting on his damned rock, looking out to sea. Propped him up."

"Go on."

"I dropped the knife. I was bent over in front of the damned seat, on my hands and knees, looking for it in the dark. I heard a shot and a bullet bounce off the rocks right beside me, then another shot and Kneisser rolled off the seat." Patel leaned forward, excited by his thoughts but set back in his seat by the pain in his feet. "That's what killed him. The rifle shot. You can't prove it was the knife. You can't prove that." He seemed secure with his argument. "I rolled his body onto the ATV trailer and hauled him to the shack. Hoped someone would find him there and see he died by the bullet. You can't prove the knife killed him. You can't."

"Did you see who fired the bullet?" Patel nodded, smiling now, traces of his old charm surfacing. "Who?"

"There were three or four people in a group about a hundred and fifty yards away. It was dark. They didn't see me on the ground, or if they did they didn't shout or say anything. Three of them were dressed in black, hoods and everything. Like house robbers. I could see their outlines. The fourth one held a gun."

"Did you know the one with the gun?" Patel nodded and looked down to watch Lillian pouring warmer water in the pan.

"Wayne Penilik," he said. "Wayne Penilik had the gun. Wayne Penilik shot Dr. Kneisser. The black ones were all pointing at the geezer in his chair, but it was Penilik pulled the trigger. Shot blew him right off his seat." Lillian's hands shook, and the water spilled on the plywood floor. "I hunkered down behind his body. They left quietly, so silent I was afraid to look up in case they were standing over me. But they killed him. Penilik killed him. Not me. Not me . . ." Masterson shifted his weight, raising his Beretta to Patel's chest.

"Kill him if he moves, Masterson," said Kennison. "He's a lying waste of space."

They were approaching Kneisser's site now, Kennison still leading. With every hundred yards, Ruby Cruz became increasingly active and co-operative. She was saying something that he couldn't quite hear, so he merely grunted. The sky was clearing, and he thought he could see stars high above. He didn't sing as he walked this time. He thought.

By the process of elimination, either Kenneth Monk or Anne Ferguson-Crewe held the journal. Kennison was convinced

Masterson was telling the truth about it being stolen—there was no upside to his lying about that, no reason to admit it existed. Kennison certainly didn't have it. Despite her mission to retrieve it, Ruby Cruz had been near death when it went missing, and Lillian, devastated by Patel's accusation that her grandson shot Kneisser in the head, had been with either Kennison or Ruby Cruz all day. Patel certainly didn't have it, or he'd have coughed it up to save his own ass. When they'd left the compound, Masterson was tying Patel to a chair with yellow plastic rope.

That left Monk and Ferguson-Crewe. Grey Anne was nowhere to be seen—Kennison had asked Cruz to do a thorough check of the Wet Tent and the Dorm Tent. Monk had been sent by Masterson to Kneisser's site to gas up the abandoned ATV and not returned. It didn't take that long to do the job. Even if he couldn't get it started, he knew the way, so could have walked back by now. He must be frozen after the petrol hunt in the storm and carrying the heavy gas can to the machine. Behind him, Cruz tripped and swore under her breath.

"These damned rocks. I'm getting sick of—"

"Hold it." Kennison raised his arm. They were close to Kneisser's site now.

"What? What?"

"Quiet." He stood still, pointing towards the shore. Ruby Cruz followed his cue and saw the ATV in the dusk, crusted with ice. Beside it, lying on its side, was the red plastic gas can, but there was no sign of Monk. In the still air, Kennison thought he heard a voice, but it could be in his head. Like the "Happy Wanderer"—he remembered that was the name of the song he'd been singing on the last trek.

He moved cautiously towards the ATV, hearing Cruz crunching snow immediately behind him. The gas container was empty.

Kennison could smell engine oil and exhaust, so Monk had already fuelled and even started the machine. Though there was ice on the seat and handlebars, the engine was clean and, Kennison thought, slightly warm. A voice seemed more distinct now, an actual sentence coming from somewhere on the wind: "Years of intense . . ."

"Monk?" he called, startling Ruby with the shout. "Monk. You there?" No response. "You hear any talking?" he asked Ruby. She shook her head, then paused as if uncertain. Maybe. Kennison moved forward up the sandy shore and wove through the boulders to the sleeping platform, to Kneisser's rock seat.

The voice was louder here. It sounded like someone giving a speech in front of a crowd. Kennison shone his flashlight on the base of Kneisser's sitting rock and pointed out the dark stains to Ruby Cruz. Now they both knew it was blood, not charred soot or lichen. Kneisser's blood, lots of it. Let by Patel, he'd said, except Kennison knew he was lying. Ruby shuddered.

The sound of the speech increased. There were distinct words now. Through a rising light wind they could hear them.

"And so it is in the very spirit of labour and discovery that I accept this tribute . . ."

Cruz made the first move, climbing over the torn piece of white tent the storm had freed, only to have caught itself between boulders. She headed towards the ridge and the grave in which Kennison had saved her life with his body heat just hours ago.

"With the respect and recognition with which it has been bestowed . . . No. With this recognition by the Society which we all, for our entire careers in archaeology, hold in such esteem . . ."

They mounted the rock ridge side by side, moving faster now, drawn by the sound. It was a speech being delivered, a thank-you speech. When it suddenly stopped, they stopped, too. Kennison and Cruz crept the last ten yards on their knees, simultaneously peeking over the grave's edge the way Kennison once peered over his childhood quarry. Below were not the fantastic oxide dinosaurs of open-pit mining, but it was still a scene that would stay with them forever. Stretched out on its back, the body of Kenneth Monk stared sightless to the sky. His hands were positioned away from his body, his palms down. His right leg had been bent slightly at the knee. There was blood in his hair and in the one ear they could see.

Beside him, kneeling on the rocks, a sylph at a sylvan pond, Anne Ferguson-Crewe slowly reconstructed what looked to be a shattered skeleton beside Monk's limp form, using it as her template. As she worked, she spoke, looking from right to left, maintaining eye contact with an audience only she could see.

"So I thank you deeply, personally for this honour, and in doing so I include my thanks . . . No. I would be remiss in not sharing this prestigious prize with those who made my explorations possible, those who laid the groundwork for my discovery, especially Dr. Karl Conrad Kneisser and his assistant, Trevor Patel, both of whom sadly passed away fighting the difficult and isolated conditions with which we—"

Grey Anne looked up slowly, sensing a real audience before knowing she had one. Her face was flushed, her smile wide, and she looked animated, attractive. Kennison thought she blushed, a young girl caught admiring herself in her mirror.

"Oh dear," she said. "What a surprise. I have been caught out then, haven't I?" She glanced at Monk's body. "This naughty boy was breaking my beautiful skeleton." Kennison thought she giggled. "Whatever will people say? Such a shame. Still, some eccentricity is to be expected, isn't it?"

The dark was a matte blanket stretched across the arc of the sky. Kennison had yet to see it blacker or hear it more silent. Standing outside the Kitchen Tent, cupping his cigarette in his palm, he patted his parka pocket to make sure the journal was still there, the book that had cost Kneisser his life and tangentially resulted in the deaths of Marie-Claire Fortier, Wayne Penilik and now Kenny Monk. Add to that the near death of Ruby Cruz. Ivan Something the pilot, too, for that matter—and himself, if not for Penilik.

Ironically, while the existence of this tatty little journal couldn't be blamed for Constable Jensen's injuries, it may have saved the lives of who knows how many in Ross Haven, if it was what drew Turqavik here, away from whatever plan it intended to carry out there. Kennison wondered if the politician—the DV—had made his damned speech about Canadian sovereignty in the North, shaken the hands of the Anglican priest and those natives deemed suitable to represent the community, and flown back to Ottawa to a cigars-and-brandy reward for having saved the Arctic once again.

They were out there now, invisible in black clothes and balaclavas. Three of them, if Patel could be believed. Lillian thought there were three as well. Kennison stepped farther away from the compound and looked to the horizon, circling three hundred and sixty dark degrees, imagining them circling, hungry Arctic wolves at the edge of a small campfire circle, snarling, starving on the barren plain, goading each other to attack first with every shrinking orbit.

Kennison had spent more than an hour skimming the journal, up to the point where Anne Ferguson-Crewe had stuffed the loose papers to mark her place. Grey Anne hadn't balked at handing over the journal. She'd stood when accused and offered Kennison her hand. He'd pulled her up out of the grave and she'd come quietly, led back on the path by Ruby Cruz. Kennison had stayed behind, sorting through the bones in the grave and carrying the surprisingly light body of Kenny Monk to Kneisser's chair, where he wrapped it in the tattered remnants of the white nylon tent. He laid it over the hood of the ATV like a mummified moose before driving back slowly along the shore to Hell, then east to the compound, arriving about the same time Ruby led Grey Anne through the Salon Tent door.

Kennison laid Monk's body, already stiffening with cold, on the ground outside the Kitchen Tent beside the green-wrapped corpse of Wayne Penilik—two young men with only the promise of accomplishment, dead long before what Sister Beata would have called "their time." Penilik might have become a force for his people in a North that was fast becoming valued. Monk, finally on the cusp of a life, died not knowing he'd made another life with Marie-Claire Fortier. Never dismissive of death, Booker Kennison despaired most over lives untried.

Kennison had left Anne Ferguson-Crewe in Masterson's care. The man took some odd pleasure in being a jailer. The informal questioning had been brief. Kennison had made things extremely simple.

"Mr. Patel, when I tossed you Masterson's deck of cards, you caught them, correct? Patel nodded, slowly, unsure of the territory. "Which hand did you use, please?" The man looked at one hand and then the other.

"He used the left hand," said Masterson. "He's left-handed. Plays cards left-handed. Trust me." Kennison nodded. Patel kept looking at his palms.

"And Ruby, you were present when we helped Dr. Ferguson-Crewe out of the grave at Dr. Kneisser's site?" Ruby nodded. "I offered her both my hands. Which one did she choose?" Ruby thought, moving both her hands, trying to reconstruct the scene.

"I'm right-handed, if that's what you're inferring," said Dr. Ferguson-Crewe. "So what?"

"According to Yellowknife, Dr. Kneisser was murdered by someone cutting his throat from behind with an Inuit knife," said Kennison. "A right-handed person."

Ferguson-Crewe made an abrupt motion towards the door, but caught herself. There was nowhere to run, nowhere she could hide or keep warm. She held out her hands for cuffs, but Kennison told Masterson to take care of her, to untie Patel who was whispering to her loudly, pleading for her to listen, making her turn away. Kennison was disgusted with both of them.

In the Salon Tent, he glossed over the entries quickly, looking solely for clues as to why anyone would find the book valuable. If he could quickly figure out what Turqavik wanted, if he could discover why they were here, it might help him defend against them. Besides, he could think of little else to do.

Masterson watched him read with a malevolence, as if Kennison rather than Grey Anne had stolen the journal from him. In the Mess Tent, Patel was finally, thankfully, silent, told by Masterson to "stop it" every time he moved a muscle. The final truth would come out when there was time to question both of them. Kennison was certain that Grey Anne had done the killing, had been clued into the journal by Patel. Whether there was more to the relationship than murder, he didn't know.

Grey Anne, bound to the chair with the yellow rope, stared at Patel as if he had betrayed her. Ruby slept—the walk to Kneisser's site and back had exhausted her—and Lillian kept to herself, walking from door to door, keeping watch, keeping busy. Mourning, in her way. Kennison could hear her sobbing softly as he turned pages.

When he'd reached the place that Anne Ferguson-Crewe had marked with loose papers, he felt he needed some air, some isolated place to think about what he knew and didn't know. That's what had brought him outside the Kitchen Tent, into a cold and dark that seemed more benevolent than it had before, even if it was masking danger, even if shared with the bodies of two dead young men.

In the courtyard beyond the compound, enclosed by the deteriorating snow fence, the stars seemed closer than their canvas, projected far forward like fibre-optic tubes with bright pastel lights at the end, pale pinks, greens, blues, faceted like cut crystals, making him wonder if he'd ever seen stars before. The stars alone offered enough light to make out the shapes of rocks and tents. He heard his own boots bleat on the snow as he walked away from the compound, becoming one with the dark. They'd shut down the generator when the satphone was recharged. It made too much noise and Kennison wanted them to have the benefit of all their senses. Besides, why show the enemy where the target lived? With no generator, there was no yard light, no light pollution. He stared into the black, wishing for the night goggles he'd had in the Balkans, wishing he could see the blue-green heat images of them circling, watching him. What did they want? Why was it so important to them?

Looking up made him dizzy, as if an infinitesimal movement of the planet confounded balance. Maybe he was still concussed from knocking himself out on Kneisser's travel chest. Maybe he was exhausted and afraid to give into it.

The sky was an earth-sized dome grounded at the horizon. To the northeast, a thin trail of transparent cloud hung suspended like some primeval vapour, a heavenly wisp, lit only by the cumulative glow of the stars a billion miles beyond it. Ancient stars, stars that had looked down on Franklin and his men, a Milky Way composed of restless wraiths, perhaps—ghosts of those who died on this land. Then, and now.

He stood perfectly still under the black dome, facing south, willing himself to feel the pressure of the turning earth on his left foot, Vitruvian man worshipping something too grand to understand, yet attuned to every nuance of movement, sound and smell. He felt guilty trying to debase this celestial awe with the common sensibility of measured man, but if, with this starlit night, he'd had a good cigar, a goblet of vintage port and someone who cared enough to read Heaney poems aloud, he'd be closer to God than he had ever been. The nuns would be pleased.

The scuff of a boot tensed every muscle in his body. He flinched, then ducked and pivoted on one foot, feinting to his right like a boxer, ready to roll on either shoulder. He was more on his guard, more wary, more ready than he realized. From the dark emerged Ruby Cruz, a crooked smile on her face.

"Out and about, looking for bad guys?" she said, pronouncing the words "oot" and "aboot," the way Americans do when they imitate what they hear as a Canadian accent.

"Always," said Kennison. "They're 'oot' here somewhere."

"You left these inside," she said. Her voice was calm, deep and thoughtful like the night. He grunted thanks and took his second-last cigarette from the pack and lit it. He'd deliberately left them inside to deny himself, to hoard them. He inhaled slowly, relishing a deep, smoky lungful. The wind was so still he could watch his exhaled smoke disperse in the vast black space. Ruby stood beside him, close, staring up at the sky, holding his arm for balance.

"Ask you a question?" said Ruby.

Kennison shrugged. "Sure."

"D'you feel at home here?"

Kennison stared into the dark. "You mean this place? The North?"

There was a silence before she answered.

"I guess I mean to ask where you feel most at home in the world."

"Wherever I am, I guess. At least in this country."

"Like some turtle? You just carry your home around with you?"

"Not really. Just don't settle, I guess. Grew up in an orphanage, sent out to foster homes and returned like an empty pop bottle for a refund. Ended up a DP, what the social workers call a 'difficult placement,' so it was mostly just me and the nuns until I finished high school." Kennison took a drag and blew the smoke out in a long exhale. "Joined the army to save the world and keep the peace in the Balkans, then the Mounties to bring justice to that land. Never really lived anywhere for long, not even when I was married. What about you?"

"I didn't know you were married."

"Neither did I, a lot of the time. Ginny had . . . problems."

"I grew up in Staten Island. We lost it—the house, I mean—when my dad came back from 'Nam. He . . . he wasn't right in his head anymore, and my mother and Karen and I couldn't keep it going. We moved to Philly—Philadelphia. Did you know Christina Aguilera was born in Staten Island and grew up in Philly?" She was silent for a moment. "But we were teased by the kids, called all sorts of names—spic, and so on, mostly because Dad was Puerto Rican.

"I think my mom died from the shame of being pitied more

than being poor. She was proud, came from what she called 'good Massachusetts stock.' My sister got in a lot of trouble—drugs and men, mostly, not sure which came first—and she killed herself when she was twenty-three. I moved to D.C., brought Dad and took care of him until he died a year ago. I worked, went to a local college to be a paralegal, one night-school course at a time."

"How come you didn't hang out a shingle? Make a fortune? Isn't everyone in the States always suing everyone else?"

"I didn't get in it to fight domestic suits or close property deals. I was big on capital J for Justice. Wanted to change the world for the better, just like you, I bet."

Kennison snorted. "So you joined the FBI?"

"Yeah. I was looking for some kind of context, some kind of club, a home I could belong to with some pride, some way to use what I learned to help people somehow. Wanted to be an agent ever since I was in high school."

"You like it there—at the Bureau?"

"Hated it, to tell you the truth. It was like showing up naked every day in the boy's locker room. Stupid looks and more stupid jokes. It's like they recruited only guys who thought the *Jackass* movies were Oscar material. I hated it until I met Harry."

"That your husband? Is he your favourite place?"

"No. Not Harry. He was like you. Harry was a soldier. An American. Like you, maybe, his country was his home more than any building or space. He was a Quantico trainer for the Bureau. Harry knew what he was about, and I was sick up to here of the office wimps who couldn't admit even to themselves that all they wanted to do was put their hand in your pants. I saw Harry as a way to get rid of them all."

"Make you happy?"

Ruby didn't answer immediately.

"I was happy with Harry, I guess, although maybe the bar I'd set for home and happiness wasn't very high. My frame of reference was lousy, y'know? Anyway, I think living with someone on a daily basis was claustrophobic for him. He was a guy's guy, and there was me and my visits to Dad and making lousy suppers that had to be eaten at certain times and asking him what he thought about paint samples for the bathroom.

"When he had the chance to run to Iraq, he did it without telling me he'd signed up. Hug and a kiss and good old Harry's off to war. See ya, sweetheart. Keep the home fires burning and I vote for the light blue in the bathroom but you do whatever you want. You know best, little woman. He was smiling when he left, grinning as if he'd been let out of prison on a day pass to go to an Orioles playoff game."

"And he was killed there." It wasn't a question and Ruby didn't answer. "Where's home now?"

"There's isn't one. I thought there was a couple of days ago, but there isn't. Not really. Not truthfully." She waved her arms at the sky and the land. "I thought it was a house, a sort of a dream house in a dream location, a place my family couldn't imagine me living. Because of all this Kneisser journal stuff, I'll miss getting it. Last week, I thought it was everything I wanted. Right now, I'm not sure, and I want to be sure for once. I want a home—not a building, but a home. Somewhere I can call mine."

"Well, I hear land around here is going really cheap," said Kennison. "Probably buy yourself a couple thousand acres for next to nothing. Before the Yanks get here and boost the prices."

"Don't bet on it. Where I come from, people already think this pile of frozen rocks is the next Saudi Arabia or Panama." She was quiet. Kennison thought that she had moved closer, but he couldn't be sure. His senses were raw and he kept turning his head, looking in all directions for movement, a set of stars blacked out by a circling silhouette. When Ruby spoke again, it was in a whisper.

"Y'know, on a night like this, here is as good as it gets. Maybe it's not where you are, but who you're with, huh?" Kennison felt her arm as if it was burning his. He coughed, raising his sore hand to his mouth, breaking the contact, backing away to tromp on his cigarette butt.

"I'm not even sure if I want this new job," she said, stuffing her now loose hands in her pockets. Her pink hat and scarf glowed softly in the surrounding dark. "I thought I did. I had it all worked out, but I keep feeling I'm forcing it, y'know? Like it's the right thing to do and all, but not right for me? That I'd be happier waitressing at some beach bar in Pago Pago or wherever?"

"I guess there are people who decide what happens to them and those who roll with what life decides for them."

"Which one are you?"

"Oh, the last one. No question. Maybe because I had no parents I knew of, nobody with dreams of me going to college or pushing me to be something special, I copped out and let the nuns decide everything for me. Even later, when I got into some bad shit, I let a priest tell me to join the army as a way of escaping a life of crime."

"They say us cops are only a gene away from the bad guys we chase. Why did you become a cop?"

"Like you. Some sense of justice, maybe. Or maybe injustice. The shit I saw as a so-called peacekeeper was stuff no one should see. Neighbours burning neighbours because of what their grandfathers did on some Serbian bridge six hundred years ago. Infants and house pets nailed to boards. Classrooms torched like they were enemy headquarters. And no matter where you went, you were the bad guy to the Serbs, the Croats, the Bosnian Muslims. They all shot at you and laughed at you for not shooting back."

"I would have shot back."

"Yeah . . . well . . . me too."

Ruby was silent, as if waiting for Kennison to tell her the story. He decided not to.

"So you became a Mountie, Sergeant Preston? Or are you more a Dudley Do-Right?"

"Very funny. At the end of our last Bosnian tour, I saw groups of civilian cops, some of them Mounties, who were sent over to comb the villages and count the bodies to try and weed out the allegations of ethnic cleansing and war crimes by all parties. It struck me that these guys were interested in finding out who the bad guys really were and what they'd done. Justice again, I guess. So I came home and applied. A bunch of us did."

"So the same reason as me, but you stuck with it."

"Well, as bad as the Mounties can be, it's not full of guys looking at my boobs and wishing they had their hand in my pants. At least I don't think so . . . never thought about it."

Ruby laughed and moved closer again. It was deep, throaty, uninhibited. A pleasant, warm sound in a cold land. Kennison hadn't heard her laugh before. She stopped abruptly, embarrassed, as if she, too, hadn't heard that sound for a long time.

"You're very good at what you do, Sergeant Do-Right. I watched you at the crime scene. You've done it before."

"A thousand times. I *should* be good at it, but it's getting harder, I think. Used to be able to tell the difference between the good guys and bad guys a mile away—"

"And now it's a kilometre?" Kennison looked to see if she was laughing. She was. He shoved her shoulder, playfully.

"Yeah. A kilometre away. You Yanks and your stubborn imperial systems and your money that all looks the same."

"Oh yeah? Give me a break. You drive with your car lights on all day long, probably because it's so damned dark all the time up here."

"No, it's not."

"Is too." Ruby shoved Kennison, laughing now. He grinned back at her, bent down and picked up some snow to throw at her. She tripped on a small rock and fell. Kennison moved forward and shoved a mitt full of snow down her ski jacket neck. Her pink hat fell off and her black hair spread on the snow that was as white as her smile. Kennison bent forward, staring at her. Her smile faded slowly as she stared up at him. He straightened up quickly—too quickly—and offered her a hand. She took it and he pulled her to her feet. Ruby brushed the snow from her suit and looked back up at the sky. Kennison was silent. Checking the horizon by habit, even though he saw nothing but black.

"You feel at home here?" said Ruby. "Like, I mean, just because it's your country, because it's Canada?"

"Yeah, I do. It's weird but I feel like I belong here, that it's mine to . . . to protect, to save or something."

"Well, who can blame you? It's your sovereign territory." She sighed. "And it's beautiful. Truly beautiful."

"Yeah. It is, isn't it? Except for the neighbours," he said, looking again to the horizon. "It's a bit too much drama for me with them around." Ruby stared into the dark.

"What do you figure this Turqavik gang wants?"

"Well, if it's not my ass, it's got to be the journal, like everyone else. I think Penilik contacted them, maybe by the satphone. Maybe he knew Kneisser had found something, maybe even watched him find it. Maybe even read it, for all I know. And I think the answer as to why they want it so badly is somewhere inside it," he said. "I just haven't found it yet. I should get back at that and stop—"

"Stop what?"

Kennison turned, suddenly a soldier on parade, and marched into the protected compound. Had she expected him to kiss her, he wondered? He felt that he'd missed something important, like a DP who'd been offered a solid family and found some weak excuse to turn it down. Maybe there was an offer on her lips, even a guilt-free chance to get lucky. Kennison believed that luck wasn't his, but when he passed the tent-wrapped bodies of the two young men by the Kitchen Tent door, he knew that that belief was mistaken.

It was quiet, even inside the tent compound. Without the wind howling, the tent sides and roofs were not flapping and the exterior doors opened quietly without forcing changes in air pressure or granting entry to gusts of snow. The silence unsettled the group gathered in the Mess Tent. Kennison had called them there as soon as he'd found the journal passage. He knew now why Turqavik was out there. He knew what they wanted, and he had it.

Masterson continued to prod Patel whenever he made a move or closed his eyes. His feet looked dead, as if they'd have to be amputated before gangrene dissolved into his bloodstream. Anne Ferguson-Crewe sat apart, looking away from the group after she grimaced at the sight of the journal in Kennison's hands. Her jaw was set with some emotion—anger, perhaps, or determination.

Ruby Cruz watched Kennison with an indefinable expression, an unborn smile, as he stood in the middle of the Mess Tent, holding the journal in one hand the way an evangelist wields a Bible. Lillian Ooqlooq moved constantly between the Salon Tent door and the Kitchen Tent door, looking out into the black night as Kennison stood and read the entry aloud.

April 26, 1848 Victory Point

We should have read the anguish in their mouths, the vacancy in smiles. My fingers ache. Even those no longer on my hand. Swarmed through the rat holes of Erebus *when we left, scrambl like vermin up ladders of* Terror *to steal that which is not there. Diffidence masked their hunger. Anger. Rest to writ more.*

On ice ridge over Vict. Pt.

A mile of rocks lrge group breaks camp. Men rise as if wraiths of snow. From nowhere. Without sound, the Silent Slaughter. Our men killed where they stand on shore without the strength to moan, perhaps they welcome death at last. Snow black with blood. Esq hack at flesh, sate themselves, depart with the longer limbs stacked like peat for future meals. Driven to survive by methods we revealed, we the civilized.

Gd save us frm our sickened selves.

The room was silent. Ruby Cruz stared at Kennison, tears welling in her eyes. For the slaughtered men? For the journal writer? For her future? Kennison didn't know. Grey Anne looked angry. Her eyes darted as if formulating a plan. Patel, looking foolish in his yellow ropes, stared at the floor with his white teeth clenched—whether from anger at the events narrated or at giving up the journal for so little, Kennison couldn't tell. Masterson stared at Grey Anne, not seeing her, his mind working, his thoughts impossible to read.

Lillian Ooqlooq broke the silence, speaking from the Salon Tent door. Her voice was loud, unexpectedly stronger than Kennison had yet heard it.

"Men are always men. Men do not change. Inuit men, white men, black Africans, Chinese men. When men are frightened, they strike back. All men strike back. When men are angry, they fight. All men fight. When men are starving, they eat what they can. All men fight to survive."

No one spoke. Lillian took a breath with a sound that might have been a sigh for her people.

"No blame to a father who steals food to save his child. No blame to a mother who kills to save her baby. No blame to any man who kills to save his life." She turned back to the window and stared into the dark. No one spoke until Kennison broke the silence.

"You know these stories. I mean, the Inuit know these stories, don't they, Lillian?" The old woman nodded. "They remember when these men died in this place." Lillian dipped her head again. Kennison could see the sentences forming in her eyes before she uttered them.

"We know the stories. They are our stories. Passed down in the dark since the English sailors came, from before that time. I said the memories of Inuit are long memories. These terrible stories are alive in us, and only this book that writes them down will share them with the world. This book is what Turqavik think must be hidden. They think if this history becomes known to white men, the Inuit will lose their power."

"No more dignified noble bloody savages at the land claims table," said Masterson, as if to himself. "No more privileged status. Just damned survivors like all of us. We'll eat shit if we have to."

"Shut up, Masterson," said Kennison as he closed the journal.

At the Salon Tent door, Lillian held her hand over her eyes and stared out the window towards Hell, her eyes moist, her breath fogging the glass.

"Closer now, Mountie," she said.

The wind was back, gusting and tossing up random miniature tornados of snow crystals like puppies playing in a winter park. If there was one thing that grated on Kennison here, one element that gnawed at his heart and mind, it was the wind, its constancy a reminder of his own childlike fickleness, its keen edge a mirror to his dithering, his wavering about women and responsibility and settling down, his inability to commit to testifying against bad men in an institution that had given him purpose and pride.

The advice of others, whether the self-protective, manipulative whining of Cosentino or what Inspector Duchesne wrapped in a tissue of warm concern, was useless. They knew only parts of the whole. They knew that if Kennison testified, Ormerod and many others would be dismissed, reprimanded. Maybe go to prison. What they didn't understand was that if Ormerod went to prison, no one would support Ginny, languishing in that expensive Gatineau rehab centre that was more a hospice, a palliative placebo for those so fucked up they could never be released. Without her father, without his money—whatever its source—she'd be tossed on the street, where she wouldn't last a week.

In the black night, Kennison walked the compound perimeter for perhaps the fifteenth time, outside the tents on this tour, close to the walls, low to the ground, checking eyelines, ensuring that his plan had the best opportunity for success. Not that it was much of a plan.

When he cried in the dark, tormented by the hard shadows of the wall crucifix, the nuns said it was only the unknown that made him afraid. "Look, Booker," they'd say as they turned on the bare overhead bulb above his bed and erased the menacing angles of the hall light. "All gone." He'd lived by that "fear of the unknown" theory ever since, whether crouched on a goat track above hill towns in Bosnia or entering an unlit basement reeking of ripe death in Kosovo. Recognize your fear for what it was; sleep with the light on.

This was different. That was logic. This ran against convention. Understanding why Turqavik was out there and what they were after did nothing to reduce the degree of threat or relieve the tension of apprehension. Rather, his trepidation was magnified. After all, Turqavik had abandoned a planned coup in Ross that must have taken months of planning and intensely secretive co-ordination with other cells. And, without compunction, they'd murdered one of their own when Wayne Penilik saw through their evil and rejected it.

"Closer now, Sargeant," said Ruby from inside as Kennison rounded the Salon Tent door. They were out there, circling like wolves, preying as a pack, moving ever closer with every circuit of their singular focus, calling attention, backing away, patiently waiting to pounce when the prey was flushed or had succumbed to pure fear. He looked up and scanned the horizon, but saw nothing.

In the Mess Tent, Kennison had counted his chickens and found them wanting. Patel was a prisoner if only by his limited ability to escape. Anne Ferguson-Crewe sat in her wooden chair, bound by the yellow ropes that had marked Patel's false confession. With Grey

Anne and Patel excluded, there were four of them to defend this fragile fort. Kennison was fully aware that any of them might easily trade the protection of the others for possession of the journal.

The book was money to Paul Masterson, either as a sale to museums or private interests or simply the pride of capturing a British document for Britain. Perhaps the Farmers had placed a cash bounty on its retrieval. For Trevor Patel, the journal was academic career leverage once he had paid to have expensive lawyers negate his part in the killing of Kneisser. For Grey Anne, miserable in her bonds, the journal was the prize of her lifetime, the Tut's tomb of the Far North country. For Ruby Cruz, whatever her decisions about her future, obtaining the book still represented a mission accomplished, an assignment completed. To Lillian, it comprised the death of her grandson and the unveiling of a secret kept long hidden. Although the journal brought this barren spot to historical life, to Kennison it simply represented motive. For the hundredth time, he patted his pocket and found its rectangular shape and weight comforting, as if it held the answer to questions yet unposed. The wind gusted again and the loose canvas flapped. At the Kitchen Tent door, he paused and said, "Eyeline?"

"Fine," said Ruby from inside the Kitchen. "I lose you on the inside corners for a moment, but that's all." Kennison walked on, along the east side of the Kitchen Tent to where it met the Wet Tent. He'd positioned someone in each module of the cross and sliced the wall canvas horizontally above the short wooden base wall to allow as close to 180-degree coverage as possible, coverage for eyes and for guns.

Ruby covered the north in the Kitchen Tent, armed with Kennison's Smith and Wesson pistol, looking over the carcasses of deflated dome tents they'd collapsed to prevent Turqavik hiding behind them. The frozen body of Wayne Penilik, wrapped in

Kneisser's green tent, lay beside that of Kenny Monk, mummified in the white nylon shelter shreds that had marked Kneisser's dig site. They lay together, already as common as furniture on the landscape.

Eyes on the black horizon, Kennison walked the north wall of the Wet Tent and turned at its eastern end. "Eyeline?"

"Gotcha, mate," said Masterson. "All the way. Bang, you're dead." He held up his 9-millimetre Beretta through the rip in the canvas and waved the barrel. Of all of them, Kennison suspected Masterson was the one looking forward to this fight. Maybe it was the first time in his life he'd been on the side of the good guys. Maybe he saw himself walking out of this as the lone survivor, journal held high, winning ticket retrieved. Yet, of the four of them, he was the least experienced in battle or with guns. Kennison had placed him facing east, inland, looking over a vast barren with few places for anyone approaching to hide.

"Eyeline?" No answer from the south-facing end of the Dorm Tent. "Lillian?"

"Yes, Mountie. I'm here. Getting water for Dr. Anne."

"You'll have to forget her for now, Lillian. I need you watching."

"I see you, Mountie. I see east the barren lands and west the burned shack. At the shore I see the three sheds at Hell." She paused. The barrel of her rifle appeared through the slit canvas and she added. "One is there, Mountie."

Kennison had kept the sniper's AK-47 and given Lillian her grandson's Winchester 70. The gun was popular with native hunters from Greenland to Alaska because it took relatively common thirty-ought-six Springfield ammunition that could stop a polar bear in its tracks. As well, its trigger mechanism was of simple, manual construction and didn't freeze up like the higher-tech rifles. That reminded him, and he checked the AK slide and clip sleeve to make sure they hadn't seized in the cold.

Kennison had taken the Salon Tent for himself, looking west to the other shore. The summer road—the same path Marie-Claire Fortier had walked to her death—was the most easily negotiated path for attack movement, despite the rocks and turns. If Turqavik wanted to move in quickly, it was a good bet they'd do so from that direction. He took one last look at the horizon before entering the tent. The movement of the door as he entered caused the tent roof to flap loosely; the cuts in the canvas had rendered it useless as a shelter and it was quickly becoming as cold inside as out. The kerosene heat dissipated quickly, making it hardly worth keeping the stoves lighted. Someone—probably Lillian—had wrapped a sleeping bag around Grey Anne, where she sat in the chair looking as unamused as Queen Victoria.

Kennison toured the interior in the same sequence, making certain everyone was in place. Ruby Cruz was at ease with the Smith and Wesson, and a quick glance told Kennison the safety was off and Ruby was ready to go. She had pushed the stainless-steel prep table on its side and crouched behind it for added protection. He checked Masterson's Beretta and made sure he had ammunition to reload. He checked Lillian's Winchester and wished he'd kept it for himself. What he really wanted was his old army C-7. He made certain that all interior doors were wedged open so that everyone could hear one another. Trevor Patel lay moaning about his feet on a sleeping bag on the Mess Tent floor, court sycophant at the feet of Anne Ferguson-Crewe.

"All right. Once more, everyone. If you see anything or even think that you see anything, shout it out and shoot at it. There's no harm in being wrong. The harm is in not letting the others know, letting others get hurt. Got it?"

"Got it," from Ruby in the kitchen, a grunt from Lillian in the bedroom.

"Masterson?"

"Aye, aye, Captain."

"Did you hear me, Masterson?"

"Of course I heard you. You're twenty feet away, for Christ's—"

"Then say so."

"Aye, aye, Captain Can—"

"Mountie?"

"Yes, Lillian?"

"I see fire." It was beginning. They were showing themselves.

"Kennison? You there?" shouted Ruby Cruz.

"I'm here," Kennison said, running to Lillian.

"There's a fire here, too. Looks like it's up near—"

"Be right there, Ruby." Kennison crawled beside Lillian and peeked out through the rip in the canvas she had lifted slightly with the barrel of her rifle. All lights, even candles had been extinguished. In the black of the night, the tall flames at Hell looked inviting, offering the light and warmth the compound lacked.

"They've torched the equipment shacks," said Kennison. Lillian nodded. "Stay here. Watch carefully. It's a diversion." Kennison moved quickly across the plywood floor to the kitchen and called back: "Don't stare at the flames. They'll blind you."

Lillian probably knew that from birth. Who was he, telling a survivor how to survive?

Ruby Cruz looked frightened. She'd stuck the barrel of Kennison's pistol through the canvas wall and now raised it to show Kennison the flames in the distance. "It's from Kneisser's site, all right," said Kennison. "Must be the sleeping platform—that was the only wood I saw there."

"Why are they burning things?" she said.

Kennison shrugged. "To distract us. To scare us. To make us think we're surrounded."

"Aren't we?"

"Maybe, but there's more of us than them. Keep your eyes off the flames. Stare into the black. Blink to regain your night vision." He turned and called out. "Anything your way, Masterson?"

"No action here."

"Keep an eye out, everyone." Kennison moved back to his position, passing Patel shivering on the floor. Anne Ferguson-Crewe was ignoring that the blanket had slipped from her shoulders. Kennison picked it up and wrapped her again. It was getting colder.

In the Salon Tent, Kennison knelt on one of the cushions he'd pulled from the futons and stared through the cut canvas towards the shore. Unless they were wearing white, they'd be hard to see, although the sky looked lighter now, oddly energized. Maybe the adrenalin allowed his eyes to dilate and increase the aperture beyond normal. By leaning forward and looking left, he could see the fires at Hell burning down. To his right, the fire at Kneisser's camp was already reduced to a glow beneath the line of sight, like the electric glow from an unseen ballpark down south. The game was on, whatever the game was.

"We had jolly big fires at school." It was Masterson speaking. "Great bloody bonfires on Guy Fawkes' Day." Let them talk, thought Kennison. It will relax them. As long as they keep watch. Kennison wondered if he saw a silhouette cross the light of the receding flames at Hell. They wouldn't be that stupid—would they?—unless they were taunting them.

"Mountie?" said Lillian.

"Saw it, Lillian. Thanks."

"We always had bonfires at home on Independence Day," said Ruby. "Great high fires in the park at the end of our street. Before Dad went to 'Nam." Ruby was silent for a moment, staring at the receding glow of the fire to the north. "I thought everyone had bonfires on the Fourth of July. It wasn't until later I found out most people set off fireworks."

"Something." It was Masterson in the Wet Tent. "Cancel that. Sorry. Nothing there."

"Good work, Paul. Keep an eye out," said Kennison. He was conscious of using leadership tools, calling his people by their first names, thanking them for their efforts, keeping them focused. The sky seemed to become brighter momentarily, but the light would hide when he looked for it.

"We always had fireworks." Patel was speaking from the floor, teeth chattering. "Tons of them. My father would spend a bundle and we'd—"

"Shut up, Patel," said Masterson. "Nobody gives a shit what your old man did, other than fuck up raising his children." Patel went quiet.

Kennison spied a strange white line out on the horizon. Uneven. Horizontal. Moving. He shook his head and blinked. It was just the thin surf lapping the shore, something he hadn't been able to see earlier.

"What about you, Lillian?" said Kennison, talking to keep alert. "You have bonfires?"

"No wood here. Sometimes we get wood from the south by summer boat, but only for cooking, or for the dark months. Light the way home for a hunter lost on the ice—"

They dove as one for the floor at the sound of the crash. Kennison fired blindly through the canvas and rolled towards the noise that seemed to come from behind him. Patel lay on the floor, kicking in fear like a roped calf. Ferguson-Crewe had fallen over and lay on her side still tied to the chair. Other shots rang, too bunched to individually distinguish. There was a groan and another single shot, a pistol shot. Then utter silence.

"Ruby?"

"Okay here. What—?"

"Keep watch. Don't move. Lillian?"

"Okay."

"Paul?"

"He's shot." It was Patel talking, his voice rising. "Oh jeez. I can see him. He's shot. Bleeding. He's dead. Oh jeez . . ." Kennison crawled quickly on his elbows through the Mess Tent. In the Wet Tent, Masterson lay on his back, crushed under the body of a large man clothed completely in black. Kennison pulled the body off Masterson and onto the floor. Masterson groaned and sat up clutching his arm.

"Keep watch, everyone." Kennison felt for the pulse in the neck of the man in black. His hand came back covered in blood. "This is one of them. One down. Two left. Paul got him. Good man, Masterson." Kennison felt stoned with adrenalin. Being in the game was so much better than planning it, than thinking about it. Than fearing it. Than estimating losses and possible results.

"Arm," said Masterson, loudly, pumped by his action and his pain. "Bloody arm. Hurts like hell. Jesus. Didn't see a thing. Came through the bloody tent like a fucking bat . . ." The canvas had collapsed from the weight of the Turqavik, covering Masterson in a confining shroud. Kennison used all his strength to drag him out of the tangle of tent and into the central Mess Tent. There was some warmth close to the kerosene heater.

"Okay, Paul. Hold on. Easy now. Keep watch, you two." Kennison ripped the sleeve from Masterson's shirt. Blood was spurting out below the inside of the elbow. It was a bad wound, not a glancing one. Arterial blood pumped dark red in the beam of the flashlight that he used for only a second or two. Kennison thought the bone might be shattered, but said nothing.

"Keep watch, people. Two to go. Keep watch. Patel, come here."

"I can't—"

"Crawl, for Christ's sake! And stop whining." Kennison waited, stemming the blood with his hands, until Patel crawled to him. "Listen to me. Stop the blood. A tourniquet. Here. Around the muscle. Use the rope. Find a stick or something. Do it. Now. Keep watch, Lillian. Keep watch, Ruby." Patel started talking, but Kennison left him, rolling through the Mess Tent to the Dorm Tent, tossing the blanket onto Grey Anne, where she lay on the floor as he passed.

"Okay, Lillian?"

"Okay, Mountie."

"Okay back there, Ruby?" he called.

"Okay here, Sergeant Preston."

"Lillian. Check your position, then come to me in the Wet Tent." By the time he returned to the Mess Tent, Patel had wrapped a length of yellow rope over a tea towel around Poncey's upper arm, and was twisting a fork knotted in it.

"Not too tight. Stem the blood flow, don't cut the circulation." Kennison moved into the Wet Tent and pulled the balaclava up to reveal the dead man's face. Lillian looked over his shoulder.

"Know this man?" She nodded.

"Sitluk. Darren Sitluk. Ross Haven. Turqavik for sure. Not the leader. A bad man. Drug man." Kennison felt for a pulse, then confirmed its lack at the man's throat.

"Dead man, Lillian. Thanks. Back to your position." Kennison rolled the body to the side and smiled at his discovery. Beneath the corpse was a C7 army-issue rifle. No, a C8 with the Elcan sight in place of the handle. He bent forward and picked up the rifle as if it was a wounded pet. This was his old Bosnian partner. This gun had been his constant companion in the army, the best friend he'd had on many dark nights. He'd practised with it and defended himself with it. He'd fired it on ranges and on missions thousands of times. He cradled it now, felt his fingers fit the trigger and guard like a custom glove. He'd killed with it. Often.

The magazine held thirty shots. He checked, and it was nearly full. He flicked the small switch that adjusted the shot to a triple burst, the sound that he'd heard kill Wayne Penilik. If his guess was right, it was also the gun that had fired the 5.65-millimetre bullet into the head of Karl Kneisser.

Unsummoned, Kennison's mind raced back to the goat paths in the hills above Srebrenica, hiding in Muslim graveyards, moving on hands and knees between the wooden post markers, many topped with round caps signifying the faithful who had visited Mecca. They'd dug in singly, above the Serb snipers, waiting patiently for one wrong move, using a single muffled shot to neutralize a soldier who'd been hiding in the forests all day, shooting to kill at children, stray dogs and his platoon members in the village—

"Sergeant?" It was Patel bringing him back to the present. "The blood's stopped, I think." Kennison checked Poncey's arm, loosening the tourniquet slightly. Masterson seemed to have passed out, but he was breathing regularly.

"Take his position, Patel. Wet Tent. Keep watch east." Masterson moaned and shifted his weight. Kennison felt under him in the dark. He was lying on the Beretta. Kennison sniffed the barrel. He liked the hot-sulphur-and-metal reek of a fired gun. "Take this," he called to Patel.

"That's my bloody—" Masterson said weakly.

"You okay, Farmer?" said Kennison.

"Cold," he said. Kennison yanked the sleeping bag from where

Patel had been lying and wrapped him in it. "Thanks," he said. "One down, eh mate?"

"One down, Paul. Well done. Not bad for a member of a former world power."

"Up yours, Captain Canada."

"Something, Mountie . . ."

What seemed like an hour with Masterson and Patel had only taken minutes, maybe seconds. Kennison passed the AK-47 to Ruby Cruz in the Kitchen Tent. Kennison took his pistol from her, still cradling the C8 in his arms. Without speaking, he showed her the AK magazine and the tracks where the clip slipped into place. He gave her the extra mags. As Kennison crawled back to his position, he heard Ruby saying something quietly, but couldn't make it out. It wasn't a warning call—her voice sounded happy, awed, like a young girl's at a bonfire. With the barrel of the C8, he slowly raised the canvas wall of the Salon Tent.

Kennison hadn't seen light for so long that the scene before him made no sense. It must be what Ruby had been oohing about. It looked like a film set, lights brighter than daylight as if mounted on towers, exposing every detail of the rocks and shore, a river of light so extensive it cast no shadows and had no distinguishable source. It flowed from purple to red to green like a mad colour wheel at a high school prom. He leaned out, staring at the sky, then pulled back, realizing how exposed he must be. And them, dammit. They're exposed, too.

"Careful everyone. Eyes on the shadows. Keep your night sight." Despite his warnings to others, he was drawn to stare at the sky where an electrical union of luminance and colour danced like a couple in a tango, indistinguishable as entities, intimate in their relationship, in their relationship to him, to each of them. He felt his right pocket for the hundredth time. The journal was still there.

"Mountie . . ." Kennison looked to his left and imagined he saw a silhouette south of the yawning woodstove at Purgatory. Closer now. Turqavik hadn't foreseen the light coming from the sky. Their own Arctic environment was betraying them, the aurora borealis their enemy. Still, two of them were still out there, their passion to obtain the journal and the smell of spilled blood filling their desperate minds with an anger that defied caution. Later, some might call it bravery.

"Got it, Lillian. Keep a watch. Ruby? You okay?" He could hear her changing her position in the Kitchen Tent. The lights outside gave them a confidence the dark could not.

"Fine. Better than fine. This is amazing. This is the northern lights, right?"

"Aurora borealis," said Patel, then grunted as if Masterson had elbowed him silent.

"*Arsaniit,*" said Lillian. "We call it *arsaniit.*" She paused. "Nothing by the shack, Mountie. Maybe a rabbit. We tell children *arsaniit* will steal them if they stay out too late."

"How could they believe anything so beautiful was threatening?" wondered Ruby.

"Men say that *arsaniit* cut off the heads of hunters who travel in dogsleds at night. Hunters slit the ears of their dogs because they believe the blood on the snow protects them."

"What's that?" said Masterson. "Look, you bloody fool. Keep watch, goddammit."

"It's nothing," said Patel. "Just the lights on the rocks."

Kennison forced himself to lower his eyes from the lights to the road. He could see the white wash of the surf on the shore plainly now, like a single strand of pearls on an African princess, a single strand divide between the black sand where the skeletons lay and the black water beyond.

Ruby started to speak, but was cut off as bullets from the north ripped through the canvas, inches over her head, striking the interior door frame and splitting the wood, careering off the cross-beam posts that supported the canvas roof. One ricocheted off the stainless-steel table, ringing it like a gong. More shots came immediately from the south, forcing Lillian to the ground behind the thin wooden base wall that was all that separated her from death.

"Down! Down," shouted Kennison, diving to the plywood floor. "Keep an eye out. All directions. This is it, people." His orders sounded ridiculous to him, but Kennison knew their primary weak spot, and that demanded a 360-degree watch. If one of the terrorists managed to creep close enough, he could hide amongst them. Tucked inches away, hidden in the inside right-angled corners of the cross where the tents met, he could knock them off one by one at will. "Know your weakness and you'll know their strength. Know their strength and you'll know your own." What was his name? The combat sergeant at Gagetown who drilled that into them each day? Brown. James Brown. "Soulman," they'd called him, but not to his face, not until they'd met again in Bosnia. His lesson had become a fighting man's mantra, repeated until it lacked meaning, like a rote-mumbled mass. Until now. It was so quiet Kennison thought he could hear the northern lights humming like an electrical tower. A chain of shots rang from the AK-47 in the kitchen.

"Anything, Ruby?"

"Maybe. Shadow. Moving your way. I hate this gun."

Kennison peeked through the slit in the canvas, keeping as much of his body back and below the wooden wall as possible.

Nothing. He looked south. Nothing. The lights dissolved from green to pink and then to purple, filaments twisting around one another, helixes making rope or making love.

"For Christ's sake, Patel. Look out the bloody slit," whispered Masterson.

"Just leave me alone. I'm not going to—"

"Shut up, you two."

"Yes, sir. Captain Canada speaks," said Masterson, unaware of what concerned Ruby and Kennison. Through the loose canvas, Kennison saw the light change from blue-green to yellow and move quickly closer. Like a comet. Understanding came later than sight, as the lighted torch twisted end over end, crashing through the roof of the Mess Tent, vapourizing the old, dry canvas as if by magic. The fire raced from tent to tent, burning the material as if it was soaked in naphtha, opening the compound to the rioting sky. Parts of the wooden wall caught fire in the Dorm Tent, spreading flames along the floor and igniting the mattresses.

"Fire here, Mountie," said Lillian.

"Do what you can, Lillian." Kennison saw a shadow and fired, trying to lead the prey. He heard his bullets crang uselessly off rocks. The heat of the barrel felt good on his arm. He heard the others scrambling behind him, shouting with fear as the flames drew close, Ruby finding a fire extinguisher in heated light and using it like a new kind of weapon.

Lillian crept up behind him. Above their heads, the northern lights gyrated, angry now where they had been beautiful, threatening exposure now where they had so recently revealed others. Little wonder the Inuit saw them as an evil.

Kennison looked around. Their fortress was reduced to a roofless, cross-shaped wooden wall four feet high, above which door frames and crossbeams rose like the skeleton of an unfinished barn.

The remaining small flames licked the charred wall, and the rest of what had burned crackled to ash. The intense heat had waned. The lack of canvas gave them full view of the surrounding territory. Although there was no longer any place for Turqavik to hide, there was nowhere for them to hide, either. It was becoming cold again with an increased breeze, as if the lights above were stealing their energy from the heat of the earth. It was silent except for the hiss of the wind and the sound of the lights, however imaginary, not silent enough to hear footsteps or the approach of any enemy. The attack Kennison had expected would follow the torch had not materialized. Where were they? What were they doing out there?

The figure ran lower to the ground than seemed possible, fast and horizontal to the rough terrain, its chest mere inches above the ground. It came from the join of the Kitchen Tent, feet from Ruby, heading towards Kennison and Lillian at full speed. The shadow Ruby had seen, Kennison thought. It had been listening to them, crouched in the inside corner of the cross. He raised the C8 and fired, but the attacker changed course, darting left, zigzagging between the rocks like a startled raptor in a video game. He turned and came on fast, mouth open in a war cry, arming himself with anger and purpose. Phosphorescent green light reflected off his gun barrel like neon, an Arctic St. Elmo's fire.

Without that light echo, Ruby might have seen nothing. She raised the AK-47 and fired as the attacker ran at Kennison. Behind the target. From somewhere, from some intelligence ingrained by endless practice, she fired again. Leading him as the attacker crashed through the Salon Tent's aluminum door towards Kennison and Lillian, snapping it out of its frame, scattering metal and glass and blood in all directions.

"Watch the south. The south!" Kennison yelled to Lillian as he threw himself on the body of the attacker. The man had cut himself badly on the glass and metal, but still held his rifle to his chest. Kennison wrested it from his arms and tossed it towards the remains of the Mess Tent, shoving the barrel of his own C8 hard between the man's lips, jamming it hard through breaking teeth, trapping his tongue, hemorrhaging the roof of his mouth. The man coughed, gurgled, choking on the blood that overflowed the corners of his mouth.

"Ruby, move to Masterson and Patel. Now." Kennison suddenly saw the attack plan as if he'd drawn it himself. Maybe too late. Simultaneous shots from north and south, then a tossed torch followed by running attacks west and east. They were vulnerable to the east, behind them. Above them, lights danced, either increased in intensity from some electron magic or excited by the battle below.

Kennison rolled off the prone body and reached for the handcuffs on his belt, rolling the form on its stomach and cuffing it from behind. Lillian knelt silently beside him, her rifle aimed at the nape of the attacker's neck. He wasn't a big man, not like the other one. Wiry, this one, a brook trout compared to a pickerel. Kennison easily flipped him on his back again and ripped off the black balaclava as the man wretched, spewing blood and vomit into the air. "Choke on yourself, you bastard. Know this one, Lillian?"

The Inuit woman nodded slowly, as if the sight of this man meant more than she wanted to tell.

"Charbonneau. Réal Charbonneau. Québec man. Part Inuit. He's the leader of the Ross cell. He's the—"

"One to go, people," shouted Kennison. He was loud with excitement, his voice as pumped as his heart. "Got the leader here. Good shooting, Ruby. One more to go. Got the leader. Stay focused. Wheee-hoo!" He hadn't felt this high since the Patsy Prévost shootout. If the truth be told, he wished he didn't like it so much, didn't need it. Must be the high that runners or cyclists felt, but this was better, without the exercise. He heard the gurgle of the man drowning in his own liquids. Then silence. Utter silence, as if the individual scene above had denied the ears sensation.

"You okay, Ruby?" His voice sounded loud in his ears.

"Okay, Kennison. Masterson's here. Pale, but breathing. Patel's okay too."

"Lillian?"

"Here, Mountie." Her voice was so close it made him start. The fire had made her abandon the Dorm Tent.

"Check on Anne."

"Okay, Mountie." The woman sidled towards the remains of the Mess Tent on her stomach. Kennison felt a moment's peace. One more to go, unless they'd made a run for it after their leader was killed. He'd expected another immediate attack from the east, but there was no movement he could see. As he turned to look behind him, he felt the shape and weight of the journal in his parka pocket. He couldn't help himself and took it out and examined it. All this death for what it contained. It was hard to hope that it was worth it.

The words on the page were formed slowly, painfully, the thick pencil lines thicker or doubled on some letters as if traced over, the style more like figures carved in stone than written on paper. In each section the writing worsened quickly, as if the writer had to re-energize his strength and thoughts before continuing.

Spent.
Tongs blck
No fingers, tose—gon.
No gangreen

Push bot up ice mtns ice
C. lies relief lies South.
V. will not last the night.
T. hugs boy, kiss frozen tears.
Our sins die w. death we pray

C. wander leder lost.
V. spews blood.
Fop to sap

Warm hands in his hot guts
gorge his toxic meet
We are who disgusted us.

They hover,
smiling like they do.

Below a slaughter
300 lgues from goal

A tomb of men,
of Failed men.

No Victory here dear gd

Kennison looked up quickly. For the moment, he'd lost his edge, forgotten his task. The sky was dancing. Lillian watched beside him, and the wind had died once more, offering an awful silence to this sorry group huddled in the wreck of a campsite. Nothing there. Nothing moving. Kennison turned the brittle page to the last entry in the journal and stared at the page, as if the lights were tricking him, as if their luminance conspired with the writer to hide the conclusion in its shadows.

There were no words, at least none he could decode. On the page were chiselled marks of pencil lead, hieroglyphs of pain on a background stain of black blood and yellow bile. The man's last message, like his last moments, was one of silence, of nothing left to say. A letter of death without reason to live.

What she said made no sense. Kennison looked at Lillian as he closed the journal, resting it on the plywood floor.

"You been to Epcot?" she said again.

"Grey Anne?" he said. "Is she okay?"

"She's okay. Angry, but okay. Wrists sore from the yellow rope. I loosened it but she will not run. Nowhere to run."

"Thanks, Lillian." She was right. There was nowhere for Grey Anne to go, especially with a killer still out there. It crossed his mind to send her as a decoy to draw out the final sniper. He'd have sent Patel if he weren't crippled.

"You go to Epcot?" Lillian repeated. What on earth was she talking about? Kennison lifted his rifle and used the barrel as a sight as he scanned the horizon from north to south. Nothing.

"I've been," said Ruby.

"Me, too. With my daughter and her daughter Simone. There were many countries side by side around a big blue lake. Mexico, Japan, Canada. Each one made up to look like another country sees it. But none of it is real. None of it true. Even the blue of the lake is added to the water."

"I know what you mean, Lillian." It was Ruby. "But it's just an entertainment thing. It's about Americans, not those countries."

"It makes other places jokes, not nations. Takes away people's pride. We saw there how people think about Canada and the Arctic. Only ice and snow. Nanook from the North. Stupid Inuit eating snow and seals. All lies."

Kennison watched.

"You're right, Lillian. That's what I thought before I came here," Ruby said. "You know, they say when astronauts get farther from the earth, the thing they notice is how the borders disappear. How it's just one world, and all earth's little territorial games seem silly, meaningless from there."

"Yeah, well, they are, aren't they?" Masterson called out in the dark. "Nationalistic crap, I say. All this bloody ownership stuff. Sovereign territory just means you can dig up your land and sell whatever's under it."

"Shadow here." Lillian poked Kennison and pointed south towards the shore, but he saw nothing moving.

Kennison shifted his weight off his right hip. He was now certain the shadow was working its way up the summer road from Hell. The lights above were throwing shadows now, shadows behind rocks, shadows where a killer could hide.

"The only reason Canada still has this shit piece of the world is because no one else wants it." It was Patel talking, and surprisingly, Masterson let him.

"Yet," he said.

"Look what's happening now, as the eyes of the world look up here and their mouths drool with the melting of the ice cap. Why is Ms. Cruz here? Masterson? Representing their interests in this sovereign Canadian land, right? And you, Sergeant Kennison? Canadian interests in the Arctic. Don't you see it? We all want something."

A small black movement between two rocks. Past Purgatory. Coming or going? Closer now.

"The bloody Canadians' idea of northern sovereignty defence," said Masterson, "is a joke. They have annual snowmobile exercises with elderly Inuit—my personal apologies, dear Lillian—carrying superannuated rifles across the bloody tundra and throw village weenie roasts with speeches in the name of Canadian sovereignty. If you can't defend it, it ain't gonna be yours for long, Captain Canada. Christ, the only sovereign territory in this country is the fucking West Edmonton Mall." The shadow left Purgatory, moving from the stove to the road with caution, a slowness undeniably human. Kennison watched.

"It's a good point," said Ruby. "If everyone wants this land, Sergeant, what's Canada going to do to defend her so-called sovereign rights? Especially since America and Europe agree she doesn't have any?"

"Jolly well said, Yank. Give us a break, Captain. We're lying on what will soon be a Lomonosov Lexus dealership." Masterson laughed. "Just down the street from Sir Johnny Franklin's Eskimo Museum and Cannibal Theme Park . . ." The man moved like a wraith. Kennison unexpectedly saw a black silhouette ten feet away, and then it was on him like snake shot fired at his face. He was forced down on his back, legs bent backwards at the knees, his C8 trapped beneath him, his wrist wracked over the Elcan sight until he thought one or the other would break. The black-clad body straddled him quickly, adeptly, like a gymnast, pinning him to the ground, digging strong thighs into the sides of his rib cage, pushing his head back to stretch his throat. Stretch it to nick his throat, to bleed him like a bullock.

Kennison relaxed his entire body, an aikido move half remembered, and his assailant moved closer as if to maintain the tension between them. Instantly, Kennison lunged upward, tossing the black silhouette off his chest and onto his back, but the figure rolled gracefully and regained his stance. Kennison turned to lunge again, feeling his spine pressed against the remains of the Salon Tent door frame, but the figure was surprisingly agile, already jumping to his feet, coming at Kennison quickly with a knife waist high, pointed forward, not held high as in a convenient training exercise but at the hip, low like a pro, ready to slice upward through the stomach. Kennison could not move backwards. The assailant sensed his predicament and moved forward, a silent shadow. One step, two. Knife drawn back for the plunge. Until he stopped dead in his tracks—stood dead still. Slowly dropping his hands. Knife clattering on the plywood floor, coming to rest beside the forgotten journal. The body falling forward.

Instinctively, Kennison reached out, catching the figure in his arms. It weighed nothing. An empty shell. Blood gushed in aortal waves from a gaping gash in its throat onto Kennison's parka, running down the sleeves and onto his hands, soon so slick with the warm, oily wetness that the body slipped from his grasp. Everything was moving in slow motion; Kennison saw the journal on the floor and pushed it away from the blood. The dead man's last rattle echoed from the gash before he hit the floor.

Kennison looked up to see Lillian standing, legs wide for balance, knees slightly bent and arms apart, a dripping *ulu* held in her hand, as natural in her ancient environment as the lichen on the rocks.

The lights raged overhead like a celebration. Slowly, as if summoned, the others moved in behind Lillian as she sank to her knees beside the body. In the shifting light, they looked like ghouls, Ruby's face white with exhaustion, Masterson's an anemic green from the loss of blood. Patel crawled forward on hands and knees, silently, tentatively, like a sheep, joined by a white-faced Anne Ferguson-Crewe, who had loosed herself from the chair.

Lillian moved forward on her knees and used the sharp, curved blade of the bloody *ulu* to slice the black balaclava, to expose the face. The only sound was her quick intake of breath as she peeled back the bloody black wool to show the face of a teenaged Inuit girl. Her voice expressed centuries of sadness. She sobbed, unbidden.

"Simone Ooqlooq. A girl I have known all her life." Her fat fingers caressed the face of the dead girl. "She loved this Charbonneau man." Tears welled and ran like clear gelatin down round brown cheeks, dripping into the pools of the girl's blood that coagulated on the floor. Her long, black hair was thick with it. "Shares my name," said Lillian. She shook her head and stood. Slowly, she bent to pick up the Winchester, checking her pockets for ammunition. The others stared, unmoving, a diorama of despair.

"You'll take care of Wayne's body, *pukitalik?*"

Kennison nodded. "I'll get his body to Ross, Lillian."

"Thank you, Mountie. Protect our land. *Tavvauvutit.*"

"Goodbye, Lillian." Lillian Ooqlooq nodded once to the others and walked into the dark. Under the northern lights they watched her, rolling side to side through the rocks to the southeast in the direction of Ross Haven, dissolving into the land and a night that would last until April.

"What will she do?" Ruby's throat was raspy and her question hoarse.

"I don't know. I don't know the rules up here. I thought they were the same as other parts, but they're not. It's not like anywhere I've been."

"Surely justice is one of the rules."

"Maybe. Or maybe justice is just the frame we impose on the picture. Maybe the picture is whatever those who survive here say it is. Or whatever the time or culture define as necessary to—" A single shot rang out, and Kennison fell to the ground in two distinct stages, first heavily to his knees, then onto his right side, a dead weight. Ruby dove to the plywood floor, rolling right and coming up on her knees, the AK cocked, panning left to right, looking for the unexpected fourth Turqavik. Outside what had been the Kitchen Tent, beside the frozen bodies of Penilik and Monk, Anne Ferguson-Crewe revved the ATV, Patel on the back waving Masterson's Beretta. With a sneer like a slit on her grey face, Ferguson-Crewe brandished the journal. Patel fired at Ruby, who dove down beside an unconscious Masterson as Grey Anne opened the throttle, lifting the front wheels off the snow and speeding towards Hell. The electric sky caromed off their receding backs like a mirror ball at a senior prom.

Kennison felt perfect peace, as if this was where he was supposed to be at this moment, as if he had finally reached where he belonged. He couldn't remember having this feeling, this wonderful warmth of a sleepy, swaddled child in a mother's arms. He heard the hum of her heart, smelled the sweet powder on her face and the warm milk in her heavy breasts. He closed his eyes to capture the moment, to savour the joy of arriving here at last, the blissfully satisfying sensation of being a marionette in someone's theatre rather than always the puppeteer.

When Ruby Cruz squeezed his blistered hand, he woke with pain to realize his serenity was that of an unconscious man. The second time in as many days. With perception came the excruciating hurt of the bullet in his shoulder. He'd been shot before. He knew the process. He knew that there was nothing to learn from it, no way to expedite the process. You only had to wait in agony for the soma to adjust to the invasive attack on its universe. The body's core regulated itself by screaming out against this violation of its borders, decrying this destruction of its cells, and its language was unhurried pain.

He opened his eyes and looked up at Ruby Cruz. There were tears on her face, and the blue-green of the electrical dance above was captured in the drops. Ruby's breathing paused a moment when he opened his eyes, hers full of things unsaid. Slowly, disappointingly, he realized the thrumming heart he'd heard was the sound of the ATV as Ferguson-Crewe and Patel raced towards the shore. He couldn't have been out long.

"I'm going after them," said Ruby.

"No," said Kennison. "Don't. She has nowhere to run."

"She thinks she does. You want her alive, right? Take care of Masterson." She tugged the cold, stiff strap of the AK-47 over her head, patted her pockets for the remaining magazine, ran out of what used to be the Salon Tent and down the road to Hell.

Kennison crawled to where Masterson was swearing to himself, conscious now, more furious that Patel had cold-cocked him with his own weapon than hurt. Kennison stood, dizzily, painfully, holding himself erect against the door frame, and looked around. The compound had been reduced to a trash tip, a collection of burned boards and boxes, their content legends encoded in the charred cardboard. They were stacked, in Daliesque fashion, in a landscape of isolated frames, a Stonehenge on a palette of dirty snow, decorated with oddly untouched furniture. Heaven had been undone.

"You all right?" asked Kennison. Masterson grunted.

"Right as rain, Captain. Hurts like hell."

"Been shot before?" Masterson shook his head and lowered his eyes, as if embarrassed to say no.

"Bugger's going for the bloody Cessna and knows where it is," he said. Kennison had forgotten about the small airplane. There *was* an escape route after all.

"Let's go."

"Go where?"

"After Ruby. After him. See what we can do."

"Oh Christ. You're serious, Captain? The halt and the bloody lame, this is. Let me grab the satphone, mate."

The road to Hell seemed more defined than it had to Ruby before—easier to read, simpler to negotiate. Maybe it was all that trekking through rocks on unformed paths that made this one appear groomed, manufactured by man. Maybe it was the lights still dancing above. She picked up speed. It felt good to run again, even with the damned rifle banging rhythmically against her butt with every step. It had been days since her Ridgley's Delight run, and she missed the workout if she didn't do it at least every other day. Like her morning coffee and a glass of wine before bed, it was a drug to her in a world that now seemed claustrophobically small.

Weaving between the rocks she could see in the light show above, she pulled off her bright pink toque and unwound her scarf, tossing them aside as she passed the remains of Purgatory. The fire that started all this seemed like it happened weeks ago instead of a couple of days. She unzipped her ski jacket to let the heat escape and loosen up her arms so she could pump them.

A kilometre ahead of her, nearing Hell, Ferguson-Crewe revved the ATV engine and turned left, down the shore, away from the landing water, away from the dig. She disappeared behind an ice-and-rock ridge that ran out into the water. Over her own breathing, Ruby could hear the whining of the engine, so she knew they hadn't stopped. But where were they going? Where did she expect to escape? Or was Kennison right? Was it best just to let them run until they figured out there was nowhere to go, that for both of them this vast land was as tiny as a prison cell? Then she remembered the Cessna was down here somewhere and Patel knew where it was. She picked up her pace.

Ruby Cruz heard the Cessna engine explode to life in the south, behind the ridge where the rocks had forced her to stop. She could feel sweat trickling down her skin, layers beneath the ski suit. Her heels hurt from the friction of the heavy boots—unlike her iPod Nikes, not meant for jogging. The rocks loomed above her, defeating her not so much by their height but by a slippery covering of ice and snow that made it difficult to climb with any speed. She could see the wide tracks of the ATV, but they didn't offer a path as much as they evidenced Ferguson-Crewe's escape route.

The single plane engine was loud and getting louder. Ruby turned and ran west along the shore to the Hell site, to the skulls and skeletons and the three small buildings that had been razed as part of the Turqavik attack.

She saw from the corner of her eye Kennison and Masterson approaching. Each had adopted a distinctive shuffle that allowed them a top speed without making their pain intolerable. Like Lillian's waddle, they covered a lot of ground quickly without seeming to be running, and without exhausting themselves.

The red and white Cessna with the oversized Krevaluk Air logo and the headlight appeared suddenly in the strait, immediately loud, revving high, moving quickly on its pontoons towards the thin strip of water on which Ivan Krevaluk and Ricky Monteith had landed. Ruby tugged the rifle strap over her head and checked the magazine. She could hear Kennison and Poncey breathing hard, even over the sound of the engines, as they approached.

"She's with the wind," yelled Masterson. She'll have to turn."

The water strip was only a few feet across now, only slightly wider than the splayed pontoons of the plane. The white parts of the plane bloomed in the northern lights like black-light night in a bowling alley. Ruby breathed deeply, calming her heart like a biathlete, raising the rifle to her eye. Kennison pulled the C8 up to his good shoulder and tried to look through the Elcan sight. It had been broken during the battle. Ferguson-Crewe was moving quickly now. Ruby thought she saw Patel smiling smugly, waving the Beretta from the co-pilot's seat.

Ruby fired, the rat-tat-tat of the AK oddly comforting after having been silent for a time. The rifle kicked at her shoulder and fired high and forward, although she thought she heard one bullet ping off the propeller. Kennison knelt for stability. He flicked the C8 switch to triple burst and fired from chest height like a cowboy, shooting to his right, leading the plane with his body, leading the prey, giving the bullets time to intersect with the plane.

Ferguson-Crewe slowed suddenly, as if she had brakes. She'd run out of channel. To the north, the ice had closed in since yesterday and she couldn't trust the delicate aluminum pontoons to break the ice. Kennison's bullets went wide to the right as he and Ruby re-aimed, but too late to shoot. Grey Anne swung the plane a hundred and eighty degrees and pushed the throttles full forward. The Cessna screamed past the three on the shore and disappeared in the channel of open water behind the ice ridge. A moment later, they watched the plane rise in the sky, the single bright headlight a launching satellite, soon out of range, using the headwind to gain height quickly.

"Bastard," said Masterson. "She sure knows how to fly." Kennison stood, the rifle hanging loosely from his good hand. Ruby moved closer to him, her AK still raised at the sky, the three of them watching the Cessna recede. Or was it?

Kennison said it first. "She's coming back. Why's she coming back?"

Then they heard the engines sputtering.

"She's out of petrol," said Masterson. "Yesss," he hissed. "Gotcha, you fucking piker." He was jumping for joy on the beach, his pain forgotten. Kennison and Ruby readied their rifles, but the sputtering plane veered away from Hell, losing height quickly, steering its own course as the engines went silent. They watched the white dot of the light dipping, faltering a moment, then falling. In the dark, an engine coughed once and went silent.

The tumble to earth transpired in slow motion, a ballet of tail swooping slowly over prop, wings yawing an impossible helix in the wind, the small craft corkscrewing at prop speed until it crashed on the ice cap far out in the strait. There was no fire—there was nothng to feed it. There was no sound they could hear. And no light.

If the ice that once held Franklin and his ships and his men in its deadly grip for two summers hadn't killed Anne Ferguson-Crewe and Trevor Patel, the cold soon would.

"Can I have a puff?" said Ruby Cruz. Kennison had lit his last Rothman's. Masterson looked disgusted, his good arm cradling the bad.

"You? Sure. Sorry." Kennison passed the cigarette to Ruby, who sucked on it like it was stick candy and coughed uncontrollably, to Masterson's delight. The three of them sat on a bench cobbled together from the charred lumber of the Hell huts, a charred plank placed on the ground, others against some rocks as a backrest. They lay back, staring at the luminous sky. Kennison had called Duchesne on the satphone over an hour ago, and now each strained to will the sound of the Otter in the distance, knowing it would be another hour or two before it could be heard.

The bullet in Kennison's shoulder was deep. Ruby had done her best to wrap it with one of the T-shirts he wore. When he'd stripped in the cold, Masterson had made some comment on physical intimacy until Ruby shut him up, saying, "I've seen all the sergeant has to offer before, Masterson. And more, huh?" She could have sworn she'd seen the man blush. The bleeding in Masterson's forearm had stopped, and Patel's rope-and-cloth tourniquet had done its work.

They hadn't much to say, like lovers or fighters having already spent themselves on each other. They leaned back like children in a movie house and watched the electronic madness, committing to the show rather than stealing sidelong peeks the way they had since the attack.

"What'll you do, Poncey?" asked Kennison.

Masterson shrugged.

"Back to the U.K. for a bit, I suppose. Have to report, you know. Stand on the carpet of the mighty. Have a job offer in the Tyrol for the winter. Ski resort. Lots of action, if you know what I mean, though I must admit I'm feeling a bit old for that . . ."

"Man, you must love winter," said Ruby. "I've had enough of it already, and it's still only November."

"Yeah, well, that was my thought before all this," said Masterson, waving his good arm to the horizon. "Now I'm thinking I have another three months on my papers, so maybe I'll hang around Yellowknife for a while. Maybe make some real money up in the diamond mines, if some Canuck will sponsor me."

"Can't imagine who," said Kennison. "Certainly no one who knows you. I can show you some good bars, though. And some really bad ones." Masterson smiled and leaned back. Kennison hesitated, wanting to ask a question but unsure of what he wanted the answer to be. "What about you, Ruby?" She was quiet. Wrapped up again in the hot pink hat and scarf Kennison had collected at Purgatory. He could hear her breathing, see her chest moving with each breath.

"Good question, Sergeant Preston." Her lightness of tone seemed forced. "I need some time to figure out the last couple of days. About what I do. About who I am. About what I want. I know a lot more about me, but I don't know what it is, huh? So I'll go home, I guess, whatever that is. Maryland? The States? Not buying a house, though. That's not the answer. Think it through—"

"This bloody awful place grows on you, don't it?" Masterson remarked.

"You read my mind. It does," said Ruby. She sounded disappointed, as if she'd lost a bet with herself. "It's really beautiful here. I mean, I'm sick and tired of the cold and the damned dark, but this place has purity to it, huh? Like we're the first people to be here, even if we aren't?"

Masterson nodded silently. Kennison reached down with his cigarette and twisted the filter tip into the snow.

"Well, it's mine, and don't you damned foreigners forget it, eh?" said Kennison. He smiled and stuffed a hand in his large jacket pocket, feeling again the comforting surface of the smooth, coloured stone he'd found in the ruined gravesite, rubbing it with his thumb.

"Just watch your Canadian ass, Captain," said Masterson. "The Yanks or the next superpower'll fight you to the death for the oil and jewels and God knows what else is under here."

"And for the rights to the Northwest Passage," said Ruby. "Oh damn, is all we can talk about wars to come?" She squeezed Kennison's good forearm and smiled. She looked good when she smiled. "Anyway, I'll be fighting for Lillian. I'm bored with all this land ownership crap. I hate the thought of this place being crowded."

"Good Lord," said Masterson. "Birth of a bloody liberal."

"If I have to go through what we just went through to get one more soldier on our side," said Kennison, "we'll all be dead before any war begins." They laughed. All of them. Kennison felt warm, among friends, like at the church camp evening fire, but with some sense of longevity, of tomorrow and years beyond. Maybe this is all sovereignty is, he thought: ownership of your too-portable soul. The thought of testifying about the corruption of small men in uniform seemed very far away.

He couldn't tell exactly when the shift began, but the light display above faded gradually. Only in its dying moments did the three of them understand it was about to end, and they moved closer together. Long after it had gone, after the mad dance had dissolved into the black, starlit stillness of an endless Arctic night, the three of them lay back, staring through the sky, smiling like the faithful in the afterglow of God.

O Alice
Forskn by gd
in the siht of You
I faled
more thn most

Dnce on my boot tps

Daisy Daisy Dai